WE LIVE

WE LIVE

THE STORY OF A WELSH MINING VALLEY

BY

LEWIS JONES

LAWRENCE and WISHART
London

First Published 1939

Reprinted in
A Workers' Library 1941

This Edition, with Introduction
by David Smith, 1978
Reprinted 1980
Reprinted 1983

© Lawrence and Wishart

ISBN 85315 469 4

AG2

This book has been republished with
the support of the English-language
Section of Yr Academi Gymreig

Printed and bound in Great Britain at
The Camelot Press Ltd, Southampton

INTRODUCTION

by David Smith

Lewis Jones was a Communist. This was the central fact of his life, the philosophical pivot around which his stormy political career and volatile temperament revolved. His politics shaped his life and coloured his writing because of his deep ideological commitment to them as the only release for a trapped society. His place and his time, he considered, allowed no other real choice. In every other respect, although hemmed in by extremely restricting public and private circumstances, Lewis Jones personified individual choice.

The argument on his lips was for collective action disciplined by political organisation, but he could never abandon the chaotic welter of individual types which made up his 'people'. He tried to combine the two elements in himself, often with disastrous results in the shining eyes of those who believed the tribunes of the people should be exemplary ambassadors of their proletarian constituents. Yet his wilful bohemianism never removed him from those he felt, with a sure instinct, he could succour through both his cockatoo personality and his tempered intelligence. The two novels he left, as a bonus from a lifetime of giving, are revealing of a public experience whose density of meaning for the literature and the history of Wales are only now being unravelled. For Lewis Jones it was the only world he knew.

He was born, in 1897, in Clydach Vale, mid-Rhondda, the pulsating heart of a South Wales whose economy and population occupied a strategic niche in the British Empire. Being orphaned early in life and so raised by his grandmother were direct signposts for the mitching schoolboy to enter the Cambrian Colliery of D. A. Thomas, later Lord Rhondda, and the model for the novels' Lord Cwmardy. That was in 1909.

Around the Cambrian Combine pits in mid-Rhondda flared the virulent strike of 1910–11 and the Tonypandy riots which, as a collier boy, Lewis Jones would have witnessed. From this couldron of turmoil came, by 1912, the pamphlet—*The Miner's Next Step*—denouncing all leadership not rooted in the men themselves. A number of idealistic leaders emerged who sought to turn theories of workers' control into practice.

Like so many other South Walian thinkers in the first half of the twentieth century, Lewis Jones was marked by the vigorous democracy evident in *The Miner's Next Step* and by that anarcho-syndicalism which, in its instant promise, framed so well the aspirations of a society as bewilderingly new as any found by an Andalucian peasant enticed to Barcelona. It was the milennnarian possibilities of this topsy-turvy world that Lewis Jones glimpsed and sought to harness.

His early mentor was the sagacious Noah Rees (on whom Ezra is based), a man wise in pit ways and educated, through Ruskin College, in fundamentalist Marxism. Clydach Vale had its own Marxian Club and Institute long before, in 1909, the Central Labour College was specifically established, as a breakaway from Ruskin, to provide independent working-class education. This too was the mulch on which the boy would feed as he sped, through an early marriage at sixteen to being, before the First World War ended, the youngest ever Chairman of the Cambrian Lodge. That war had shown the bargaining strength of a mining work-force which was in excess of 250,000 in South Wales by the early 1920s. Lewis Jones tied himself to it further by relinquishing his studies in mining engineering for headier visions. He attended the Central Labour College in London, on a scholarship, between 1923 and 1925. At this time, like Len his main fictional protagonist who is an amalgam of himself and other close friends, he joined the youthful Communist Party. During the lock-out of 1926 he was sent on a speaking-tour of the shaky Nottinghamshire coalfield: this led to his prosecution for seditious speeches and a three months' prison sentence.

After the collapse of the General Strike all struggle was defensive. The work-force was halved, non-unionism set in again, unemployment rates in Rhondda went over forty per cent, and a rival, non-political union was supported by the coal owners.

Lewis Jones did not know how to defend: his refusal to work with blackleg labour led to his dismissal as checkweigher in 1929 and to the start of his final decade of work amongst the unemployed whose wretched condition now symbolised the coalfield in a grim reversal of its pre-war buoyancy. By this time he was an orator of unrivalled gifts, able to articulate the emotions of people with whom, in all other ways, he merged. He became a Welsh organiser for the National Unemployed Workers' Movement under whose auspices he led three Hunger Marches from South Wales. Within the coalfield he was active in arranging demonstrations and meetings, culminating in the huge protests against the Means Test in early 1935. That these were all-party demonstrations based on the entire community confirmed his belief in the potential for total, political involvement inherent in his society, if only the scales of illusion and mutual suspicion could be permanently removed.

To the end he argued for unity within the Labour movement and, in the heyday of the Popular Front, shared many platforms with Labour politicians. At a by-election in 1936 he was elected, from mid-Rhondda, to the

Glamorgan County Council as one of only two Communist County Councillors. The international struggle against Fascism was seen as an extension of the daily fight against exploitation at home; his speeches had him bound over by the law yet again.

He volunteered to go to the Spanish Civil War but was considered more valuable as a domestic propagandist. Besides, his earlier brushes with the conventions then considered proper in a leading Communist party member did not augur well for the kind of harsh political discipline required in Spain. As if to quell all doubts about his political drive, he worked unstintingly in the cause of Spanish Aid and it was in this cause that he died when his heart gave out after addressing over thirty street meetings in a day. That was the week in January 1939 in which Barcelona fell to Franco.

Lewis Jones was no martyr, however, if martyrdom suggests passivity, resignation in the face of overwhelming odds, the victim's brave acceptance of his fate. The point of his life, on the contrary, was its aggressive activity, its breezy, vital lustiness that refused, in the name of others, to be graceful. This is the legacy, too, of the novels he managed to write despite his intensely packed life.

We Live appeared, as a sequel to *Cwmardy*, in 1939 after Lewis Jones's death. The proofs, which had been worked on, were seen through the press by D. M. Garman (of Lawrence and Wisnart) who wrote the brief foreword, and Mavis Llywelyn, a schoolteacher and Communist Party activist, who had helped Jones greatly with the mechanics of both books.

It is, superficially, the more interesting of the two since it moves rapidly from one major event of working-class struggle to another, until it ends with Len's heroic death in Spain. This eagerness to highlight each incident is the book's major weakness as a novel, since it causes Lewis Jones to turn almost all of his characters into automated abstractions whose fictional duty is only to spill the historical

Introduction

beans. What is of decided interest, though, is the retelling of party discussions, pit-meetings and political arguments, often through long speeches that are highly effective as isolated moments, and the impelling need of the author to convey the undoubted importance of the matters he puts before us like quick-fire cinematic images. This he does by investing his novel with the aura of a romantic heroism which, he is certain, in real life will produce the political fruits he desires.

The book was written at the height of the decade's feverish political whirl and stands as an earnest, insistent piece of propaganda. The problem it poses as a novel on the interwar years in the coalfield cannot be glibly dismissed for all that, because its blend of melodrama, sentiment and collective action is uncomfortably close to a reality, in which it was possible for 'the People' to be eulogised as a stage army even by those, like Lewis Jones, who knew them (as he showed in *Cwmardy*) too intimately to reduce them elsewhere to less than their particular selves. The forced creation of a South Walian working class from the late nineteenth century meant that people wrenched from the closeness of personal and rooted traditions into an impersonal and a-historical world required – in order to have a sense of themselves as a proletariat – an identity that could only be their own if mediated through ballads, games, choirs, jokes and anecdotes which mirrored their own collective endeavours, courage and self-deprecation. That new tradition, for all its ambiguities, was neither crushed nor passive. It spawned, in addition, an organically-related intelligentsia who were keenly aware of the self-making of this manufactured working-class. Lewis Jones was a spokesman of their human potential who became less concerned to depict the subtle contradictions of a forgotten people as he grew more anxious to trumpet, in his fiction, what they had already shown in their struggles – the fact that *We Live*.

April 1978   *University College, Cardiff*

FOREWORD

LEWIS JONES died on January 27th, 1939, suddenly and unexpectedly, after addressing thirty meetings during the day through a loud-speaker in the streets of the Rhondda, appealing for food for Spain. The last hours of his life were spent serving the cause to which for a quarter of a century he had devoted all his energy and imagination, the cause of the working-class ; and not the least of his services was the writing of his two novels—*Cwmardy*, which was published in 1937, and *We Live*, the proofs of which he had corrected shortly before his death.

This is no place to attempt an estimation of his achievement either as a political leader or as a novelist, but a few facts about his life may help towards the understanding of both. He was forty-one when he died, and, with the exception of very short intervals, all his life was spent in the Rhondda. His last home faced his first across the valley, in the small village of Clydach, near Tonypandy. Like most boys of the South Wales mining valleys, born before the epoch of mass unemployment, he went straight from school to work in the pits, and for the next fifteen years or so he was to experience every phase of the miner's life ; the long gruelling hours in the depths of the earth, lock-outs and strikes, trade union organisation, struggles with the police. His work-mates in the Cambrian pit recognized his abilities and appointed him Check-Weigher, a post which he filled until he refused to work with blacklegs.

Shortly after the war he won a scholarship to the now defunct Labour College in South Kensington, and it was while there that he joined the Communist Party in 1923. Before he went to the College, young as he was, he had been chairman of the Cambrian Colliers Committee, and when he returned to the Rhondda he resumed the exhausting life of a militant. Already he was known as an orator of the first order, and he travelled to meetings up and down the country, but always coming back to his beloved Rhondda, the nerve centre of his activities and of his imagination. Here, amongst his own people, he won a reputation for his courage and his ability in leading their struggle. His class enemies and his political opponents respected him, and the ordinary men and women loved him for his humanity and humour, and for the glowing imagery of his speeches. Several times he led them on hunger marches, and at a bye-election in 1936 they elected him to the Glamorgan County Council. He used to take the bus down to Cardiff to attend meetings after signing on at the Tonypandy Labour Exchange.

This is a background of activity which many working-class militants will recognize. The bare facts, however, convey little of the qualities that made Lewis Jones so lovable as a friend and so inspiring as a man. No one, I think, who talked with him, even for a short time, could have failed to be impressed by the restless energy of his mind and the boldness of his imagination. New ideas, new experiences delighted him, yet he was not interested in ideas for their own sake ; they were valuable to him in the degree to which they could be translated into action. Thus, though he only began to write during the last few years of his life, the process of imaginative creation was not new to him. What he had previously formulated in action and in the lovely cadences of his oratory, he now expressed in his novels, and he brought to the art of writing the same qualities —a rare tenderness for the humanity in people, an objective understanding of the struggle of his class, a lyrical appreciation of natural beauty and a high sense of drama.

Such a combination of qualities is enough to make him a forceful and original writer. If his natural gift was as an orator—and he had perfected this as an art —he had, I feel convinced, progressed far enough in the practice of literature to make, with his two novels, a real and vital contribution to the culture of our times.

D. M. GARMAN.

CONTENTS

CHAPTER I

Clouds over Cwmardy

THE wind howled over the mountain and swept down on Cwmardy as though chased by a million nightmares. Dark corners roared and whistled when they encountered the onslaught, while telephone wires twanged under the pressure. Street lamps turned the moisture into miniature rainbows that glistened on the slimy road. The tumult echoed high up over the valley, where the tempest spied the fissures in the mountain and battered its way in, to return with increasing fury on the village beneath.

A tall smokestack stuck its head through the ruddy glow of the pit furnaces, too proud to notice the clamour of the storm, above which sounded the " chug-chug " of the pit engines, broken at short intervals by a " clanketty-clang " as the pit spewed two trams full of coal into the storm and sucked two empties out of it. The wind howled more loudly still at the theft, but to no avail ; for immediately the empty trams were in the grip of the cage it tore them from the elements and plunged them into the blackness of the pit. The heavy wooden droppers on the shaft-head beat back the chasing wind and rain, which sought revenge on the houses lower down the valley.

The little lights in the cottage windows of Cwmardy winked at the storm, inviting it to burst open the doors and share with the family inside the cosy heat of the open fire-place. Behind one of these windows an old woman sat patiently darning a sock. Her drawn face, with its yellowish skin, reflected the shadows from the fire, before which she sat with parted knees. A huge man was stretched languidly in an armchair nearby. His slightly bowed shoulders and silver-streaked hair betrayed advancing age, and his face was remarkable for its long, stiff moustaches and the black scars that emphasized its lines.

I

For about the twentieth time in as many minutes the old woman raised her eyes from the wool in her lap and looked towards the window, down whose cracked panes the water streamed.

" I wonder what in the world our Len and Mary do want out on such a night as this ? " she muttered disconsolately. " They will be sure to get wet to the skin, and with her bad chest that will mean pewmonia so sure as God is my judge."

She stopped for some moments and listened to the squealing storm, while the old man grumbled a curse at the smoke which every now and then belched from the chimney into the kitchen where the old couple were sitting. After a while she turned her attention to her companion.

" Fitter if you went out to look for them, James, instead of sitting by there on your backside, like if they was safe and sound in the house and you didn't have a worry in the world," she complained.　Jim looked at her a moment, then spat heavily into the fire before replying.

" Huh !　What you talk about, 'ooman ?　If the son of Big Jim is 'fraid of a little drop of water and a little puff of wind, it is time for you to ask what is the matter with you," and with this trenchant remark he placidly resumed his pipe.

The steel-rimmed spectacles on the tip of her nose quivered with her indignation.　" Shame on you, James, talking 'bout your only son like that !　But there, I do only waste my time talking to you.　Huh !　It is all right for you to talk, with your body so big as a bull's and your head just so dull as one."

She got up from the chair and went to the door, which she opened just wide enough to push her head through ; but though she shouted her son's name at the top of her sharp voice, it got lost in the wind even as the cry left her lips. Big Jim turned his head and growled.

" Shut that bloody door, Shân fach, or this smoke will make me into a kipper.　There's nothing for you to worry 'bout, mun.　I 'spect they have gone to a meeting and 'on't call here 'cos it is too rough to come up the hill."

Shân banged the door and shuffled back to the chair, her unlaced boots flapping on the stony kitchen floor with every step.

" That's how you men always is," she grunted.　" Always

your own comforts first, never mind 'bout nobody else.
No, not even your own flesh and blood. Well, well!
There have never been such a night since the 'splosion, and
there you be, James, so happy as a tomcat on the tiles,
knowing all the time that they are out in the middle of it."

This brought him erect in his chair. " Hell-fire, 'ooman!
Have I not told you they is safe enough ? You be nuff,
mun, to give a man the bile and diarrhœa all in one. And
you do call this a storm—ha, ha ! It is nothing but a sun
shower. Good God ! I 'member once in Africa—— "

Shân forestalled the threatened reminiscence.

" I don't want to hear nothing 'bout your old Africa or
your storm. No. Pity it hadn't took you then ; it 'ood
have saved me a lifetime of worry and trouble."

She bent her head and went on with her darning, raising
her eyes every few minutes to glance at the ticking clock,
whose rhythmic monotone for some time dominated the
kitchen. Big Jim went on smoking contentedly,
occasionally spitting into the grate and twisting his soap-
stiffened moustache with a slow, dignified twirl. He
looked up once at the garishly painted almanack on the
mantelshelf, and a distant look stole into his eyes when he
remarked.

" Duw, duw ! The years is slipping by pretty quick
now, Shân fach. Only the other day us was in the middle
of the 'splosion, and here it is 1924 already. The years
are going over our heads like months, muniferni."

Shân glanced from her darning to reply softly : " Aye ;
you are right. Us is getting on now, James bach, and the
earth will soon be calling to us."

Outside the house the storm seemed to have swept the
streets clear of humans, but the structure known as the
" Fountain " on the village square glistened as the lights
from the Boar's Head chased the shadows over its body of
rusted iron.

Ben the Barber's doorway looked like a black blob
painted into the darkness stretching beyond the rim of
light cast from the windows of the Boar's Head. But
occasionally the blob was pierced by a tiny gleam as the
two policemen crouching within the door exposed a button.
Both were well protected from the storm, but this did not

prevent the moisture dangling from the end of their noses. The taller of the two raised his head from the keyhole for a moment to whisper excitedly : " I'm sure I heard something about lock-out."

His mate merely growled.

" Huh ! I wish they'd pack up for the night. Perhaps we could sneak into somewhere dry, then." He noticed the other's head still lifted from the keyhole, and broke off his grouse to say : " Keep your bloody head down, mun, or we might lose something important, 'specially if you heard right about the lock-out."

The other obeyed, at the same time retorting : " Huh ! What do that matter ? We can always put it down in the station the same as if we have heard it, can't we ? "

A shuffle of chairs came from the room and he sprang erect immediately, with a sibilant warning. " Sssh ! They've finished and are coming out."

His mate, draping the cape more closely about his shoulders, hastened towards the fountain to be pulled up sharply.

" Not that way, you fool. You'll be right in the light there."

He hurriedly retraced his steps and the two had hardly pressed themselves into the black recess of another doorway when a number of people came out of Ben the Barber's.

One of the men muttered to the woman next him, as he buttoned his coat up to the neck and watched her do the same : " Good God, what a night, Mary ! "

" Aye, Len. Terrible, isn't it ? We'd better run or we'll be soaking long before we reach your mother's."

He caught her arm and both ran into the driving rain, burying themselves in the darkness beyond the fountain. Half-way up the hill they came to an involuntary stop, panting and dripping. Len put his arm round the thin shoulders of his wife as he heard her breath wheeze in her throat, and gently drew her small form into the shelter afforded by the pine end of a house. A racking cough suddenly tore at her chest, and he helped her wipe away the stained sputum that wetted her lips, his slim body nearly hiding hers.

After a while she broke the silence that had followed the fit of coughing, her voice still harsh with the strain.

" I'm sorry I went to that meeting."

He stooped a little to peer more closely into her face as he voiced his surprise. " Sorry ? What have you got to be sorry about, Mary ? "

" Oh, I don't know. Only I thought, when you asked me to come, we were going to hear something definite about all these rumours of a lock-out. But instead of that, all I've heard is blabbing about revolutions and politics."

He drew himself up in a hurt manner, his arm still about her shoulders. " Half a minute, Mary. Don't say that politics is nonsense. Didn't you hear the chairman say that politics is everything for the workers ? Good God ! If we had more politics we wouldn't be in the hole we're in now."

She interrupted him petulantly. " Oh, shut up for goodness sake ! You take everything that Harry Morgan tells you as if it was gospel. You make me sick, Len. Here we've been talking all night about revolutions, when very soon we might want all our strength to face the lock-out that is coming if what our women say is true."

Her words stung him and he lost his temper. " Aye, women's cackle—with their arms folded on their bellies, while we are in work ! Huh ! You'd sooner listen to rubbish like that than to sense the same as you had to-night. But I don't care a hang ! You can say what you like, I'm glad I joined the Party to-night."

She looked up into his face, and even in the darkness he saw the whites of her eyes gleam as she said : " Aye, I know that. But what else could I expect from a husband whose head is as soft as his heart ? "

Len swallowed audibly and tried to say something, but the words wouldn't come. He was used to her vehemence, particularly when she felt something deeply, and had only asked her to the meeting in the hope that Harry Morgan, the Party leader, would have shaken the convictions bred in her by Ezra Jones, her father, the local miners' leader. He was himself susceptible to the same influence and always hesitated when they combined forces against him in an argument, although he never admitted this fact even to himself.

To cover his discomfiture he suggested that they proceed, and neither of them said any more as they plodded up the

hill. They entered Shân's house without knocking; but
the old woman looked up from her darning when she heard
the latch rattle.

" Huh! Fine time of the night, indeed, for a young
stripling of a boy to be out," she began, at the same time
making place for them near the fire. " When I was your
age, my boy, I 'oodn't dare to be out after seven o'clock,
and here you strut in with Mary fach and her bad chest
at 'leven 'xactly like it was first thing in the morning.
You ought to be ashamed of yourself, Len."

He said nothing, and squatted comfortably in a chair,
but before he had time to settle down properly she ordered:

" Come here. Leave me feel if your clothes is wet."

" Oh, let me alone, mam. We've only been to a meeting,
and it's bad enough to have Mary nagging without you
helping her," he replied petulantly.

" Ah, answering your only mother back, is it? Don't
forget my boy, when I was your age I 'oodn't dare to look
at my mother twice, let alone answer her back, God bless
her!" She raised the canvas apron to her nose. " But
there. What is the use of arguing? Children to-day is too
big for their boots and half of them don't know they are
born. Huh!"

She turned to Mary. " Take your wet clothes off, my
gel, and put them by the fire while I do make a cup
of tea."

" Don't bother, mam. We'll be going before long,"
Mary replied, at the same time drawing her chair up, and
continuing: " What do you think have happened
to-night?"

Shân interestedly cocked her ears up at once and Mary
went on, without looking at Len, who wondered what on
earth she was driving at.

" Our Len have joined Harry Morgan's Party."

Shân gave a little scream: " What? Joined those
infidels?"

She was overcome with emotion for some moments,
during which Jim slyly opened one eye which he immediately
closed when he saw her looking at him.

" Wake up, James," she demanded. " Something awful
have happened to our Len. Oh, Duw! After me rearing
him tidy and 'spectable all these years and taking him to

chapel every Sunday like a clock—and now to come to this ! ''

She covered her eyes with her apron, and did not see Jim stirring awkwardly and blinking his eyes like a man suddenly awakened from a deep sleep.

'' How be, Mary fach. What is all this bloody fuss about ? '' he greeted them.

'' Our Len have joined the Party,'' Mary informed him.

'' Huh ! Well, that's better than joining the militia, in't it ? ''

Len smiled at the remark, knowing by it that his father was siding with him against the two women.

Shân turned to Mary. '' There ! What did I tell you ? The man have got no shame in him. You can see now what I have had to put up with all these years. No wonder my hair have gone white years before its time.''

This statement stung Jim, and he drew himself erect in the chair. '' Don't you listen to all she do tell you, Mary fach. I have been man and wife to her for more than forty years, and she have got nothing to say against me.'' He lost his temper. '' Hell-fire ! What can I help if our Len have joined the Party. He haven't kilt nobody, have he ? No, by damn, and if I was only twenty years younger, I 'ood do the same as him.'' The challenge brought no response, so with many sighs and groans he stood up, and Mary let him take off her wet coat and arrange it on the brass rod over the fireplace.

Shân was busily buttering some bread when her wandering glance noticed thin spirals of steam ascend from Len's trousers. She stared hard for a moment and bent her head to have a better look before declaring triumphantly.

'' There you are ! Whatever I do say is always wrong, but now you can see for yourselfs. Look at that trousers, Mary. It is wet to the skin. Come on, my boy, off with it this minute.''

There was some commotion while Len, realising the futility of argument, changed into an old pair of his father's trousers, which hung about him like a blanket. Thus satisfied, Shân called them to the supper table, and it was some time before the rattle of crockery and the crunching of home-made pickles was interrupted by her abrupt query.

" How is your father, Mary fach ? I haven't seen him since old Mrs. Davies, Ty-top, was buried."

Mary hastily swallowed the food in her mouth. " He's not half well." Then, turning to Big Jim, she said : " I believe he's worrying about all this talk of a lock-out. He went off early yesterday morning to see somebody or other, and he's been moping like a bear ever since." She sighed. " I wish I knew what is the matter with him, but he won't tell me or Len a word."

Jim sucked the drops of tea from the end of his moustache with his lower lip, then commented : " Well, I don't know what you do say about it, Len, but there's something in the wind. Look how us was on stop to-day for more than an hour waiting for trams. It never used to be like that. No, muniferni ! Aye, gels ; I heard Shenkin the fireman tell Sam Dangler that they have closed two of the pits the other side of the mountain and have rosed the horses."

" Why is that, Len ? " asked Shân, now anxious to placate him. " I thought they did only rise the horses when there is going to be a strike or something like that, and I have never heard of a strike over the mountain. No, nor have Mrs. Jones, Number two, either, because she was talking to me to-day and she never said a word, although she have got brothers working over there."

" No, mam. The men are not on strike, but the owners say that they have shut the pit for good and are sending some of the horses over here and selling the others."

Mary had remained singularly quiet during this conversation, but she now broke in sharply : " That's what makes me so mad, and why I went to the meeting with Len to-night—worse luck. They'll find work for horses. Aye, they'll see to it they are not left to wander about the pit ; but they don't care a hang what happens to the men." Her voice rose passionately. " No, they'll be left on top with no one to find work for them or to see that they are fed."

Big Jim leaned forward in his chair and tapped her shoulder patronisingly with a huge forefinger. " Aye, aye, Mary, my gel, you is quite right. If old Cwmardy and the company do close down our pit, they will see to it that the horses is all right, but us will have to look after our bloody selves. That's the way of the world, my gel. It have always been like that ever since I have knowed it, and always will be. What say you, Shân ? "

It was Len who answered. " That's one of the things for which I joined the Party to-night," he declared, glad for some reason to justify his action. But Shân only glared at him, and Mary opened her mouth to say something when the donging tones of the clock interrupted her. They looked at it simultaneously and Len got to his feet in a flurry, the ends of the trousers dragging under his boots. " Come on, Mary," he pleaded ; " five o'clock in the morning will soon be here. I can call for my trousers to-morrow night after I come home from work."

They all rose to their feet and the young couple, after bidding the others good-night, left, with Shân admonishing : " Now, be careful where you do tread, 'cause it is the easiest thing in the world to break your necks on a night like this."

Meanwhile two policemen in the station were slowly removing their waterproof leggings. One was too fat to bend sufficiently and had to wait until his mate could help him.

" Ah," he gasped, straightening his tunic, " thank God that lot's over."

" What lot—your leggings ? "

" No, you silly fathead ! I'm talking about that bloody meeting."

A head poked itself around the door of the mess-room in which the two officers were sitting, and a voice hissed : " Look out, boys. He's just come in."

The fat policeman gulped nervously, then said : " Funny for the old man to be around this time of the night. I thought he'd be safely tucked up in bed with one of his dames by now."

" Don't you worry about them tales, mate. Old long 'un is more concerned about his duty and these bloody Bolshies that are springing up all over the valley than he is about women."

The door opened and the two men sprang to attention as the inspector, followed by another uniformed individual, walked in. Their salute was barely acknowledged by the painfully elongated man who walked direct to the fireplace and then turned his back to the flames. From this point he scrutinised the remaining inmates of the room with eyes that were red-rimmed, as though he slept little or drank much. A short, bristly moustache emphasised the thickness of his lips, and he stared at his subordinates for some time with a fish-like, glassy look. When he spoke his voice was as thin as the hair he tried to spread all over his head.

" Well, who was at the meeting ? "

" Harry Morgan, Fred Lewis, Len Roberts and his wife, sir—— "

" Yes—yes, hurry up and don't eat your words ! " he snapped, gently stroking his posterior as the heat warmed his flesh.

The man so addressed coloured and hastened his recital of names. When he had finished, the thin man remained thoughtfully silent for some moments before saying : " Hmm. Len Roberts and his wife, eh ? It seems this chap Morgan is beginning to spread his wings. Hmm."

He looked up sharply to ask : " What did they say ? "

The two policemen looked uncomfortable and fidgeted uneasily without speaking.

" Come, come. Haven't you heard what I said ? "

The fatter constable drew himself erect and saluted again. " Well, it's like this, sir. It was such a dirty night and the wind was howling so much that it was impossible to hear a word of what was going on inside except a blur of voices."

The thin face before him turned from red to purple and a little time elapsed before the lips parted to bark out : " What ? Do you mean to tell me you heard nothing ? That you listen to a nest of Bolsheviks plotting sedition and have nothing to report ? "

He swallowed hard, then turned abruptly from the flabbergasted constables : " Inspector, I want a full report of that meeting first thing in the morning."

The inspector saluted and both left the room, but the discomfited policemen remained standing for a long while, both looking miserable and awkward.

At last the taller gave a deep sigh. " Ah well. The old man must have been upset about something. Perhaps he's had a row with his old woman."

" Maybe. But that's no reason why he should have his

bang out on us. No good arguing about it now, however. The best thing we can do is to prepare that report."

They pulled their coats off and drew the table nearer the fire.

Outside the station the wind still howled round the streets of Cwmardy, seeming to gather greater fury because the rain had deserted it. A group of men, their heads bent to the beating wind that ballooned their coats behind them like bustles, battled past the police station and its two busy occupants.

" What a hell of a night ! " one remarked, his words partially strangled by the wind.

" Aye, but we can be thankful the rain have stopped, or we'd be soaked long before we reached the pit," another remarked.

" Not much odds about that. You want to see Dai Cannon's heading. The water pours down from the top, and bubbles up from the bottom. Gee ! And the stink— ugh ! It's like a thousand lavatories and polecats all in one. He's got to work under zinc now to keep the water from his body."

" Ach ! Zinc be damned ! What bloody use is that to a man ? He can't carry it about with him from the face to the tram. Better for him to stick the water than try to dodge something that can't be dodged."

They continued to fight against the wind and presently one of them asked : " What's all this talk about us going to be locked out ? "

The reply came instantly : " By damn, they might as well shut the bloody hole for good for any use it is to us on the wages they pay now."

Further conversation was lost in the noise of the pit-hooter, which suddenly split the air with reverberating blasts that echoed through the crevices of every house in the valley. The group of men hurried their pace in response to the command, and in a short time Cwmardy was left to the mercy of the wind as the clanking of hob-nailed boots on stone died away.

CHAPTER II

Another Victim

THE following afternoon Len wearily dragged his feet out
of the pit-cage and was glad to find that the storm had
blown itself out and a yellow sun was poking its thin rays
through the murk of the valley. The sight and the cool
air invigorated him and he wasn't long reaching home, where
Mary was busily cooking his dinner.

Before pulling off his dirty coat he asked : " Where's
your father, Mary ? "

She looked up from the saucepan over which she was
bending, and although her face was flushed with the heat
from the fire, he noticed that her eyes were sad in the dark
shadows that circled them.

" I don't know, Len. He's been out again since early
this morning." She paused and stirred the contents of the
saucepan, then continued, without looking at him : " I've
told him you joined the Party last night."

Len stopped short, his coat hanging loosely from one
arm. " What did you want to do that for ? " he demanded
sharply. " But there, what does it matter ? He was
bound to know sooner or later."

He went on with his preparations for dinner, and while
she was serving it up he asked : " What did he say ? "

She waited until she had shared the dinner on three
plates, one of which she put on the hob, then answered :
" I don't know what he said altogether. Here, eat your
dinner ; we can talk after." She sat tiredly in the chair
beside him and pecked at her food, leaving half of it
untouched. Having finished his dinner, he noisily moved
his chair back and reached up to the mantelpiece for a
cigarette, while Mary poured him a cup of tea. He puffed
away silently, trying to look unconcerned, but all the time
watching her through the smoke that left his mouth, as
she patiently began clearing the dinner things.

12

At last his impatience bubbled over and he again asked :
" Tell me, Mary, what did he say ? "

Her hands trembled fretfully when she replied : " Oh,
for God's sake don't let's bother our heads about that
nonsense now ! " She went on with her work and after
it was finished sat down, drawing her hand across her
forehead.

Len became immediately solicitous, and tried to soothe
her. " Your head is bad, my dear ? " he queried. " Why
don't you take a powder and have a lie down. I can
manage by myself now."

The gentle tones made her ashamed of her irritability,
and she looked at him affectionately as she replied : " It's
all right, Len. Only I'm worried about Dad."

She paused to wipe her perspiring hands on her apron.
" I don't know what's coming over him. He's getting more
miserable every day and hardly touches a bit of food. Oh,
Len, he's breaking up fast and is not the same Dad I've
known in the past."

Len, conscious of how deeply she loved her father and
how she was affected by the change taking place in him,
hardly knew what to say, but managed to murmur : " Aye,
I've noticed him myself these last few weeks. It must
be his age," he added consolingly. " Look at my old
man—he's getting so miserable that it's hellish to work with
him. We'll be the same ourselves when we're their age,
I suppose." He tried to laugh, but the half-hearted
attempt drew no response from his wife.

Len knocked the light off his cigarette and carefully put
the stump back on the mantelshelf before going out into the
backyard to fetch the tub, which he placed in the centre
of the kitchen. This done, he pulled off his dusty shirt
and wet singlet ; then, naked to the waist, lifted the boiler
of hot water from the fire and poured it into the tub, where
Mary cooled it with panfuls of cold water. Bent double
over the edge of the tub, he began bathing, and Mary
gathered together the discarded pit-clothes.

His head was a mass of black lather when he heard her
say : " There have been more compensation cases here
for you to-day."

Len hurriedly swilled the soapsuds from his head and
sat on the tub-rim while she handed him a towel. He

wiped himself, but his hair was still damp, although his face was pink with rubbing.

" Who's been, Mary ? " he asked.

" Oh, old Reuben and the boy with the broken back," she answered, washing his back vigorously, then taking the towel from him to use it herself.

Len stood up and, unbuttoning his trousers, let them fall about his feet before stepping naked into the tub.

" Well, well," he said while he soaped his legs. " It's a shame the way they're mucking about with the compo people." Mary watched the ripple of the skin over his ribs as he raised water with his cupped hands to swill his legs.

" Yes, you're right, Len," she commented bitterly, her mind focused on the thin body before her. " The company have now offered them a lump sum each to square them off."

Len's amazement was demonstrated by the way he let his hands drop limply to his sides and looked at her, utterly unconscious of his nakedness. " What ? Offered them a lump sum ? " He clicked his tongue against his teeth in audible disgust. " Well, well. That means the rotters want to wash their hands of them, now the poor dabs are no use. No wonder your old man is worried, by damn."

He came out of the tub and began dressing in his evening clothes. He had already pulled the clean shirt over his head, when a new idea entered his mind.

" But why do they want to buy the compo men off, now ? " he asked in bewilderment.

Mary shook her head. " I don't know, unless it's something to do with all this talk that we are going to be locked out," she replied hesitantly.

Len shook his head, as puzzled as she was, but he made no further comment as she helped him take the tub back out.

A further smoke revived his spirits and he asked her to come to the pictures.

" I'm sorry, Len, but you know I've got a Woman's Guild to-night, and I can't let them down," she replied.

This upset him again, and he muttered half savagely :
" I don't know, but whenever I ask you to come with me, Mary, you've got this, that, or something else on. I tell

you straight I'm just fed-up." He began to shout. " I would be treated much better if I was a lodger."

Mary seemed to compress her body into knots as he continued his tirade, but she kept control of herself until he said, " Only last night, you were nagging me about joining the Party, but you don't say a word about yourself and this Guild, which is only a bloody gossip-shop, I expect."

This brought her bounding to her feet. " Don't you dare say that about our Guild, Len Roberts ! Those women do more work in a month than your Party, as you call it, can do in twelve."

" Aye," he sneered, " they'll work blue hell organising mystery tours and trips round the coast in a charabanc, but when it comes to anything that counts, they're all blab."

Mary's face went white. " Oh, so that's what you think, is it ? Now we know where we are. But let me tell you this, you and your Party will be glad to come on your hands and knees to our women for help before you'll be any good."

Len laughed loudly. " Ha-ha-ha ! That's a good un ! Ha-ha, the best I've heard for a long time ! Come to you for help—there'll be something wrong with us when we do that."

The sneer stung her deeply. " I don't know so much about that. You are all pretty good talkers. Aye, you'll talk all night about revolutions and Russia or anything that doesn't concern our people. But when it comes to a lock-out or something about the pit you're all dumb."

She challenged him with a direct question. " Tell me, how much time was spent last night talking about conditions in Cwmardy ? " She answered herself without giving him time. " Five minutes and not a second more. Bah ! Fitter if you and Harry Morgan thought a bit less about people in other countries and a bit more about your own."

This was unexpected and caught Len awkwardly, but he tried to defend the position. " Half a minute, Mary. You've got to understand the conditions all over the world, mun, to know how to alter things here. Good God ! Haven't we got something to learn from the Russian revolution ? You're talking like a sledge, mun."

She made no reply other than with her eyes, which

looked at him pityingly as she rose from the chair and prepared herself for the Guild. When she was ready, he put his coat on and took his cap from the peg near the door.

Mary smiled quietly to herself and asked : " Where are you going, then ? "

" Oh, I might as well come with you down the road. I might see Will Evans or some of the boys," he replied in tones that made Mary regret her sharp words, but neither spoke again as he accompanied her down Main Street and left her at the house where the Guild held its weekly meetings.

Len continued his way aimlessly, his mind occupied with the row he had just had with Mary. But he soon forgot this and began to think of the work he had to do next day. He planned to go down earlier than usual so that he could stand some timbers before the haulier came. Having settled this, his thoughts wandered to the compensation men and the talk in the pit.

" It's a funny thing," he mused. " Ten years ago next August the Great War started, and now, nearly exactly ten years after, there's all this talk about the pit shutting down and all of us being thrown out of work. It's like as if things go in waves every so often."

He was deep in meditation of the problem when his attention was attracted by someone shouting his name. He stopped and looked behind to see two young men hurrying towards him, whom he recognised as Will Evans and Fred Lewis. The former was slim, but even with his clothes on his body gave an impression of sinewy strength. His cap, pushed carelessly to the side of his head, and the blade of grass which dangled loosely from his mouth were symptomatic of his whole approach to life. He never troubled about his appearance, and his eyes gleamed with a mischief which prompted him to see the humour in everything. He had a habit of bursting unexpectedly into a loud laugh. that rolled in recurring gusts and rising resonance from his mouth in a manner that made it irresistibly infectious. Fred Lewis, his companion, was the opposite in every way. Rather tall, his black hair made his face sallow and exposed the fallacy of the " hail, fellow, well met " demeanour which, in a patronising way, he deliberately cultivated. Fred boasted to everyone that

he was among the first to join the Party and was no less
assertive in declaring that he was its foremost theoretician.
But he never told anyone he hated Ezra, the miners' leader,
because of the latter's influence over the workmen, and
detested Harry Morgan because of his growing ability and
eloquence. All other men he regarded with contempt, as
nincompoops made to follow people like himself. Will had
long ago at work detected these weaknesses in his mate,
and never failed to take advantage of the fact, secure against
all retort in his extreme lack of self-consciousness.

The pair came up to Len, who greeted them with a casual
" How be, boys ? " But Will was bubbling over with
impatience and made no attempt to return the salutation.

" Is it true what I have heard, that you have joined the
Party ? " he asked.

Len merely nodded his head and Fred said, " There you
are. Will you believe me now ? "

Will Evans looked at Len with open mouth, then began
to laugh unrestrainedly. " Well, by damn, I never
thought you had nuff sense, Len, to do a thing like that.
Ha-ha ! Ho-ho-ho ! "

Len appeared hurt by this doubtful compliment, but had
no time to say anything before Fred interjected : " Oh,
I don't know about that, Will. Len has got the average
intelligence, and in any case he can always turn to me for
help when he's in a knot."

Will turned to the speaker, his eyes filled with admiration.
" By damn, Fred, if you keep on you will so sure as hell
land up in Parliament one day."

Fred unconsciously expanded his chest. " Well, there's
many worse and less clever than me there, so I don't see
why not."

Will glanced at Len's face, but the misery he saw on it
made him change the subject. " You're looking like a dog
with the colic. Buck up, mun," he remarked.

" Oh, I'm all right," came the dejected reply. " Only
I thought to go to the pictures to-night, but Mary went to
the Guild instead, and I was wandering about on my own
till you chaps came up."

Will burst into another guffaw of laughter, which impelled
a passer-by to ask : " Happy, to-night, in't you, Will ?
Have the old man lost a leg, or what ? "

" You mind your own bloody business, Twm. Len by here have lost his missus in the Guild, and he don't know what to do with hisself."

The new-comer, although uninvited, joined the company, and the conversation continued for a long time. It was only eventually interrupted when Fred's restless eyes saw a cortege of men in pit-clothes slowly coming towards them down the street.

" Hush, boys, somebody has had a tap." In an instant the whole street was silent but for the sharp " tip-tap " of iron-shod boots as the men, four of them carrying a stretcher covered completely with brattice cloth, passed by.

Someone whispered : " Who is it ? "

To be answered in a softer whisper : " Si Spraggs. He was caught by the journey, poor dab, and never had a chance."

The news passed from mouth to mouth as quickly as a telephone message, and even before Len reached the door of the Guild-room the women were already coming out, their eyes full of fearful queries till he told them who it was. They immediately became relieved and solicitous.

One stout woman who had reared a houseful of children, all of whom were now working, muttered disconsolately : " Well, well. There have been nothing but worry and trouble in that house ever since I have knowed it." She outlined the history of the bereaved family while the other women listened attentively, at the same time inwardly congratulating themselves that the corpse did not belong to them.

When the recital was finished, one asked, " She is going to have another baby, in't she ? I fancy I saw her looking like it the other day in the shop, but I didn't have much time to notice."

They went back into the house and continued the discussion there. Before they finished they had planned to provide a wreath, and had allocated themselves in pairs to be responsible for the widow's house and to keep her company until the body was buried.

Len felt like following Mary, whose face had gone grey when she heard the news, into the Guild-room. Common sense held him back, and he retraced his steps up the street, to find his mates had disappeared. This did not worry him, however, because the tragedy had swept everything else from his mind and he automatically followed his feet while his imagination ran riot.

His first conscious knowledge of direction came with the increased palpitation of his heart. He stopped to rest and looking around saw below him the narrow strip of valley which Cwmardy headed like a black bonnet. The evening was now brilliantly fine, and the air on the mountain clear as he slowly continued his way to the top. But the thought of the corpse followed him and stamped itself more deeply into his brain with every step he took across the mountain, till he sighted the valley on the other side. He sat down, and after a while his thoughts drifted and he began to appraise the scene before his eyes. He compared the gloom of the village beneath and the thousands of dark lives it contained with the bright sky and clear air above in which the larks tinkled their tunes. Len followed the ascending music and wondered if the larks sang because they were happy. The people he knew mostly sang hymns, which were always sad and seemed to harmonise with their sorrows. He let his eyes wander down the length of the ragged valley and saw the smokeless stacks of the idle pits near its end, a sight which prompted him to wonder how soon Cwmardy pits would be equally silent and dead. It seemed that everything he saw and heard was a portent of impending dereliction and despair, a thought which made him mentally forgive Mary the quarrel for which he was at least equally responsible. He sighed and turned in the direction of the Channel, which glistened in the distance like a ribbon of light.

His boyhood's romantic ambition to become a sailor had evaporated with the passing years, but a strange tenderness and longing still surged through him whenever he caught a glimpse of the sea. It always took his mind back to the time his mother had taken him on the chapel excursion and to the day in Blackpool at the beginning of the War, when he had first made love to Mary. Musing in this manner, he lost all consciousness of time until the night began to wrap him in its cold blanket. Presently he began to shiver, and rising to his feet, he slowly made his way home down the mountain.

CHAPTER III

The Lock-out

THE Big House, perched on a jutting crest half-way up the mountain, brooded whitely in the dusk. Its windows, already reflecting the lights behind, shone through the trees that surrounded this mansion belonging to the colliery company. From its altitude it looked down on the pits and valley its occupants dominated.

Lord Cwmardy, head of the company controlling the pits, rose from a chair and looked at the three men who sat with him in the drawing-room of the Big House. They sat in different postures, but each of them accepted the warm invitation of the cushioned chair which nearly buried him. Cwmardy's square, clean-shaven face with its silvered hair and the poise of the broad shoulders demonstrated the strength and the self-confidence of the man. Pouring himself a glass of liquor from the decanter on the table, he sipped it appreciatively, then began to speak in deep tones that fitted in with his general build. He told his listeners the banks were pressing and that nothing faced the company but liquidation followed by complete reorganisation of the pits. His voice shook a little when he explained that the working conditions and price-lists would have to be drastically altered. He had been born in Cwmardy and reared with its people, and always felt a vague sentimental attachment to them, but he soon gripped himself as he concluded his report.

Mr. Higgins, the representative of the banks, stretched his long body more comfortably in the chair and carefully stroked his grey moustache, with a hand noticeable for its slender whiteness, before saying, " I believe Lord Cwmardy has explained the position fully. I don't pretend to understand the technique of mining. That is your business, gentlemen ; but I do understand it is high time something

was done to ensure payment of interest on the money we
have invested."

He kept on for some time, and when he finished his statement there was a long silence which was eventually broken
by Mr. Hicks, the general manager of the pits.

" I don't believe the men will accept lower price-lists,"
he commented hesitatingly.

Mr. Higgins drew himself from the chair to say coldly :
" That is their responsibility. We have done all we can,"
and the conversation drew to an abrupt close.

There was an awkward pause ; the bottles on the table
glowed in the firelight, some blood-red, others bright yellow,
like gold. At last Mr. Higgins introduced a new subject.

" What is this affair I understand you are presiding
over, Lord Cwmardy ? " he asked with assumed interest.
The coal-owner's eyes sparkled immediately.

" Oh, it's a kind of musical festival, a *gymanfa ganu*, as
our people call it," he replied. " We usually get some very
good singing, and I enjoy attending them."

Once started on this subject he was in his element and
for a long time entertained his listeners with anecdotes
relating to it. When his guests retired, Lord Cwmardy
strolled to the window and watched for many minutes
the twinkling lights of the valley. Something like a sigh
escaped him as he turned back to the room.

Next morning Len was sleeping like a log and Mary had
to shake him roughly before he woke. Once down the
stairs, however, he soon recovered his faculties and began
dressing in his pit-clothes, while Mary, her nightdress
covered with Shân's shawl, prepared breakfast. Before
the meal was finished they heard sounds from her father's
bedroom, followed by his entry into the kitchen. Ezra's
hair was bushy but grey, and the ends of his once-trim
moustache were ragged, as though they were continually
being gnawed. His eyes, dark like Mary's, were sunk into
his head. The brows were so thick that his eyes appeared
to be half closed ; but the shortish, broad body showed the
essential alertness which, together with a stubborn tenacity
in doing what he regarded as right, irrespective of other
people's opinions, were his main characteristics.

Mary hastened to pour her father a cup of tea as he took

his seat in the armchair at the side of the fire. This helped
to ease the tightness in his chest a little, and he asked :
" Did you hear anything particular in the pit yesterday,
Len ? "

Before he could receive a reply, the old miners' leader
hastened out at the back, where he coughed painfully for a
while then returned to the kitchen.

" Ah, that's better," he gasped, licking his moustache.
" Hand me that cup, Mary." He took a sip of tea and
continued : " What was I talking about ? Oh, I know.
Yes, there's something big in the wind. Lord Cwmardy is
down again. That's the third time now, and he doesn't come
here for nothing. I wish I knew what was in his mind."

His voice had become puzzled, and he stuffed his pipe
with the herb mixture which Big Jim was prepared to
gamble his life was the best cure for asthma.

Len looked over the rim of the saucer he held to his lips,
gulped down the tea in his mouth and nodded his head as
he commented : " Aye, Will Smallbeer was talking about
it yesterday. The trams have been coming pretty slow
these last few days, and he said we can expect short time
before very long now."

Ezra looked up sharply. " Will Smallbeer ? What does
he know ? What he says isn't worth taking notice of.
But, all the same, listen to what the men are saying, Len.
Their guesses are never far off the mark."

Len rose and put his coat on, wondering what Ezra was
driving at, but he made no further remark. When he
was dressed he kissed Mary, bade the two good morning,
and left them alone together.

Big Jim was ready and waiting for his son when the latter
reached his parent's house, where, as usual, Shân insisted
on his drinking the cup of steaming cocoa she had waiting
for him. As the men left the house she warned them :
" 'Member to take care of your selfs."

Jim merely laughed and waved his hand airily as he
joined the long line of silent men making their way to the
pit. Before they had reached half-way a whisper ran back
through the line. " No work to-day. Stop trucks." The
men stopped and looked questioningly at each other, as
though someone had pulled a lever that tied their feet to
the paving-stones.

The spell was broken by a loud shout from Jim : " Good God, couldn't they have telled us before we put our dirty clothes on ? Now us will have to bath all over for nothing. Blast 'em ! " He spat disgustedly into the roadway. A group of men came down the hill, pouring water from their jacks and loudly declaring :

" It's no good, boys. The sidings is full of coal ; not a bloody empty to be seen anywhere, and the lamp-men have been ordered to give no lamps out."

Dai Cannon, one of the local preachers and Big Jim's close friend, indignantly pulled his overhanging belly back under the leather belt, while his loose lower lip dangled wetly beneath his moustache.

" Why didn't they blow the hooter to let us know there was no work ? " he demanded of no one in particular.

All the men now began pouring their water into the road and some of the younger ones started to sing lustily as they turned and retraced their steps to the strains of :

> Mae bys Mary Ann wedi gwiwo
> A Dafydd y gwas sy'n cael y bai.
>
> [Mary Ann's finger is swollen
> And David the servant gets the blame.]

Bedroom windows were hastily lowered and tousled heads pushed through to see what was the matter, but the men shouted reassuringly to the women folk.

" Don't worry, gels. It's only stop trucks. Go back to bed ; the old man will soon be with you. Ha-ha ! " The laughter at these quips rippled through the ranks like wind through grass.

For three days in succession the men had to return home. On the third occasion they did not pass jokes at the expense of the women ; the useless trudge up the hill each morning had made them too resentful.

" Bloody wasters, drawing us out of bed like this for nothing ! " said one loudly. " By gum ! In the trenches they ought to be, where we was. We'd soon bring them to their senses, or blow out the bit they've got." This state-ment met with general approbation.

Shân knew the men were returning even before Big Jim and Len opened the door. The miners made sufficient

noise to advertise their coming. She looked up when her
men entered and waited until Jim had pulled off his coat
before asking : " What, again ? However do the company
think we are going to live ? "

Her hair hung in graceless wisps over her nightdress,
deepening the lines in her face. " Three turns in one week.
Oh dear, dear, it is more than a poor 'ooman can bear."
Neither of the men replied to her wail, but Len stayed to
prevent the quarrel he thought was brewing.

The silence got on her nerves. " Can't you say something, dyn jawl ? " she asked Jim. " Or have your tongue
got tied to your head ? But there, what do you worry,
so long as you do work sometimes and have your pocket-
money regular. Huh ! It is me who have got to ponder
my poor brains out how to stretch the little bit of pay twice
so far as it is 'sposed to go."

Jim could stand her accusations no longer, and began
shouting back : " Hell-fire ! Think you us have come back
for fun, 'ooman ? What think you us is, mun—tomcats
to go up and down the hill as you do shout to us ? By
damn, if you do think that you is thinking wrong, my gel.
Take that from me, muniferni ! "

He caught a glimpse of the fire kindling in her eyes and
changed his tones. " Don't blame us, mun, that there is
no work. Us can't help it," he cajoled. But Shân knew
his tricks and was not deceived.

" Oh, no ! Nobody is to blame, I 'spose, but it is me who
will have to face the peoples who have been good enough
to put food in our bellies. What to tell poor old Evans
Cardi the good Lord alone knows. I can never do it."

She wiped her eyes in the hem of her nightdress, exposing
her withered legs. Her tears always affected Jim, and he
now reluctantly tried to soothe her, grunting : " All right,
left it to me. I'll go down and see the old ram."

Shân withdrew the nightdress from her eyes and glared
at him. " For shame, using them words before your only
son ! Huh ! You, indeed." There was a world of
contempt in her voice as she repudiated what he had
thought a magnanimous offer. " Clever man you are to
see anyone. No, James. The best thing you can see is
in the Boar's Head, where there is plenty of rams every
night, more shame on you."

Jim started to make an indignant protest but she gave him no time. " And don't you never think you can wear the trousers and the petticoats ; one of them is quite enough for you. You look after your own business and leave mine to me, if you please." She drew her bent form erect with great dignity and her eyes flashed a challenge at him.

Jim looked at her with open mouth, into which the ends of his moustache drooped, but he had no fitting retort and the matter dropped when Len said : " Don't worry, mam. Dad can't help it. I must go up the house now. So long."

During the idle days rumours of the impending lock-out had spread like fire, and the people could talk of nothing else, everyone professing to have inside information, although actually all of them were completely in the dark. On the fourth day the pits began again. Len and his father were among twenty-seven other men and boys who worked the same conveyor face. On the day of the restart the men chatted to each other as they cleared the stones and rubbish that had fallen on the iron troughs during the stoppage.

Will Smallbeer gave his opinions to Len while both were engaged in lifting a huge stone that had fallen flatwise on the conveyor. " There is something funny about all this business, Len, you mark my words. I have been working in this old pit for going on forty years now, and have never knowed her having stop trucks for nothink."

Len was as puzzled as the old man, but did not like to expose his ignorance. " Perhaps the company is going to go bankrupt because they can't make the pit pay," he suggested hesitantly.

Will Smallbeer lost his temper and let the edge of the stone he was holding drop back into the conveyor with a bang, as he straightened his back the better to say. " Ach ! Don't pay to hell ! No man can never get me to believe that. Why ! Here us is filling coal for shilling a ton, when us can get the trams, and the company do charge twenty shillings for the same bloody coal on top."

" That might be," Len retorted, unwilling to be beaten in an argument now it had started, " but the company have got much more to pay than our wages, mun."

Will lifted his lamp to the level of Len's face and looked into his eyes. " Poor boy," he muttered as he lowered the lamp again. " Poor dab ! You do want to have your head read. Pity ! " He sighed like a man deeply grieved.

The conveyor began to clatter into life and further conversation became impossible.

Len's limbs tugged wearily on his body when he entered the kitchen after the shift was over. Mary was busy preparing his dinner, but he noticed she looked ill.

" What is the matter ? Have you had another pull ? " he asked anxiously.

She shook her head somewhat wearily. " Don't worry, Len. I'm all right. Just a bit of a cold."

He knew she had avoided his question, but, aware of her obstinacy, he did not pursue the matter. Ezra was sitting in the armchair in exactly the same attitude as when Len had set out for work in the morning. His white hair gleamed in the glow from the fire. He did not say a word till dinner was over, and while Len bathed and dressed merely resumed his pipe, the peculiar stench from which nearly choked the other two. At last the miners' leader casually looked from the fire to say : " I've found out the company's little game at last, and what our men have been talking about isn't far off the mark."

Len sat down and gazed with deep interest at his father-in-law as the latter continued more slowly and seriously : " Mr. Hicks sent for me this morning to tell me that the pits will close down unless we are willing to meet the company half-way."

Len's eyes opened wide. In spite of all the talk about a lock-out he had never thought of the possibilities in such a tangible way as Ezra was now putting them, but the elder man gave him no time for conjecture or comment.

He had bent again towards the fire and it seemed he was now musing rather than talking. " Clever, clever ! Shut the men out just as winter is coming on us—huh ! We've had six years of peace since the end of the War, but it was too good to last."

He raised his head and they saw that his face had become prawn and his eyes sad when he asked : " Will you go round the committee-men, Len, and tell them there is a special meeting to-night ? "

Len did not question him, although he glanced in a puzzled way at Mary, who turned her head away. He had shut the door behind him before she noticed his cap still hanging on its peg. She pulled it off and hurried to tell him about it. He was already half-way down the street when he heard her shout and looked behind to see what was the matter.

" You've forgotten your cap, Len."

His hand went automatically to his head and found it bare. " Never mind," he shouted back. " I shan't be long, and a bit of fresh air 'on't hurt me."

When Len had notified all the committee-men he made his way to Ben the Barber's, hoping to have a hair-cut before the meeting started. He found the shop empty, but sharp whistling and the noise of chairs being shifted in the inner room urged him to peep round the door. Ben was hobbling about, preparing seating accommodation for the committee meeting. Chairs, benches, a table, and an old-fashioned stove with a stack that penetrated the centre of the ceiling occupied all the available space.

Ben stopped whistling when Len asked : " How's trade, Ben ? I see you're busy."

The voice that replied was as sharp as the whistle that preceded it. " Huh ! It's on tick, like that clock by there," pointing to the mantelpiece.

" Never mind, times will soon get better," Len soothed.

The lame little barber continued his hopping between the chairs, grunting all the while : " Better ? Better ? Ha-ha ! That's good, hmm ! That's why the committee is meeting special to-night, isn't it ? The last time it met here was during the strike, and take it from me there's more trouble brewing. Aye, my old nose can always smell it."

The shop-door opened to admit members of the committee and he kept silent as they sat down with various salutations. Len forgot his hair-cut and joined the conversation which Dai Cannon started. Ezra was the last to enter, and the miners' leader wasted very little time before taking the chair and beginning his report. He told the committee how the company was unable to hold its contracts on the market because of the high cost of production in the pit

and the competition from other countries. His report
did not take long, and he concluded with the remark:
" That is how the position was put to me, fellow workmen.
The company says it can't keep the pits going as things
are. Either we lower the cost of production—that means
we fill more coal for less wages—or the pits close down.
The matter is now in your hands."

Whenever Ezra did this, the committee-men knew from
long experience he had already come to a personal decision
which was distasteful to himself.

Len sensed the man's mood and wondered why he had
not hinted in the house what he intended doing. He saw
the glare from the fire deepen the lines in Ezra's face and
fancied his eyes had become dismal; but his attention
was quickly drawn back to the room by a shuffling of chairs
as Dai Cannon rose heavily to his feet. Dai's bottom lip
hung lower and wetter than usual as he growled : " Huh !
I seem to have heard that yarn before. Going bankrupt,
eh ? That's always the tale when they want something
from us."

Ezra stopped him with a wave of the hand, and his words
exposed the decision he had come to. " Either that, Dai,
or close down the pit for good and get no work and wages
at all."

The discussion now became heated and bitter, Harry
Morgan being particularly vehement as his voice rang
through the room like a bell.

" That's the new line of leadership," he declared
raspingly, staring hard at Ezra. " Because the company
say ' more work for less wages, or no work at all ' we are
expected to tell the men that half is better than nothing.
Bah ! In this way the company can get everything it
wants and our Federation becomes the agent for giving it to
them. If that's all the advice Ezra can give, he'd better
go over to the company openly. That would be cleaner
than acting as their servant in our ranks." His voice rose
passionately as Ezra's face went whiter. " No, we can
never accept this. If we do, we destroy our Federation
and play right into the hands of the boss. We must fight
the lock-out as we fought the strike ; and if the company
can't keep the pits open, then let's force them out of the
way and get on with the job ourselves."

This challenge was greeted with a burst of applause and Ezra's chin sank more deeply on his chest as he felt the temper of the men vibrate in the close air, but when he rose to his feet he was his old indomitable self, and his voice, though deeper, was as cutting as Harry's when he replied to the latter's accusation : " I was fighting this company when Harry was in petticoats. Yes. I lost a wife and a home through it, which is more than Harry has ever done or is likely to do. It's quite easy for a man with the pride of a peacock and the brains of a sparrow to strut bravely for a short minute in this room, and easier still for him to use a soapbox to slander better men than himself ; but let him tell us what to do without hurting our own people more than we hurt the company."

Harry bawled out, " Struggle or starve."

Ezra laughed in his face and remarked : " You mean struggle *and* starve." The others now joined in, and the place became a bedlam of conflicting and challenging voices.

Across the road Mr. Evans Cardi was slowly putting up the shutters of his stores. The corrugated-iron sheets which had been placed over the windows during the big strike were now stiff and heavy. His wife came out to help him, and in a short time the windows were covered and the light blotted out. John's shoulders drooped as he walked into the kitchen ; the high forehead that jutted over his eyes made them look even more morbid and sunken than they actually were. The old couple ate in silence the meal she had prepared, and after she had cleared the dishes away, she sat opposite her husband and began knitting. This, for some reason, seemed to irritate him and he peevishly exclaimed :

" Put that knitting down, Maggie, it gets on my nerves ! "

She obediently dropped the wool into her lap, with a patient gesture, and asked : " What is coming over you, John ? You get more miserable every day."

He looked at her queerly before rising to his feet. " Do you know how much we have got left in the bank ? " he asked, his voice hoarse from the fatigue induced by worry.

" I don't expect we have much, John."

" You are right. We haven't got enough to meet our

bills this week." He rose to his feet, agitatedly ruffling his hand through his sparse hair. " But how can we help it ? " he groaned. " Big Jim's wife and many others didn't pay anything off their bills this week again."

" Did you let them have more credit, John ? "

" Of course I did. You see, Maggie fach, if we don't give them credit they won't come to deal with us when the pit is working full, and that means that we lose their custom and what they owe us," he explained apologetically.

" But how are we to carry on, John ? There's Ron's college fees due again." She clasped her hands and dropped them helplessly on her lap where they tangled themselves in the wool. " Oh, God ! What are we to do ? " she moaned in a frenzy of self-pity. " I can see nothing before us but the workhouse and my poor boy on the parish, after all we have done for him."

Her head dropped until her eyes were on a level with the fire, in whose flickering tremors she saw the shattering of her dreams. Her attitude alarmed John, and he tried to soothe her. " Hush, my gel. Things are not so bad as that. Ron will surely get a job as a teacher or something when he finishes his studies. Don't worry ; everything will come all right yet."

The harassed woman rose and, placing her hands on his shoulders, while the wool made a pool about her feet, looked him squarely in the eyes.

" Do you really believe that things will ever come better in this valley, that puts a blight on everyone that comes to it ? " Her voice was an echo of the incredulity that consumed her.

John tried to brighten her and answered reassuringly : " Of course they will. Once we are over this depression, and the company conquers the foreign competition threat, we will be drawing dividends again from our shares in the pit."

The poor woman's eyes warmed a little, but her tones were still sad when she said : " I hope you are right, John bach. Yes, I hope you are right."

The night pressed darkly on Cwmardy as two uniformed men left the fountain, where they had been watching what transpired in Ben the Barber's, and methodically paced their way up the Main Street, focusing their lamps on every doorway they passed. Before they reached the hall of the Chapel, next-door to the police station, their heavy tread was lost in the sound of singing. Lights streamed through the painted windows in a variety of hues that seemed to quiver in the caresses of the music.

The two officers hesitated a moment, until one exclaimed, " It's the Gymanfa Ganu that Lord Cwmardy is leading. Let's go in for a bit to hear it."

The other agreed, and they tip-toed into the Chapel, which was packed with miners and their families. The men sat on one side of the aisle, and the women, dressed in their Sunday best, lent a brightness to the other.

Lord Cwmardy stood in the pulpit, his face beaming with pleasure as he led the singing. The beautiful voices seemed fastened to the end of his baton, as it lifted them into ascending crescendoes, then dropped them into deep throbs. Occasionally the sopranos rode the heavy basses like a flock of seagulls on a wave.

Lord Cwmardy's baton flashed more quickly and his face became a mask of concentrated hope as he worked the choristers towards the final stanza of the hymn they were singing. The initial mournful hopelessness of the tune was lost in the tempo of the finale, which swept the voices together into a vocal unity that awed the policemen at the door.

Wiping the perspiration from his forehead and rolling the sleeves of his white shirt more firmly over his elbows, Cwmardy looked at the languid form of Mr. Higgins, with a glance that seemed to whisper: " What do you think of that ? There is nothing like it in the world ! " The coal-owner was very fond of music, and thought his work-people the finest choral singers in the world.

Whilst the festival was still in progress, the committee-meeting ended and the men came into the street, where a heavy drizzle was beginning to fall. Each raindrop, impregnated with fine coal-dust, became a lump of mud before it fell on the earth of the valley, where the rain had all the effects of a deep fog smothering the lighted windows and pressing drearily on those it touched.

Len and Ezra walked quietly home, their coat-collars buttoned tightly to prevent the black moisture running down their necks, but Len's bare head was dripping before

they had gone twenty yards. The ascent made Ezra
wheeze and his chest bubbled wetly as he fought for breath.
What the miners took to be asthma was now demanding a
heavy toll from his one-time vigour.

They were in the house before either spoke, and Mary
solicitously took the wet coat and hat from her father, at
the same time scolding Len for going out without his cap.
He merely grunted in reply, and she turned impatiently to
her father to ask : " Tell me, Dad, what happened in the
committee to-night ? "

Ezra kept on gasping, while his eyes bulged with exertion,
and it was Len who answered : " We have decided that we
can't accept the terms offered by the company. The only
man in favour was your father, but I don't blame him. Let
every man stick to his opinion." He became enthusiastic.
" By gum, Mary, you ought to have heard Harry Morgan."

Mary looked at him while she gathered her thoughts.
His reference to Ezra had stunned her for a moment ; but
at last she muttered : " So we are in for another spell of
misery." Then her eyes brightened as she went on :
"But, Duw, Len, it's good to know the spirit of the
big strike is still in us, even though so many years
have passed."

Ezra recovered his breath, shook his head disapprovingly,
and said : " It's easy to talk like that, my gel. But there,
I suppose it's natural for youngsters like you. Aye, I used
to be the same myself once, but a lifetime of fighting against
the company has taught me it's useless running your head
against a stone wall."

Len squared his shoulders. " I don't agree with you,
Ezra. I believe the committee is right and that Harry
Morgan hit the nail on the head when he said that this was
a new stunt by the company to get rid of their debts and
smash down our wages and conditions."

Ezra, with his customary astuteness, let Len run on,
knowing this was the surest way of finding out all he was
thinking. Len's eyes were gleaming as he entered into the
spirit of the argument.

" I know it is hard, but isn't all our life hard ? I understand what it will mean if they shut the pit ; but we can't
let them use the pit like a sledge against us, just to make us
accept everything that they say. Oh no ! Don't forget,

Ezra, hundreds of our men were hurt and some died so that we could be where we are to-day."

"Aye," said Mary, "that's right, Len. But we can't get from the pit something that's not there, can we?"

She always sided with her father, feeling his wider experience to be a surer guide than Len's exuberance. Her outburst startled Len. "Something that is not there? What do you mean?" he asked.

"What she says," answered Ezra, a smile softening the lines of his face. "If competition makes it impossible for the company to pay the present wages, then it means, as far as they are concerned, that the wages are not in the pit and therefore the men can't have them. Mind you," he added, somewhat hurriedly, "that's the argument of the company. But there is something deeper in the whole business than you see on the surface. It's all right for Harry Morgan to tell us we must fight or go down. Aye, it's all very well for him to say we should do as they've done in Russia, and take the pits over for ourselves. That's very brave talk, but no one yet has told us how to do this."

Mary tried to help her father. "It took ten days to do that in Russia; but it's taken us hundreds of years to build a trade union in this country."

Len turned sharply in surprise. "What? Ten days? God Almighty, mun, it took Lenin a lifetime to plan with his comrades what happened in Russia!"

"Ha! So it took more than ten days to shake the world, then," she scoffed.

Ezra cynically interrupted: "There you go again, wandering all over the world. We started talking about the pits and now you two are bothering your heads about what happened in Russia."

He stopped pacing the kitchen and stood facing Len. "Listen. You know that no one wants to smash the company more than I do, but, my God, to do that I'm not prepared to smash the people. What I see in the future if we let the company lock us out is our men slowly drifting back one by one to the pits, after they have reached the end of their tether—and that won't take very long, believe me. No, Len, you must learn that there is a time to fight and a time not to fight. If I could only see some hope of winning, I'd agree with what the committee decided

to-night ; but I can't, I can't. All I can see in front of
us is collapse, and when that time comes I hope I will be
dead, because our valley and our people will be finished."
He bent his head on his hands as though he wanted to blind
his eyes to a picture they saw.

The hopelessness of the words tugged at Mary's heart,
and she put her arm round his neck with a protective gesture
which showed her whole mind was fixed on his sorrow and
not his outlook on the future.

But Len, with no bonds of blood to bind him to sentiment, although he felt deeply the breakdown of confidence
implied in the words, sprang restlessly to his feet. He
was one of the workmen and knew their every whim and
mood.

" I don't believe you," he stated abruptly, even while he
felt amazed at the manner in which he was addressing his
old mentor and leader. " You know I have got every
respect for you, but if what you say is right, then there is no
hope for us. It means that, after all we have done and
worked for, we have now got no future except misery."
The very thought of this outcome to the struggle of the
people made him offensively assertive and his voice shrill
with disbelief. " No, Ezra ; I don't believe you, and I
wouldn't believe anybody else who said the same thing
as you."

Mary felt she wanted to challenge him and defend Ezra,
who had again recovered his composure, and was now
lighting his pipe with a long spill of paper, quantities of which
he always kept on the hob ; but Len gave her no time.

" It's no good you standing up for your father, Mary.
He'll be the first to tell you that you have got to think for
yourself, as he told me years ago. Gee, mun, use your
common sense. Isn't it us that sunk the pit ? Of course
it is, Mary, and by gum it's only us can save the pit."

Len was always like this. Whenever he was engaged in
a tussle with Ezra, he vented his spleen on Mary and carried
the fight to Ezra through her. She knew this, and its
effect was to make her more determined in her support for
her father even when, sometimes, she sensed he was wrong,
as she did on this occasion. But she said nothing as Len
continued expounding his convictions.

" Why, if we give in to the company now, it means that

we really end where you don't want us to. Harry was right
when he said our only chance is to keep on struggling.
How do we know," he demanded, glancing at Ezra, then
hastily turning back to Mary as he saw the hot eyes fixed
on him, " how do we know that if we give in at the start
the company 'on't come after us again in six or twelve
months with the same yarn ; and down we go again. And
so it will carry on, down—down—down until we reach the
farewell rock, then everything will be finished and we can
put our tools on the bar for good."

Len's face was flushed and his eyes were bright with
emotion as his own vehemence strengthened the convictions
in his mind.

Mary rose and began clearing away the supper things,
remarking at the same time : " Oh well, it's no good
arguing now, I suppose. The committee has decided,
and we'll have to put up with what's coming."

The words bred a new idea, and after a short pause during
which she flicked the crumbs from the tablecloth into the
grate, she turned with the cloth in her hand and demanded
passionately : " Why is it we have got to suffer like this
year after year ? We are no sooner out of one thing than
we are bang into another, and all our lives is nothing but
trouble and strife."

" It's the way of the world, Mary ; and neither you, or I,
or anybody else can alter it," Ezra replied.

Len shuffled restlessly in his chair before saying : " I
can't agree with that. The world, after all, is only what
we let it be or make it."

No one replied to this and the conversation languished,
each becoming preoccupied with the thoughts generated
during the evening. At last Mary reminded Len : " You
had better get coal and sticks ready for the morning, or
we'll be forgetting." He went out of the back door, and
after a time returned with a bucket of coal in one hand and
a bundle of sticks under his arm. By the time he had put
the sticks in the oven to dry and had washed his hands,
Ezra, with a muttered " Good-night, both," had gone to
bed. Mary and Len followed shortly after.

Mary waited until her husband was in bed before stating
quietly : " So you are still siding with Harry Morgan and
his communists against my father."

He raised his head from the pillow and, reaching up, took her small face in his two hands.

" It's not that altogether, Mary, but I'm bound to agree with anybody who thinks the same as me, in't I ? " he queried half regretfully, for the first time realising how deeply he had hurt her.

She made no reply and shook her head free from his hands, turning her back to him when she came to bed and falling asleep with nothing more said.

During the remainder of the week, life apparently went on as usual in Cwmardy, but when the men came up the pit on the following Saturday they were confronted with a huge printed poster, pasted on the end of the bridge that separated the colliery from the village. The miners nearest read its contents out loudly, so that those behind could hear. Every two minutes or so the number of men increased as the cages brought them to the surface, but the whispering voices soon acquainted them with the news.

CWMARDY CONSOLIDATED COLLIERY CO., LTD., (1924)

PUBLIC NOTICE.

> The official receiver herewith announces to all concerned that the affairs of the above company and all its undertakings are now in the hands of Sir William Wheeler, who has been appointed the official liquidator to wind up the company.
> All who have claims upon the company must make them to the liquidator within one month from this date. No applications can be considered thereafter.
> The collieries will be open for work on and after next Monday on the following conditions and price-lists.

The surrounding men listened avidly, many of them with their mouths open, to the recital that followed. The items passed from mouth to mouth as they were read, so that even the miners on the fringe of the crowd were aware of the new conditions almost at the same time as the readers. When the words " Any workman not prepared to accept these conditions need not present himself at the colliery " were read, a roar of anger deadened the sound of the pit engines. It was heard in Cwmardy, and women rushed to the doors with frightened eyes to ask each other what had happened.

Big Jim looked furiously about him. He and Len stood practically in the middle of the angry mass of shouting miners.

" Ha," howled one, his voice ringing sharply above the others, " so this is the new way of robbing us, eh ? "

" The frigging blackguards ! Put a bit of lavatory paper with words on the bridge and think we will say ' Pity ' to ourselves, and then go back to the pit for whatever they do want to give us. Huh ! Babies in dirty napkins 'ood jib at that."

Another loud roar stopped him. " Bankrupt to hell ! "

" The swindlers are running away ! "

" Bloody robbers ! "

" Let them keep the pits ! "

This latter cry grew louder and more insistent. It was taken up by increasing numbers, until nothing else could be heard.

" Let them keep the bloody pits ! " and with this challenge the miners marched down the hill to their homes.

When Monday morning came the hooters blew their raucous command through Cwmardy as usual, but no lights suddenly responded in the cottage windows. Before 6 a.m. John Evans Cardi stood staring through the bedroom window of his stores into the empty darkness outside. He drew the curtains a little further apart and squinted up the street in the direction where the pits were silently brooding as though they had missed something they wanted very much ; but the only light he could see was the one which gleamed from the police-station. John shivered as the cold air played about his bare legs, and a groan gurgled in his throat.

His wife drew herself from the sheets and beseeched him :
" Come back to bed, John bach. It's no use you worrying and catching your death of cold standing by there."

The old man slowly retraced his steps and got into bed, making her shrivel as the cold clamminess of his flesh touched her own. " Duw, duw, you are freezing," she complained.

John paid no heed to the remark, but Maggie heard him

murmur : " At last it has come. This is the end of everything."

She shook him sharply. " Come, come, one would think the end of the world was here."

He turned his head and something bright dripped from his eyes and glistened for a moment in the lamplight.

" Well, what is it, my gel, but the end of *our* world ? Every penny gone out of our savings, the company bankrupt, and our last hope killed by this morning's silence in the street."

He hesitated and looked hard at her with misty eyes, then moaned : " Tell me, Maggie, how are we going to live ? We have nothing left. Nothing. The men have made their minds up and the pit is dead." He turned on his belly and buried his face in the pillow while she tenderly smoothed the thin hair on the back of his head.

About a fortnight after the beginning of the lock-out, Len called at his parents, a practice he had whenever he was worried or had time to spare. He found them quarrelling ; Shân was dabbing her eyes with the corner of her apron. The old couple paused while Len made himself comfortable, then Shân began where she had evidently left off.

" How on earth us is going to live after this week the Lord alone knows," she moaned. " Poor old Mrs. Evans Cardi was crying to me only yesterday about the money they have got out and nothing coming in, poor dab. Well, well, between everything, I don't know what the world is coming to, no, not I ! "

She began weeping into her apron again, hoping by so doing to provoke Jim. She succeeded.

" Hell-fire ! " he bawled. " You do talk to me, mun, as if I was boss of the bloody company. What can I help if they shut down their frigging pits—they don't belong to me, do they ? Why the hell don't you go up to the Big House and nag Lord Cwmardy—not have your bang out on me all the time ? "

He turned appealingly to Len, the sight of whom seemed suddenly to give him a new line of defence. " Ask Len," he demanded. " He have got a better head than me and can answer you back in your own brass."

This gave her the opportunity she wanted. " Ha !

That's the sort of man you are, is it ? Willing to put your burdens on the back of your own poor boy that have got enough to do to carry his own, what with this lock-out and his wife dying on her feet with her chest. Ach ! Call yourself a man, indeed ! Huh ! I have seened better ones in old Sanger's circus before now. Duw, even a dog will fight for his own ! Shame on you, James ! '' Her face was both pitying and contemptuous when she turned away from him.

Jim leapt to his full height like a bouncing ball, at the same time involuntarily squaring the droop in his shoulders and inflating his chest the better to express his indignation as he shouted : '' No man can call me a dog, specially you, Shân. No, by damn, I am a better man than all your family put together, and don't you forget it ! ''

She interrupted him, anger in her very poise. '' Don't you dare to say anything 'bout my fambly, James Roberts. They are too good for their names to be on your tongue. Yes. Where would Len bach be,'' she demanded, '' if they didn't look after him and our Jane, now in her grave, God bless her, when you runned to the Boer War, not caring if us had a crust to share between us.''

Big Jim collapsed under this tirade, and sat down, his moustache now drooping wearily. '' All right,'' he announced, '' I will go over the mountain to-morrow to look for work somewhere else, and I do hope when I get it that my body will be smashed to bits by a fall. That will bring you to your senses, and you will be sorry for all that you have said to me.''

Len burst out laughing at the sheer incongruity of the remark and the manner in which Jim said it, but there was no mirth on Shân's face.

'' What,'' she queried like one who could not believe she was hearing aright, '' you will leave your own home, your wife, and children, so that you can be buried by a fall, God knows where ? No ! Never ! Not while there is breath left in my poor old bones.''

No more was said after this, and a little time later Len bade them good-night and went home.

CHAPTER IV

Conflicting Loyalties

THE weary weeks dragged on until the lock-out was in its eighth month, without either side making any move to re-open the pits which moped stagnantly at the head of the valley. Relief stations had been opened in the chapels, and once a week long queues of people waited patiently for the food-notes doled out to them from the rates. Lack of cash made it impossible to buy clothes or pay Federation dues, and each week the people became more shabby. Women looked enviously at the smoke curling from the stacks of pits surrounding Cwmardy and silently longed for the day when theirs would once more be pulsating with similar life.

Coal was as scarce as cash, and one evening Len told Mary: " Put my working clothes out to air to-night ; me and dad are going up the level for some coal in the morning."

Mary looked sadly at the lines marked deeply into his thin face and the weary posture of his body.

" We can manage for this week again, Len, if I go careful with what we've got. I hate to see you going up that level," she burst out. " Your body can't stand it ; you are fading away before my eyes and are looking like an old man. Nobody would ever think you are only twenty-four next December."

Len understood her solicitude and was glad of it, but he tried to ease her mind when he replied. " Don't worry about me ; I'm all right. Let's get as much in as we can now, before the company blows the levels down, as it has threatened to do."

Mary did not answer, but before going to bed she dragged the box containing his working clothes from the dark hole under the stairs and arranged them on the brass rod fixed to the mantelshelf.

Early next morning, as the dawn was being spawned in

the smoke that fogged the valley, they rose from bed. Mary prepared the breakfast of dry toast and tea, which was all the relief-note enabled them to obtain since the lockout, while Len donned his pit-clothes.

" Is that old tater sack still here ? " he asked. She fetched it from the back and laid it down on the mat before the fire.

Len looked through the window and remarked : " It's not worth drying it, Mary. The weather don't look at all too good."

After breakfast he kissed her and, advising her to go back to bed, wearily made his way towards his father's house, where he found the old man waiting on the doorstep staring at the heavy sky with its restless clouds.

" It's looking pretty dark, Len bach, and us had better hurry up," he announced.

Before they reached the summit of the mountain, the mist had turned into a drizzle that soaked through their clothes in spite of the sacks draped across their shoulders.

Big Jim spat disgustedly into the air and muttered : " Huh ! Every time you and me do come for a bit of coal, the rain do come pelting down 'xactly like if someone is watching to spite us out."

Len said nothing, the clammy clothes clinging coldly to his body making him too miserable for words, but followed his father up the steep path towards the mine level, driven horizontally into the side of the mountain. Several men passed them before they reached their destination, each bent nearly double beneath the sack of coal straddled lengthways across his shoulders.

" How is things up there to-day, boys ? " Jim asked.

" You'll find plenty of muck and water, but bloody little coal ! " was the grunted reply as the men gingerly made their way down the mountain.

Len and his father continued the climb towards the level, and when they reached its mouth they sat on the sopping grass to recover their breath. The hole into which they intended to go was driven flush into the earth, and seemed hardly big enough to admit a sheep. An endless torrent of water tumbled noisily out, swirling round the heavy wooden box on sleigh-like runners that obstructed the opening to the level.

Len was the first to rise to his feet, and, shaking the wet sack from his shoulders, took hold of the rope attached to the box, at the same time remarking : " Come on, dad. We might as well get going."

Big Jim grunted, took a huge lump of half-chewed tobacco from his mouth, carefully wrapped it in paper which he put into a brass pouch, then followed Len into the level.

They crawled on their hands and knees, Len pulling the box while his father pushed. Before they had gone a dozen yards they stopped to light a candle each, which they then stuck in the tin holders fastened to their caps. The tiny glimmers glinted on the black water as the two men went more deeply into the entrails of the mountain. By the time they reached the small seam of coal, both were exhausted and half sat, half lay in the water for some minutes to recover.

Big Jim took advantage of the rest to look about him, but a glance was sufficient to send him into a temper.

" Muniferni ! Same bloody trick agen ! They have tooked all the loose coal and have left nothink but stiff dead ends and muck to us. By Hell, call themselves butties, mun jawly ! Huh ! They don't know what the name do mean ! "

" Never mind about that now," Len interrupted peevishly. " Let's get on with the job before the other men come, or we'll be here all day ! " Thus admonished, Jim stopped his grunting and helped Len get the tools from the bar on which they were locked. They each took a mandril and shovel and went towards the coal-face, which was a little drier than the roadway.

For hours they punched with all their might at the hard overhanging roof that prevented their getting to the thin vein of coal underneath. But eventually they hammered it flush with the coal, then took it in turn to fill the box with the stones and rubble. Each time the box was full, Len pulled it to the mouth of the level, where he unloaded the rubbish, occasionally watching the larger stones roll down the mountain with increasing momentum. When the rubbish had all been cleared away, they started working the coal. The idleness enforced by the lock-out had softened the men's bodies and made their muscles less supple. Len felt his hands burn intolerably. The mandril became a red-hot iron that seared more deeply into his flesh with every blow he struck, while the confined space forced him to contort his body until it lost all human semblance. His posture added to the strain on his shoulders and drove pins and needles into him in currents that made him long to scream. He turned on his belly, stretching his limbs in the water that covered them as he lay. This eased the cramp for a little, but his hands burned even more ferociously when he took hold of the mandril again.

He was glad when they had sufficient coal to fill the box. Even the crawl through the foot-deep water with the rope tearing at his shoulder as he dragged the loaded box behind him was better than the paralysing cramp of the coal-face. By the time they had finished filling their sacks with coal, more men had come to the level. These helped to lift the loaded bags on to the shoulders of the two men before going into the level themselves, leaving Len and Big Jim to get down the mountain as best they could.

Before they had proceeded far, Len began to feel the weight on his back grow heavier with every stride. Each lump of coal became a nail that stuck into his flesh with maddening persistence. He jerked the sack to shift the pressure and pain from a particular spot, only to feel others that were even more agonising. The weight forced his shoulders nearer to the ground and pressed his feet more deeply into the wet earth, making it a strain to drag them from its grip. When he lifted a foot to take a step forward, he felt he was lifting the world with it. The pressure on his body forced his mouth open, and he sucked in the air with audible gasps like a swimmer in a heavy sea.

They had not covered half the distance down the mountain before Len was in a state of collapse. He closed his eyes, hoping thus to shorten the distance to his home, but when he opened them again, Cwmardy seemed further away than ever through the dull skeins of rain that dangled from the skies.

He groaned, and only the sight of Big Jim steadily plodding ahead prevented his dropping to the ground with the sack of coal across his neck. Although his brain was numb, the red-hot needles in his back forced him to break the shackles that held his feet to the earth. He thought each step he took would be his last, but somehow the last was always the next. His knees lost rigidity and his bones seemed to melt so that his feet dragged along the ground, at no point entirely leaving it. He lost all sense of space and time until he bumped into Jim when the latter stopped by the wall that separated the colliery siding from the road leading to the village. His father helped him lift the bag of coal onto the wall so that he could rest.

Len felt his body float in the air and a lifting sensation fill his head. He sat down abruptly and closed his eyes.

Presently he heard a sudden clang of iron and Shân's voice saying : " You haven't got much further to go now, Len bach, and us have brought two buckets to help you."

He jumped to his feet and saw his mother and Mary before him. Pride made him ashamed of their action and he blurted out savagely : " What the hell did you want to bring those buckets for ? Do you think I'm still a little kid, mam, and haven't grown up ? "

Shân looked at him reproachfully, the wet shawl, swathed round her head, dripping moisture on her face. Len turned away and rested his arms on the wall while he looked at the long lines of coal-filled wagons the other side. Here and there he caught sight of a policeman on guard. Big Jim remained squatting on the ground, placidly chewing the tobacco he had so carefully saved before entering the level. Suddenly Len turned to his wife and pointed to the pit sidings.

" Look, Mary. In't it a shame ? Those thousands of tons of coal, that me and dad have helped to fill, now rotting in the rain, have been there since the lock-out began, while we have got to kill ourselves to get a bag full from the level. It's bloody maddening ! Aye, and we're all mad. Why the hell don't we all get together and empty those wagons, instead of slogging our guts out in the mountain ? "

His voice became squeaky with excitement and exhaustion, and Mary, knowing his moods, did not reply, but Big Jim, looking at his son slyly for a moment, remarked : " Aye, aye, Len bach. You are quite right, my boy. Big Jim's son must always be right, muniferni ; but be careful the bobbies don't hear you or catch you looking at that

coal on the sidings, or you will have a summons, sure as
hell ! Ha, ha ! "

Shân felt it necessary to add her quota. " Aye, indeed,
Len. Many a poor old dab have been fined or put in jail
when they tooked coal because they didn't have no money
to buy some."

This sentiment found a responsive chord in Len's mind.
" By gum," he said, " I'd never seen it in that way before,
mam. They lock us out of the pit ; then give us food-notes
instead of money ; and when we take coal because we
haven't got money to buy some, they make us pay twenty
or thirty times its value in fines, and when we can't pay
that they make out that we are criminals and send us to
clink."

Big Jim looked at Mary with a glance that seemed to say :
" There's a clever man for you, my gel. Not many scholars
in Cwmardy could put it together so quick or so good as
that, eh ? " But he confined his remarks to : " And who
is on the bench to send you down ? Why, Mr. Hicks, the
general manager, in't it ? " No one replied.

When they were ready to go Len resolutely refused to
allow the women to fill their buckets from his sack.

His mother looked for some moments as though she
were prepared to use force to compel him, but she cooled
down sufficiently to say : " All right. You will come to
your senses one day. But you shan't spite us out. No,
not if us have got to go round the back lanes and scrape
cokes from the ashes to fill our buckets. Huh ! You have
comed a big man all of a sudden, haven't you ? "

Len knew from past experience how advisable it was
that he say nothing, so he worked himself under the sack,
which now felt heavier and more painful than ever, and
followed dumbly in the wake of his father. Shân noisily
rattled the empty buckets, and Len prayed that none of his
mates would see the two women before he reached the
house. He clenched his teeth and kept his eyes fixed on
the ground until he came to the little tin chapel and heard
a murmur of voices.

Big Jim stopped and turned round to ask : " What is on
there, Len ? It can't be a service or your mother 'ood be
there."

Len was too exhausted and miserable to answer, but he

also wondered as he slowly dragged his body and its burden towards the house.

Inside the chapel a congregation of preachers, shop-keepers, and others was listening to a prayer offered up by Will Smallbeer, who had been converted during the lock-out. The sound Big Jim had heard was the deep " Amen " from those present when the prayer was finished. This was soon followed by a lament about conditions in Cwmardy, and Mr. Evans Cardi summed up their feelings when he said :

" This lock-out is taking us to ruin. I can't see any hope of our getting back the debts the people owe us, and now, after eight months, we are no nearer the end of the stoppage. It's bankruptcy, it's ruin ! " he wailed despairingly.

The village doctor, whose double chin hid his tie, helped the discussion that ensued. Clearing his throat, he rose to his feet, and was immediately given a respectful silence which enabled him to say without lifting his hoarse voice : " Yes, gentlemen. It's ruin for all of us unless something happens very soon. The people expect me to treat them just as they did when they were working and paying for my services. But I must live. I have to pay for the powders and medicine I give them, but it is impossible to carry on any longer, impossible."

A bitter moan ran round the chapel, whose tin walls made the echoes even more melancholy. After a while, Mr. Hughes, the preacher from Calfaria, the chapel where most of the officials worshipped, rose from his seat.

" There is no sense in it, friends," he began. " The men are being led unwisely. No one can say there is a dispute on, yet Ezra persists in treating it as one. The Com-munists are using Ezra's stubbornness to further their own political ends, and he is too weak to stand up against them. I say there should be no politics in the Union." Another moan, interspersed with cries of " Shame ! " interrupted him for some moments. " O God ! If we could only gain the ear of the people and show how his obstinacy is bringing despair and dereliction to Cwmardy," he was continuing, when Will Smallbeer jumped up excitedly.

" I know, I know ! " he shouted. " Why not go up the Big House to see if the company have got something new to

offer ?   We can then go to the people, 'specially those who
go to Chapel, with something definite that many of them
'ood be only too willing to accept.   Once we can get a few
of them going back to the pit, the rest 'ood soon follow.
I say the same as Mr. Hughes—keep politics out of the
Union and the pits."

His beer-drenched waistcoat glistened queerly in the dull
light of the sacred edifice.

A few evenings later, a group of men with hats pulled
down and coat-collars turned up, made their way slowly
up the tree-bordered drive leading to the Big House.   The
trees, bending in the cold wind, seemed to beckon each other
to listen to the subdued tramp of ascending feet and the
request they were taking to the company.

Will Smallbeer shivered and whispered to the preacher :
" Cold night, in't it, Mr. Hughes ? "

The latter's acquiescing nod could not be seen in the
darkness, and no more was said, although the wheezing
breath of Evans Cardi was audible through the leafy
rustling.   The men paused a while when they reached the
main door of the Big House before ringing the bell, but the
speed with which the ring was answered showed they were
expected.

" Round the corner to the servants' entrance," the foot-
man announced without any preamble or explanation.

As the flunkey shut the door in their faces, Will's eyes
glared in the lights pouring from the windows and he
swallowed noisily.

Mr. Hughes broke the tension when he said, in what he
obviously intended to be a propitiating manner : " A
small misunderstanding, I expect.   Lord Cwmardy will
probably explain when we see him.   Come, let's go round
the back."

The others docilely followed him, although Smallbeer
continued snorting as though a straw were tickling his nose.

It was late in the night when the men came back out
through the front door, where Lord Cwmardy shook each
of them, with the exception of Will, by the hand.   The
deputation was half-way down the drive when the dogs
guarding the grounds began to howl mournfully, the
echoes running between the trees with eerie reiteration.

Mr. Evans shivered coldly at the sound, but Smallbeer seemed to find it stimulating.

" The dirty sods ! " he cried vehemently. " They know they got us in a vice now we've been up to them, the rotten bastards ! "

" Ssh," whispered Mr. Hughes and Evans Cardi together in shocked sibilance.

" You forget yourself, William, but don't forget the friends who are with you."

" I know ! " bellowed Will. " You think because I have stopped drinking since the lock-out and attend the services regular, that I have forgot where I come from and the butties who fought with me in the strike. Never, never ! " he shouted, his voice rising in temper with every word. " Give me Big Jim and Len before the bloody lot of you ! "

He quickened his pace before they could reply and his curses, floating back to them through the night, mingled with the moaning of the dogs and was soon lost in the distance.

Len left his chair and went to the door when he heard the tramp of heavy feet hurry past the window, but all he could see was the back of the man running up the street. Something peculiar in the gait puzzled him.

" What was it ? " Mary asked when he returned to the kitchen.

" Someone running. I couldn't make out who it was, yet I could swear that I know him."

The puzzled frown remained on his brow for some time after they resumed their conversation, then suddenly he remembered.

" It was Will Smallbeer ! " he declared dramatically. " I wonder what he's been up to ? "

Mary supplied the answer in a moment. " He was one of the deputation picked in the chapel meeting to see Lord Cwmardy. More than likely they've finished and have come back," she said.

Both remained gazing into the fire for a long while after this, until Mary looked up at the clock and queried :

" I wonder what is keeping dad. It's not often he's out so late as this." She paused, then moaned : " Oh Duw ! He worries me more with every day that passes."

Len shook his head and both resumed their meditations, until Mary again broke the silence.

" This will finish him. If the chapel people have made an agreement with the company, it will mean that dad will have reached the end of his rope. Aye," she added bitterly, " it would have been better if you and the Party had listened to him in the first place. All this misery wouldn't have happened then, and our men would be working and solid in the Federation, instead of as they are now, split up and ready to go back to work on the conditions offered in the beginning."

Her thoughts turned to Ezra again and her eyes filled with tears. Len watched the shadows play over her face, and they reminded him of the reflection of moving clouds on the mountain. She grasped his arm tightly. " Oh, Len, I'm afraid this will change dad altogether. He doesn't seem to have his old strength to fight both the preachers and the men who want to go back to work." She began to weep quietly, at the same time wailing through the fingers that covered her eyes. " Oh, Len, I wish the men would decide to go back, all together, and put an end to this poverty and worry that is slowly killing us. If it keeps on much longer, there'll be nobody left in Cwmardy ; those of us who are not in the cemetery will be tramping the country looking for work."

Her words and demeanour worried Len. He had never seen her so completely broken up before and so obviously a victim of her emotions. But he said nothing in case his remarks should further disturb her, although he felt that matters were reaching a crisis. His mind switched back to the discussions in the Party, particularly the one where Fred Lewis advocated that the Party should support Ezra and urge the men back to work. The scene which followed Harry Morgan's taunt that Fred was ratting lived again before his eyes, and his mouth unconsciously shaped to the arguments he had himself used to prove the accusation.

He forgot the kitchen and the softly weeping Mary near him, and his eyes became blind to everything but the indignant form of Fred, when he rose to his full height and walked out, flinging back over his shoulder the retort : " Call yourselves Communists ! Bah ! If you were in Russia, the bloody lot of you would be shot as anarchists ! "

An impatient rattling on the door-latch brought him back
to his immediate environment, and he turned his head to
see Ezra walk in. The miner's leader looked like a very
old man who had lost all vitality, and he hardly glanced at
his son-in-law as he sat down wearily. Mary wiped her
eyes hastily, hoping the tears had left no betraying signs
upon her face. The silence that followed the elder man's
entry was heavy with unspoken thoughts until Ezra himself
gave them voice.

" We have now got to make up our minds. Either the
committee takes the men back to work, or the preachers
and shopkeepers will."

There was at once a hopelessness and yet a kind of
desperate determination behind the statement that egged
Len on to say something, but Ezra stopped him with a wave
of the hand that seemed to sweep the whole of Cwmardy
into its grip.

" It's no good arguing now. Everybody knows the
position, and like cowards we have all been keeping it to
ourselves, hoping that something would turn up to prove us
wrong. Aye, cowards." His voice began to quiver with
a passion that was unusual in this stern man, and it rose a
little as he went on. " If you had only listened to me at
the beginning, these months of hunger and sorrow would
not have been. But no ; it was easier to call me a renegade, as Harry Morgan did in the committee, than to face
up to reality. But now, all of you, do you hear . . . all of
you, have got to face it," he shouted. " There is no
committee, the men are not paying the union, and unless
we give the terms for going back to the pit, the others will ;
and that means the end of the Federation in Cwmardy.
Already there is talk of a new non-political union, and there
are many of our own people who will welcome this—yes,
welcome it in the hope it will smash the Federation for
good."

Mary grew alarmed at his vehemence, and hurriedly
rose from the chair to place her arm about his neck when he
drew his hand across his eyes like a man whose sight is
fading.

" Oh, dad, don't take it so hard," she implored ; " no
one will ever make me believe that the people are not
behind you now, as they were during the strike."

Len, who had been a silent listener to Ezra's outburst, saw her gulp back the sob in her throat and came to her aid, although he sensed that words would no longer have weight with her father. He hardly knew what to say in the circumstances, but forced himself to declare half-heartedly : " All of us who count are behind you, Ezra ; and you can bet on it the Party will back you all the way against those who want to give in to the company. You can have faith in that," he concluded rather apologetically.

Ezra lifted his head sharply, letting them see the dull glow in his pouched eyes. " Don't talk to me of faith," he almost snarled. " That's what the preachers you condemn say they have, but I've got none of it. No ! I've always had to go on facts, not faith. Nine months of semi-starvation is enough sacrifice for our people, and rather than see others, who have no business to interfere, put an end to it, I'll do it myself. Yes. There is nothing for it now, any more than there was in the beginning. When there are two evils that we have got to choose from, we must always choose the lesser." His voice was husky when he concluded and he caught Mary to him, making her sit on his lap as though the contact brought consolation.

Len felt himself devoid of argument in face of the crisis as Ezra had presented it, but faith in the Party persuaded him that there was a solution somewhere, even though he couldn't grasp it at the moment.

He was saved further pondering by Mary, who said quietly, in tones showing she had a complete grip of herself once more : " I agree with you, dad. You are right and we must put an end to this lingering. I'm sure the most sensible of the men who used to be on the committee will agree as well when you put the position to them." Both men immediately saw a glimmer of hope in the sentiment, although each hoped a different outcome.

Ezra lifted her from his knee and, rising himself, stood near the fire with his back turned to it. He recited a number of names and asked Len if he'd go round their houses in the morning and invite them as old committee-men to a discussion on the new development. Len agreed, but insisted upon adding Harry Morgan's name, which Ezra had for some reason omitted. There was an argument over this, and Ezra only finally gave way when Len

threatened to drop the whole matter if Harry wasn't
invited.

Next day most of the invited men turned up to the committee. Dai Cannon, Sam Dangler, and Big Jim sat near
each other ; the latter commenting audibly about the
others present.

" How be, Reuben ? " he greeted a coal-scarred veteran,
who at the beginning of the lock-out had been given a lump
sum in commutation of the weekly compensation he had
received for an affliction to his eyes, which the doctors
said was nystagmus. The man so addressed turned around
to look at his questioner. His eyes were large and seemed
to be all pupil, that blinked and quivered in the dull
light of the room. He carried his head slightly sideways
on his hunched shoulders, as if this made it easier to concentrate his gaze.

" Hallo, Jim. Glad to see you," he growled.

He had no time to say more before Fred Lewis strode in,
walking arrogantly past the men already there and
squatting himself in a vacant chair near the table, from
which he turned round to nod patronisingly to his
acquaintances.

Jim bent down a little to whisper in Dangler's ear :
" That's a clever chap for you, mun."

Sam nodded his head disparagingly. " Aye, he's clever
all right. So clever that he do always look after number
one first, never mind a hell about anybody else. One day
he'll leave all of us in the dirt, 'spite of all his big talk."

Jim did not like to be contradicted in this manner, and
hastened to defend his position. " Hell, mun ! I
didn't say anything 'bout that, did I, Dai ? " turning
to the latter, who shook his head in confirmation. " All
I did say was that he is a clever man. As for the other thing,
why, you do know so well as me that any man born above
the Boar's Head can look after hisself without asking anybody for help. In't that right, Dai ? " turning again to
his mate for support, then immediately adding : " Mind
you, I don't say he be so clever as our Len. Duw, there's
a scholar for you ! I bet he's the smartest man in the four
pits, muniferni. It is a pleasure to hear him arguing with
Shân when she is in her tantrums. Duw ! He do blind her
with science."

Fred Lewis sensed he had something to do with the conversation, and hearing the word " clever " turned round and smiled at Big Jim, who solemnly nodded his head as a greeting, at the same time twirling one end of his moustache.

Ezra now rapped the table and Jim hurriedly whispered to Dangler : " Give me a bit of the 'bacco you do owe me, Sam, before he do start." He rubbed the proffered lump carefully on his patched trousers to loosen it as Ezra began quietly speaking.

Len sat next to Harry Morgan, whose high forehead and large spectacles made his face appear all eyes as he listened intently to the miners' leader. During the first half of his statement, Ezra stressed continually the poverty wrought in Cwmardy by the lock-out, until old Reuben grunted loudly : " Cut it out, mun. Don't us know all about that, without you preaching by there about it ? "

Harry clapped the interruption loudly, and Big Jim, thinking it was Len, did the same, although the latter remained perfectly quiet. Ezra, always intolerant of opposition, immediately threw aside the factual sternness with which he began the meeting.

Fixing his attention on Harry and not even glancing at Reuben, he raised his voice heatedly. " Can't you forget your politics and your prejudice for a while, man ? " he demanded. " Or have you come here with your usual tactics of disruption, not caring what will happen to the workmen so long as you and your Party have their way ? "

Harry jumped to his feet to make an indignant repudiation of the charge, but Will Evans' loud, rolling bursts of laughter were before him. " Ha-ha ! Ho-ho-ho ! That's a smart 'un ! Hit the other bloke first when he's pulling his coat off. Ho-ho ! Ha-ha-ha ! "

Will's thin cheeks rippled with the laughter, but he soon became quiet again when he saw the serious faces around him remain impervious to the attempted joke. But it had served its purpose, because Harry had resumed his seat during the brief interlude, leaving Ezra's statement unanswered.

The miners' leader continued his speech where he had left off before the interruption, and when he reached the end he was pleading vehemently that the committee should ask the company for the terms and advise the men to accept them.

" Unless you do that," he said tonelessly, like a man to whom talking has become a sudden burden, " we will destroy even the little organisation we have left, and rather than that, I am prepared to admit defeat."

He suddenly noticed the tense look in the men's eyes, and his own filled with a pain that he tried to hide in an outburst of temper. " Don't stare at me like that ! " he cried. " It hurts me more than it does you to have to say these words. I never thought I would see the day when my own men would leave me and follow others." His voice quavered, but he had hardly time to sit down before Harry Morgan began speaking.

Len listened to the Communist leader, following every word with an intensity that made him oblivious of the fact that the other men were equally interested. The high-pitched voice sounded louder than it actually was as the words rebounded from the walls of the small room. Harry always addressed a dozen men in the same manner he did a thousand and this occasion was no exception. With a bite in every sentence, he explained the tactics of the company ever since the strike, how they began by separating mates in the pit, then introducing strangers to further estrange the men.

" And when they had done this," he continued, " what after ? They came to us in seam after seam saying we would have to lower the price-list and give them more output or the seam would have to be closed."

Ezra started to his feet but Harry hurriedly checked him with the remark. " I know I will be called a disrupter and all the rest of it for what I am going to say, but that won't stop the Party of which I am proud to be a member from speaking what it thinks is the truth."

Fred Lewis jumped up excitedly. " I'm as much, if not more, a Communist as you are, and I say we must always be prepared to change our line. I believe we are wrong and that Ezra is right."

Big Jim guffawed loudly. " Ha-ha ! If I do know my P's and Q's you 'on't be a Communist after to-day, mun jawly."

No one took notice of him, and Harry continued as though there had been no interruption. " Ten months ago they flung their bombshell. They said accept what we give you or finish in the pit till you do. That was an ultimatum, a threat that tried to rob us of our voices and make us puppets of the boss. And after sticking it for nearly ten months, Ezra now wants us to give in because a few preachers and what-not are interfering. I say no ; and if Ezra says differently, he's of more value to Lord Cwmardy than all the officials in the pit."

As he developed the argument, his passionate utterances electrified the men present. There was a momentary pause when he finished, until Len cried out : " That's it ; Harry's right. To give in now will be to play right into the hands of the company."

He went on at some length, repeating the arguments already made until he sensed a restless fidgetting among the committee-men, one of whom shouted : " We've had enough speeches. Let's vote."

Big Jim was on his feet in a jiffy. " Don't you shout my boy down, if you do know what is good for you," he howled. " Fair play for everyone I do say and don't none of you forget it." Dai Cannon caught the tail of his coat and jerked him back to the seat, but not before Len also sat down.

When Ezra put the matter to the meeting, the vote for standing firm was decisive. His face went even paler and he opened his mouth to say something, but changed his mind and rose from the chair without another word. He turned when he was near the door and looked back at the silent men, whose eyes were fixed on his. Hot saliva rose to his throat and he swallowed hard, his drooping shoulders looking pathetically lonely as he left the room.

Len did not return until late that night, and when he at last entered, Ezra was already in bed, but Mary sat crouched over the fire. Her posture was sufficient witness to the despondency that consumed her. It hurt Len to see her in this frame of mind and he put his arm consolingly round her neck, at the same time using his free hand in an effort to turn up her face so that his eyes could look into hers. But she avoided him with an impatient motion that made him halt involuntarily.

After a while, during which he stood awkwardly near her, not knowing what to do or say, he muttered : " Let's go to bed ; the fire's going out and you'll only catch a cold down here."

She made no effort to answer him or to move, and when he realised her intention he became impatient. Bending down, he put one arm under her legs and the other round her shoulders, and, although she struggled feebly, carried her up the stairs.

He knew that Ezra had already prejudiced her regarding the night's decision, but her attitude had stirred his pride too much to permit him to ask what his father-in-law had actually said. Both of them silently undressed and went to bed.

Len was up early in the morning. He pulled on his trousers, then glanced down at her sleeping face, bending to kiss her softly on the lips. The tightly drawn little wrinkles about her eyes told him the depth of her worry, and he felt sorry he hadn't tried to coax her during the night. She stirred restlessly, but did not wake as he quietly closed the bedroom door behind him. He lit the fire, made tea and some toast, which he took up to her. She was awake when he entered.

" I'm sorry, Len, I was so nasty to you last night," she apologised, taking the cup from his hand.

" Never mind, you are worried."

She hurriedly put the cup on the chair near the bed as he said this. " Oh, Len. Yes, I am worried," she emphasised. " I'm sure dad won't accept the decision you took last night. I'm sure he won't."

Len looked hard at her. He felt she was hinting something to him, but could not grasp it. Mary saw the puzzled look in his eyes and longed to tell him what was bubbling on her lips ; but, instead, she hastened to console.

" Don't bother your head, Len. Everything will come all right in the end."

He left her in bed and went to meet Harry Morgan and the other Party members, who had planned to chalk the roads and poster the hoardings with slogans. It was so early that the streets were practically deserted, but Will Evans and another man posted themselves at each end of the street to watch for any wandering policeman while Len and Harry hurriedly chalked huge letters on the roadway : " People of Cwmardy, don't go back to the pits till the old conditions are granted. Stand solid behind the committee. Demand the council feed our children in the schools. Don't listen to those who want to break our resistance."

In every street the same advice was written, while posters with much the same message were pasted on the pine ends of houses and other places. The continual bending put a pain in the small of Len's back, but he refused all requests from the watchers to change places. He felt more proud of his handiwork with each slogan he chalked, and was determined to finish the job on his own.

He little thought while he was doing this, that Ezra, with Mary at his side, was making his way up the drive towards the Big House. Half-way the miners' leader stopped abruptly and grasped his daughter by the shoulder. Mary could feel in his fingers the conflict which gripped him, but she faced him without flinching when he stared into her eyes. His voice sounded like a croak when he spoke.

" Tell me, Mary. What else can I do ? " Before she could reply, he rushed on : " I know you are against my seeing the company now the committee has decided, but that's not good enough for me. No. If it wasn't for Harry Morgan and Len, the others would have seen the same way as I do and we would now be doing the right thing. Remember that, Mary," he pleaded. " If there is anything wrong in what I am doing, the committee is to blame and not me. They should have been men enough to do what is best for the people instead of letting themselves be influenced as they were."

He drew a hot hand across his brow and Mary led him gently to the grassy verge of the drive, where he sat down wearily. The poverty and the deadly inertia of the last ten months made her believe with all the strength of her mind that her father was right in his desire to call the lock-out off. But the long experience of discipline and obedience to leadership which he had carefully nurtured in her forced her to disagree with his present action. The very training he had given her throughout her life was the instrument which now made her condemn him, although she took care not to let him know the extent of her opposition.

Mary took the bent head in her hands and pressed it to her bosom, but the contact seemed to acquaint him with

her innermost thoughts and he hurriedly shook himself
free.

" I know what you are thinking, Mary," he asserted
hoarsely. " Yes, I know." He paused a little to recover
himself and when he continued his words came more slowly
and deliberately. " You believe that the committee is
right, and that I am weak. That's what Len and the
others think. But you're all wrong. Do you hear me ?
All wrong. I have led the people of Cwmardy for thirty
years, and I know their every mood. Ha ! If I let them
dribble back to work one by one until the return became a
rabble, you would think I was strong eh ? But I've led
too long to fall into that trap and I know—are you listening?
—I said that I know the only way to lead is the way the
people want to go, and you must take them altogether
or you'll be left on your own."

The despairing monologue appealed to Mary's desire and
emotion, but she failed to efface completely from her mind
the consciousness that she had heard similar statements
from him before in a crisis. The continual conflict of
opinions between Len and her father was slowly developing
an independent outlook in her, but this was not yet strong
enough to beat back the devotion she had for Ezra, which
always made her support him when she failed to convince
him.

Without being conscious of it, she now tried to reconcile
her love with her opinions. " I don't agree that the committee is right, dad," she declared sadly. " But I don't
believe the people won't follow you now as they have
always done, if you ask them to. What I can't understand
is why you are going to the company in spite of the committee, instead of going to the men. Oh, dad, I'm sure
they'd do what you want them to, never mind what the
preachers say."

He stopped her sharply. " That will do, Mary. You
are too young to know what is best." His voice became
softer as he begged : " But in your ignorance don't you also
desert me, Mary. No, don't you do that, my dear, because
that would mean the end of everything."

His plea conquered her and the tears in her eyes made
them scintillate when she answered. " How ever can
you think such a thing, dad ? Whatever happens and

whatever anybody says, where you go I'm coming, never mind where it is."

She helped him to his feet, and the windows of the Big House seemed to grin maliciously at them as Ezra left Mary waiting, and went to the front door with bent head and heavy feet.

Half an hour later he returned and dumbly handed her a document which she subconsciously knew contained the terms on which the men could restart work.   She read as she walked, and her eyes were flaming by the time she had finished.

" The men will never work on these terms," she exclaimed.

Ezra did not look at her when he replied : " Too late now.   I've already agreed to them, and all that is left is to explain them to the men."

This shook her severely, for she had not for a moment thought he would have gone so far as this, and she stopped to blurt out : " But, dad, you shouldn't have done that. You ought to have let the men see the agreement first, since they are the ones who will have to work under it. At the very least you ought to have showed it to Len and the committee."

His silence quieted her, and she said no more as she followed him down the drive, but, buried in meditation, Ezra failed to notice that she made no attempt to return the document.

During the remainder of the day Mary burned to show the agreement to Len, but she restrained herself till they were alone in their bedroom.   Len knew her moods and lay quietly in bed watching her undress, although his heart beat more quickly each time he saw her thin body.

When she had finished she sat in her nightdress on the edge of the bed and handed him the document, saying : " Here, read this."

He sensed by the throb in her voice that something serious had happened, and, in a sudden surge of emotion, he drew her backwards across his body, pressing her to him.

She struggled from the embrace and gasped : " Read that first, perhaps you won't be so anxious after."

Len forced his eyes to the paper, but before he was half-way through he sprang out of bed and began pacing excitedly, his shirt swishing like a kilt about his bare legs, while he muttered to himself.

His movements got on Mary's nerves, and she grasped his shirt. " For God's sake, sit down, Len. You give me the creeps talking to yourself like that."

He glanced down at her. " Creeps, to hell. I know somebody else who will have the creeps when the workmen know about this lot," he declared, at the same time sitting on the bed beside her, while he read the agreement again.

" Good God, the men'll never accept this ! "

" They have already been accepted," Mary said quietly.

Len jumped to his feet, stared at her for some moments, then burst out as though he doubted his ears. " Accepted ? Who's accepted them ? "

He was obviously bewildered, and she averted her eyes when she replied. "Dad agreed to them with Lord Cwmardy to-day. I was with him."

Len took her face in his hands and fixed his eyes on hers in spite of her efforts to avoid him. When he spoke, the words were hard and incisive. " If your father did that he is a traitor."

A muffled sound came from Ezra's room, followed by a groan. It galvanised Mary into sudden life, and tearing her head free she jumped up, her heaving bosom betraying the tumult the accusation induced in her. She forgot all her previous doubts as the blood love in her body clouded her intellect and forced her to her father's defence.

" You coward, to slander your best friend, the man who has taught you all you know!" she shouted passionately.

Len came towards her and would have spoken, but she checked him with a gesture that showed her contempt. " Don't come near me," she gasped, and the cough that lingered in her throat made her words sound more bitter when she continued : " You, of all men, ought to know how much my father has sacrificed for the people and the Federation. I was there when he told you how my mother died of a broken heart when the owners sold her home up because of dad."

Len nodded mutely. He felt uneasy, but she gave him no time for words, as she went on with her tirade while the tears rolled down her cheeks. " My father has always in

every way been a man of the people ; and now when he is in
the greatest need of help, they snub him and turn from him."

A spasm of coughing racked her chest and checked the
torrent of words.   Len picked his trousers from the bed-
rail and extracted a handkerchief, with which he wiped
away the phlegm that stained her lips.   He drew her
tenderly to the bed, where both sat for a while as she
regained her breath.

When the spasm was over, she took up again the threads
of defence, but her voice was now more subdued.

" You've told me scores of times, Len, that the workers
never desert their own," she said.

Len immediately saw what she was driving at.
" That's true," he stated categorically, as though there
was no room for doubt.   There was a pause before he took
the initiative and challenged her.   " But you can't expect
them to stick to a traitor, can you, Mary ?   You're not soft
enough to believe they'll stick to somebody who's got no
faith in them.   If you are, then you'll believe any bloody
thing."

Mary coloured and asked, in tones that were again
beginning to quiver with temper : " If what you say about
them is right, why have they turned from dad after he has
given everything, his life, home, and happiness, to them ? "

Len looked at her pleadingly.   He had known this fight
was bound to come off sooner or later, and dreaded it because
he was aware it could lead to a lasting cleavage between
himself and Mary.   Her passionate devotion to Ezra had
often raised jealous queries in his mind, but he had always
evaded the issue.   Her words showed he could do so no
longer and must face it whatever the ultimate result.   He
drew himself together with a tremor and said with all the
gentleness he could command.

" Mary, my love, why don't you try to listen to reason.
You know how hard it is for me to say these things, but
they have got to be said, mun, or I'd be less than a man and
not worth any love you might have for me."   He swallowed
bitterly as the thought flashed through his mind that she
had very little love to give anyone after Ezra had had his
share.

The pause encouraged Mary to believe he was weakening.
She also knew the issues at stake, but confident from past

experience, she felt herself stronger than he on vital matters and had already made her mind up for him. She began to plead : " Oh, Len, if you can say these things about dad, what can we expect from those who don't know him so well ? "

Len realised she was trying to keep him on the defensive, and the knowledge gave him courage to protest. " I don't agree with you that either me or the people have deserted your father. No, by gum, Mary, the boot's on the other foot, if it comes to that. You know as well as I do that ever since the big strike and the shootings, he has drifted further and further away from the struggle and the principles he used to believe in. Be fair, mun, and don't shut your eyes to things they ought to see."

Mary jerked herself taut and her eyes flashed into his. The essential truth of his remark had struck her like a blow, but she stubbornly continued to challenge him.

" You have got to prove that," she declared harshly.

Len looked at her helplessly. He ached to catch her in his arms and his head hummed with the effort he was making to control his emotions, but the love he had for her, which had often been a weakness, was now the source of his greatest strength. He shook his head slowly before saying in tender tones that none the less showed the depth of his conviction :

" It is for you to see the facts, Mary. You will find all the proof you want in them. Think, girl," he pleaded, " only for a little minute. Isn't it true that ever since the strike he believes that the men can never beat the company, that it is always better to meet them half-way than it is to fight them ? Of course it's true," he answered himself. " He has lost faith in the people, and, because of this, thinks the company is invincible. That is why he always tells us that half a loaf is better than nothing. You have heard him say that yourself a dozen times, haven't you ? "

She nodded her head without thinking what she was doing. He saw the gesture and it gave him confidence to go on. " Oh, Mary, I know you love your father to the bottom of your heart, but don't you also love all the people who have suffered the same as you from the lock-out? Haven't us all sacrificed as much as each other to beat the company and make the pit fit for men to work in ? "

Mary's head dropped slowly while he spoke, until her chin rested on her chest, and she sobbed quietly to herself.

There was silence for some minutes, during which she gathered new energy. " The Party is jealous because dad has got so much influence over the men," she challenged him. " They want to break him so that they can have control of the Federation."

Len caught her shoulders and bent his head sideways until her eyes looked into his. " You are saying anything now, Mary, because you are too weak to give in. You are only telling me something that your father has told you, and you know in your heart that it is a lie."

The downright assertion and his manner of making it conquered her, and she made no effort to continue the argument. Len's face flushed when he realised she had capitulated, and a warm glow ran through his body. He drew her head towards him while he murmured in her ear.

" Don't worry, Mary ; it's always better for us to face reality than to run away from it. Your old man has often told us to look at things as they are, and not only as we want them to be. And he was right, although it often hurts us to the bone to do it."

Her submissive acquiescence spurred him on, and he felt her tears wet on his cheek as he carefully turned her body until it rested recumbent upon the bed.

" Oh, my dear, it is only by our love for the people that we can measure our love for each other." Without conscious effort he caught his silent wife to him and squeezed her body to his flesh with hot intensity.

Mary sighed softly and Len felt desire sweep over him from head to feet as she relaxed herself in his arms and her upturned face looked trustingly into his eyes. With excited haste he pressed her backwards on the bed and his kisses stole the blue from her lips, replacing it with a living red. Her head now rested on his arm and her flesh quivered with vitality as his hand sought its intimacy. Though neither spoke a word he saw the smile on her lips melt the shadows in her face before he clasped her to him and both were buried in each other.

Some time later, he turned on his side and carefully covered her with bedclothes, before drawing her body tenderly to his and stretching his hand to extinguish the light.

CHAPTER V

Back to Work

NEXT day Len reported Ezra's action to a special Party meeting which he called for the purpose. It was decided that if Ezra did not call a meeting of all the people, the Party would, with Len as the speaker making the report. On the other hand, if the miners' leader convened the meeting, then Len was to be chief spokesman in opposition to the terms.

The news of what had been done soon filtered through the doorways of Cwmardy, and for the remainder of the week nothing else was talked of. Ezra sent a crier round to announce a mass-meeting on the Sunday, and the message gave delight to the preachers and shopkeepers, the vicar going so far as to liken Ezra to Moses leading his people out of the desert.

Many of the miners, however, wondered what was wrong with their leader, but the increasing torment of their poverty together with their inherent loyalty inclined them to his support.

Mr. Evans Cardi rubbed his hands gleefully when one of his customers told him what had happened, and a smile parted his lips as he hurried into the inner kitchen to let Maggie know.

"We have reached the end of this misery at last, thank God," he said. Her face was flushed when she looked up from the account books and waited while he told her what Ezra had done. When he had finished, she gave a little sigh.

"He is a good man, but pity he didn't do it little bit sooner ; we could have let our Ron finish his studies then," she remarked. Her husband, looking years younger already and the lines on his face seeming less harsh, interrupted her. He was anxious that nothing should spoil the joy induced by the knowledge that Ezra was leading the workmen back to the pit.

" Don't worry about that," he consoled. " I have been talking to some of the councillors about him, and if we use our heads and scrape some money together, they might find him a job as a teacher when he comes back."

" But you know, John, that he doesn't want to be a teacher," she retorted.

" Tut-tut. He will get used to it in time, and perhaps later on he'll be able to look round for something better." A knock on the counter took him back into the shop, where Shân and another woman with a baby in a shawl were waiting. Evans could not conceal his exultation and greeted them with : " Better times ahead now, eh ? Ha-ha ! " At the same time washing his hands in invisible water.

The woman with the baby grunted. " Hmm. From what I can hear, I don't know so much about better times. Our Si told me that the only difference will be that we will be getting parish pay just the same, only now we will have to work for it."

" Tut-tut," Evans interrupted impatiently. " Hard work will never hurt nobody."

Shân cocked her ears up. " What ? Never hurt nobody ? Well do I know that it 'on't, if a man can get a bellyful of good food and a clean home after doing it ! I don't believe in these old strikes and lock-outs no more than anybody else, but I don't believe in a man working for nothing, neither. Oh no ! Come you, Mr. Evans."

The grocer hurriedly served them, then went back to the kitchen, where he and his wife planned their son's future in every detail before retiring for the night, happy in the belief that they were on the brink of a new prosperity.

Very early Sunday morning, three buses droned through the drizzly rain towards Cwmardy's police-station, waking many of the inhabitants long before their usual time. An occasional eye squinted through carefully parted window curtains, but none saw the buses unload their cargo at the police-station. One of the higher ranks surveyed the new-comers critically as they stood rigid and awkward in the cramped space of the station. His eyes were coldly vacant as a carp's when he told them : "We don't expect any trouble, now that Ezra Jones has come to his senses, but those Bolshies may try to turn the people against him." He spoke at some length before he allowed the tired men to rest on the benches and chairs brought in for the occasion.

Ezra had spent a restless night, and after tossing about for hours he rose from bed and quietly made his way to the kitchen. The cold dampness made him shiver, and he hurried to light the fire and make some breakfast for himself. He had not finished this when Mary came down, her nightdress covered by an old shawl of Shân's.

"Where are you going, dad?" she asked in surprise when she saw her father.

"Just for a little walk, my girl. A bit of fresh air will do me good."

He tried to hide the turmoil which was consuming him, but Mary's senses were too acute to be deceived. "You can't go out in this weather, dad. It's raining, and you'll be soaking wet long before the meeting."

He gave her a quick glance as he put his coat on and when he was near the door turned to say heavily : "It's not the rain that harms, Mary. Life would be easy and happy if we only had to contend with that. Yes, easy and happy and men could die in peace." Without another word he opened the door and went out.

Later in the day Len tried to persuade his wife not to come to the meeting. She had told him nothing of what had transpired between herself and Ezra ; but he guessed there must have been something, and the fact worried him. She made no reply to his hesitant request, but he knew by the drawn expression on her face that she was intensely worried and he longed to console her in some way, although he felt that words would sound empty in the circumstances. He had already told her of the Party's decision to fight Ezra's policy in the meeting and this helped further to estrange them, so that he left the house alone.

Len found his father impatiently waiting for him. The rain had now stopped, although the sky was full of buffeting clouds, which neither of them noticed as they joined with the others who were making their way to the meeting-place on the rubbish dump. The turmoil in the sky found an echo in the valley, where, louder than the drone of countless voices, the pit engines filled the air with a preparatory "chug-chug" that beat on the bent heads of the people.

"What think you is going to happen to-day, Len bach?" asked Jim in his deep guttural voice, before suddenly bending his huge body and dismally emitting a curse. "What in bloody hell is the matter with me these days? My back and legs do feel like they are on fire and I can't walk two cams without wanting a whiff." He checked himself with a groan, his face contorted with pain and disgust.

Len always felt unhappy when he witnessed these periodic evidences of his father's decline, and he now paused sympathetically, hardly knowing what to say.

"Why don't you go to the doctor, the same as mam have asked you?" he demanded rather curtly.

Jim looked at him a moment as though he thought he had to deal with a man who had suddenly become deranged, then he roared out loudly enough for everyone in the vicinity to hear.

"Doctor to hell! What good can his powders and water do for a man like me, who have looked after hisself all his life and can work better'n any two men in the pit any day of the week. Doctor, muniferni!" He spat contemptuously on the ground, rubbing it viciously with his foot before saying: "Come on. It is only a touch of the bile after those chips your mother maked for dinner."

He thought over this for a while as they continued their walk. The words had implanted a new reason in his mind for the pains he was enduring. He was immensely proud of his once magnificent body and always loath to admit that excessive work and age were now beginning to take toll of his strength.

"Aye, that is it," he muttered, "chips." He stopped again and looked at Len queerly. "Huh! I can see taters in your face as well, my boy. And no bloody wonder. For the last ten months us have had nothing but chips in our guts come day, go day. By Hell, it's a wonder our skins is not like tater peelings by now."

This explanation appeared to invigorate and anger him at the same time. "Hell-fire! How can you 'spect an old sodger like me, who have fought in two wars, to thrive

on bloody muck like that ? Ha-ha, tinned dog and taters.
Ha-ha ! ''

Len said nothing, but Big Jim chuckled all the way to the
dump near the sewage-contaminated river, where thousands
of people were already assembled.

Ezra sat alone on the lorry that was to be the platform.
His posture, with his chin cupped in his hands as he drearily
surveyed the mass of faces before his eyes, denoted the
melancholy and solitude which enveloped him. The white
patches in his hair gave him a pathetic appearance, although
his face still conveyed his dominant strength even in defeat.
The delay began to make the waiting people restless, and
an impatient murmur eddied through their ranks, breaking
into Ezra's thoughts and bringing them back to the job
in hand. He appeared a weary man when he rose to
his feet, but the upraised hand, commanding silence,
betokened the same power he had carried in moments
of victory.

The characteristic gesture thrilled Len as it always had
done in the past, and for some reason it made him think of
Mary. He wondered if she had remained at home, even
as he realised this was impossible for one of her temperament. More or less unconsciously he looked around for
her, and saw scattered here and there amongst the crowd
of hungry faces a number that looked healthy and well
fed ; but before he had time to ponder the problem, his
wandering eyes caught sight of Mary and Shân, and he
immediately started edging his way through the throng
until he reached their side.

Mary's whole being was fixed with staring concentration
upon her father, and Len knew by her attitude the struggle
going on within her. He touched her gently on the arm
and she started at the contact, although she tried to smile
when she recognised him.

"Oh, you frightened me for a minute, Len," she
apologised. He made no answer other than to clasp her
arm more tightly to him as Ezra's husky voice broke through
the dead air.

The miners' leader explained the misery that had followed
the lock-out and the hopelessness of expecting to defeat
the company by adamant inaction that only prolonged the
agony for the people. His whole demeanour tanged

with hate as he outlined step by step the measures taken
to break their ranks.

"Men who have lived on your backs for so many years
now interfere in your pit affairs and want to break up the
Federation. They have been doing all in their power to
turn you against me and have divided you in such a way
that the only hope left is to go back to work together and
admit we are defeated," he declared bitterly.

Will Smallbeer's heavy voice flung itself into the momentary silence that followed these words: "That's right.
Back to work, boys, before they put strangers in our places,"
he boomed with all the force of his lungs.

The cry was taken up and rolled through the crowd.
"Back to work!" "Back to work!"

It rose higher and mightier until another cry, which
gathered impetus and volume with every second, began to
chase it: "What for?" "Let's know what for."

For many moments the two impulses shook the mass of
people until they swayed like trees in a tempest. Len, still
holding Mary's arm and followed closely by Jim and Shân,
pushed his way to the lorry, on which he immediately
clambered, leaving his family pressed against the wheels.

But as Len climbed up a messenger ran to the man who
waited patiently in his car on the main street for news.
He listened to the hasty report, then gave curt instructions
to the messenger, who hurried back to the field where Len,
having succeeded in getting some measure of order among
the people, was shouting at the top of his voice:

"Ezra is betraying us. His words show he is becoming
a deserter."

Ezra clenched his fists until the knuckles drew the skin
so taut that they looked as white as Mary's face. But
Len saw neither.

"Let's know in shillings and pence what the new terms
mean. Let's know the exact conditions before we start,"
he cried, his voice cracking with the strain.

Someone shouted: "Get down, you bloody Bolshie!"

Others howled: "Give the chap a chance. Let him
speak. Go on, Len."

In a flash the air became electrified, and Len's further
statements were drowned by the noise.

Mary looked nervously around the excited mass, and the

hollows in her cheeks became deeper as she hesitated. Then she scrambled on the lorry before Jim and Shân could check her. The wind billowed her skirt over the back of her knees, but no one took any notice of this as they recognised her haggard features and she rushed towards her husband and caught his wildly waving arm.

" Stop. For God's sake stop. It is madness. Madness ! " she cried. Len did not hear what she said, but he read her lips when she shouted : " Leave it to dad. He's the only one who can handle them now."

The big men who were scattered about drew closer together as Ezra once more rose slowly to his feet. He had made no effort to calm the tumult while Len was trying to speak, and now waited until it subsided, which it soon did as the people became aware that he intended speaking again when they made order.

When at last he spoke, the words throbbed in his throat. " You've heard what Len and his Party have to say and will think what you like. I have a duty to you and intend doing it whatever is said. The pits will be open to-morrow for all of you that want to go. Those who don't can stay away. I have finished."

With this he gave Mary a glance that bored into her bones, gulped hard, then abruptly jumped off the lorry and left the field.

The people looked in amazement after his retreating form, until the big men started to hustle and order them to move on. Slowly they began to drift away, muttering and arguing as they went, until only Len and Mary, Big Jim and Shân were left on the deserted field that had become as silent as a cemetery. They looked at each other dumbly for some moments, then turned and followed the people as the pit-hooters blared the fact that the pit had found new life.

Len and Mary went home to his mother's, and when they were all seated Shân asked in a casual manner : " What do you think to it, James ? Do you think the men will act sensible ? "

Jim said nothing, the long stand had made his body sore, and Len's failure to get a hearing had increased his irritation. But at last, seeing that no one spoke, he condescended

to say : " I don't believe they do know their bloody selves
what they are going to do."

This knocked Shân off her mental perch for a moment,
but she soon recovered herself. " Huh ! Don't know
what they is going to do, eh ? And the hooters blowing
like it was New Year's Eve. But there, perhaps it was you
was too dull to understand what Ezra said."

The words made Mary's cheeks go even whiter, a fact
which the old woman immediately noticed. Repenting
the effect of what she had said, she put her arms round the
girl's neck and tried to console her with flattery.

" There, there, my gel. What are you worrying about ?
Your father did do quite right, as everybody with sense
do well know." She looked significantly at Len and Jim
as she said this, but neither of them took up the challenge,
though Len began to feel very awkward and wished he
had gone straight home. He was on the point of suggesting
this course when his father asked :

" Do you think they will work to-morrow, Len ? "

" Yes, dad. I'm afraid they will," nodding his head
sadly.

" 'Fraid ? How comes that, Len bach ? " asked Shân
with assumed surprise.

" Hell-fire ! Don't start nagging the boy so soon as he
do come in," shouted Jim in exasperation.

Len stemmed the impending storm. " It's all right,
dad. Mam and Mary are worried about the shop and the
rent. It is they have got to stand the brunt of that ; we
know nothing of what it is."

He bent down to pick up a black beetle crawling over
the sand near Mary's feet, and threw it into the fire. They
all watched the squirming form turn the hues into blue and
green, which worked up through the red of the flames.

" Duw ! That was a pretty sight, mun," said Jim
admiringly. " See if you can catch some more, Len." And
he looked at the soot-grimed wallpaper in case any should
be crawling there.

Shân resumed the conversation with a plea. " Tell me,
Len bach, what is you and your father going to do to-
morrow ? "

Len had feared this direct question and looked at her
before answering. The worry he saw in her face put a

grief in his heart, and he hardly knew how to reply. He turned to Mary for support, but her gaze was fixed on the fire, and it was obvious by the droop of her body that the events of the day had robbed her of what little strength she had. Bracing himself, he huskily tried to placate his mother, at the same time hoping his words would justify his action in Mary's sight.

" I know it is hard for the two of you, mam. But what else could I do ? We can't go against our principles and go back to work to-morrow after we have told the other men not to, can we ? "

Shân, as usual when she was deeply upset, raised the corner of her canvas apron to her nose and moaned, " O God, bach, where is it all going to end ? "

The smoky air in the kitchen weighted the words in the ears of the two men when she continued. " Whatever can us do ? Ten months without a penny piece and head over heels in debt, and me without a shimmy to my back ! Oh dear, dear ! There is nothing before us in our old age but the workhouse." She stopped her moaning and turned sharply to Len to declare bitterly. " But I knowed it ! Yes, so sure as God is my judge I knowed it 'ood come once you started mixing with those old Bolshies ! "

She paused and sniffed, hoping Mary would come to her aid, but the latter did not appear to be listening to what was going on in the kitchen, so Shân continued on her own, her voice rising with her temper. " Don't you dare to bring that Harry Morgan, with his nice tongue and sly ways, inside my door agen. No, and if you are wise, Mary fach, you will keep him from yours too. It is him that have turned the head of our Len."

None of them interrupted her and she stopped of her own accord, only to resume, with greater vigour, in a direct attack on Jim, who had been silently congratulating himself that he was out of it.

" There is nothing stopping you to go to work like other men, James, because you did never have no principles, whatever the old things is ! "

The sudden turn in events shook Jim, but he squared his chest indignantly and his eyes flashed red in the fire-glow as he retorted : " Be careful what you tell me to my face, 'ooman. Don't you never dare to say that Big Jim have

got no principles. Huh! Many a better man than you
have lived to regret those words all their lifes. But there,"
he added resignedly, as though it had just struck him that
the argument was beneath his dignity, " what am I bothering to you about principles for ? There have never been
one in your fambly, so what can us 'spect ? "

Shân stared at him with open mouth as he went on.
" Let me tell you, once for all, Shân, that if Len and Mary
is Bolshies, then, by damn, I am one as well, and a bigger
one than the two of 'em put together ! See ? "

With a dignity amounting to arrogance he raised his
hand to his moustache and twirled its stiff ends about his
fingers. The action thawed the glare in Shân's eyes as
she sensed the rigid loyalty of her husband, and looking at
Len, she saw the same pride there.

" All right," she sighed. " Have it your own ways this
time agen. But so sure as God is my judge, one day they
will have to break the door down with sledges to find our
dead bodies starved to death on the floor."

Big Jim, whose pride was stung by this last remark,
interrupted her. " If any man will ever find me starved to
death, it 'on't be on the floor, but decent and tidy in bed
like every 'spectable man did ought to be. Yes, muniferni ! If you do want to die on the floor, Shân, you will
have to do it by yourself, and I tell you straight now."

When Len and Mary eventually left the old couple and
went home, they found that Ezra, after leaving the kettle
on the hob, had gone to bed.

CHAPTER VI

The Breaking of a Friendship

ON the Monday morning after the mass meeting Mrs.
Evans Cardi was awakened long before her usual time by
the sound of singing. For some half-dazed moments she
failed to understand what was happening and her hands
groped aimlessly under the bedclothes, until she suddenly
realised that her husband was not beside her. She sat
up in a frenzy of alarm, and when she bent over to light
the candle her fingers were trembling.

The singing seemed to get louder and she fancied she
recognised the voice. Gathering her courage she got out
of bed and went cautiously down the stairs into the shop,
where she found John, his nose pressed against the window-
pane as he peered into the street, happily humming :

> " At five in the morning,
>   As jovial as any
>   The miners were leaving
>   Their homes for their work."

Accompanying the tune like a staccato baritone was the
" tramp, tramp " of hob-nailed boots.

"Whatever are you doing down by here, John ? " she
asked in amazement.

He did not take his face from the window, but called
over his shoulder : " Come here, Maggie fach. Come and
see them going to work. Ha-ha." He laughed with the
exuberant happiness of a child. " Our troubles will soon
be over now. Come, look at them going up the hill to the
pit. Ha-ha ! We won't have long to wait now before
trucks of coal will be rolling down the line, and the ships
in the docks will get up steam and we will have dividends
on our shares in the pit." He began to shout as the
picture gripped him. " Then, Maggie, we can pay off the

74

mortgages, get rid of our debts, and have enough money to
get our Ron a better position than teaching on the council."

Maggie's eyes gleamed with joy, but she urged him back
to bed and he reluctantly left the window, unwilling to lose
sight of a single unit in the long line of black-clothed men
silently trudging their way to the pit. He was enamoured
of the tiny pin-pricks of light that stabbed the morning
darkness through the cottage windows, but her exhorta-
tions reminded him that the hair on his naked legs was
stiff with cold and excitement.

He followed her upstairs into bed, marking each step with
a happy little chuckle. She tucked him in beside her,
stiffening her limbs involuntarily when he wound his cold
legs about hers and fell to sleep like a baby with his face
resting on her bosom. She had followed him before the
hooters howled the news that the last man was down the
pit.

The echo of the hooters had died at the bottom of the
valley before the specially imported police had left their
hiding-places in the dark corners and alley-ways of
Cwmardy.

On the way to the station one of them said loudly :
" Good job that's over. We'll be able to sleep in peace
now."

Someone muttered a warning. " S-sh ! Do you want
all the men who haven't gone to work to hear you ? "
They spoke in quiet whispers after this.

" About how many do you reckon went to the pits ? "

" I should say about four thousand."

" Huh ! That means there's over a thousand that
listened to that bloody red Len Roberts, and are now in
bed while their butties are working."

Another butted in : " Aye, it's a shame. I say all these
bloody Bolshies ought to be rounded up and sent to Russia.
They wouldn't be long finding out which side their bread is
buttered then, and would be damn' glad to come back to
the old country to work."

They slithered in single file through the half-open door
of the police-station and carefully drew the blinds.

The police officers had hardly settled down to sleep after
their all-night vigil before the sun poked its rays across the

sky and into the black pall belching from the smoke-stack which threw them back at the windows of the Big House, where Lord Cwmardy sat with the earpiece of a telephone pressed to his ear.

He seemed very interested in what was being said from the other end on the colliery yard, and when the voice had finished, asked : " How many did you say, Mr. Hicks ? . . . Hmm. Very good. Better than I thought for the first day. Yes. Eh ? What did you say ? No, no, man. Don't delay. Put the notice up immediately. Give them till Saturday to present themselves for work and let them know if they're not there by then their places will be filled with men from other areas. . . . Oh, by the way, Mr. Hicks, have you seen to it that the old part-nerships have been broken up and the working-places inter-changed ? . . . Very good. Very good, indeed, Mr. Hicks. . . . No, there is nothing more, good morning."

He replaced the receiver with a smile and made his way to the dining-room, where his daughter, a robust young woman, sat awaiting him. Lord Cwmardy patted her hair affectionately as he passed her on his way to the chair she had ready at the breakfast-table. He settled himself comfortably while she poured the coffee, after which he remarked.

" Well, my dear, the men have come to their senses at last and we can look forward to some tranquillity in this valley."

His eyes became reminiscent and his voice strangely soft when he said. " Do you know, Margaret dear, I love this old valley and the people in it ? It was here your grandfather sunk his first pit and laid the foundations of the company as it is now. Yes, your grandfather was a fine man. Strong enough to know not only what he wanted but also how to get it. Often is the time when I was a little boy he took me down the pit and made me sit on the side while he helped a collier to fill his tram if there was a rush for coal."

He sighed at the memory, and his daughter looked at him from under her eyelids.

" Do you think the men will quietly accept the new price-lists ? " she asked.

He squared his shoulders abruptly, spilling a drop of coffee on his trousers, but taking no notice of this.

"Accept ? Of course they will. We have broken the backbone of their resistance and need have no further worry. You see, my dear, these pits here have always been a storm-centre, our people being the first to fight and the last to give way. But we have ended all that now Ezra Jones, their leader, has become more sensible. A fine man, Ezra. He used to be a firebrand and caused us a lot of trouble for many years, but he's getting wiser as he's getting older." He strangled another sigh in his throat and asked her to pass the marmalade.

While Lord Cwmardy was having this conversation with his daughter and the hooters were blasting the valley with their blare, Big Jim was trying to light the fire in the kitchen grate. It was only after persistent nagging that Shân had persuaded him to get out of bed first. Her deliberate restlessness while he was sleeping made him grunt continually and had at last awakened him.

Rubbing his eyes, he sat up on his haunches and growled : " What in hell is biting you, Shân ? I thought you had poisoned all the bugs. For hell's sake go to sleep, 'ooman, or get up and let a better man sleep in peace."

" Fitter if you got up yourself for once, like other men. There 'ood be some shape on living then," she retorted.

Jim remembered looking at her for some moments in amazement before bursting out. " What ? Me light fire ? Good God ! What is coming over you, my gel. Don't forget I am a man, not a bloody dish-cloth. Huh ! It has always been against my principles to do a 'ooman's work."

He had begun to curl up under the bedclothes again, but her next words brought him back to his haunches with a jerk.

" Bah ! Principles indeed, what are they ? I have never seened one and nobody else have neither. Will a principle put food in our bellies or clothes on our backs ? " she demanded of her dazed spouse. " No, never in your life. It is only work will do that."

This shot compelled Jim to remark with ponderous slowness, as though she had committed sacrilege. " A principle is like God. It is something you can't see, but it is deep down in your heart all the same."

Shân had looked at him scornfully before replying :

" Huh ! Your heart 'on't take you far when your belly is empty of food."

It was this final remark, spoken caustically, that had sent Big Jim shamefacedly down the stairs in his shirt, vainly trying to maintain his dignity by flinging back with a grunt over his shoulder what he thought was a crushing retort :

" For shame on you, 'ooman, for thinking a man's guts is more 'portant than his heart. If somebody heard you, mun, they 'ood think you have never been inside a chapel in your life. Huh ! "

He now tried to analyse her statements as he held a sheet of newspaper before the fire to draw the flames more quickly up the chimney. He felt that somehow she had got the better of him, and, pondering over the problem, forgot all about his work until a draught of air tore the paper from his hands and sucked it up the chimney, where it set the soot on fire with a roar.

The noise startled him for a moment, and he sprang back just as Shân, half-dressed, came rushing down the stairs to see what was the matter.

Jim immediately grasped his chance and shouted at the top of his voice : " Hell-fire ! Is this bloody house witched, or what ? "

She gave a glance at the fireplace, then began to pull her skirt over her head while he made frantic efforts to extinguish the flames, howling instructions all the while.

" Get some salt, Shân ! Quick, now ! "

" There is none in the house," she moaned, at the same time unconsciously patting her disordered hair.

" Hell-fire ! This is not the time to prink yourself up, mun. Get some sand, then ! "

" That is all gone too. Oh dear, dear. This will mean a summons so sure as God is my judge, and us without a penny in the house. Why for was a man so useless ever brought into the world ? "

She sat resignedly in the chair and muttered : " Ah well, us might jest as well be burned to death as starve to death. It is quicker, anyhow."

The neighbouring women rushed out into the street and saw the dense fumes of smoke and flame pour from the chimney. They gazed sympathetically at the sight for a while, then one said : " Poor old Shân will have a mess to clean up after this."

" Aye," another replied, looking at the curling smoke and folding her arms aggressively on her stomach. " And no need for it at all, if Big Jim did only do the same as our Dai and sweeped it down once and agen with the cane brush, it 'ood never catch fire. But there, what can you do with a man who do always say, whenever you tell him anything : ' One man, one job ' ? "

This started an argument, and the fire died down while the women gossiped.

Later the same morning Len took a stroll through the main street, nodding here and there to the various groups of men scattered about. All of them were opposed to the new terms, and their resentment was expressed in their thin faces and the heat with which they discussed the position. Each time a strange policeman came near they turned their backs to him and audibly spat into the roadway as he passed.

Dai Cannon was the centre of one group that hailed Len, who returned the greeting and joined them.

" Aye," the irascible old man was saying, " Not so very long ago they was shouting like anything for the Federation and now the twisters have sneaked back to work like dogs scrounging after a bitch in heat. Ach, they do listen to Ezra like as if he was God."

The keen attention which the listeners paid to his words encouraged him and he spoke more loudly : " No man is good enough for that. No. What have Ezra done for us after we have paid him well all these years and gived him a nice house and enough money to wear collars and ties every day of the week ? " He blew his nose before answering himself. " Nothing. He have turned on us like the rest. I tell you, boys, it's every man for hisself these days."

Will Evans, a muffler dangling rakishly from his neck and his cap stuck at an angle on the side of his head, thought it time to help. " That's right. They're all the same, self first and everybody else last, from what I can see of it. Look at Fred Lewis. He's supposed to be in the Party and have been preaching revolution like blue hell for years ; but now he's crawling round licking Ezra's arse.

Bah ! I wonder what Ezra had from the company for this sell-out," he concluded insinuatingly.

Len felt his face go red, then white, and was about to break into the conversation when someone warned : " S-sh ! Here they come. Talk about the devil, muni-ferni ! "

Ezra, his head bent and his hands behind his back, came slowly towards them. Fred Lewis was with him, talking volubly, his hands in continual motion as he tried to emphasise something ; but Ezra did not appear to be taking any notice of him. The miners' leader quickened his step a little as he came near the group and his head sunk more deeply between his shoulders, until he heard someone hiss : " Traitor ! "

The word jerked him erect, and he stopped to scan the faces before him with glittering eyes. He stared at them, one after the other, until he saw the white face of his son-in-law. For some seconds the two men's thoughts were centred on each other and completely oblivious of anyone else.

Len felt a vague pity run through him and he would have given anything if he could have apologised for the remark, but Ezra's features were set with a hardness that allowed for no compromise. His voice rasped like a saw on steel when he said : " Did you hear it ? ' Traitor ' was the word they used. And you and your gang taught them to use it. Huh ! After what you have said and done behind my back, you should know what a traitor is."

His voice broke for a moment but his eyes were more adamant than ever when he shrugged his shoulders and without another word walked on, leaving the men gaping on the kerb. Lewis, nonplussed by the suddenness of the incident and feeling very awkward, sheepishly followed, but the attack made Len feel giddy. His head swirled, making his mouth dry and his stomach sick. Will Evans saw the emotional strain he was undergoing and patted him sympathetically on the back.

" It's no good worrying, Len. That have just about finished everything between you and your father-in-law," he consoled.

Others joined in the talk that followed, but Len had lost all interest in what they were saying.

During the afternoon most of the men who had stopped from the pit again gathered round the street-corners to see the others return. Len sensed the cleavage between the two sections as the black-faced men walked past the groups. He saw one-time mates look bitterly at each other and pass in silence. The sight sent a thought flashing through his brain.

" Good God," he muttered to himself, " we have forgotten all about the company and now see each other, instead of Lord Cwmardy, as enemies." He continued to look on helplessly and all the time the conviction grew on him that something new had developed in the valley over night. He began to wonder if the Party were right when it advocated that the men remain out in spite of all that had happened. Wouldn't it have been better to keep the men together and accept the inevitable, rather than have them turn on each other as they were now doing ?

These and other thoughts crowded themselves on him until he heard a shout.

" You'd better all get back, boys, because they're starting strangers next week if you don't."

The news beat into Len's mind like a blow, and he hurried away. By the time he reached the house he had gripped himself somewhat, although his hurried entrance betrayed the tumult still within him.

Ezra sat quiet and morose in his customary place, and did not even raise his head when Len entered. The latter ate the food that Mary had prepared even while he noticed that her downcast eyes seemed to lengthen her face, giving it an appearance of loneliness. She motioned him to a chair near her when he had finished his food, and the action bore out his feeling that something unusually serious had happened. He tried to catch her eye, but she avoided him and all he saw was the twitching of her face. He sat down and for a time the only sound was that of heavy breathing. Then Ezra broke the silence and his words dripped like melting icicles into Len's heart, where their very coldness sent hot flames through his body.

" Len Roberts ; there is no room in this house for you and me together. One of us has got to get out."

Len sprang to his feet, but Mary's look dragged him down before he could say anything, as Ezra went on without

raising his gaze from the fire. "Well can you look to
Mary—you, who have made her father's name a byword in
Cwmardy ! " The miners' leader rose to his feet and rested
his hand on the mantelpiece. " You heard what I said ?
Either you or me are leaving this house to-night. Too
long have I stuck all the sneers and taunts that have been
flung at me, and the time has now come when it's going to
be ended, inside these doors at least."

Len felt like a child tossed into a flood. The words
buffeted about inside his head and he was unable to grasp
their import clearly, although spontaneously he thought
of Mary. He was unable to conceive of anything happening
to himself unless it happened to her, and the first question
that broke from him was a puzzled : " But what about
Mary, then, Ezra ? "

The very innocence of the query shook the elder man,
who had prepared himself to face a scene and never expected
this. He hesitated, then answered : " Mary will do what
she thinks best. She is old enough to think for herself,
but all I hope is that she will stick by her father for the
short time that is left to me." Something in his throat
clouded the last words and nearly made them inarticulate.

Len looked from father to daughter dazedly, then something hot simmered within him and he jumped up as for
the first time he became aware of the full weight of
Ezra's ultimatum. His chest was heaving when he
shouted :

" Ha ! I see what you're driving at now. You want
me to leave my home. You want to kick me out like a dog,
and think I'll go with my tail between my legs ! " He
swallowed hard and went on more hurriedly, as though the
words were bursting in his mouth : " But you're thinking
wrong. Yes, by gum, you're thinking wrong." His arms
were now beginning to wave wildly and Mary tried to
pacify him, but he only cried : " Don't interfere, Mary.
If your father isn't man enough to stand up to opposition,
then he's not man enough to lead the Federation. Do you
think that because I am your husband I have got to believe
everything he says and do everything he wants me to ?
No ; not on your life ! I have got a home to go to, don't
worry—the one I had before ever I came here, and I'm
always welcome there."

" Hush, Len," she implored. " Dad's bad and don't mean half of what he's saying."

Ezra had now resumed his seat, and his dejected demeanour had the effect of dampening Len's temper as quickly as it had flared up. This emotional volatility was one of his main characteristics, and it always found expression in his relationship with Ezra and Mary. All his mature life had been influenced by the miners' leader, and even now, despite their many differences, he regarded Ezra as the strongest and most dominating man in Cwmardy. Coupled with this was his intense devotion to and pride in Mary. They had been reared together in the village and drawn into the struggles of the people from early childhood. This had the effect on Len of mentally fusing father and daughter together as an indissoluble unit, and he could never think of one without at the same time thinking of the other. He wondered now what she would do in face of what Ezra had said, knowing that the ultimatum applied to her as well as to himself.

Throughout the scene, Mary had remained practically silent, although she was aware of the personal issues at stake. She was her husband's superior intellectually, having the capacity to think more coherently and feel less acutely, and when she now spoke it was obvious to both men that she was expressing her deepest convictions.

" Dad, Len. I'm sorry that this has happened, especially when all of us know there was no need for it."

Ezra shuffled restlessly, but she gave him no time to intervene.

" I know what you feel, dad, about what's happened, but you can't blame Len for that, although he belongs to the Party."

" Can't blame him, Mary? Don't talk foolish, girl. Isn't he one of the leaders and isn't he the one they always put up to fight me on every issue ? "

" I know, dad, I know," she patiently assented. " And I wish in my heart he had listened to me and never joined it. But what's the good of talking about that now."

Ezra stopped her curtly. " There's every reason why we should talk about it. His Party called me a traitor and it's a lie . . . a lie ! " He shouted the last words, but gained control of himself immediately. " I have spent a lifetime in this movement, Mary, and your mother got buried in it. Yes, I know the struggle from A to Z, and I won't allow any man to call me a traitor because I won't do what he or his mates want me to do. What I have done I have done with my eyes open, and the people have listened to me. I am sorry there are still a few soft enough to follow Len and his Party."

Len's temper began to rise again, but Mary intervened hastily.

"Don't start quarrelling again, we've got enough to worry about without that."

"But he told me to leave the house, Mary, and I want to know if he means that."

Mary knew immediately that Len had precipitated the crisis in spite of her efforts to avoid it, but she tried to mitigate the effects by taking the offensive from Ezra's hands at the beginning.

"Yes. That's true, Len. Dad told you to go."

"No, I didn't, Mary, I said one of us would have to go." The tones in which Ezra said this were as heavy as lead, but they acted on Mary like a stimulant.

"Oh, why do we beat about the bush like this?" she asked. "Both of you are feeling nasty and bitter, but to-morrow you will be sorry for what you are saying now." She gulped a little. "Listen, the two of you. Both of you know how much I think of you, but you are asking me to choose, dad, and it's not fair. There's room in this house for all of us, as there has been ever since Len and me were married, and I don't see why you should talk to him as you did just now because you have quarrelled about something else."

Ezra stirred in his chair again. "Don't talk so lightly, Mary," he said sharply. "This is not a simple quarrel. For years you know that Len and me have been getting further apart on everything that counts, and now we've reached a point where there can be no harmony between us while we are together. That's what I mean when I say there is no room in this house for both of us."

Len felt obliged to interpose and, turning to Mary, he exclaimed: "That's just the point, Mary. Your father and me can never agree on many things. Anybody can see that after what he's done about the lock-out. Good

God, I'd say the same thing about my own mother if she
did the same thing as that. So what's the good of arguing ?
I've followed Ezra through thick and thin all my life, and
it cuts me to the bone that it's got to come to this. But
it's not my fault. Neither you or him can expect me to
bury all my thoughts in what he says and does. No. He
has taught me to think for myself, and what I haven't
learned from him I've learned in the battles of our people
and in the pit from my butties. And that's good enough
for me." His voice became bitter as he took down his coat
from the back of the door. " Your father has told me to
leave. How easy he said it, knowing it's his house and
I've only been here on sufferance all this time ! I can
hardly believe I have been so blind as not to see it before.
Never mind. We're never too old to learn." His anger
got the better of him, although he had been trying to control
it, and he blurted out : " But I remember the time when
he left us all without being told to go. Aye, left us when
he thought we were in a hole and the company was beating
us. That's the sort of leader he is . . . good when everything is going all right, but cruel and selfish when the odds
are against us and he can't get his own way."

He put his hand on the latch and was about to lift it
when Mary sprang up with a little cry. " Don't, Len.
Don't go and leave me. Dad doesn't mean what he says.
Do you, dad ? " She appealed to Ezra, but he made no
response. She went to him and took his head in her hands,
while Len stood immobile, hardly knowing what to do at
this new development.

It was obvious that Mary had made her mind up during
the last few seconds and was now tensed to express her
opinions whatever the consequences.

" Dad," she challenged gently, " you are not only nasty
with Len because of what's happened about the lock-out,
but also because you are jealous of him."

This stung Ezra to retort immediately. " Jealous ?
Jealous of him ? Ha-ha ! "

" Don't laugh, dad. I'm very serious, more serious than
I have ever been in my life. You are jealous because you
are afraid that Len and the Party are going to get more
support than you from the people of Cwmardy and because
you believe I think more of him than of you. I don't

believe in the Party any more than you, but I'm bound to say, dad, that I think you did wrong when you didn't give the men a chance to have a say about the agreement, although in everything else I believe you were right."

The two men were now listening intently to what she was saying, each conscious of the fact that she was determining their future.

" But, dad, when you tell Len to leave the house it means you are asking me to leave either him or you. Yes, you are asking me to choose which I love most, and I can't, I can't," her voice broke and she paused while she recovered herself.

" Can't you see, dad, that I love the two of you equally as much, but in different ways. I'm not a little child now, only doing what I'm told to do. You have reared me to think like a woman and have always taught me to have an opinion of my own. Oh, dad, don't you remember when you used to take me to the workmen's committees and meetings because I was too small to be left in the house on my own after mam died ? "

Ezra knew what was coming and his head slowly sank until it had slipped from her grasp, when she went on very softly.

" Don't you think, dad, that had an effect upon my mind ? Of course it had. When the men used to challenge you on something, I used to hate them in my childish mind for daring to say anything about you. I used to be thrilled when you and them would be talking of the strikes and the other things connected with the pit. I was happy when I was old enough to join with our other women and do something myself, as well as listen to others. Yes, all of these things you've reared me up to, and that is why, dad, Len can never steal me from you, but neither can you steal me from Len.

" That's something you must both learn. You tell Len that he must go. That means that you are throwing me out as well, because if he goes, I go with him—not because I love him more than you, but because I have to take his part when you are unfair, dad, and take advantage of him. I know now as sure as the morning will come that if I choose to stay with you after Len has gone that you will want me to agree with you in everything, as you now want Len to do. You will want to rob me of the independence that your own training has given me. You will love me so long as I agree with you in everything. No, dad. That's something Len has never asked me to do. If he goes, I go with him."

Her eyes filled and she caught Ezra's head to her breast and felt his heaving shoulders as her words sank home. She silently nodded to Len to go to bed. Before the door had properly closed behind him, Ezra broke down completely and she heard him sob for the first time in her life. Her own tears fused with his as she tried to soothe him.

CHAPTER VII

Speed-up

LEN was glad that the threatened domestic break-up had not matured, but he was very worried about affairs in the pit, and during the days following the quarrel, his mind was concentrated on the problem of work. He felt uneasy and wondered if he and the others who remained out were doing the right thing ; but he dreaded the thought of going back to work after the stand the Party had made against the terms and the restart. He hesitated to tell anyone of his thoughts in case he would be regarded as weak, but towards the end of the week he determined to seek Ezra's advice, although there was still a certain tenseness between them.

The opportunity came one night at the supper-table when, instead of asking Ezra direct, he asked Mary : "What do you think me and dad should do ? I don't fancy it's right for us to go back to work just because the company says it will put other men in our places." He paused. "But somehow I feel unless we do something quick, they'll keep us out for ever. I don't know what to do for the best," he concluded dolefully.

Mary looked dubiously at her father, but the latter appeared to be deep in thought. All along she, in common with many of the women, felt there was no purpose served in remaining out now most of the men had restarted ; but she had mentioned nothing to Len about her opinions. His straight query and evident puzzlement, together with Ezra's apparent lack of interest, prompted her, after a brief hesitation, to be frank.

"I hardly know what to say, Len," she muttered, looking at him helplessly, then blurting out : "But one thing is sure, we can't carry on for ever with nothing coming in. Oh, I wish to God the men had never got divided like this."

She knew she was on dangerous ground even as she uttered the words, but both men fortunately seemed to miss their import. Her outburst, however, brought Ezra from his abstraction, and he raised his head with a tired motion.

" There's two lessons I've learned in life. One is that the next best thing to victory is to know when you're beaten. The other is always to keep with the men wherever they are."

Len looked at the man and wondered what was coming next, but he made no effort to say anything, as Ezra went on, his dark eyes a little less moody :

" And no one can question that we've been beat this time. How can we expect to win," he demanded, " when we are fighting not only the company but the Government as well ? "

He paused, realizing immediately the slip he had made, but Len, impelled by the opportunity, gave him no time to recover before asking : " But it's a Labour Government, Ezra, and how can they be against us ? "

The miners' leader coughed, pretending to clear his throat, then said : " Yes, it's a Labour Government, but what power has it got ? It's only there on sufferance and can be put out at any minute."

" But, Ezra, if it's kicked out for doing something for the people, then that's just the way in which the people will put it back with full power, isn't it ? "

Len was getting excited as he began driving his points home, and Mary became a little anxious as she saw his exuberance. " Let's stick to the point and not start talking about politics that will lead us nowhere," she advised in an effort to avoid the argument she knew was brewing.

Ezra willingly followed her cue. " You're right, Mary, and the point's perfectly clear, in my mind at least, and I should think to every other sensible man or woman."

Len opened his mouth, but he had no chance to speak, as Ezra interrupted his unspoken thoughts.

" Oh, I know all about principles and what not, and I know it's very nice to feel oneself to be a martyr. Ay, indeed, very nice and comfortable. But I've never yet seen what good it's done anybody, least of all the people it's supposed to help. That's why I advised the men to go back to work."

Len could hold himself in no longer, and he broke the
momentary silence that followed Ezra's remark. " But,
Ezra, the position's different, mun. You told us to go
back when we were all united, and by telling us that you
broke us up, as you can see for yourself now."

" Yes, Len. But that would have happened in any
case because of what you and the Party did. If you'd
only listened to me and put those wild theories out of your
head, the men would have gone back together and there
wouldn't be any of this bitterness." His eyes became
hard again and his face set. " You can thank the Party
for the present position in Cwmardy."

Len hastily swallowed the food he had put in his mouth,
while Ezra was speaking, but Mary interrupted him before
he could make himself articulate. The partial reconcilia-
tion between the two men had given her a happiness she
had not felt for a long time, and she knew whatever she said
would be accepted by both as her honest opinion, even if
she were wrong.

" I don't think you're right, dad," she said, " I believe
you've got enough influence with the workmen to hold
them, especially when you have the committee behind you,
as you did."

Ezra started to say something, but she went on : " All
the same, I believe the same as you about Len going to
work. His place is there with the other men, and even if
they were wrong that's no reason for deserting them."

Len rose agitatedly from the table : " You can't say I'm
a deserter ! " he exclaimed. " There's such things as
principles that one must stick to through thick and thin."

A slow smile passed over Ezra's face, softening it for a
moment as he said : " That's where you're wrong. When
I was your age I used to think the same, but experience—
and you will agree it has been a fairly wide one—has taught
me that principles which go against the workmen must be
put on one side."

The argument now became more heated and continued
until very late, but at the end of it Len agreed to apply
for his work back if the Party and the workmen still out
agreed.

Early next morning Len went round the homes of all the
Party members he could get hold of, and it was decided to

support Ezra if he called a meeting. This was done ; Len
and two other Party members going round the streets with
a bell to announce the meeting, which was held the same
afternoon.

After much bitter recrimination and bad feeling, all the
men decided to go up to the pit the next day and apply for
their work.

Before the first hooter had started to blow the following
day, Shân was out of bed and had lighted the fire in the
kitchen. Her face was glowing with happiness when Jim
came down, and she fluttered around him like a hen.

" Ha-ha, James bach, it is good to see you in working
clothes once agen. Aye, indeed, mun."

" Huh ! I do agree with you," Jim grunted in reply,
at the same time bending to pull his trousers over his feet.
" Don't be long with that toast ; our Len will be down
any minute now."

" Tut-tut ! Don't you worry 'bout my business. This
is not the first bit of toast that I have made. Oh no."

The old couple were seated at the breakfast table when
Len walked in. Shân immediately jumped from her chair
to wet the cocoa she had prepared for him. " There, Len
bach, put that down your little belly." Len never refused
this, because he knew it gave her pleasure.

In a short time the men were ready to leave and, as they
were about to go, Shân warned them. " Now, 'member,
mind to take care of yourselfs to-day. You have been a
long time from the pit now, and 'on't be so quick as you did
used to be."

Big Jim's happy laughter rippled round the kitchen like
a drum beat. " I have worked in that old pit going on for
forty years and you can venture there is not much about
her that Big Jim don't know, you take that from me."

With this, they both kissed the old lady and left the house.

When the two men presented themselves at the lamp-
room they were told to wait outside the manager's office,
or " insulting room," as Jim always called it.

" Funny bloody game this, in't it, Len ? " he asked
bewilderedly, as they made their way across the colliery
yard towards the office where a long queue of men were
already lined up.

Len did not answer, although he was equally surprised by this unusual procedure. They fell in at the tail end of the queue and waited, while they watched the twinkling lights jogging from the lamp-room to the pit-head. The indignity of the wait galled Jim, and at last, unable to contain himself any longer, he bawled out to no one in particular.

" Frigging hell ! What do they think we are—doorboys, or dancing fleas, or what ? I have never seened such a insult in all my born days." No one replied, and this drove him frantic. " By damn, they can spit on me, but no bloody man breathing can rub it in, muniferni."

The words were hardly spoken when a rustle ran through the ranks as the office door opened and the colliery sergeant came out, shouting at the top of his voice : " Only fifty wanted to-day. First come, first served."

The waiting men stood immobile in amazed silence until the sergeant bawled : " Come on there. Who's the first to start ? "

In a flash the ranks broke and the men rushed for the door. The fifty men required were signed on in a very short time and made their way to the lamp-room, while the remainder were advised to come up again next morning, when perhaps more men would be needed.

Jim looked dazedly at Len, hunched his shoulders, swallowed hard, then turned his back to the office and walked away, saying deep down in his throat : " Len bach, they got us by the short hairs."

Next day the rain swept Cwmardy in gusty spasms that soaked all it touched, but men were waiting at the pit-head long before the first cage went down. Len and his father were drenched when they reached the office, water streaming down their faces and the backs of their necks. Jim wanted to remain at the front of the queue, but Len urged him, grunting and swearing, to the end. Everyone waited tensely for the sergeant's voice, each man ready to rush for the door at the first sign. When it opened, however, both Mr. Hicks and the sergeant came out. The two proceeded along the line of anxious men, Mr. Hicks occasionally calling a man out and feeling his biceps. If he was satisfied with the result he sent the man to the lamp-room ; when he was not, he sent him home with the advice to try again some other time.

A number of men had already been instructed to start before Mr. Hicks reached Jim, but he unhesitatingly told the old workman to get his lamp, without bothering to ask him questions or feel his muscles.

" The fireman will tell where you are to work," the general manager advised, as Jim started on his way to the lamp-room like a man in a trance. But before he had gone far, he turned sharply on his heels and demanded, " What about our Len ? "

" Oh, we'll find something for him later," was the complacent reply.

Jim snorted. " Later to hell ! That is no bloody good to me. Either he do start now with me, where he have always beened, or not one of us will start."

Mr. Hicks knew this was an ultimatum and that it would be no use blustering, but he was anxious to have Jim back in the pit because of his capacity as a workman.

" Oh, all right. As a special favour, you can take him with you." Without another word the two men fetched their lamps and made their way to the pit. Before entering the cage, Len looked back at the queue of waiting men, then took a sigh with him into the iron carriage.

The " bang . . . bang-bang " of the wooden droppers falling into place as the cage dropped out of sight sounded strange to Len and the hot, fœtid atmosphere of the pit, after the long period of fresh air on the surface, made him choke. He tasted it thick in his mouth and retched like a man who had never been down a pit before. The sensations took his mind back to the day when he had first started work, and his imagination ran more quickly than the falling cage. He felt glad he had been destined for the pit and laughed inwardly at his one-time longing to be freed from it. The dangers and the struggles, the hatreds and the humour had become part of his life. His body and mind had been moulded in the pit by his fellow workmen, and without them he knew his world would be empty.

Big Jim, beside him in the crowded carriage, groaned, then growled : " I wish that engine man 'ood be more careful with his brakes, instead of jerking our guts into our mouths like this. If his back and legs was paining like mine he 'ood have a bit more care, muniferni."

The darkness of the pit-shaft did not enable Len to see

the man who answered. " Aye, you are right, Jim. But
what can you 'spect from these crots of kids that they have
brought in to work the engines ? Bah ! The old 'uns who
have worked this cage all their lives have been chucked on
one side like muck. I tell you, boys, this old pit is going
all to hell."

There was no time for further conversation before the
carriage floor bumped on the wooden planks that covered
the water sump at the pit bottom. The men got out,
separating according to the side of the pit in which they
worked. Len waited for his father and they walked in
company with other men towards the stable a hundred
yards or so from the shaft bottom. They had nearly
reached the heavy planked door which covered its entrance
when Jim pulled up sharply and whispered.

" S-shh ! Didn't I hear somethink in the stable then ? "

The men stopped and listened. Above the whistle of air
through the cracks in the door came sounds similar to those
made by wildly scrambling hoofs, then a muffled voice :
" Hold his head, mun ! Keep his bloody arse in towards
the manger ! " A short silence, then : " Whoa ! What
the bloody hell are you doing ? Whoa, boy, whoa ! "
Then more excitedly, " Get hold of that twitch. Quick
now. Ah that's better." The scrambling ceased and the
men looked at each other, their faces dull shadows in the
darkness that pressed on them.

One remarked : " They'll have a job with old Dangler
to-day. It's his first day down since the lock-out, and I
pity his poor haulier."

" Huh ! You can keep your pity for yourself. He's
working your heading to-day," remarked another voice,
adding as an afterthought : " You needn't worry about the
haulier. Sam's got him and you can bet your life that he
knows how to handle Dangler. They're old butties."

Suddenly the noise of the whistling air stopped as the
huge stable door was tugged open by those inside.

Someone shouted : " Hide those blasted lamps and get
out of the way." The waiting men hurriedly clambered
on the sides of the roadway as a file of horses, each with a
haulier at its head, came out. The horses were restless
and excited, the whites of their eyes shining wickedly in
the semi-darkness. One of the hauliers warned in passing :

" Watch Dangler. He's the last. Keep well away from his arse if you're wise."

Big Jim picked from the roadway a short piece of stick as thick as his forearm, and muttered to Len : " If he do try any of his funny trickses on me, I'll put him down so flat as a pancake."

Len did not reply as Sam, clinging tightly to Dangler's head and talking in his flattened ear, led the horse past with swishing hoofs that made the air rustle like a ballet dancer's skirts. The men kept a respectable distance behind the horses, whose feet disturbed the coal dust and lifted it in fine clouds through the enclosed air, where it tickled their nostrils like snuff.

Will Evans sneezed loudly, blew his nose, and said for all to hear : " I'm sure old Sam do train Dangler so that nobody else can drive him. That's the only way he can stick to his extra turn a week for working a dangerous horse."

" S-shh ! " came the sharp warning. " We are near the locking hole and the fireman might hear you."

The men's lamps were examined in the big hole driven into the side of the roadway, and they were given separate instructions by the fireman before proceeding on their way.

The official welcomed Jim with a smile. " Hallo, Jim. I'm glad you're back, mun jawly. It's about time they sent some real workmen down, instead of these strappers that are here."

Len cocked his ears up at this but said nothing as the fireman went on : " I have got orders to send you to Mockyn Bobby's heading, Jim."

Before he could say any more Jim's surprised voice interrupted him. " Mockyn Bobby's ? What the bloody hell do I want there ? Me and Len have got our own place, without going to anybody else's. Ha-ha ! Come on, Shenkin bach, stop pulling my leg, mun."

" Indeed to God, I'm not pulling your leg, Jim. I have got more respect for you than that, and well you do know it. But them's the orders I have had from the big boss."

Jim bewilderedly pulled his cap off and wiped it over his face as he asked. " But what's the matter with my own place ? I have droved it in from the engine parting, and I

am not going to leave it for any big boss." He lost his
temper and began to shout. " No, I 'oodn't leave it for
The Devil hisself, and that's telling you somethink,
Shenkin."

" Come, come, Jim bach. Don't be so stubborn, mun,
you know that I can't help it. Another man is working
your place and you have got to shift, that's all about it."

Jim, his eyes bulging in his blackened face, held his
breath a moment when he heard this, then gasped, as
though he doubted his ears : " What did you say ?
Another man working in my place ! Arglwydd mawr !
If any man have touched my coal and my timbers, I'll chop
his head off with his own hatchet ! " He swallowed hard
then howled. " Who is it ? Come on, tell me quick. Who
have got the cheek to work my place while I am idle in the
bloody house, standing Shân's nagging because I am man
enough to fight for a principle ? "

The fireman became alarmed at his vehemence, but he
felt he had to carry out his instructions whatever the
consequences. " It is not your place any more than it is
mine," he asserted. " All the pit do belong to the company,
and they can do what they like with what they own, can't
they ? "

" Not my place ? " Jim challenged. " Who the hell
drived it in ? Who ripped it down and timbered it ? "
His voice became shrill with thwarted pride. " Who risked
his body and slogged his guts out to keep it tidy so that
there was always a tram of coal ready on the road and two
in the face ? Not my place, indeed. If it is not mine,
who the bloody hell's is it ? "

The fireman did not attempt to argue further. " Them's
my orders, Jim," he said, " and if you don't like them, then
all you have got to do is to go back up the pit ; and I would
be sorry for you to do that."

This ultimatum shook the old workman and put a glazed
glare in his eyes like that in a cow's that has just been
poleaxed, but pulling himself together he hurriedly thought
out another line of action in defence of his place.

" If us have got to go to Mockyn Bobby's, then where
is Mockyn working ? " he asked.

" Oh, they have sent him the other side of the pit," was
the reply.

Len had been silent throughout this argument, although he saw the new tactics the company was adopting to break the men apart and scatter them among mutual strangers in various parts of the pit. He caught his father by the arm.

"Come on, dad. There's nothing for it but to go where we are sent." Jim looked like refusing, but after a brief hesitation he responded to the appeal and walked away from the locking hole with his head bent and his lips cursing.

After twenty minutes' walking in the humid air, the clothes sticking to their bodies with sweat, the couple reached the place where they had left their tools before the lock-out. The clamour of coal being thrown into a tram stopped as they drew near and Jim walked up to the man who was working, at the same time tilting his lamp so that the light fell full on the stranger's face.

There was an awkward pause while Jim scanned him up and down before asking heavily : " What for did you come here and work another man's place, butty ? "

"What else could I do ? I either had to start here or not at all."

"That's right, dad. It's not his fault," Len broke in, fearful that the old man would lose his temper again.

Jim sighed. "Ah well. Perhaps it will all work out square in the end, Len bach." He turned to the stranger and advised : "Take care how you do work that face, butty. It is hellish funny and you have got to keep your butts clean and cut the right-hand side in front of you all the time if you want to work her as she ought to be worked. And you want to watch the top. It is very sly and you can't trust to test it with a mandril, because it will ring like steel one minute, then, before you can blow your nose, it will drop ' bump ' like a shower of lead."

The man thanked him for the advice and the couple, sharing the tools between them and bent double beneath their weight, left him. By the time they reached their new work place, Big Jim was again in a temper generated from weariness. He rested for a while to look about him, then spat viciously at a passing cockroach before saying disgustedly :

"Huh ! I thought so. Rippings behind, coal worked square till it is left so hard as concrete, muck all over the place. Huh ! A navvy have been working here, not a collier. In a muck-hole he ought to be or digging trenches on the tip."

Len took no notice and began pulling off his clothes. The heat was intolerable and the percentage of gas in the air made the blood pound at his temples. He felt exhausted already, although he revived a little when the upper part of his body was naked to the hot air.

The two men had half-filled their first tram when the fireman came round to inspect the place.

" How many is this, boys ? Your third ? " he asked.

Jim threw his mandril violently to the ground. " Who the flaming hell do you think you are talking to—white mice or what ? Three, muniferni ! Ach, that little fire-man's lamp have gone to your head."

" Gone to my head or no, Jim, you can depend on it the Big Boss will expect eight a day from this place."

" Eh, eight a day ? Ha-ha, you have made a mistake, Shenkin, you are talking to men now, not donkeys. There's no man in the pit can fill eight a day in this bloody muck-hole without pulling the roof in on him, and you can venture Big Jim is not going to do that. Ho, no ! When I will be buried alive it will be up in the sun, where I can enjoy myself."

The fireman grunted uncomfortably, and stroked the moustache over his mouth with a thick forefinger. " Ah, well. If you 'on't do it, you can bet the buttons on your coppish they'll find somebody who will, Jim."

This put Jim on his dignity, and swelling his chest he declared : " You can tell the Big Boss from me that he can get to hell out of it, and if he can find a better workman than me there, let him send him down. Till then, tell him to keep his chops shut when he is talking to men who was working when his father was carrying him about in his trousers pocket."

The fireman gave it up and went on his way, his lamp-light getting progressively smaller until it looked like the red-hot point of a needle.

Len and his father kept on working in silence for a while after the official had left, until the former, who was heaving shovelfulls of coal into the tram, asked : " You can see the game, dad, can't you ? "

" See it ? Of course I can. Clear as ink. They are
going to try to break our hearts, boy bach. Make us do
twice so much work for half so much pay. Bah ! A tad-
pole could see it, mun, if he had eyes."

Putting his hand to the small of his back the old man
bent his body and groaned. " Ach ! What is the matter
with me ? To hell with everything ! Aye, and myself as
well."

For the remainder of the day he worked with less haste,
and Len noticed that he made no effort to lift the huge
lumps of coal into the tram without first breaking them up
into smaller pieces. At the end of the shift both men felt
sore and tired, and although the fresh air on the surface
revived them a little, it was some weeks before their bodies
again became inured to the strain and cramped positions
of the pit.

CHAPTER VIII

Strife in the Valley

NEARLY twelve months passed by, but hundreds of the original workmen at the pit were not restarted. Their places were taken by families who lived outside Cwmardy, many of whom moved into the valley when the menfolk found jobs. The native unemployed drifted to the rubbish dumps and mountain sides to dig for coal during the winter, while some unloaded the rubbish wagons on the pit-head, displacing the men who had been paid wages for this work. Overtime became rampant and new divisions and bitternesses developed among the people.

During this period the cleavage between Ezra and the Party on the issues of the lock-out had widened until they now embraced nearly every issue that rose in the pit and the valley. Ezra was made a J.P., an honour which, the Party claimed, proved he had irretrievably betrayed the people, and as a result Harry Morgan was put up against him as candidate for the former's council seat. Harry was defeated, but he continued to attack Ezra on every possible occasion. The logic and arguments of the Party's fight had Len's full approval, although he was allowed to keep in the background as much as possible to avoid further crises in his domestic life. The uncompromising attitude of the Party, and the statements its members made against him, embittered Ezra, and he came to regard them as greater enemies than the company. Len, on the other hand, found that the struggle against his father-in-law widened his ideas and gave him a better appraisal of Socialism and all that it meant. The old illusions bred in him by Ezra, and later by Fred Lewis, regarding revolutions and politics were shattered, and, altogether, he gained a basis of knowledge that made him an able lieutenant for Harry Morgan and a formidable opponent for the miners' leader. Mary unconsciously helped him a great deal to get this mental balance and clarity.

Since the quarrel she had tended to become more critical of everything that was said and done by her father and Len, and found herself, without knowing it, being drawn nearer to her husband not only emotionally but intellectually. But she would not join the Party, out of loyalty to her father, who, she felt, was fast breaking up in every way.

One day Ezra was called to London by the Federation. He remained there a week, and on his return looked gloomier than ever.

The discontent in Cwmardy seemed to be common throughout the country, and rumours began floating about that there was to be a general strike of all the workers in the land against the threat of the coalowners further to reduce the miners' wages and conditions. Ezra confirmed the rumours at a mass meeting, and this brought men back into the Federation. His report of the discussions in London became the foundation of definite discussions in the pits and the meetings. Len's experiences in the pit, apart from what he learned in the Party and the Federation, made him convinced that the time for action was again approaching. The knowledge made him introspective as he thought of the poverty Mary and his people would have to endure once more, but he brushed this mood away when he visualised the possibilities of victory for the men.

Despite this, he came home from work looking unusually gloomy on one occasion. Mary noticed his depression, but waited until he had had his dinner and bathed before asking:

" What's the matter, Len. Have you had a stiff day ? You look more than tired out."

He stretched his legs wearily before him and lit a cigarette. " I expect I do, Mary. I'm just about fed up with the pit since I started after the lock-out. None of us know from one day to the other what job we will be expected to do once we get down the pit. If the officials ask us colliers to unload muck, we've got to do it or they'll say, ' There's plenty of men on top of the pit who'd be glad of the chance ! ' "

The light on the cigarette burned his finger and he bent forward to flick the dead ash into the grate before querying,

almost hopelessly : " Can't you see what it is all leading to,
Mary ? The men are afraid to trust one another for fear
anything they say will go back to the boss and every week
the company is quietly dropping our money, until they
don't even pay the price-list they themselves forced on us.
Good God ! I remember before the lock-out all of us used
to pass our pay-papers around, but now you can't get to
know what the man next to you is having for his work."

Mary shook her head disconsolately, but tried to
encourage him as she sensed the despondency beneath his
words. " It's no good worrying, Len. We'll get nowhere
by doing that. It's rotten, I know, but the men are bound
to turn one of these days." She sighed and drew her chair
nearer the fire as though she felt a cold chill fill the air.
" It's a wonder to me how they stick it," she went on restlessly. " They must be smouldering on the quiet and
one day that will burst into a flame again, then something
will have to move." A pause, then : " I hope something
real will come from this general strike which dad is talking
about. I fancy it's not so hard and cruel when we're all
fighting together as it is when we're on our own." Another
thought came to her and she whispered : " Remember
Black Friday, Len ? "

He nodded his head and she rose from the chair and sat
on his knee. His hand aimlessly caressed the strands of her
brown hair, which reflected the brightness of the brass
candlesticks on the mantelpiece. The contact suddenly
awakened something within him, and he pressed her close
to his body. Her eyes softened as she continued :

" But one day our people will get their own back on the
company and the traitors ; then dad will be back where
he belongs . . . with the people as their leader. It's
bound to come, especially if the Federation can get the
other unions to take part officially in the general strike."

Len felt her vibrate with feeling and her body magnified
itself despite the sunken chest hidden beneath her blouse.
Her assertiveness in some vague way made him aware that
power did not depend alone on bulk.

At the next Party meeting, a few days later, Harry
Morgan gave a report of what the Miners' Executive was
doing to further the general strike. " We must make the

national leaders agree to stand by us for a strike against
the demands of the owners," he declared, his high forehead
gleaming in the lighted room and his spectacled eyes
looking as large as an owl's. "That's the first move—get all
the country into action. Then our Party will have to help
the executive to work through the other unions and
industries so that all the people will know the justice of
our case, and when the attack comes, they will be ready to
meet it with us."

The large room in the library where the meeting was held
was crowded with people, all of whom were blended in a
tense anticipation of what was to come. When Harry
continued, his voice kept rising into a falsetto as the excitement gripped him :

"Yes, comrades. For the first time all the people in
this country will fight together in a common cause against
a common enemy."

A murmur rolled round the room, and one old man,
who was the founder and deacon of one of the local chapels,
rose to his feet. Even above the subdued whispering, his
chest could be heard rattling like a bag of marbles.
Numerous blue scars were scattered over his hands and face
like tattoo marks, but when he spoke, his voice, though
hoarse, carried a timbre that made it sweet in the ears of
his listeners. Job Calvaria, as he was known to the
workmen, had won the respect of the people by his devout
efforts throughout his life to practise in the pit and in
Cwmardy the principles he preached each Sunday in the
chapel. He was now tremulous with emotion as he said.

"Twenty years have I waited for this. Twenty years
of work and pain as I have seen my butties go one after
the other down the hill to the cemetery, each poorer after
all he had done than when the good Lord first sent him into
the world. And now, when my own race is nearly run on
this earth, what I have prayed for so long is about to come.
Oh, my fellow workmen, how glad I am to know that these
old eyes of mine will see you free and happy before they
close forever on the sins of our masters !"

The eyes he spoke of bubbled over and the tears ran
unheeded down the furrows in his cheeks, wetting his
moustache.

The murmur that had preceded his speech now become a

rumble of sharp claps and stamping feet that brought the meeting to a close.

Outside in the street, groups of men and women were gathered heatedly discussing a special article in the evening paper. Len bought a copy and with a single glance at the glaring streamer across the top of the page hurried home to show it to Mary and Ezra. He handed the paper to his wife before pulling off his coat and waited while she read it aloud.

REDS PLAN GENERAL STRIKE.

" Agents of Bolshevism, who have been allowed with impunity to preach their pernicious doctrines in this country in spite of numerous warnings we have given, are now plotting a general strike as the first step towards a revolution which they hope will take government out of the hands of the people. They hope to bring about a dictatorship in place of the democratic parliament which has for untold years been the heritage of British people. They want to bring their pernicious political creeds into the trade unions of the nation.

" Much now depends upon the statesmanship of the trade union leaders, and we are not without hope that they will again come to the rescue, and prevail upon their men to undertake no foreign methods in this country to settle disputes which can always be disposed of by machinery already set up for that purpose."

Ezra laughed broadly when Mary read this with due emphasis on the relevant paragraphs. " Ha-ha ! The usual red herring, and we should have expected it. You take it from me there will be much more before the strike begins . . . if it ever does."

Len took the paper from Mary's hand and remarked : " They want to split us up at the start by making people believe that we miners are only a bunch of agitators paid from Moscow to make trouble here. Ach ! What a bunch ! Harry is right when he says that from top to bottom, from the Government to the colliery company, they are all linked up like stinking sausages on a string." He flung the paper into the grate with a gesture of disgust. " The dirty hounds. They'll sink to any depths and say any lies to get their own way over the people."

He hung his coat behind a chair before sitting down. Mary's eyes glinted wickedly as she saw that his anger arose from agitation and not thought.

" Oh Len, for shame," she twitted, " fancy a Communist losing his temper because he thinks the capitalists and the Government are unfair—ha-ha ! "

Ezra joined in his daughter's laugh at Len's discomfiture, and this checked Mary immediately. " Shoni Fairplay is dead in this world long ago," she declared. " Aye, ever since one man began like a bug to live on the back of another."

Len caught the spirit of her new mood and entered into it with a gusto that was strange to him. " But bugs feed so much, Mary, that they get helpless and easy to kill. My old man have often told me, Ezra," turning to his father-in-law, " that he would sooner a flea a thousand times to a bug, because a flea will have a go for his life, but a bug after he have been feeding on you for hours will stand and stare you out as brazen as brass."

They all laughed at this, until Mary, unwilling to be beaten in this debate of similes, continued : " But don't forget, Len, that many a bug has saved himself by the stink he makes from his own rotten body. Oh yes, he takes blood from us and this makes him so fat and lazy that he can only lie back and smell, but he always comes for more when the first lot is gone. And that's what happens with the capitalists. They can't either live or protect themselves without the people. After they have robbed us, they protect themselves with those they have taken from our own ranks."

Ezra leaned forward as the significance of this struck him. He fancied he saw its full implications and wanted to divert the others from this.

" Take what happened during the last strike, as a start," he broke in. " As soon as the Government saw we were beating the company, they sent the police into Cwmardy ; and when they found that police and batons couldn't drive us back to work, they sent soldiers and guns."

Len's eyes sparkled as he saw his chance. " So you believe in revolution, Ezra ? "

" Not at all, my boy. I believe in the ballot box and democracy."

The reply was somewhat hesitant, as though Ezra felt himself off guard, but Len pushed his advantage further. " How can you say that when just this minute you said that the Government sent in soldiers against the people of Cwmardy after we had with a single voice said we didn't want any more cuts in our pay."

Ezra had now recovered himself. " Ah, that's a different question. The police and soldiers were sent here because we haven't yet learned how to vote in the right way. That's it, my children ; if we put our enemies in power when we have the chance to shift them peacefully, then it's no use grunting when they whip us."

This last remark drew Mary upright in her chair, and her chest heaved as a new idea grew in her mind. Even the ticking clock seemed to hush itself when she spoke, her husky voice adding emphasis to the words. " But the people put a Labour Government there in 1924, daddy, and the police were used as much against us then as under any other government. If parliament is power, why did our labour leaders take sides with the owners in every strike that took place ? "

Ezra's face went grey at the question, until he bent his head to poke the fire into a red glow. When he rose he was ready to answer.

" That was not the fault of the Labour Government ; they were only in office and didn't have any power."

Len felt that the lameness of the answer made it an apology, and he hastened to turn the subject before Mary could continue the argument.

" Never mind about that now. The big thing is to bring this general strike off ; then we will settle the question of power." He became reminiscent and asked : " Do you remember, Ezra, when you used to tell me that power wasn't something on top of the pit only, but that it was also underground. You said it's not enough to have a good Federation ; we must have unity underground in the coal face as well ? "

" Yes. And I still believe that. But government is a different thing."

There was a long silence after this, before Len rose

from his chair. "Let's go for a walk before bed-time, Mary."

She consented, after telling her father they would not be long.

The young couple walked slowly up the path that ran gently from the foot of the mountain to its summit. Half-way up, they stopped to sit down and look at the black mist that already hid the valley from sight. The gleam from the pit furnaces broke through the darkness and covered the mountain with a blanket of red in which were streaks of yellow. A thought, generated by the recent discussion, sprang to Len's mind at the sight.

"Funny, isn't it?" He began rather sadly. "During the strike we all carried the red flag in our demonstrations and meetings and every one of us was proud to do it. Somehow or other, it seemed to be the spirit of our struggle, but now the only people who still cling to it are those who believe the same as the Party. Aye, for some reason the others have put yellow into the red, just like those beams that are bursting from the furnaces." He pointed in the direction of the pits.

The analogy appealed to Mary, who was still somewhat upset. "Yellow is the symbol of cowardice," she remarked slowly, then stopped, as though the words had given birth to a new idea. She folded her arms across her breast and squeezed them tightly to her before resuming hesitantly: "But I can't believe that dad is a coward to-day, any more than he was when he led the strike. No, no. He can't ever be a coward. It must be that the yellow is the sign of compromise which you say the Party believes to be his policy. Yes. That must be it."

She shivered and, rising to her feet as she turned up the collar of her coat, bade him come. They descended the mountain a different way from that they had climbed, and soon found themselves in Main Street, where Mr. Evans Cardi was idly standing in the doorway of his darkened stores. His voice was heavy when he greeted the couple: "Good-night!"

Len noticed the old man's hands were trembling and would have passed after returning the greeting, had not the other pleadingly asked him: "Do you think they will come out on strike again, Len?"

" Yes, of course they will, Mr. Evans. There is nothing else we can do, is there ? "

The shopkeeper said no more, and with lowered head retreated into the shop, where his wife, seeing the hunched shoulders, asked plaintively : " What is the matter with you now, John ? "

He told her and there was a stillness for some moments before she said in desperation : " But it can't last long, John. It can't. You have told me that the men are divided and that the Federation is smashed. How can they go on if that is true ? "

John gloomily shook his head without looking at her, and muttered : " That won't stop them. Ezra is with them again and the Communists are supporting him, so that they are all behind him and will fight so long as he tells them to."

Agitation conquered his wife and she expressed in words the dominant desire of her mind, when she exclaimed : " But the Government is bound to step in. They can't let these people ruin the valley in this way. Oh God," she wailed in a spasm of despair, " where is it all going to end ? First the explosion, then the strike, then the lock-out, and now this."

Her emotion affected John deeply. He had no answer to her plea, so placed his arms on the table and buried his face in them, moaning all the while more to himself than her.

" We will have to get our Ron from college now. The bank manager was telling me only this morning that we can't get any more advances from him. Oh, Maggie fach, we are worse off than when we started forty years ago." He jumped angrily to his feet and shouted : " If the people would only pay what they owe us, we could carry on. But no ; they are going to the Co-op and the big shops after we have fed them all through their troubles."

He broke down and cried like a child in sheer impotence while she tried to console him even as her own tears dripped on his sparse hair.

CHAPTER IX

Night on the Mountain

THE pits in Cwmardy once again became hot-beds of agita-tion, which the officials failed to check, as renewed con-fidence from the prospect of a general strike swept the men nearer each other than they had been since the lock-out.

The headquarters of the Party at the library was too small to hold the men and women who joined, and at each meeting numbers had to sit on the floor and window-sills to make room for all who wanted to enter. Even the elder men and their wives generated new life and entered into the arguments with as much vigour as the younger members.

The Party held regular street meetings, where they took it in turns to explain what was happening to the people elsewhere, and why the Government was already preparing to take sides with the owners against the working men and women. Sometimes miners from other parts of the country were brought in to speak to the miners in the valley. Everything helped the people of Cwmardy to prepare for the strike with vigour and determination, confident that this time they would be victorious.

Dai Cannon, who had again broken the pledge, summed up the general feeling very neatly one Saturday night when he and Big Jim were drinking in the Boar's Head.

" What think you of the big strike that is coming off, Dai ? " asked the latter.

" Short and sweet, like a donkey's gallop," was the terse retort.

Jim thought the reply a very good joke all through the week-end and was still chuckling over it as he made his way to his working place on the Monday morning. He had to wait some time in the face before Len arrived. The old man was in the middle of his recital when a light appeared back in the roadway and jogged its way towards them.

Jim ceased his story-telling and gazed with open mouth at the diminutive form that confronted them.

The little lad, his lamp nearly dragging the floor, broke the silence first : " Shenkin the fireman have sent me to work with you," he declared categorically, as he began pulling off his coat. The sight of his puny body drove Len suddenly frantic. It revived memories of the day when he had himself started to work in the pit and all it had meant to him since. He remembered his mother telling him, when he left the house that first morning : " You be starting, Len bach, what only the grave can take you away from." The thought made him wonder how long this little lad would be a slave to the pit.

" Is this your first day down ? " he asked the boy, only to receive a contemptuous reply, uttered in a pitying voice.

" Duw, duw, no, mun. I have been working for going on three months now."

Len lifted his lamp to have a better look at the boy's face. " You must be gone fourteen, then," he remarked, " if you have been working this last three months."

" Oh, that's easy, mun. Don't you 'member my old man ? He was kilt about five years ago ; and ever since then my old 'ooman have been having compo for him. Oh, aye, the company have been very good to us. They let me cheat my age a bit, see, so that I could start to work sooner than the other boys and help my mother. Aye, aye. I'm boss of the house now, of course," he added in a confidential tone.

" Oh. Are you a good workman ? " asked the discomfited Len, while Jim looked on with admiration in his eyes.

" Good workman, indeed. I should just bloody think so ! If you don't believe me, ask my last butty."

He lowered his voice confidentially. " That was a good butty, mun. He thought I was the best boy in the pit and gived me trumps regular as a clock every week."

Len smiled at the subtle hint, while Jim covered his desire to laugh with a gruff : " Argllwydd mawr. They be sending them down these days before they be tucked properly, muniferni ! "

The two men ordered the lad to remain near the tram and made their way to their respective places in the coal-

face. Some time later a number of lights gathered around
the tram and both men squirmed back through the face
once more to see who the visitors were. They found Mr.
Hicks with three other officials and a tall, healthy-looking
young stranger awaiting them. The little lad unconcernedly went on putting coal into the tram until Big Jim
stopped him. The lad's body oozed sweat, which washed
the coal-dust off his chest and soaked into the waist of his
turned down trousers, making them shine oilily. Jim
gave the lad a glance and bade him sit down, then turned
his attention to the officials.

Mr. Hicks coughed, and said : " This is David, the son
of Lord Cwmardy. He has come down to see the pit and
you boys at work."

The tall young man held out his hand to both Jim and
Len, saying at the same time, " Pleased to meet you. I've
heard a great deal about the two of you."

Len said nothing while his eyes examined the magnificent
body before him, but Big Jim was ready with a reply.

" Glad to meet you, butty. I hope you will never come
so bad as your old man." The officials were flabbergasted
at this retort, and Mr. Hicks indignantly took Jim to
task.

" For shame, James, talking like that to the son of the
man who employs you," he stated.

Something cold ran through Len's body and chilled his
blood. He raised his lamp, showing up in white relief
the fresh, well-filled features. His voice was hard as the
steel wedge he used on the coal when he asked quietly :
" Where do you work, mate ? "

" I don't work. I'm at college," came the good-natured
retort.

" At college, eh ? How old are you ? "

" Twenty. But why do you ask ? " There was surprise
in the query, but Len took no notice.

" Hmm. Twenty years of age, at college, and not
working. Hmm ! " The officials stood silently by, but
Cwmardy's son kept smiling good-humouredly.

" If you don't work, how do you live ? "

" Oh, my father pays my college fees and gives me an
allowance."

" I see. Yes. I see ; your father keeps you." A brief

pause, then : " But where does your father get the money from ? "

The sudden question, put so artlessly, swept the smile from the young man's face. He took a step towards Len, clenching his fists tightly, but he stopped abruptly when he saw Big Jim also move forward.

" What the devil has that to do with you ? " he demanded, his voice shrill with indignation.

Len's words ran into each other as he replied, pointing his fingers at the boy, who was sitting interestedly on the big heap of coal near the end of the tram.

" That's where the money comes from to keep you in college with an allowance at twenty years of age. That child has got to come down this damned muck-hole day in, day out, year after year, until he gets too old and weak to fill more coal. After that, if he's not killed before then, he'll have to rot on top of the pit until he pegs out and is ready to be buried in another hole."

Len's chest heaved as he made his denunciation, and the officials stood motionless, like rabbits facing a stoat, so that without interruption he continued : " Your father makes that little boy by there work eight hours a day for thruppence an hour so that you can live without working."

Mr. Hicks broke the spell and sprang to the aid of his discomfited charge, shouting loudly : " Stop these insults. If it were not for Lord Cwmardy giving the boy work, he'd have no wages and he and his mother would starve. You should be glad he's been given something to do."

Len looked wistfully at the manager when the latter was speaking and replied gently : " Aye, you are right, Mr. Hicks. I can see it now. When we won't work, we starve whatever our age or size." He paused a moment as though he were mentally trying to solve a puzzle, then continued : " Yet Mr. David by there don't starve although he don't do any work. His body is bigger and stronger than mine can ever be, yet he can get a new kind of thrill by coming down the pit to see us and that little boy working. Aye, a thrill, more shame to him ! " He began to shout with rage. " That's it. We work and sweat and slog our hearts out to fill the rotten guts of louts who think that work is beneath their dignity." He lost all control of himself and howled : " Go ! Get back to where you came from. Spend the allowance your old man gives you from the last ounce of our strength.   See the blood on every pound-note you change, taste the battered bodies on every bit of food you eat, see the flesh sticking on the coal you burn.   Aye, and when we refuse to work to keep you fat and idle, send your police in to baton us down.''

The outburst staggered all his listeners, and Mr. Hicks murmured hurriedly to the officials : '' Come.   Let's go. The man's mad.''   They obediently followed him till they came to a huge lump of coal Big Jim had levered from the face, and which now obstructed their passage.

One of them shouted back : '' Break this up for us to pass.''

'' Break it your bloody selfs,'' Jim replied, throwing his mandril towards them.   The crestfallen officials and their important charge retraced their steps, and without another word or glance at the two workmen made their way up the road, followed by Jim's exultant shout : '' Ha-ha ! Ho-ho ! That will show you that our Len is so clever as any of you, college or no college.   Put that in your pipe and smoke it. Ha-ha !''

Len and his father sat silently for some time after the departure of the visitors, while the boy looked at them with awe and admiration.   Unable to contain himself any longer, he rose to his feet, swelling his little chest in such a way that his navel became a pool holding one bubble of sweat which shone in the light from the lamps.

'' Gee,'' he exclaimed, '' that did take some doing, mun, to tell the boss's son off like that, and in front of his own face, too !   In't you afraid to have the sack ?   But there, I 'ood have done the same myself if he gived me any of his bloody cheek.''

Len burst out laughing, then ordered : '' Let's forget it, and get on with our work.''

At the end of the shift Mr. Hicks was awaiting them as they stepped from the carriage.

'' Get away to hell out of it,'' he screamed, spitting out the words and waving his stick frantically.   '' Here I go out of my way to get better relations between the men and the owners and you turn round and insult the very man I bring down to do it.   Yes, that's the one,'' he shouted to the interested workmen who had gathered round, at the same

time pointing his quivering stick at Len. " That's the
man who wants to spoil everything."

His anger got the better of him and stepping forward
he raised his arm threateningly, but not before Big Jim
had barged between them, with the quietly spoken command
to the manager :

" Put that stick down.   Come, quick now, before I splash
you against that bloody wall."

His fierce demeanour cooled the general manager, who
slowly lowered his arm and walked back into the office.
The excited men gathered round, began asking questions,
but after a brief explanation, Len led the way to the pay
office, where Big Jim picked up their joint wages, from which
he took some coins before handing the remainder to his son
with the remark : " Here, take your pay from this and give
the rest to the old 'ooman.   Tell her I 'on't be long, but I
must have a pint before ever I can walk up that bloody
hill."

Len was long accustomed to the procedure and the
excuse, so he made no reply and went alone to the house
where Shân was waiting.   He gave her Jim's wages and
waited for the inevitable question, which she always
answered herself.

" Where is your father ?   In the Boar's Head, I 'spose.
Huh !   One day he will repent all that he is doing and will
be glad to sit quiet in the corner by there with me to tend
on him hand and foot.   Ach !   One of these nights I will
lock him out, so sure as God is my judge."   She placed the
wages in her purse, which she then replaced deep in the
bosom of her dress before turning to Len again.

" I wonder how many more pays us will have before the
strike will be on us ? "

He looked into her eyes.   " Don't worry, mam fach.
It won't last long this time, because all the workmen in
the country are behind us."

" I know, Len bach.   I know," she replied quickly, as
though she wanted to dispel a doubt.   " Don't think I am
downhearted.   Oh no, my boy.   When it is a fight, your
old mam is with you all the way."

Len left her and slowly made his way home to Mary,
where he soon forgot his weariness as he recited the events
of the day.   Dinner was over by the time he had finished,

and he anxiously waited for her comments while she emptied boiling water into the bath-tub. But she said nothing as he pulled his shirt off and he was on his knees leaning over the tub before she remarked softly :

" There's a silly thing to say to the boss, Len. You are asking for the sack. Yet I can't help feeling it was splendid to stand up to them like you did." The warmth of her words soothed him as she went on. " How is it you are so kind and gentle and patient in most things, yet you have these sudden spasms of temper ? "

He would have replied, but she stopped him with a laugh as she pictured the lad making his defiant challenge after the officials had gone. The laugh ended in a sigh. " Ah, well. Never mind about those things now, Len. Bath. Then we can talk about the strike."

Len hurried over his bathing, wiping his head while she washed his back, and in a short time the couple were immersed in an argument during which Len explained why the strike must necessarily be a short one. His old pessimism was evaporating as the strike drew nearer, and he could see nothing but complete victory before them.

Mary shook her head and looked into his eyes, where she saw her own face in miniature. " I wish I could believe the same as you, Len," she began. " But somehow I don't think it is going to work out so easy as all that."

" Of course you don't, mun. You are a woman and don't understand these things. But tell me why you don't think we are going to have a quick win ? "

" I can't say, Len. Oh, dear, there's something in the back of my mind that makes me think of what dad did during the lock-out."

Her tones were sad and he tried to comfort her with an off-handed : " Ach, we all make mistakes one time or another, and your father is a different man now."

" That's just it," was her retort. " But you see, Len, what mistakes can lead to. What happened in Cwmardy during the lock-out can happen again in the strike. Not all of those who are going to lead it want it, and those who don't want a strike they are leading will always look for a way to end it." She paused a moment, then continued more vigorously : " Look at Fred Lewis for a start. I know he's in the Party, but no one will ever make me believe he is sincere. Give him half a chance and he'll use it to push himself on."

Len laughed. "You're miserable to-night. I'd like to see the leader who'd dare to break this strike. Why, the people would kick him right out of the movement for ever."

"I'm not so sure. There's so many ways of doing a thing, and don't forget we'll have the Government against us," she replied slowly; then shook her head and added in dismissal of the subject. "Come. Let's go for a walk before it gets too late."

It was already dusk when they left the house, and a few pinpricks of light, breaking through the murk, rimmed the streets of Cwmardy as the pair sauntered along the edge of the mountain. When they were nearing the railway line that ran from the pits through the valley, Mary suddenly stopped and gripped Len's arm tightly.

"Did you hear anything?" she asked nervously. He shook his head and strained his eyes to peer into the blackened distance. Then he heard a sound like a low moan creep towards him, and pressing her arm to his side he whispered: "I heard something then. It was like some-one moaning."

"Yes. It came from over by there, near the quarry." A pause, then: "Oh, Len, perhaps some poor dab has tumbled over it."

He swallowed hard before saying, "You stop here while I go and see." But she still grasped his arm as he cautiously groped towards the sound. Their feet loosened a large stone that rolled before them with increasing speed. Len stopped again and pointed excitedly to a vague black shadow that seemed to skim the dusk on the right of the quarry.

"Isn't that someone running?" he asked, a quiver in his voice.

"Yes," was the hurried reply. "Look, Len—that was a button shining."

They hastened their descent till they reached the quarry, from which the moans now came more clear and piteous. Len lighted the way with matches, taking care that Mary kept near him. They had only walked a few paces when

Mary, her voice shaking with apprehension, whispered :
" Hush. There's somebody talking ! "

They both heard it simultaneously : " Oh mam, mam !
Oh, my poor head."

" Come quick, Len, it's over there," Mary darted off with
Len close at her heels. He nearly fell over her when she
suddenly bent down to scan a form at her feet, her hands
moving quickly and impatiently over it.

" Light another match, Len."

He immediately obeyed the low muttered command,
carefully shading the flame in his cupped hands. The
flickering light fell feebly upon the body of a boy in working
clothes, who lay stretched out upon the stony floor of the
quarry. The match-light died and buried itself in the
surrounding darkness before Len could strike another.
Mary became impatient.

" Get some paper, mun. Look through your pockets."
He found an old pocket-book and hastily tore out some
pages, which he twisted and lit. The increased light shone
on a black face with closed eyes and slowly moving lips.
Mary caught the head to her, gently resting it in her arms.
Len brought the light nearer and saw the blood flowing
through the hair until it ran down the boy's face, streaking
it with red. All the time, the lad's lips kept moving.

In a frenzy, Len lit more paper, and parting the dirty
hair saw the gash that split the boy's skull. He felt his
stomach turn and his head go light, but pulled himself
together when he heard Mary say :

" Pull my petticoat off. Quick ! I mustn't move or he'll
bleed to death." Len fumbled at the end of the garment
trying to tear off a piece, but it was too strong. Mary
slowly bent her head till it touched the earth behind her,
arching her body. " There—hurry," she gasped, all the
time trying to keep the lad's wounded head still and steady.

Len hastily put his hands under her skirt and tore the
fastening of her petticoat loose from the waist, pulling the
garment intact from her body.

" Rip some strips off," she ordered. Len did so and
between them they cleaned and bandaged the wound, after
which they both remained stupefied for some moments,
neither knowing what to do next. The continual moans
flayed their nerves, while the flame licking at the remaining

end of the paper died down, then suddenly flickered to life
again.   As the light finally faded into the night, the moan
took shape.   Len hurriedly bent his head to the lips and
heard them whisper tiredly :

"Oh mam, mam !   Oh, my poor head."   A long silence,
during which Len and Mary held their breath, then : "He
hit me and run away.   Oh, mam, mam, where are you ? "
The low plaint ended in a sob that brought tears to Mary's
eyes, but Len nearly pressed his ear on the cold lips in his
anxiety to hear every word that oozed from them.   He had
to wait some time before the limbs stiffened in Mary's arms
and the lad burst out explosively : "The rotter hit me,
then run away.   But I saw him, it was a bo . . . " the last
word died on the first syllable and the body relaxed again.

"Oh, he's dead, Len, he's dead," Mary moaned, and Len
frantically put his hand on the chest beneath the wet
shirt.

"No," he said somewhat hysterically, "his heart is
going a bit, although it's very soft.   Oh, Mary, my dear,
what can we do ? " he asked.

Mary shuddered.   Her arms were cramped and her body
quivered with the strain.   "Go down quick," she muttered.
"Fetch your father and mine.   Fetch anybody you can
find."

Len jerked himself erect and replied sharply : "No ;
I can't leave you here by yourself in the dark."

He could not see the flash in her eyes but he felt the
harshness in her voice when she said : "Don't be childish.
Do what I tell you, Len.   Can't you see that perhaps this
boy is dying and every minute counts ? "

Len said no more and hurriedly scampered from the
quarry.

When he returned he was accompanied by a crowd of
people, many of whom carried lamps, and a stretcher
borrowed from the surgery.   They took the lad from
Mary's arms and tenderly placed him on the stretcher,
while Big Jim picked up the cramped girl like a baby.
The procession then slowly retraced its steps down the
mountain to Cwmardy, Len holding Ezra's arm and
helping him over the steep track that snatched away his
breath.

The people left in the village were waiting to receive

the procession with its burden, and their excited muttering faded into silence as it approached. The stretcher was taken straight into the surgery where the doctor prevented the entry of everyone except Big Jim and Ezra.

Very few people slept in Cwmardy that night, they were too busy wondering what had caused the injury to the boy, who had not opened his mouth since the last statement Len heard. The general puzzlement found an echo in Mary's home. Len confided in his father-in-law, and when the recital was over Ezra began pacing the kitchen, as he always did when perturbed.

" Whoever did it, did it for the boy's pay," he asserted. " But what I can't understand," he continued, stopping to look hard at Mary, " is who could be so low and brutal to rob a lad of his wages ? " He turned to Len. " You are quite sure you didn't hear the last word he said ? "

Len shook his head. " No, Ezra, but it sounded like something that begins with a ' B,' " he replied.

Ezra went on with his pacing, at the same time muttering, half to himself, " B ? B ? What can that mean ? Bowen, Bevan, Brown ? " Len interrupted him. " I don't believe it was a man's name he wanted to say because an A came before the B sound, didn't it, Mary ? " turning to his wife who now joined the conversation.

The excitement of the night had affected her deeply, but when she replied her voice, though low, was emphatic. " I believe he wanted to say : ' But I saw him. It was a Bobby.' "

Ezra's face went grey as she asked Len : " Do you remember the shiny button we saw for a minute on that running shadow ? "

Len nodded his head and she continued : " That might have been one of the silver buttons that only policemen wear."

Ezra interjected harshly : " Hold your tongue, Mary. For God's sake keep such thoughts to yourself. You can't prove anything, and if somebody heard you say such things as that, you'd get us all into serious trouble. And in any case," he added as an afterthought, " what would a policeman want with a boy's few shillings ? "

Len, who had taken umbrage at Ezra's tone, answered : " When he heard us running down the mountain he might have pinched the pay packet to make us think it was a common thief who had beat the boy about.''

" No, no, Len. It doesn't work out so easily as that and you and Mary had better wait until you have definite proof before you ever speak of the matter again.''

But Mary, having started on this train of thought, was not satisfied, and despite her father's strictures took it further. " The wicked scoundrel might have been waiting for one of our men who take coal from the trucks and carry it down the line in the dark, dad,'' she asserted.

" There, there. That'll do,'' commanded Ezra brusquely. " Don't let's have any more loose talk that might land all of us in prison.''

This closed the discussion and little more was said before Len and Mary went to bed, leaving Ezra staring into the ashes that cumbered what was left of the fire.

Next day, Ezra had a telegram calling him to London again for a meeting of the National Executive, at which a final decision was to be taken regarding the contemplated general strike. He was away for some days, during which the main topic in Cwmardy was the strange accident that had since resulted in the boy's death. Most of the people were convinced there had been foul play, and they were quite ready to believe the rumours that somehow began floating around to the effect that a policeman was responsible.

At the inquest Mary tried to give her opinion, but was abruptly silenced by the coroner who told her : " We want to know what you saw, not what you think.'' Shân voiced the general opinion when she told Jim after the inquest.

" I think our Mary fach is quite right. There is nothing too bad for those pleece to do, and I 'oodn't trust one of 'em not a inch further than I could throw him. That's gospel for you, James.''

The talk and gossip soon died down after Ezra's return, with the announcement that the general strike would begin in a fortnight's time if the owners still insisted upon reducing the miners' wages. This news revitalised the people and meetings were held almost every other day to make preparations for the coming fight. But in the minds of many, the lad who died in the quarry was not forgotten.

CHAPTER X

Preparation for Struggle

A SHORT time prior to the strike Harry Morgan, who had been speaking all over the country on behalf of the Communist Party, urging all people to support the miners and the coming strike, asked Len: " How would you like to go to the city for the Party, to help the comrades there ? "

Len did not answer for some moments. The request made so abruptly took his breath away. When at last he spoke, both his words and face expressed incredulity.

" What, me ? Go to the city ? Good God, mun, you're talking through the back of your neck. How can I help the Party or the people there ? Ha-ha, that's a good un, Harry ! "

Harry smiled, a twinkle glinting behind his spectacles. " You can help them all right, Len. Your experience in the last strike was second to none, and since you've been in the Party you've become a passionate speaker who can win the people to our point of view when you try."

The compliment made Len laugh again, but he checked it as another implication of the proposition struck him. " Are you asking me to leave my own butties in a fight ? " he asked incredulously.

Harry's smile widened. " Why not ? Do you think they can't carry on without you ? "

The quick retort abashed Len, and he blushed as he replied. " I didn't mean that, Harry, and you know it. But my place is with my own people, and there I'm going to stick in spite of all your sneers."

Harry's smile vanished. " Your place is where you are wanted most," he declared sharply. " You see, Len, this fight can lead to great things that some of us can only dream of now. Think of it," he exclaimed, his voice rising with enthusiasm, " the whole working class entering into action together, behind the miners, against the

bosses and all that it means. The Government is bound
to show its hand as the agent of the capitalist class. It
will take sides with them against us and expose the fight
to our people for what it really is—part of a struggle for
political power. It's possible for us to do what Lenin
and the Russians did—that is, get rid of the parasites for
good."

Harry went on in this strain for a long time, giving Len
no chance to say a word until he had finished, by which
time he had drawn a word picture of such immensity that
it frightened Len, although the logic of his life experiences
forced him towards it.

He made no reply, but turned away with a muttered :
" So long.   I'll see you again."

Harry was astute enough to make no attempt to detain
him or say any more.

For the next few days Len could think of nothing but
what Harry had said.   He pictured all he had heard and
read about the Russian Revolution, and tried to apply
the conjured images to Cwmardy.   But always he checked
himself with a plethora of mental queries.   Would the
owners and the Government give way peacefully to the
desires of the people ?   Would the army refuse to obey its
generals if the Government tried to use it against the
people ?   What about the Air Force, manned by men
like Lord Cwmardy's son ?   These and other questions
tumbled through his mind incessantly, keeping time with
his mandril as he drove it into the coal.   Accompanying
these questions and running through them were thoughts
of Harry's request that he should go to the City during the
strike.   He wondered what he would have to do there if he
went, and who he would meet.   He felt he could do nothing
once he was away from his own people and, subconsciously,
feared things would go wrong if he were not with them
during the strike.   Already he was beginning to sense his
own power and influence.

He sought Mary's advice on the whole business and they
talked it over for hours one night, but failed to reach any
definite decision.   Already extra police were being drafted
into the valley and the atmosphere was getting tense, but
the workmen and the Party were once more solid behind
Ezra, who was confident the strike would be short and

successful and that, as a result, the Federation would be united under his leadership again. He had continual discussions with the railway and other union leaders in Cwmardy, and a joint strike committee was set up.

The people of the valley echoed this confidence, a fact which found expression in the Boar's Head on one occasion when Will Smallbeer and Big Jim were the centre of a group of drinking pals. Jim had already drunk sufficient to make him patronisingly philosophical. " Aye, boys. It is just like Buller and the Boer War. He let them do this and do that till they thought they was beating us, muniferni ; then all of a sudden, after he had drawed 'em where he wanted 'em, bang-bang, just like that, and the war was over ! " He shifted a lump of tobacco to his cheek and placed the half empty tankard of beer to his lips, while Will Smallbeer wiped the ale that dripped from his moustache to say ponderously :

" Strategy. That's the thing, strategy. Us might have to lose two or three or four, aye, perhaps more battles before us get into position to win the big 'un. But it is worth it in the end, and that's where us is now. For years and years we have been fighting here and fighting there, but never all together at the same time." His eyes gleamed with memories and beer, as he went on. " But we are there at last, boys bach. Ha-ha ! This time all together at the same time, and nothink can stop us winning now. Our Lord's words are proving true—' Righteousness shall always prevail.' " He closed his eyes to repeat the last statement, then took another drink from his pint mug.

The conversation became general after this, and young Will Evans struck a discordant note when he said : " Huh ! Us is all bragging like blue hell to-night. Make sure us isn't barking at the wrong dog. I heard stories like Will Smallbeer's during the lock-out. Aye ; us was all big men then and thought we was cocks of the walk. But don't forget, boys, what happened in the end. Mark my words, some waster will so sure as hell let us down again."

" Don't talk so bloody soft, mun," was the reply he received from several quarters. " Isn't the T.U.C. calling us all out this time. There can't be no selling now, and Smallbeer is quite right."

Will closed an eye in an impish wink, looked at the

fire and spat into the grate with a smacking sound before saying, without raising his head : " That's it, boys. Old Smallbeer is quite right, in't he ? Of course he is. He always was, wasn't he ? Even when he went up the drive to the Big House during the lock-out, eh ? Ha-ha ! "

His queerly pitched laughter rumbled round the room as he raised his head triumphantly, and Will Smallbeer slowly and with great dignity got to his feet. The old man's whole demeanour showed he had been greatly hurt, but that he was prepared to forgive because his traducer did not understand. Everyone became silent as he chided them.

" For shame, boys, to kick a man, and a butty at that, when he is down. Everybody with any sense in his head do know full well that what I done in the lock-out was quite right. If us hadn't gived in then Ezra 'ood have kept us out forever and our bellies 'ood by now be fast to our backbones. Aye," he continued in a paternal manner, gratified by the attention being paid to his remarks, " a good fighter must always know when to give in just so much as he must know when he is winning, in't that so, Jim ? " He turned to his mate for support.

Thus appealed to, Jim twirled his moustache and nodded. " Aye. That's right, Will bach, only that a good fighter have never got no need to give in." This unexpected statement brought a loud laugh from all present and the discomfited Smallbeer sat down without another word.

The week immediately preceding the strike, Mr. Evans Cardi called a meeting of all the tradesmen in Cwmardy. His tall form looked thinner than ever and his thin moustache dropped loosely over his mouth when he rose to address the meeting.

" I have called you together, friends, so that we may decide what we intend doing during this strike. Most of us have now reached the end of our tether and, speaking for myself personally, I won't be able to give any more credit to the strikers." He broke into a wail he could not control. " My God ! We have suffered enough. Our savings gone, our investments useless, and now our business ruined. This valley and its people are like a blight." His sentiments were repeated by most of the other speakers, but when it came to deciding action, none of them knew what to do. They were lost in a wilderness of conflicting emotions and interests which crushed each other at every point of contact.

Davies, the butcher, tried to survey the position for them. " The multiple shops that have come to Cwmardy will not give credit, but they will bring in cheap stuff and sell it at a price that would ruin us. The Co-op, with its huge capital and backed by the Federation, can afford to give credit, knowing it is guaranteed. That's the position, gentlemen. If we don't give credit we are ruined, because the people won't come back to us after the strike ; and if we do give credit we won't be able to pay our wholesalers because the people will never be able to pay us."

He brushed his fingers through his hair like a dazed man, still trying to find something he could not see.

Late that night, when Mr. Evans Cardi returned to the stores, he heard voices in the kitchen and vaguely wondered who was there, but he was not unduly curious because his mind was still fixed on the problem of credit and the final ruin that faced him. He pulled off his hat and coat and quietly opened the kitchen door, but before he had time to look about someone clasped him round the head, pressing it passionately, at the same time murmuring :

" Dad, dad. I've come home. Look at me."

The arms released the old man's head and he looked up to see the square, well-set form of his son, Ron. Mr. Evans turned, and through the wet haze blinding him saw Maggie sitting quietly near the fire. He walked unsteadily to her, putting his hand affectionately on her shoulder before again looking at Ron.

Gulping back his tears, he exclaimed : " Ron, how well you look, and how glad I am to see you, my boy ! " He paused and his face clouded. " But what brought you home so soon ?"

Ron laughed happily. " Why, I wanted to see you and mam, didn't I ? "

" Yes, yes. I know. But there is something more than that."

A further hesitation while both men looked each other in the eyes, then : " Don't hold anything back from me, Ron bach. If you have done something wrong, you have no need to be afraid to tell me."

Maggie, her face a series of interlinking lines, interrupted. "Don't worry, John. Our Ron couldn't do anything wrong. He came home because he felt there was something out of place here. I told you not to tell him anything in your letters," she added petulantly.

The old man brightened for a moment. "Is that so? Good, very good indeed." Then another cloud covered the happiness on his features. "But what are you going to do, Ron? Have you got a position anywhere?"

Ron sensed how the conversation was developing and could almost feel his father's rising hysteria. He took a vacant chair, and placing it near the old lady, pressed his father into it, before saying as he stood before both his parents:

"Mam and dad, you know I love you two more and owe you more than anyone else in the world. I could read in every one of your letters, although you did your best to hide it, how things were faring with you in the shop, how everything has been going out each week and practically nothing coming in. Do you think, knowing this, I could stick at my studies while you were suffering here with no one to help you?"

The old people looked up at him and pride made their features soft when he continued: "No, dad and mam. My place is by your side, helping you through. I have won a degree and am now a certificated teacher. With these qualifications, it won't take me long to get a position." He stopped when he saw the gleam in John's eyes and coughed.

"Wait a minute," his father said slowly, dragging every word from his throat. "Don't think for one minute that qualifications are enough to get you a decent position in Cwmardy." He began to shout a little. "No, they don't count a lot here, although you must have them as a matter of form."

His shoulders drooped, and his next words were without bitterness or anger. "To get a position here under the council you must buy it." The last two words were whispered, as if he feared someone would hear them.

Ron looked at his father in amazement, then burst out indignantly: "What? Buy a position? If that's so, haven't you paid enough, haven't you and mam scraped

and slaved to pay the rates and give me education enough
to win qualifications ? "

His mother checked him.   " That is so, Ron bach.   But
we are not the only ones who have done that, and you are
not the only boy in Cwmardy who has got degrees and is
now looking for a job.   Your father is right."   She became
slightly hysterical.   " To get a position we will have to
pay for it, and we have no money, my boy, no money at
all.   Oh God," she moaned and suddenly buried her face
in her hands.

As the full implications of what they were saying struck
Ron, he turned white.   " Well, if that's so, there's nothing
before me but the pit."

His mother jumped to her feet, letting the tears run
unheeded down her cheeks.   " There will be no pit for
you while there is sight in my eyes and blood in my
body," she hissed.   " Your father and I have not sacrificed
all these years to see you end in the pit."

The wailing tones of John followed immediately.
" Besides, how can you go to the pit when the men are
on strike ? "

" Oh, the strike won't last long," Ron asserted, although
all his ideas were crashing to the ground.   " Once it's over,
your old friends among the officials will be able to squeeze
me in somewhere."   His father looked at him earnestly
for some moments, then rose from his chair to confront him.

" Ron bach, forget the pit.   The officials have no more
authority under this company than doorboys.   No, less
than that, because doorboys have the liberty to stay away
from the pit."

He quietly resumed his chair, leaving Ron erect.   The
young man felt himself standing in solitude astride a world
that was crumbling beneath his feet.

The fire crackled in the hearth and drew his attention.
He looked into its depths and slowly forming in the flames
he saw a picture of the pits.   This changed even as he
watched and he saw it become transformed to a likeness
of Len's face.   He sighed and sat quietly near his parents.
Neither of them moved till the fire had burned out and the
glow from the cokes had died in the ashes.

Very early next morning the police-station hummed

with subdued excitement. The police officers had been awakened sooner than usual and were busy polishing their boots and brushing their uniforms in readiness for a special inspection. The imported extras marched from their various billets in squads, and in a short time all the police were paraded in the large yard hidden by the high walls behind the police-station. Most of the imported constabulary had never been in the valley before, although all of them had heard of it. Its reputation made them nervous and fidgetty. One half-turned his head towards the officer next him and whispered from the corner of his mouth :

" What sort of men are these miners of yours ? I've heard a lot about them, and if half of it is true they must be pretty hot."

" Yes. They're hot all right, and tartars at that. But we manage them all right when there's no trouble about, and that's—— . . . sssh."

He broke off abruptly as a group of men came out of the station into the yard. The paraded police instantly drew themselves to attention while the inspection took place. They looked an imposing body of men with their bright buttons, erect posture, and huge bulk. The inspection over, they were addressed by a squeaky voice that seemed to add emphasis to the uttered words.

" Shortly you may be called upon to keep the peace in this valley. Those of you who have never been here before, need to know now that you will be dealing with men of violent passions and extreme views, men who don't care to what extremes they go in times of crisis like the present. Among them are a number of agitators and Bolsheviks who are always ready to take advantage of every opportunity to stir up trouble. At the first sign of this I want you to take stern measures to avoid repetition. When you strike, strike straight and strike hard. It may save a lot of trouble later on. If the first blow is insufficient, keep on until you have done your work. Remember these men fight to the last and are always dangerous while they have strength. I don't ask you to go out of your way to look for trouble ; on the other hand, don't avoid it or try too hard to prevent it."

Later the same day Len coaxed Mary to come with him for a walk. He always tried to keep her as much as possible in the fresh air, because her chest was getting worse and was really alarming him, although she never mentioned anything about it.

" Let's go up the mountain," he pleaded as she wiped the dishes after dinner. " We must settle the whole business one way or the other to-day, because Harry's been on to me again about it and told us to make our minds up," he added as a clincher.

Mary looked at him and saw the shadows in his eyes. The sight put speed in her hands, and in a short time she had distributed the dishes in their places on the dresser and was ready to accompany him.

They made their way up the street and out of the village towards the quarry where they had found the injured lad. When they reached it they stopped to rest while the emotions of that night once more swept through them. Stretching before them countless spirals of chimney-smoke rose lethargically into the air and the barking of dogs came gently from the distance. The occasional sharp, long-drawn cry of a mother calling her child split the air like the flight of a bird, but the other sounds floating from the valley were mellow and round, like the strumming of a giant harp.

The placid serenity of the panorama enthralled Len and he placed his arm round Mary's shoulder, at the same time becoming reminiscent and sentimental until she checked him with a remark : " Don't be silly, Len. You know those pimpers with their spying glasses are everywhere, and very likely are watching us now."

He responded to the admonition, sitting with his chin on his knees and fixing his attention on a procession of small figures in single file slowly winding its way up the incline towards the quarry. He gazed for some moments, then drew Mary's attention to it.

" Look ! Can you see them ? " he asked, pointing with his finger in the desired direction. She nodded her head and he went on. " They are walking as solemnly as if they were in a funeral."

Both continued watching the procession come near enough for the individuals to be distinguished, when Mary said : " The boy in front looks as though he is dragging something, Len."

" Yes, and some of them look to me as if they are crying. I wonder what's the matter," he queried in reply.

The problem was too much for them, so they waited for the mysterious pilgrimage and the burden so solicitously being dragged with it.

At last the procession reached the mouth of the quarry, where it stopped while the children scanned the unexpected occupants. After a brief hesitation the boy who appeared to be the leader recovered his courage and silently led the way over the stones to the grassy rim, pulling an old pram covered with sacks behind him. The other boys and girls followed him in single file, as they had done up the hill, paying no further attention to Len and Mary, who looked curiously on. When the leader stopped they all gathered around him. Suddenly a small girl began to sob pitifully, but this was the only sound that broke the silence as one of the lads lifted the edge of the sack on the pram and drew out a big ball of tightly rounded paper, a broom handle, an old rag doll, a bag of something that rattled like marbles, and then a fire shovel.

With this latter implement he began digging vigorously into the soft earth while another lad reverently extracted another rag-covered bundle from the recesses of the pram, and held it rigidly in his outstretched arms until the first boy had dug a hole.

Len wondered what it was all about, when Mary nudged him and nodded towards the weeping girl. They saw one of the boys look at her hesitantly a few times as though he wanted to say something but was too shy to make the attempt. At last he pulled himself together and, walking towards her, put his arm about her shoulder before bursting into tears himself.

Len felt a lump rise in his throat and turned his head away. The hole was now ready and the leader tenderly lifted the rag from the form held by the other, and exposed the battered carcass of a small puppy. Taking it in his own hands, he very carefully placed it in the little grave. The children now filed past the hole, each looking down at it before walking on ; then they all waited while the grave was refilled and the puppy covered in. When this was done one of them took a short piece of stick and a piece of cardboard from the pram and, tying them together, stuck

the improvised monument on the grave. After this cere-
mony had been completed, the sacking, fire shovel, and
all the other paraphernalia were bundled back into the pram,
the weeping girl lifted astride the lot, and the procession
began its trudge back into the valley.

When it was out of sight, Len and Mary bent down to
read the crudely written epitaph in white chalk :

> Our Toby.
> Kilt by a Kart.
> All the gang is greefed.
> By order.

Mary glanced into her husband's eyes, not sure whether
it was his or her own that were misty, and they continued
their walk in silence.

Presently she said :

" Isn't it wonderful, Len, how our children copy what
older people do."

He did not reply for some moments, and when he did, it
was slowly and thoughtfully : " Yes, Mary, it is. And if
they can grieve like that for a dog, how deep is their desire
for love."

It was a long time before either spoke again, but when
they left the mountain they had agreed he should go to the
City in the morning.

" You see, Len," Mary had persuaded him, " one day the
people will want you as a leader, and you must have as
much experience as possible, not only in Cwmardy but all
over the country, like Harry Morgan. After you have been
to the City seeing new people and new ways, you will know
much more than you do now. That will come in useful
for us later on. And it won't be for long," she twitted
him, " because you yourself believe the strike will be a
short one."

Len had argued no more after this shot. " Take care
of yourself while I'm away, and write to me every day to
let me know how the strike is going here," he muttered,
rather hurt by the fact she had said nothing about being
parted from him. It began to drizzle as they walked home
and the lights from the Big House winked coldly through
the drops.

Next morning Len and Mary were up early, the absence

of hooters and the throbbing of the pit leaving the dawn
dead. Breakfasts and other preparations were soon completed and they made their way to his mother's house,
where Shân fussed about him like a broody hen.

" Now 'member, Len bach," she warned. " You are
going to a strange land among strange peoples who you have
never seed before. Look after yourself and mind to keep
away from the public-houses, although, fairplay, I have
never had cause to worry about you and that, different
from your father, thank God."

Big Jim stopped soaping his moustache and raised his
head from the cracked mirror into which he had been
peering. He glanced round at the company and chuckled
deeply in his throat.

" Ho-ho ! Telling Big Jim's boy how to look after
hisself ! Ho-ho-ho ! That's good, mun jawly ! Why,
Shân fach, you did ought to know by now, mun, that it is
like putting water on a duck's back, it do go in through
one ear and out through the other."

Saying which he bent hurriedly to the mirror and thus
escaped the glare Shân cast at him.

The old woman nearly broke down when Len caught
her to him and kissed her cheek before leaving the house.
Her eyes followed him till he turned the corner by Evans
Cardi. Big Jim airily waved his hand to her as he followed
Len and Mary out of sight, and Shân went indoors with her
apron to her nose.

During the wait for the train Jim, with Mary hanging
tightly to his arm, advised Len what to do in the city.
" Take heed of your mother's words," he warned ; " they
be good and sound. But don't never be a mollycoddle—
no, by God, don't let it never be said that Big Jim made
and reared a jibber. If a bit of fun come your way, take
it and care not for no man."

" But I'm not going for fun, Dad. I'm going to help the
Party in the fight," Len interjected.

His father looked at him with patronising affection and
drew himself erect, at the same time inflating his once
magnificent chest. " Aye, aye, boy bach. I do know
that well enough without you remembering me. But you
must 'member you will never be so old as me so long as I
live, and I do know better than you of the ways of the

world. Duw, duw, aye. Did I ever tell you of one day on the Rock ? "

Len heard a puffing in the distance and hurriedly interrupted the threatened reminiscence. " Come, dad. The train is just in."

Jim picked up the little attaché case that contained Len's one change of underclothes and a few handkerchiefs, and pretended to fumble with the carriage door while Len caught Mary tightly to him and tried to crack a whispered joke that died on his tongue. The guard blew his whistle, there was a quick scramble, and before either of them knew it Len was in the carriage leaning through the window and pressing something into his father's hand, with the words.

" Here, dad. Take this and have a pint while I'm away."

The train moved forward as Jim gazed at the coin and then at Len. " All right," he said with a kind of sigh. " Since you do press me so hard to take it, I will, because I have never been a man to go against his own children."

The train was now half-way out of the station and Len shouted above the din of the engine : " So long, Mary. So long. Look after her and mam, dad. Tell Will Evans I'll write to him as soon as I get a chance."

He kept leaning further out of the window, waving his hand until a bend took him from sight and he sat down to watch the houses and the valley he loved float past the window. A lump rose to his throat and he wished he had not undertaken the task. He began cursing Harry Morgan and the Party for taking him away from Mary and his people. This mood did not last long and he soon dozed off to the drone of the wheels, asking : " What's before me ? What's before me ? "

CHAPTER XI

The Big Strike

DURING the next ten days Cwmardy seen from the mountain looked like a dead village on which the silent pits frowned as though in disgust. But in the streets the aspect was entirely different. Squads of police periodically paraded the entire area, seeming anxious to find an excuse to break through the suppressed excitement of the people, who met in huge meetings each day to receive reports of what was happening throughout the country and in Parliament. Groups of men and women gathered in every street to read and discuss the latest *Labour Bulletin* dealing with the strike. Everyone felt that the testing time had come and that the owners of the pits were about to suffer a severe defeat.

Mary helped the Party members to distribute leaflets from house to house, in each of which they explained how the Government was solid behind the owners and against the workpeople. This activity gave her new strength and put a glow in her cheeks. The close contact with her people made Mary a different woman and helped to dissipate the pessimism that had grown in her following upon the defection of Ezra during the lock-out.

In one mass-meeting, called to receive a report from Ezra of the latest discussions in the Executive, a man whom Mary hadn't seen before began asking questions. He sat a few seats in front of her, and something in his manner of speaking drew her attention to him. She felt in a vague way that his sentences were not uttered in the same manner as they would have been by the people in the valley. Unable to see his face, she watched his waving arms as he addressed the meeting, and thought it strange his women-folk allowed the padding in the shoulder of his coat to be visible through a big tear in the cloth.

" Perhaps he's only a poor lodger on his own," she thought

to herself, and sympathetically concentrated her attention on what he was saying.

Ezra had adopted his customary posture, elbow on knee and chin cupped in his hands, as the man started to speak, but he jerked himself erect when he heard :

" I say the time has come when we have got to do something. What's the good of being on strike and just sitting about twiddling our thumbs ? That's just how our leaders like to see us . . . nice and peaceful like rabbits in a field." Loud clapping and stamping feet interrupted him for some moments, and when he continued it was with more vigour and confidence. " The Communists are just as bad. Harry Morgan is away in another part of the country, pleading there is a danger of a section of the men breaking away and forming a new union. I say a leader's place is in his own home, not trapesing about the country. Take Len Roberts—he's gone away as well, and who sent him ? Not you, no not on your life ; he had orders from his Party and had to obey, whatever you might have thought."

Someone started applauding again and Fred Lewis shouted : " Hear, hear, a Communist's place is with his own men."

This brought Big Jim to his feet immediately, his moustache bristling. " Don't you dare to speak bad of our Len behind his back," he bawled. " If you have got anything to say when he is not here, say it to his face."

Loud laughter silenced him and the speaker continued. " What we want is action. Why should we put up with all these strange police ? That's what I want to know. I say we should march from here to the police-station and hound them out of Cwmardy."

The unexpected sharpness of the challenge sent a momentary shock through the meeting, until a few jumped to their feet shouting. " That's right. Action—that's what we want ! " Others sprang up at the call, and in a short time the meeting was in an uproar, some scrambling for the door, others bawling for order, and a few hesitantly advising prudence.

Mary felt the excitement press on her and she wanted to shout with the rest. Through her mind flashed the thought, " Why should we have them here ? We didn't ask for them and everything is peaceful." The knowledge increased her indignation, and she was on the point of rushing to the door with others when she caught Ezra's eyes fixed on her. He was now on his feet with fists tightly clenched and face white as the patches in his hair.

" Stop ! " he shouted, and the one word ran through the hall like a bell bringing to a standstill those who were milling towards the doorway.

He waited a moment, then went on harshly. " Do you want to play into the hands of the Government ? Do you want to give them an excuse for batoning and shooting, when our national leaders are calling for cool heads and public order ? " He paused again, but no one replied, and a number began to sit down. This action soothed the others and a sort of sigh crept into the air.

Ezra felt he was again master of the situation, and his next words showed this. " You are men, not sheep to follow the whistle of any shepherd. Who is the man that called for riot ? " he demanded. The people looked round to the spot where the first speaker had stood, but his place had been taken by someone else during the excitement. Mary glanced suspiciously about her, but failed to see the torn coat. Uneasy thoughts entered her mind, but she had no time to ponder them before her father's voice again cut through the hall.

" Did any of you know him ? "

There was no answer.

" I thought so. A stranger sent into our midst to provoke us to disorder—yes, I thought so. We should have expected this."

The assertion was followed by a noisy hubbub, and the temper of the men rose once more as the full import of the incident came to them.

Ezra closed the meeting shortly after, but the discussion continued on the streets and in the houses. Jim and Mary reported the affair to Shân, whose legs were too bad to enable her to walk to the meeting.

Jim concluded his recital with the sentiment : " I knowed there was somethink wrong about him as soon as I clapped eyes on his dirty chops. Muniferni, if I had him by here now, I 'ood bust him between my finger and thumb like a monkey-nut."

Shân snorted. "Yes, easy for you to say that now, but I 'spose you was jest so ready as the others when he spoked his nonsense."

Jim looked at Mary like a man deeply hurt. "There, what did I tell you on the way up?" he demanded.

Mary had no time to conjure up the imaginary conversation before Shân broke in. "Never mind 'bout that. What is in the soup kitchens for dinner to-morrow?"

Mary took advantage of the question to change the subject. "I believe it's corned beef stew, mam, but I'm not sure."

"Huh! Corned beef stew agen. Fitter if they gived us enough money to buy our own food decent."

Mary listened to a long harangue, in which Jim joined, on the difference between food values and cooking in the good old days and now, then made her way home to make tea for her father, who, she knew, would be tired and irritable after the strain of the meeting.

On the tenth day Cwmardy was again in a ferment. The clang of hob-nailed boots ran in repeating echoes round the streets, adding to the clamour of voices.

Ezra, with Mary at his side and a telegram in his hand, paced the kitchen, his face putty-coloured and pitiful. Suddenly he reached for his cap, stating abruptly: "I'm going out to them."

"Wait. I'm coming with you," she replied.

Together they made their way through the village to the Square. To every excited query, Ezra, the telegram still clutched in his hand like a death-warrant, declared: "Yes. We are smashed. The strike is over."

The people fell in behind and followed them to the Square. On the way down the growing procession was met by some policemen, one of whom shouted.

"Stop. You can't demonstrate without a permit."

The words were drowned in a roar: "Permit to hell! Get out of the way! Chuck them in the fountain!"

The Square was soon packed with people, and Ezra climbed onto the fountain bowl and, turning slowly to face all the people, read the telegram:

"Strike called off. Advise your men return to work without delay."

A short silence generated by mass paralysis followed the words, then a shout that increased in volume with every second as the strikers grasped the significance of the instruction. The shout rose to a roar that broke through the walls of the Big House and the police-station before bounding back to run round the valley in reverberating challenge.

" The rats ! "

" They've sold us ! "

" We refuse to go back to work ! "

" Our strike goes on ! "

The slogans grew louder and higher, became more incoherent and confused as they reached a climax, then became clear again as they fused into triumphant song :

> " Though cowards flinch and traitors sneer,
> We'll keep the Red Flag flying here."

The tumultuous chorus struck Len's ears just as he left the carriage in the railway-station. The sound sent the blood pumping to his head. Without thinking he dropped his case and rushed to the Square, where the people were already forming up in preparation for a march round Cwmardy.

Big Jim, now alongside Ezra, who was still on the fountain, was the first to see Len. He stared hard for a moment at the unexpected vision, then began to howl at the top of his tremendous voice :

" Whoa, boys ! Whoa ! There's our Len, back from the City."

Mary hastily pushed her way nearer the fountain at the news, and another roar swept the air : " Len ! Good old Len ! Let him speak."

Flushed and panting, Len pushed through the mass of people, until, impatient with enthusiasm, some of them lifted him on their shoulders, where he was held in a vice despite his struggles. By the time the new tumult had died down, he had recovered his wind and his voice was clear and vibrant as, catching sight of Mary, he began to speak.

"Comrades. I just want to say how proud I am to be back again among you, in the valley to which I belong. It is true that the general strike has been betrayed by a small group of politicians who call themselves leaders of labour. Yes, it's true—they went round the back door of Downing Street to sell us, like butchers with cat's meat.'' He was interrupted by a storm of booing :

" The traitors ! "

" Kick 'em out ! "

" White-livered rats ! "

" They're no more labour than my arse ! "

When the uproar had spent itself out, Len continued. " But our fellow workers haven't let us down. They are still behind us to a man and a woman.'' Again he was interrupted, but this time by cheers, which continued for several minutes. " Yes, comrades,'' he went on, when he had a chance, " the Government, as our Party said all along, sided with the capitalist class, but let the Labour Party and the councillors use the local council to feed our kiddies in the schools, and our fellow-workers in every part of the country will see to it that we will not starve. Let us keep on fighting until victory is won and this Government brought down.''

Again the stormy cheers moulded themselves into music that helped to marshal the ranks for the delayed march :

> " Then raise the scarlet standard high,
>   Beneath its shades we'll live or die.''

The rhythm timed the marching feet, whose heavy " tramp—tramp " maintained a sonorous monotone to the song. Len kept close to Mary all the way, pressing her closely to his side in the crush.

" This is life,'' she whispered, stretching herself to bring her lips near his ear.

" Yes,'' Len replied, " because it shows the way to revolution and freedom.'' Her hand sought his, and they both joined in the singing as their feet took them on.

The strike of the miners continued throughout the country. Things got worse each week that passed for the people in Cwmardy. The Federation funds became exhausted and no strike pay could be doled out. The local Co-operative Stores came to their help and gave credit to the soup kitchens which the committee opened in the chapel

vestries and the school yards. The men supplemented
this by occasional raids over the mountains after wandering
sheep.

In the meantime Len had renewed his boyhood friendship with Ron, and they spent hours together discussing
how the Labour Party could save the position through
Parliament and the council. The discussions sometimes
became very fierce, when they differed on matters of policy,
but always they met again to pursue the argument. Len
was adamant that no solution to the troubles of the people
could be found through Parliament and was fond of
reiterating a statement :

" You can depend on it, nothing will ever come to us
except through the trade unions and revolution. The
pits and factories are the fortresses of the working-class
and only through them will we free our people."

Ron was equally adamant that if the Labour Party
worked correctly and sincerely in Parliament there would be
no need of a revolution. " Before you capture the pits,"
he asserted on many occasions, " you have got to capture
political power."

This always stumped Len, particularly if Ron accompanied it with a challenge. " After all, isn't your Party
a political Party, striving to organise the masses to take
power out of the hands of the capitalists ? "

Ron's parents kept much of their poverty away from him,
but even so he had a fairly shrewd idea of their circumstances, and the knowledge tore at his heart until he
dreaded the chasing thought that never left him. He had
tried everywhere to find work, only to find in its stead that
his father's words were true.

One day in sheer desperation he asked Len : " Do you
think, Len, if I explained to Mary she would use her
influence with her father to get me a position somewhere
under the council. I understand he is the chairman this
year, and a word from him will go a long way."

He coloured self-consciously when Len looked at him,
but tried to cover his confusion with an apologetic
explanation. " You see, Len, my position is entirely
different from yours and the other men's. I am not a
workman, have never been trained for one. My parents
thought to make me a cut above that. Do you remember,"

he asked wistfully, " when I used to boast of my going to college instead of to the pits ? "

Len nodded sympathetically, his heart aching at the tragedy unfolding itself before him.

" Well, I've been there for years, as you know, and have now come back with all that education can give me. Yes, knowledge, degrees, and all that these things mean. But when I come back to my own home, where it was intended my training should make me a big figure, I find myself unwanted and useless. Oh, God," he moaned in a spasm of realisation, " if my father doesn't find enough money to buy me a job I must remain idle all my life."

He paused for a moment to regain control of himself, but before he could continue Will Evans strolled along, his cap set rakishly on the side of his head and a blade of grass in his mouth.

" Hallo," he casually greeted them, " how be ? "

Both returned the salutation, after which Len asked : " What's on to-night, Will ? Anything important ?"

He noticed Will scanning the street uneasily even as he answered. " Aye, of course. There is something important every night if I can find one."

He pulled the blade of grass from his mouth to spit and, lowering his voice, whispered confidentially : " You haven't seen Will Smallbeer about, have you ? "

Len replied, while Ron shook his head : " No, he haven't passed us and we've been here about half an hour, Will."

A dreamy look came into Will's eyes and he muttered, more to himself than the others : " I wonder where the old blighter is gone to ? "

A brief pause followed, during which he appeared to be making up his mind about something, then, with a resigned shrug : " I s'pose I'll find him after he have spent the bloody lot."

He turned to Ron. " You see, butty, we sold a bag of coal to the doctor yesterday and put it all on a horse, and it have come in at a big price."

Len tried to console him. " Don't worry, Will bach. Old Smallbeer is as honest as the day and wouldn't do you down for the world."

" Yes, I know that, Len, only once a man gets four or five pints in him he do forget what honesty is. Ah well,

no good worrying, I s'pose, only next time us will sell a
bag of coal I'll make bloody sure who'll handle the money."

Len turned the subject. " Me and Ron have been talking
about a jam he's in, Will. Perhaps you can give us some
help."

" Oh, aye," Will commented interestedly. " Well, you
can depend on it, butty, when you fail, I 'on't, although I
admit you are a bit cleverer than me in most things."

Len and Ron laughed loudly at the complacent back-
handed compliment.

" All right," said the former, " let's see what you'd do if
you was in Ron's position."

Ron repeated his statement, and in the telling forgot
everything but his own woes. Will listened with
exaggerated intentness until the recital was finished, then,
like a professor propounding the solution to a problem, he
commented :

" Hmm. Yes. That is a tough 'un, to be sure." He
turned his attention directly on Ron to whom he addressed
his next remarks. " You see, they do say—I can't prove
it mind you, but it is common talk all the same—that to
get a job on the council you have got to give the councillors
your first year's wages. Huh, 'scuse me," he apologised,
" I mean salary. But even then you can't be sure of a
job, because somebody else might give more than you."
He screwed his eyes up and continued. " But even then,
once you've got in it's a pretty good bargain, for you are
right for life afterwards."

The sheer starkness of the statement battered at Ron's
last hope. " But my father hasn't got any money to give
them," he complained bitterly, realising his friends were
unconsciously digging a grave to bury his past. " There
have been so many strikes and lock-outs and so on in
Cwmardy and he's given so much credit that he's now
ruined and doesn't know where to turn."

Will glanced at him with the same quaint look. " Oh,
aye, so that's it, eh ? Your father is further back than
when he started. Nothing left after all he have done, like
Len's old man and me and all of us in the pit. Hmm.
Pity, pity." He closed his eyes like a man deep in prayer,
then suddenly opened them again to say. " I know, Ron.
Tell him to come out on strike with us."

The two men looked at him in amazement, Len being the first to recover his composure. " Don't talk soft, Will mun," he pleaded. " How can Mr. Evans come on strike when he's not working for anyone except himself and his family ? "

Will took some time to absorb this. He screwed his face into furrows, then looked into the dirty air before stepping forward a pace to aim a kick at a lump of horse-dung in the roadway. He watched it smash in pieces and let his gaze follow one bit that travelled towards Ben the Barber's window. He sighed disappointingly when it fell short, then resumed the conversation as though there had been no interruption.

" Well, there might be something in what you say, Len, now I come to think of it. Aye, I do give in to that." He turned abruptly to Ron. " Look here. If your old man haven't got no money the best thing you can do is fight with us, see ? When we got money, everybody have got it, because it is no bloody use to us unless we spend it."

With this parting shot he fixed the cap more tightly on his head, gave them a nod, and strolled away with a final remark. " If you see Smallbeer, tell him I haven't forgot about the bet."

Len looked after the retreating form of his mate with amusement which he failed to conceal, but Ron's look expressed amazement.

At last he asked : " So you think nothing can be done, Len ? "

" No, Ron. Nothing except what Will said—struggle or starve." He paused, as though sorry for the pain he was going to give his friend, then went on with greater vehemence : " Look at my people. They have lived on bread and taters and tea for months, yet not one of them complains or talks of giving in. We are fighting not only the owners and the Government but our own leaders, who are a majority on the council. We asked them to feed our children in the schools, and they refused, Ron. They refused because they say there is no money there, and even if there was they wouldn't have power to use it in this way." He saw the sad hopelessness that crept over Ron. It melted the hardness of his words and turned them into a plea. " Don't think I am harsh, Ron. It's the last thing in the world I want to be. But I must tell you the truth, mustn't I ? I know my people are blamed for bringing the valley to ruin, but all they are doing is what you are trying to do, only in a different way. They are trying to get a living from their strength, just as you are trying to get one from your education.''

Ron looked hard into the far recesses of the sky for some minutes before replying softly, like one who had found sudden conviction in momentary contemplation.

'' Of course you're right, Len. Didn't I study the theory before sending the books to you ? But the study was so easy, comrade, and the necessity that now makes me put that theory into practice is so hard. Yes. Very, very hard.'' He shook himself sharply, then said : '' Forgive me, Len. I have been selfish and cowardly.''

Len caught his hand and pressed it warmly. ''Don't apologise to me, comrade bach,'' he begged. '' I'm not worth it. How often have I lost faith because I didn't understand ? How often have I failed because I wasn't strong ? Don't worry, Ron. Keep close to the people. When we are weak they'll give us strength. When we fail, they'll pick us up and put us back on the road again.''

The intensity of his emotions robbed him of further words for a while and both of them stood silently awkward until Len somewhat lamely suggested : '' I tell you what, Ron. Let's tell Mary that you're prepared to join the Party if she will. Then the three of us can fight together now, like we used to play together when we was in school.''

Ron shook his head slowly. '' I must think it over, Len. I have to consider my father and mother, and you know what their feelings are regarding the Party. You see, Len,'' he added apologetically, '' dad has to be friendly with the councillors and he must be careful, particularly now when the Party is fighting the council.''

Len's face dropped in disappointment, and the other, noticing this, hurried to make amends by saying : '' I know I must come to it some day, but they have done so much for me that I can't bring myself to hurt them just yet.'' He felt the lameness of his answer, hesitated a while, then blurted out : '' But I'll come with you on the demonstration for school feeding and parish relief at the end of the week.''

This news brightened Len, and he began explaining what the Party intended doing on the demonstration. The two friends talked of this for some time before parting.

On the day of the demonstration Ron rose early and had cleaned the house and lit the fire before his parents had got out of bed. He toasted some bread and went into the stores to look for something to go with it, then he called them from the foot of the stairs. A lump had risen to his throat when he saw the empty shelves, that made the shop look nude and obscene, but he choked this back as he heard his parents shuffling about in the bedroom. He was worried about the old people. His mother was obviously ill, and on a number of occasions he had caught his father looking vacant and strange, like a person who had lost his memory or his mind. Ron hastily brushed the thought away as they came down the stairs and entered the kitchen. After the frugal breakfast was eaten he kissed his mother and patted his father's shoulder affectionately before reaching for his coat. He had put this on when he heard the rough scrape of a chair hurriedly shifted. The sound, so unexpected, awakened a hazy fear and he turned round to see his father standing at the side of the table with one hand outstretched and a finger pointing accusingly.

"Where are you going, Ron?" The tone in which the question was put made it more ominous than the words. The old man's eyes were fixed on his son in a stare that frightened Maggie without her knowing why. She rose unsteadily to her feet and put her hand on the sleeve of her husband's coat.

"What is the matter with you, John? The boy is only going out for a walk."

He made no answer other than to shake her hand away. Ron felt his flesh pucker as he caught the stare of his father.

"Why do you look at me like that, dad? I'm only going for a stroll, as mam said."

"Don't lie to me, boy. I asked where are you going?" The old man spat the words out as though they were venom on his tongue, and Ron knew further evasion would be futile. Still clutching his cap, he took a chair and sat down near his mother, who bent sideways a little and put her arm protectively round his neck. The brief period of suppressed emotions that followed got on Ron's nerves and made him reckless. The stillness in the kitchen was so deep that when he spoke he thought he was shouting, although his voice, apart from a little quiver, was quite normal.

" If you want to know, dad, I'm going on the demonstration to the council."

John wrung his hands, slippery with sweat, then slumped to a chair, only to spring up again immediately. " I know. Yes, I knew it all the time. Oh, God ! Oh, Maggie fach, our only son has been deceiving us all the while."

He clasped his head in both hands and squeezed desperately as though hoping in this way to crush certain things from his brain. Maggie grew alarmed and tried to soothe him.

" Leave the boy have his fling for a while, John. He is young and will soon come to his senses."

" Young, young ! Don't tell me that. He is older in knowledge than both of us put together." He started pacing the kitchen, his temper increasing with every stride, until he could no longer contain himself. Turning abruptly on his heels, he flung himself towards Ron and tried to tear the coat from his shoulders, at the same time shouting in a snarling voice :

" You shan't go out ! I won't leave you disgrace the family that has sacrificed its all to give you education. Let me go, Maggie," he screamed as the latter, frantic with fear for the safety of her son, tried to drag him away.

Ron rose to his feet, slipping his arms free from the coat so that it dangled loosely in his father's hand.

He felt again the same helplessness as on the night when he had returned from college and had been told there was no hope of work for him in Cwmardy. His cheeks paled as he realised that battle was simpler and less harsh than the one that now confronted him. Then it had been economic desperation that had caused the scene, but now it was ideological hatred. He felt the world, that had suddenly come between himself and his parents, swirl about him like a fog and wondered vaguely where his feet would land. A voice from miles away impressed itself through his thoughts. It reminded him, for some reason, of the bell tolling in the cemetery as the gates opened to admit a corpse.

" To think that we have reared and kept close to our hearts an infidel, an unbelieving Communist, a son that associates with the scoundrels who have ruined Cwmardy and our home ! Oh, God, what have we done that this should be our final tribulation ? ''

Maggie helped her husband to a chair into which he slumped like an empty sack. Her own face had hollowed during the short time the scene had already lasted, and Ron knew that deep in her heart she felt the same as his father, but that love for her offspring was greater than her faith.

John weakly raised his head from his arms and looked again at his son, who stood so immobile and silent nearby. Their glances met and fixed for awhile before the old man's eyes dropped as they melted with pathos. " Ron, Ron.'' The name, so slowly repeated, seemed to ooze from his heart.

" Tell me, my boy. Tell your mother, whose body bore you safely through the travail and blood of birth, tell us, whose lives were fused in yours, that you'll mix no more with that crew of atheists.''

Ron shuddered coldly and came out of the trance that had gripped him. He fought desperately for arguments to justify his actions, for reasons that would destroy the intolerant prejudice of his parents. Although they had never mentioned a word to him he knew that his boyhood association with Len and the contact between them ever since had been a painful knowledge to his parents, who had aspirations that transcended such friendships. Being aware of this he could not help sympathising with them, even now in this crisis, as he thought of the tremendous shock they must have suffered with the realisation that the friendship had now become not merely personal but political. Up to this moment he had been prepared to drift along on the fringe of the movement, as his reply to Len's plea had implied, but the sudden outburst from his father had involuntarily destroyed all his emotional vacillations. He now squared his shoulders and faced the old couple, whose stares burned through him.

" Why are you so bitter against the Communists, dad ? They have done nothing to you.''

" Done nothing to me ? Ha ! Haven't they ruined

this valley and my business ?   Don't they always and everywhere advocate strikes ?   Don't they preach disorder and
revolution ?   Haven't they drawn the people from their
chapels and religion ? ''   He began to get excited again,
but checked himself with a moan.

"Oh, Ron.   We reared you to become a decent, law-
abiding citizen.   We held out hopes that you would
become a leading light in the life of Cwmardy.   Yes, a
well-respected man.   And here you have linked yourself to
everything that is foreign to our people and their beliefs.
You are a friend of the riff-raff in the valley.''

This sneer stung Ron to a hasty retort.   "You can't say
that, dad.   Len's people have been dealing with you all
their lives.   His mother goes to chapel as regularly as
anybody, and Len himself is as gentle as a lamb.   It's
your blindness and the narrowness of your life that makes
you so intolerant of any opinion that happens to be opposed
to yours.''   He spoke very low, but each word was
emphatic as he continued.   "You want things to remain
stagnant, to be to-day as they were in your boyhood.   You
are not willing for people to learn, not prepared to see them
struggling.   You want them to be like a river that doesn't
flow.   But it can't be.   No, it can't be, whatever you may
feel or think.   As water, to be clean, must keep on flowing,
so must the people keep on struggling to get security and
happiness in this world.   How can it be otherwise ? '' he
entreated them both.   "Water that is stagnant is fœtid
and deadly, and people who won't struggle are dull,
apathetic, and sordid.''

Both the old people gazed at him dumbstruck, silent in
the pause which preceded his next words.   "I respect
your faith, mam and dad.   I know you are sincere in
them, but so also I know that other people are equally
sincere in their principles, although you do not agree with
these.   They are not wrong because you disagree.   Oh
no.''

John could stick the indictment no longer, and sprang
to his feet, his whole body quivering as he shouted:
"That's enough.   Get out of this house with your infidel
ideas !   Go to those you call your friends and see if they
can help you in your poverty—see if they will do and suffer
for you as me and your mother have done for thirty years.

And when you find out the truth, come back here and see what you have left." His voice cracked and an odd look crept over his face. Maggie was now openly crying, and Ron half started towards her, but changed his mind, and hesitantly putting on the coat he had retrieved from his father, he turned and slowly walked out.

The old man and his wife waited until they heard the door slam, then looked at each other in silence, each seeing a face that was lined and worn. Maggie saw strange fires glowing in her husband's eyes, but was too weary to wonder why they came or what they portended. The scene had robbed her of volition and they sat pensive and practically motionless for some hours, once or twice letting their glances wander round the room.

In spite of extreme poverty, their pride had forbidden the sale of any of the furniture, each piece of which they regarded with an affection second only to that which they had felt for their son. The various wooden articles filling the house symbolised for them the stages and episodes in their married life, and they now reminded Maggie of the past. A tear worked its way down her withered cheek, following every intricate groove till it reached her chin, from which it dropped when she coughed. John placed his arm round her bony shoulders, pressing her head to his breast, while the glow in his eyes deepened, as did the furrow on his brow.

" There, there, Maggie fach," he crooned in her ear. " Don't take it so hard ; it is no good grumbling or grieving at our lot." He paused a second and tried to lighten his tones. " Ron will come to his senses again, when the people who owe us money pay their debts and make it possible for us to get him a position."

She was seized by a fit of coughing which left her gasping, but she at last gathered sufficient breath to groan : " What is the good of talking like that, John ? You know the people can't and never will pay us." She stopped again to cough, then began to moan. " Oh, Ron, Ron ! Whatever is to come of you ? I had such lovely dreams of what you were going to be. I saw myself as the proud mother of a great man and now, oh dear, dear." She turned to John, and repeated : " Yes, a great man, and here we are as poor as church mice not knowing where to turn. It's enough to make anyone a Communist." She relapsed into silence and John shook himself restlessly. He seemed to be struggling with some idea, and eventually said with infinite slowness, as though he were answering a difficult question that had been put to him.

" No. We can never go to the parish for help, and we can never lift our heads while Ron is an infidel. Better for us to die here and now than face that disgrace." His face seemed even thinner and the shadows more numerous as he whispered the thought and his fingers dug passionately into her shoulder.

Maggie looked into his eyes and her own opened wide at what she saw there. He seemed to read her thoughts before she hoarsely spoke them, nodding her head in time with the words. " Yes, John. You are right. Better that than the other thing. But how ? " She exclaimed sharply as the idea began to fix itself in her mind. John lifted her tenderly to her feet and they stared at each other with an intensity that made them alone in the world. She felt a pain in her chest as though rats were gnawing at the bones, but watching his look become more fixed and horrifying, she did not cough. The visible tremor of his body told her he was trying to fight away some inevitable action, but she felt no fear.

At last he spoke, every word deliberate and emphatic. " Maggie fach, we have lived together many years now, and have seen many ups and downs, but through it all we have stuck together as man and wife should. Yes, my dear, that has been our life." A sob came into his voice but he checked it immediately and clasped her head in his hands. " Oh, Maggie fach, as we have lived, that is how I want to die . . . together." He flung his arms wildly into the air and his voice rose hysterically as despair conquered him. " Yes. Ron has left us alone and we must die together . . . and now." He screamed the last words twice, before staggering to the ornate sideboard, where he began frantically searching for something in the drawers.

Maggie watched his every movement but she made no effort to hinder him. Instead, she slowly sank back into the chair, looked into the dying flames that gasped in the grate, and sighed. A smile clung to the corners of her lips and her eyes grew bright. She scarcely seemed to notice that he had left the sideboard and was now standing over her with an open razor in his hand. His whole body was trembling and he kept mumbling incoherently, but Maggie paid no attention. Once or twice she shaped her lips to say something, but the words did not come. Then presently, almost as though she were crooning gently to herself, she whispered :

" John. John bach. So this is the end." It was not a question but an assertion. There was no sadness in her voice and her face was placid.

Suddenly she caught the hand that held the razor and dragging it to her lips kissed the open blade. " There is no room for us any longer here," she murmured, " but God has provided a place for us somewhere else where we won't be a burden on our little Ron."

John bent his head and she felt his hot lips burning through her hair. " Come, John bach," she coaxed him, " there is no need for us to wait. I'm ready to come with you."

He appeared not to hear her, for he continued muttering to himself, blind to everything but the loose skin on her neck. With passionate eagerness his fingers traced the veins and sinews whose throbbing seemed to fascinate him. He closed his eyes as his hand jerked up and drew the razor across her throat. He felt the blade slice through her flesh, but when he opened his eyes again, Maggie's were still staring at him, though blood was pouring from the wound. He fancied she wanted to say something, and bent his ear to her lips, unconscious of the spurting blood that drenched him. But all he heard was a whimpering gurgle. He lifted his head a little, wondering what she wanted, when her fingers closed over his hand and slowly lifted it to her neck.

The action flashed to his brain knowledge of what she desired and he carefully searched for the wound with his fingers. Finding it, he parted the edges, placed the razor inside and slashed again, her hand still gripping his and following the sweeping stroke. He felt her grasp tighten convulsively on his wrist, as her head sagged forward on her chest.

John freed himself from the clasp and stood back a pace. " I'm coming, Maggie fach, never fear," he muttered, and,

hearing no response he caught her head in his hands,
heedless of the blood streaming down her dress to the
floor beneath his feet ; then, seeing the razor which he
still clutched, he flung it with all his strength into the grate.
His glazed eyes stared at it for a long time as it lay resting
in the ashes, and the only sound was the mocking " Tick-
tock, tick-tock " of the clock on the mantelshelf.　This
eventually forced itself in upon his senses and he raised his
head to look again at Maggie, whose eyes were now closed.
He went to her and stroked her sticky hair with his lips for
a time, then suddenly jerked himself erect and his feet
slipped in a puddle of blood.

He looked at this helplessly for a while, then sprang to
the back door through which he hurried, returning in a
moment with a length of rope, used to tie orange boxes.
Jumping on the table he fastened one end of the rope to a
hook in the ceiling, leaving the other looped end to dangle
about a foot lower.　Then he scrambled off the table,
each action becoming more hysterical, and made for Maggie's
slumped body.　He lifted her head and gazed at her.
The lips were already curled back from the teeth, but he
kissed them, while he mumbled to himself : " I'll soon
be with you."　He closed his eyes for a moment, then
jumped back on the table and placed the loop about his
neck.　Its touch sent a cold shiver through him, but he bent
his knees to allow the full weight of his body to fall on his
neck, and scrambled with his feet to find the edge of the table
and kick it away even as he heard loud shouts in the street
and Ron's voice calling : " We are marching for bread
and extra relief."

The table crashed over and the old man felt his chest
bursting.　He opened his mouth, but no air came.　He
began to kick wildly and his body swung like a pendulum
on the rope, which swayed for a long time after the demonstration had passed the shop.

CHAPTER XII

Len goes to Gaol

WHILE this was happening in the stores of Evans Cardi, the drizzling rain curled over the rim of the mountain and swept down on Cwmardy in visible gusts as the people gathered about the Square for the demonstration to the council chambers. The wind moaned along the telephone wires, lashing the people's faces and bending their heads to the muddy earth. Harry Morgan and Len stood on the fountain, with Ron and Mary nearby in the centre of the crowd. Harry's arms waved wildly and his voice crackled through the rain as he shouted :

" Where are those who are supposed to be our leaders ? Where are those we put in Parliament and the council ? Here we are about to march, not to the Big House against the owners, but to our own leaders who we have put in power on the council. We are marching for relief and school feeding. I ask again, where are they now ? "

A loud howl followed this :

" Where are they now ? "

" Where is Ezra ? "

" We gave them power. They must give us bread."

Len saw the skin on Mary's face twitch, and it made his burn. Pulling Harry's sleeve, he pleaded : " Don't keep them too long, comrade. Let's start the march. Our people are getting wet, standing here."

Even as he made the request Mary had left Ron's side and was pushing her way to the fountain, which willing hands helped her to mount. The waves in her brown hair shone wetly in the wind, which ruffled the strands across her face. Brushing them aside and paying no heed to the surprised couple with her on the fountain, she began to speak, her words vibrant with feeling.

" Our leaders have deserted us," she declared, " because

they think the fight is only in the pit, between us and the company. Yet they once asked us to put them on the council and in Parliament because the struggle is everywhere. When they were only a few on the council they pleaded with us to give them more seats, to give them more power, because they were helpless. We gave it to them— all the power they wanted. We put them in control, and now they tell us that although they have power they can do nothing because they have no money."

Someone shouted harshly : " Don't forget your father is one of them."

She went white as she turned in the direction of the sneer and for a moment Len thought she was about to fall off the fountain, but before he could move to help her, she had recovered herself and began speaking again, although a little huskily : " I know he is one of them, but I also know he doesn't agree with the others. If he felt there was any way to help us, I know he would take it. But what can he do alone ? Although he is true, he is helpless."

The struggle between filial love and the objective reality of the present situation weakened her, and Len caught her arm as she stumbled. His voice was harsh with affection as he said : " That will do, Mary. Don't kill yourself. We'll start off now."

He never remembered the exact statements she had made, but he understood the changed outlook behind them and marvelled as his glance roamed over the crowd that faced him. He saw glimpses of the police at the rear hustling the people, and knowing what the action portended, he immediately took command, shouting as loudly as he could :

" Keep together, boys ! Don't let anyone break your ranks and don't let anyone provoke you."

He jumped from the fountain, Mary and the others beside him, and the march to the council chambers began, the people clamouring and shouting as they followed their leaders. A red banner was hoisted into the misty rain, which soon soaked it into limp sogginess.

Mary was the first to notice the number of police that fell in alongside the demonstration from every street and lane. She mentioned it to Len, who looked around and saw the truth of her remark.

When he turned to her again, his look was worried, but he tried hard to be casual when he said : " Well, we expected them, didn't we ? "

" Yes," she retorted urgently, " but can't you see what it means, Len ? During the long strike they came to protect the company ; then they came to protect the black-legs, as dad often told us ; but now they come to protect our own leaders."

He paused momentarily as the full effect of her words struck him, but the pressure from behind pushed him along again as he replied : " By gum, you're right, my dear."

They kept on marching without saying any more for a while, during which he appeared to be gathering his thoughts. Then quite unexpectedly he said to her : " Of course, that's right. It's the logic of the whole struggle, although I never saw it that way till you showed it to me now. The councillors start off by being our leaders against the company. The Government sends its police in to help the company and the blacklegs, in the name of law and order. This makes our leaders lose faith in our ability to win the fight, and because we won't listen the police are sent in to help them. Well, I'm damned," he concluded, " it's funny how the struggle sieves us out, in't it ? "

No more was said until the council chambers were in sight, by which time all the demonstrators were drenched to the skin ; but the banner was pushed higher into the air when they saw the strong cordon of police blocking the entire road.

Len went white and his lips closed tightly for a moment. Then he grasped Mary's arm and grimly warned her : " Now, remember. You say nothing. Leave this to me and the other boys."

Mary did not reply, but a defiant look flared in her eyes. The procession only stopped when the front ranks were right up against the cordon, but it was near enough to the council chambers for the strikers to see the ashen faces of the councillors through the windows. A loud howl immediately broke the air.

" Come down here where you belong ! "

" Baby starvers ! "

" Traitors ! "

The police ranks drew in ominously and each constable

grasped the looped strap that dangled from his trouser pocket. The inspector in charge stepped forward a pace and faced Len, whose body looked insignificant against the other's.

"Come on! Break up!" came the harsh command. "You can't march any further."

"We don't want to march any further," Len retorted. "All we want is to send a deputation into the council."

The inspector hesitated a moment and the shouting became more wild. It seemed to irritate the police officer.

"That'll do," he said. "I don't want any of your bloody cheek, and you can't send a deputation, because the council has just told us it doesn't want to see you."

The strikers near heard this and the shouts grew into a roar at the news. A wild movement began to sway the people, and without any warning the fight started. The police charged into the crowd, hitting madly at every head within reach. The councillors hurriedly retreated from the windows of the chamber as the bodies began to flop to the ground, where they tempted heavy booted feet.

Len felt himself hurtled about like a log in a flood. He looked about frantically for Mary, and seeing someone grasp her roughly by the arm, the world went dark and he snarled at the top of his voice: "Keep your dirty bloody paws off her," at the same time furiously pushing and fighting his way towards her. A sudden pain brought him to his senses as he felt his arm being twisted behind his back in agonising jerks. He moaned with the pain and shouted hoarsely: "Let me go, you cowards. Give me a chance." A further twist brought his head down till it nearly touched the ground and he heard from far away someone saying harshly: "Take him inside." He kicked wildly behind him, then felt something crash upon his head, and as he crumbled up he fancied he saw a huge black boot coming to meet his stomach. But he did not hear Mary scream wildly: "Oh, my God, they're smashing Len up and taking him in!"

Hours later Len was lifted roughly from the stony floor of the cell into which he had been flung. He vaguely sensed he was being dragged along a dark passage, but didn't take much notice. He wondered if he had two heads and how far apart they were from each other. He knew they

were on fire because of the fierce burning in them. His
eyes pricked him like red-hot needles and he was afraid to
open them, but the bright light in the room to which he
was taken seeped through the lids and forced them open.
The momentary glance showed him, through a steamy
mist, a large number of uniformed men. He raised a heavy
hand to his head, then dropped it again, wet and sticky,
to his side. A murmur of dim voices came to his ears, but
he made no effort to distinguish what was said as his knees
began to wobble and he crumpled face down upon the
floor.

The next thing he remembered was the sound of low
moans and a trembling that shook his limbs like jelly.
He slowly gathered his thoughts and drew himself to his
knees, all the time wondering what had happened and
where he was as he rose unsteadily erect. His head still
throbbed, but the burning agony had gone, although his
ears were filled with a funny buzz that somehow made
him think of the mountain in summer. He stood swaying
for some seconds, then thrust his arms before him and
stepped out—one pace, two paces—before his knees touched
an obstruction. Bending down, he let his fingers run over
the coarse cloth that covered something like a bench.
Straining his eyes to see what was there, he fancied the air
became lighter, and looking at the floor behind him he saw
a shadowy pattern beginning to form on it. He kept
watching this, his whole soul in his eyes, until he distinguished black bars with panes of light between them.

Slowly lifting his head, he saw the small window high up
on one side of the cell wall. Turning away, he gazed around
the cold emptiness that surrounded him before wearily
making for the bench to sit down. The clammy air made
him shiver, but he did not think of the blanket beneath
his body as, with his head clasped in his hands, he drew
to his mind all that had happened. His eyes filled with
tears as he again saw Mary in the grasp of the huge policeman and the bodies of his mates upon the wet earth.

A thin, squeaky noise, percolating from the street into
the cell, disturbed the painful soliloquy. Len listened and
heard a newsboy shout " Special Edition." The sound
made him happier in a moment, as it gave him contact
with the world outside. He thought it sweeter than the

music of his mountain larks and walked hurriedly to the
cell window the better to catch every syllable.

" Russians imprison British subjects." He stretched
himself taut at the words and breathlessly waited for the
rest. " No free speech in Russia. Englishmen in danger.
The Government takes stern measures."

Len wondered what had happened and for a moment
forgot his own predicament. He slowly resumed his seat
upon the plank, and as he thought more deeply over the
newsboy's cry a bitter smile curled his lips.

He never remembered how long he sat without moving,
but he suddenly felt the cold steal through the flesh into
his bones. He shivered and pulled the solitary blanket
over his shoulders in an effort to keep the cold at bay.
Finding this insufficient and his muscles beginning to
quiver involuntarily, he rose and paced the cell, the blanket
dangling to his feet like a robe. The rhythm of the walk
began to work itself into his brain, which made a song of
each step. " Eight steps up. Stop. Five steps across.
Stop. Eight steps up. Stop." He sat down again to
get away from the maddening reiteration, and tried to
retrace the events of the day. But tales he had heard
of what policemen did to prisoners in the cells insisted upon
intruding into his thoughts. The affair of Syd Jones the
wrestler came to his mind with stunning force. He
remembered the night Syd was frog-marched to the station
and brought out next morning dead from heart failure.
Big Jim always insisted the man had been beaten to death.
Other incidents and anecdotes crowded into his mind,
where they became a panorama of living pictures that bred
in him a slow-developing fear. He looked about the cell
for a weapon, but saw nothing, and suddenly realised it
had become pitch dark. He sat down again, closing his
eyes tightly in a vain attempt to shut out the pictures
that passed before them.

He began wondering what the police intended doing with
him. His imagination illuminated the cell and he saw the
iron-studded door open to admit a number of great hazy
forms. He jumped up in a frenzy, only to find the darkness
more intense than ever. Fearing to sit down again, he
paced the cell once more. This time the thud–thud of
his tramping feet made him think of boots and he smiled

when he remembered the old saying that all policemen had big feet. But the smile faded into a pitiful twist of the lips with the thought that boots made fine weapons. Better than batons, he thought, when a man was down. He saw them, big, black, and shiny, staring at him from all parts of the cell, and their cold, glittering hardness appalled him. He felt them driving into his head and body, and closed his eyes to sweep them from sight. But they followed him, scores of them, lifting, falling, kicking, thudding. " No-no," he shouted hysterically, burying his face in his arms. " Not that, not that. You can't kill me here."

His breath came in gasping sobs and he sat down to steady himself. The thick darkness seemed to press on him, but when he raised his head he fancied the walls had drawn closer together. Perspiration ran in trickling streams down his face and the hair on the back of his neck bristled. He stopped breathing and tried to brace himself, but all the time the walls came nearer and nearer, until he felt they were nearly on him and ready to crush him in a clammy embrace.

He sprang erect in a panic and raced to the door, which he missed in the darkness, flattening himself against the opposite wall. Rebounding from this, with increasing panic he hurled himself in the opposite direction, and sensing he was against wood began to kick madly at the door, at the same time screaming : " Let me out ! Let me out ! For God's sake let me out ! I'm smothering."

There was no answer and he kept on kicking and screaming until, when he was nearly exhausted, he heard the shuffle of feet outside the door and the clanging of keys. He felt the door pressed open against his body and retreated more deeply into the cell, where a flash of light suddenly blazed full on his eyes, completely blinding him.

" What the bloody hell is all this fuss about ? " he heard a voice ask roughly.

The sound and the knowledge there was another human being with him sent Len's courage back to him in surges. Still seeing nothing, he pulled himself erect and answered : " Nothing. I only wanted some company "

For a second there was amazed silence, then :

" You cheeky little bastard ! " came the indignant

retort. " Who the hell do you think you are, Lord Muck
or what ? " Another pause before the voice continued.
" Here, mate, we'll soon put a stop to his damned nonsense.
Anybody would think he was in a public house or something, making all this damn noise. Help me to pull his
boots off."

Before Len could make any remonstrance he was pushed
flat on his back, while one policeman sat on his stomach
and the other pulled off his boots. In a short time Len
was again alone. He wrapped his feet in the blanket
and tried to sleep, but his mind was too restive.

After what seemed hours he heard the clang of keys
and the door open again, but, thinking it was the police,
he did not move or open his eyes. Then a small hand, soft
and cool, pressed upon his burning forehead, and springing
to his feet he caught Mary to him in a clasp that melted
her body to his. She eased herself gently away with a
blush as she saw the grinning policemen.

" Hallo, Len my dear. How are you ? " she asked,
trying to speak casually although her voice was trembling.
She looked at his face, where she saw the dried blood and
bruises. Tears clouded her vision, and this time, heedless of
the presence of anyone else, she kissed him hungrily. What
she had seen for some reason flashed her memory back to
the battered lad on the mountain, and something told her
that her suspicions were correct.

The waiting police grew impatient. " Come on, hurry
up," said the sergeant ; " we can't stop here all bloody
night to watch you two spooning by there."

Mary looked at him indignantly.

" It's your fault we are here at all," she retorted
heatedly ; " and now you've got to wait till I finish my
business."

" Pretty bloody cocky, in't you, missus ? " he replied
with half a smile. " But never mind. Get on with your
business and don't be too long."

Mary turned to Len and inquired what he was charged
with. He told her he didn't know and began explaining
all that had happened when he was interrupted.

" Cut that out. That's not business."

Mary bridled up again, but Len checked her with a weary
gesture. " Never mind about that, Mary my dear. We'll

know soon enough. Tell me, have any of the boys been hurt ? "

She told him a few had been badly battered but he was the only one arrested. His eyes subconsciously travelled over her body, but she showed no signs of injury. Clearing his throat and drawing her into the far corner of the cell, he whispered in her ear. " Will your father be on the bench to-morrow ? "

She went white at the question and was some time before answering. " No, Len. I've tried to coax him, but he says if he sits on your case it will show he's taking sides and would do you no good."

Len's body jerked and he would have shouted out but for the pressure of her hand upon his wrist. Controlling himself, he mumbled bitterly. " Huh ! When he asked the committee to let him accept the position as J.P. he said he'd be able as a magistrate to see that our people had fair play when they were brought up in court. And now the very thing he'd do if he had the position, he says he can't do because he's got it."

He saw the pain in her face and hastened to soften her palpable grief. " There, there. Don't take no notice of me. We're all unfair to you, my dear. Whatever your father does we throw up to your face as if you could help it ; and all the time you are fighting with us, not only against the company and the police, but against your love for your father. Oh, Mary, forgive me," he begged.

She patted his bent head caressingly.

The sergeant bawled out. " Come on there, time's up. No more sloppy bloody nonsense."

Mary looked him straight in the eye before saying : " One day, my friend, you'll get what you deserve. And you'll find it will be something very different from what you desire."

She kissed Len again and walked to the door, where she turned to say : " Cheerio, Len. Keep your spirits up. All the boys and your father and mother are thinking of you, and one day our turn will come."

He strained his ears to listen for the patter of her little feet, but the heavy thump of her escort's drowned it. His emotions had been soothed by her visit, and shortly after her departure he fell into a deep sleep.

He was still asleep when the door was opened early next morning, and the policeman had to shake him roughly before he woke. Len looked up with a start, then remembered where he was, and, stretching himself, he rose. Although he still felt sore all over, his mind was clear and alert and he was prepared for what was to come. The policeman placed a mug of dirty-looking tea and a piece of dry bread near him, with the remark :

" Don't be long shoving this down. It's nearly time for the court to open."

Len looked at the stuff contemptuously, then at the police officer. " You can take that stuff back to where you had it from," he replied. " All I want is a wash and a shave."

" Ho ! Want to be a bloody swank, do you ? Well, you can't have a shave, see."

Len looked the surprise he felt. " Why not," he asked innocently.

" Because we don't want you cutting your throat, the same as some of the others have done in my time," was the astounding answer.

Len's eyes filled with horror, and the policeman, repenting the confidence he had intended as a barb, begged : " Don't let on that I told you that, or I'll get into trouble."

His words went unheard by Len, whose mind was busily traversing the possible reasons why people should commit suicide. " Poor devils," he muttered to himself, and sighed, then visibly pulled himself together before telling the policeman : " Don't worry about me cutting my throat. There's too much rubbish needs cleaning from this world yet."

The officer took him to the lavatory where Len swilled his face under the dripping tap. This done, he returned to the cell, where he was left alone with his thoughts. But he did not have much time for further meditation before the door opened once more and two brightly polished constables marched in and, placing themselves either side, led him down the narrow passage and up some stairs, whence he emerged into a small box-like structure in the middle of a strange room.

Len peeped over the side of his cage and saw that the court was half full of people, among whom he immediately noticed Mary and his father and mother. They looked at

him yearningly when they caught his glance, and Shân
half rose from her seat to come to him, but Mary tugged her
skirt and made her sit down again. Big Jim waved one
hand airily, while the other curled his moustache, as much
as to say : " Don't worry, boy bach. Big Jim is with you
now."

Somewhere from without the court came a deep muffled
drone of voices. Len wondered what it was even as he
noticed the hasty passing backwards and forwards of the
numerous police in the building. The drone grew louder
and heavier until it seemed to shroud the building like a
shawl and he heard the strains of a song battering against
the walls :

> " Then comrades, come rally,
> And the last fight let us face.",

Something swelled in his chest and he felt the air swirling
about his ears. He momentarily forgot the court-room
and, lifting his musical voice, he joined in :

> " On our flesh too long has fed the raven,
> We've too long been the vulture's prey."

His action electrified the people in the public gallery, who,
as though drawn by the music of his voice, instantly
rose to their feet and accompanied him, Mary's sweet
soprano riding Big Jim's deep bass. After a momentary
paralysed silence there were loud howls for " S-s-silence "
and posses of police, white-faced and fearful, stormed into
the court, where they looked at each other stupidly, none
of them knowing what to do.

Len stood square and erect, his head thrown back a little
and his eyes glistening proudly as the last notes faded into
silence and three men entered the court from behind a heavy
plush curtain. Police sprang rigidly to attention to a
loudly barked " S-silence ! " and the magistrates took their
seats on the raised dais that faced the court.

Len scrutinised them with interest, realising they were
the persons who held his liberty in their hands. The one
in the middle had a pinky bald head, a clean-shaven face
with hanging cheeks, and a pair of rimless pince-nez which
he carried on the tip of his nose. The other two Len knew
as the alderman who had read the Riot Act during the long

strike and Mr. Higgins, the financial advisor to the company. The man in the middle, whom Len assumed to be the chairman, bent across the desk to whisper something to a small awkwardly built man in the well of the court, who had to stand on his toes to get his ears near enough to listen. When the conversation was finished, the latter, screwing up the muscles of his face to give himself an appearance of sternness, addressed himself to Len.

" You are charged with unlawful assembly, breach of the peace, riotous behaviour, assaulting the police, and impeding the police in the execution of their duty."

Len's eyes grew larger with each statement and he looked dazedly at Mary, but the only consolation she could give him was a wan smile which put a blight on her own even as she gave it. He heard the small man ask sharply :

" Do you plead guilty or not guilty ? "

Realising the question was addressed to himself, Len pulled his wits together and answered heatedly : " Not guilty, of course. I'm a working man, not a criminal, and it's all lies."

This created a sensation and the police looked at each other with shocked faces, as if something indecent had been said.

The chairman rebuked Len. " Please answer the question and don't make political speeches."

For some time after this Len hardly followed the proceedings, his brain joined with the singing outside, until a policeman went into the box and gave evidence of the violent assault that had been committed upon him. Len looked at the huge bulk of the man with interest, then began to realise as he followed the evidence that it was he himself who was supposed to have maliciously battered the witness.

At the end of this evidence he was asked if he wanted to cross-examine the witness. The question startled him for a moment and he blurted out : " Yes, of course I do. It's lies, wilful lies."

A dozen police gathered round the dock as his voice began to rise, and Big Jim fidgeted restlessly in his seat. The chairman rebuked Len again. " You can ask any question you like on the evidence," he warned, " but you can't use this court for propaganda. Don't forget we are men of experience on this bench and know how to deal with stubborn people." The police and officials laughed heartily at this quip, the other magistrates joining in.

More witnesses went into the box to repeat the evidence of the first. The monotonous repetition sent the alderman to sleep. At length Len was asked if he wanted to go into the witness-box or preferred to make a statement from the dock. After a brief hesitation, during which he tried to decipher the difference between them, he elected to remain where he was. Despite several interruptions from the chairman and the clerk he managed to recount the events of the day up to the time of the fight. By this time his modulated voice was firm and distinct, every word as clear as a music note.

" You don't want us to believe that the police were responsible for the riot, do you ? " asked the chairman in amazement.

" Yes, I do," replied Len sharply. " They carry batons, not wings, don't they ? "

Big Jim laughed loudly and it was immediately taken up by the other people in the public gallery. The police rushed about like hens, bawling : " Silence ! Order ! " as loudly as they could.

The chairman, his face purple with injured dignity, warned those present : " If there is another such unseemly outbreak I shall order the court to be cleared at once."

Len took no heed of the threat and continued his statement. " This court has already made its mind up against me," he declared. " You are biased from the beginning because I am one of the strikers, and are ready to accept as God's truth every lie that the police have brought against me. This is the first time I have ever been in a court of law, but I've been here long enough to know that no working-man can ever hope to get justice in such a place as this." He was interrupted again but he took no notice and began shouting to get himself heard above the others. " If justice is fair, why am I tried by a coal-owner instead of by my own fellow workmen ? " A policeman stepped into the dock and gripped his arm tightly. This calmed him a little but he gave one parting shot : " This bench and the police work hand in hand."

His tirade had electrified the people present and Big Jim was already on his feet when the chairman looked at the other magistrates, slyly nudging the alderman, who had dozed through it all. Each of them nodded assent to something that was unspoken. The chairman then beckoned to the chief constable, who had sat quietly near the clerk throughout the proceedings.

" There are no previous convictions," he stated, then coughed and rubbed his forefinger along his little moustache, " but the police know him as a desperate character who associates with revolutionaries and other disorderly elements. He is in the forefront whenever there is any trouble among the workmen, and is always the first fomenting them to acts of violence."

The magistrates looked sternly at Len during this recital, at the end of which the chairman addressed him. " We are sorry to see a young man like yourself in this position, charged with such serious crimes against the peace. But we can't tolerate foreign methods of agitation in this country, and in all the circumstances we are agreed that you must go to prison for six months with hard labour."

An unearthly scream cut through the court like a sword, followed by a mad roar, but Len did not see where the police rushed, as he was hustled down the steps back into the cell out of sight.

CHAPTER XIII

Mary joins the Party

DURING the remainder of the day Len was like a man in a dream. He heard the shouting that continued outside rise on occasions until it became a wild roar that hammered his ears. His whole being yearned to know what was happening ; at the same time he wondered how long it would be before they took him from the station to the prison.

It was very dark when at last the cell door opened and he was taken into the charge room, which was full of pale-faced policemen. The chief stepped towards him in an ingratiating manner, saying : " We want you to be reasonable, Roberts. We are taking you to the railway-station, but there are many people outside waiting and we want you to see that they do nothing foolish." Len sensed at once that the delay in transferring him was due to the fact that the police were afraid of the people. He warmed at the thought, but he said nothing as he fell in between two sergeants, one of whom bent down to whisper :

" If you try to make a dash for it, I'll bash your bloody brains out before you go two steps."

Len looked up at the threat. " Don't worry," he answered ; " I won't run away. If you think I will, why not handcuff me ? " holding out his wrists.

The sergeant was about to follow this advice when the chief yelled : " Put those things back, you damned fool. Do you want the people to tear you to bits ? "

Abashed, the sergeant returned the handcuffs to his pocket. Len could not see how many police surrounded him as the procession made for the door and entered the street, where the people were waiting. The lights from the lamps and shop windows seemed to flow with the water on the road and the sight fascinated him, but he raised his head when he heard a terrific shout :

" Here he comes ! "

He caught glimpses of the densely packed mass through occasional gaps between the police escort which swayed under the pressure as it slowly forced a path to the railway station, where the train was already panting impatiently.

The police each side of Len gripped him tightly as though they feared he would float away from their ranks on the crest of the shouts that vibrated all over Cwmardy. As they neared the station, outside which a cordon of police was lined, the ranks were broken by a sudden rush and Len found himself surrounded by his own people, among whom were Mary and his parents.

Shân, tears streaming down her cheeks faster than the rain that dripped from her hair, flung her arms about him like a hen covering her chicks before a barking dog.

" They shan't never take you," she declared, her eyes flashing as her body swayed in the undulating movements made by repeated police dashes into the crowd to recover their prisoner. This only made her crush Len more tightly, and his body had to follow the motions of her own while, his face pressed flat to her breast, he struggled for breath.

During the tumult he felt someone press his hand, and bursting free, he saw Mary beside him, both women guarded by the towering bulk of Big Jim. Mary glowed with excitement as she asked : " What shall we do ? Make a dash for it ? "

Len hesitated for a moment, then said : " No, comrade bach ! It will only mean postponing what is bound to come and it will mean more pain for us all. No ! Better for me to go now."

She nodded agreement and kissed him passionately before forcing her way, Jim close behind, back into the middle of the crowd. Len heard voices raised in song ; and still clasped tight in Shân's arms and surrounded by people, he began again the walk to the railway station, where the engine was puffing and blowing like a fat man who had run far. The cordon of police opened, then closed behind them ; but not before Big Jim and Mary had dashed through and fallen in alongside Len and Shân. The remaining police came running up, and in a short time the platform and waiting-room were full of them. The same two sergeants hurriedly got hold of Len and tore him

from Shân's grip, bundling him into a reserved carriage.
The other passengers craned their necks through the
windows, anxious to see what all the excitement was about.

Shân fought like a mad dog to get into the carriage with
Len, but Jim caught her by the shoulders and held her in a
vice despite her kicks and threats. The engine gave a piercing scream and the people lifted their song to even greater
resonance and strength. Shân wept tears of sheer impotence.

Mary chokingly cried : "Don't worry, Len ; we'll get
you out before your time's up."

Big Jim waved his free hand, and the train slowly
gathered a puffing momentum that took Len away from
Cwmardy and his people.

Before the people reached their homes, they knew what
had happened to Ron's parents. This knowledge and Len's
imprisonment pressed on them like a physical weight.

Mary lay awake for the greater part of that night. The
heavy air gave her a choking sensation and forced her out
of bed. She paced the room for a while, casting an
occasional glance at the pillow where Len's head used to
rest. She opened the front of her nightdress to let the air
cool her chest, but the action only made her think of his
hand, and increased her misery. At last she made her
mind up, and, picking up the candle, went into her father's
room. When she entered, Ezra, still dressed, was brooding
over the little fire which he always kept going all night.
His hunched shoulders and drawn features made him look
very old and ill, and Mary felt for a moment something of
the tremendous emotional strain that was tearing at him.
The little dancing flames from the fire played over his bent
head, giving it a lurid life which his dull eyes, when he looked
up at her, betrayed as false.

Mary's heart went soft and moisture dimmed her vision,
but she quickly regained control of herself and asked
quietly : "Why in't you in bed, dad ? "

Ezra merely shook his head and replied : " I can't sleep,
my dear. My brain is burning with thoughts of Evans
Cardi and Len, so what's the good of going to bed ? "

She sat near him for a while, laying her head on his
shoulder before beginning softly : "Yes, it's awful. The
world is upside down somehow." She sighed and went on :

" We must get our Len out of jail as soon as possible, dad."

She felt his bony body quiver when he answered : " Yes, quite right. But how, my dear, how ? "

Mary rose to her feet, the helplessness in his voice astounding her so much that it took her some time to reply. " We must ask the Federation and the people to have protest demonstrations."

" But that is the very thing he's in prison for," was his quick retort.

The words struck Mary like a blow, sending a cold anger through every vein. " Yes, that's true," she almost shouted. " But he wouldn't have been locked up and beaten about if you and the other councillors had done your duty and had been with us on the march."

The look that leapt to his eyes frightened her, but she went on, although more quietly : " Oh, dad ! Can't you see our Len's in jail because he led a demonstration to you and the council, to his own leaders, and you told the police you didn't want to see us. Didn't this give them the excuse they wanted ? "

The gravity of her challenge appalled her after she had made it, and she dropped to her knees near him. " Oh, dad," she moaned. " Can't you see where you are going ? Don't you know that Len and the Party are right when they say you are being driven closer to the company and the police every day because you have stopped being a fighter with the people ? I have followed you blindly all my life, but now I'm beginning to see how right Len and the Party have been. I know you are still as true, dad ; but things have gone beyond you."

Ezra shook himself like a dog whose coat is full of water or fleas. " You don't understand, my dear," he said bitterly. " The councillors know better than you or Len or his Party what our people are suffering, and no one feels this more than us. Don't forget that Len hasn't got a monopoly of sympathy for the poor. But our hands are tied at every turn. Yes." He paused awhile and bent to the fire again, to continue sadly : " It's true we have a majority on the council, but we can do nothing with it, because we have no money and the Government hems us in at every point. Hundreds of pounds are spent in relief for the strikers and income from the rates is falling every week."

Mary felt the room go black and rose agitatedly to her feet. Ezra's gaze followed her, and he saw the thin limbs shadowed dimly on her nightdress as she paced the room. A hard lump rose to his throat, breaking through his efforts to keep it down. To cover his discomfiture he tried to speak harshly and aggressively.

" Why should Len help those Bolshies to bring the people against me just because I am a councillor ? Isn't he concerned any longer about the company, that he wants to fight me and the other leaders ? None of us can do the impossible, and he has only got himself to blame for what has happened. I've told him times out of number to come away from Harry Morgan and the gang mixed up with him, who think of nothing else but disorder, and everybody but themselves as traitors."

His daughter stopped her restless walking and drawing near looked steadily into his eyes. " So your enemy isn't the company any more, dad ? " she grated through her teeth, even while she hated what she was saying. " It's now your own workpeople, like Len and Harry." She broke down and stopped, although no tears came to help her ; then went on pleadingly : " Oh, dad ! Why don't you join forces with them instead of thinking them to be wasters and enemies ? "

Ezra caught her by the shoulders rather roughly, his mouth a thin strip that added to the shadows on his cheeks. " How can I join with people who have nothing in common with me ? All that I believe in and fought for they think is ' Social-Fascist ' and ' reactionary.' In all their meetings they say openly that everything I have done has helped to betray my people." The gall in his words thickened. " How can I join with people who believe in violence and revolution, who want to use the Federation and the whole Labour movement to this end, who act like spies in every organisation ? " He lowered his voice. " No, Mary ; to join with them would be to betray all I have lived and struggled for."

Mary drew herself from his grasp and made quietly, as though she were afraid of disturbing something, to the door, where she turned to say sadly : " All right, dad. Let's hope that by refusing to work with them you'll never find yourself in the position of having to work with the company and all that it stands for ; although, God help me, whatever you did, I would still love you."

Ezra half started forward, but she closed the door and went back to her own room before he could say any more.

Next morning she got out of bed flushed and heavy. Her chest burned with a cough that tore her lungs and left her listless. But despite this she hurried over her house-work and prepared breakfast for her father, who had not yet come down. She thought once of going out without seeing him, but changed her mind and went upstairs to his room. She saw at once that he had not slept all night, and a wave of solicitude swept over her.

She bent down and kissed him on the forehead. He began stroking her hair and presently his fingers were caressing the lobe of her ear. The old affectionate touch revived sentimental memories and she murmured softly : " Forgive me, dad, for speaking like I did last night. You see, dear, it isn't my fault, is it, if I now see things with different eyes ? But whatever happens I'll always love you as much in the future as I have in the past."

He drew her to him and whispered half sadly, half triumphantly : " I know, my dear. I know that you will never desert me. But I can't understand. I have tried to teach you all I know, and now it looks as if the very things I taught you are weapons you use against me." His brow puckered into a puzzled frown. " Something strange is happening. Things are moving too fast for me," he sighed, and added : " Let's leave it all there, Mary. Let's keep as father and daughter and keep politics outside the front door."

He followed her down the stairs and looked wistfully after her when she went out, leaving him alone with his breakfast.

Some hours later, she saw Harry Morgan walking towards Ben the Barber's, and, quickening her pace, she caught up with him before he entered the shop.

" I've been looking for you all the morning," she exclaimed a little breathlessly.

He made no reply, but waited for her next remark.

" I want to see you about our Len."

" Well, what about him ? " was the curt retort, which took Mary aback somewhat. But she soon recovered her composure, although she went a little paler.

" I thought he was a comrade and that you and the others would be worried about what's happened to him."

He softened when he realised how she was suffering. " We are, Mary. In fact, I have called a special Party meeting to discuss it now, and that's why I can't talk about it with you, because you are not a Party member and we haven't yet worked out a line on it."

Mary looked perplexed. " Can't discuss it ? " she repeated questioningly. " Why not ? In't I interested in the business as well as you, and haven't I got the same principles as your Party ? "

Harry laughed shortly and retorted : " That's what they all say. But you can't be a Communist outside the Party."

Mary started to say something, stopped, then said something else. " But Len always told me that Communists are not born, they are made. Experience, knowledge, life, struggle is necessary to make us into Communists, and it is your place to help us into the Party, not put obstacles in our way."

Harry blushed a deep red at the reproof, and Mary, turning her back, walked away with her head held high and her teeth clenched hard.

Later in the day, Mary called up to see Shân, whom she found busily washing clothes. The old woman was flushed with exertion and heat from the steaming water in the tub, when she rose to greet her daughter-in-law. She hastily wiped her hands in her apron, while Big Jim sat morosely in the armchair, smoking his favourite clay pipe, which sent Mary into a racking cough.

Solicitously knocking out the hot ash, he invited her to sit on the stool near the fire, with the kind advice : " You will find that big enough for your little arse, Mary fach."

Shân glared at him, but he took no notice, and in disgust she turned to Mary.

" Why are you washing so early in the week, mam ? " The latter asked, more to gain time than information.

" Oh, my gel ! I must do something to forget our little

Len in that awful prison, as if he was a fief or a murderer, God bless him."

She raised her apron to her nose and began to sniffle.

Jim grunted audibly, and said to Mary: "I hope to Christ your nose will never come like Shân's, my gel. It is worse than a bloody tap that is leaking before you touch it. I never seed such a 'ooman in my life for crying, muniferni."

His own eyes looked a little wet as he said this. Mary feared that Shân would take up the challenge and start a quarrel, so she joined the conversation.

"I must start washing as soon as I can, too, so that our Len can have a change of underclothes. He's had the ones he's got on for over a week now."

Jim growled: "It's no good your doing that, because they 'on't let him have them. You see, he's in a jail, not a infirmary."

Shân dried her tears and stared at him as though she thought he had suddenly lost his senses. "What you said? 'On't let my boy have his own clothes? Huh! Why not, James? Don't forget that you are not boss of the jail yet, big man though you think you are."

Jim tried to patiently explain to her, but she interrupted him with a snarl. "The jawled! God forgive me for saying such words! To smash my boy up, then put him in jail for nothink, where he will have to mix up with all the old riff-raff that I have never reared him up to."

Jim interrupted her. "Shut up, mun! Good God! What if he was in a military jail, like his father have been? It 'ood be time enough to make all this fuss, muniferni." He turned to Mary. "Did I ever tell you, Mary fach, about the time they put me in jail on the Rock?"

He went no further with his contemplated anecdote. "It is all right for you to talk," Shân interjected. "You are big enough and dull enough to take care of yourself; but our Len have only once been away from his own home, and is not used to roughing it like you old rodneys in the militia."

Jim stretched himself to his full height. "Don't you dare to say to my face, 'ooman, that I was in the militia! I am a guardsman and have been all my life."

Mary warded off Shân's ready attack. "It's no good

us worrying," she told the old woman, who again put the apron to her nose. "It won't do Len any good and would only make him miserable if he knew."

She remained with them for some time longer, and, after she had sipped down the tea which Shân insisted she should drink, she went wearily home.

She did not go outside the door for some time after this visit. She felt ill and depressed, but one day while doing some shopping she heard someone shouting, and hurried her steps till she came to a meeting being addressed by Harry Morgan. This was the first time Mary had seen him since their altercation. He stood on a beer box, borrowed from the Boar's Head, and she noticed there were very few women among the crowd of fifty or so that listened to the speaker. Harry's face was shining with the perspiration induced by the vigour of his gesticulations, but Mary would have passed on had she not heard him refer to her father.

"The Reformists have become Social-Fascist," he announced, "and Ezra is the leader of them."

Something cold clutched at her heart, and she felt her whole body shrink as Harry went on.

"If the councillors fed our children in the schools, if they had joined with us on the demonstration, Len would now be among us instead of rotting in a prison cell."

The truth of the statement paralysed Mary for a moment, until she saw Ron standing near the box, holding a red banner. The tragic death of his parents recurred to her immediately, and she scrutinised him more closely. He looked much thinner and taller than when she had last seen him, but he bore himself in the same proud manner as hitherto. She had heard he was now lodging with Will Evans' mother, but that he intended going away shortly to look for work.

When Harry had finished speaking, Ron took his place on the box. His cultivated voice and calm demeanour gave added weight to the sentiments he expressed, sentiments which were echoes of what had already been said. But his presence upon the box excited Mary and turned her thoughts to Len, who was responsible for this transformation in Ron. She kept thinking of this all the way home,

and was unusually quiet for the remainder of the day.
Ezra noticed this and attributed it to her depression.

" Come with me to the public meeting organised by the
Labour Party to-night ? " he asked her.

She was on the point of refusing, then remembered it
would give him pleasure, and consented with a thin smile.
Ezra found a place for her in the gallery of the theatre
where the meeting was held, then left her to take the chair.
The platform was full of local notabilities, among whom
she noticed the M.P. for Cwmardy ; but for some reason
her attention was mainly fixed upon the dress and appearance of the people on the platform. They looked so
prosperous, and she could not help comparing them with the
strikers and the street-corner meeting in the afternoon.
She glanced about and noticed that Ron, Harry, Will
Evans, and other members of the Party were scattered
about the hall. Ezra opened the meeting and welcomed
the M.P., who had just arrived.

The latter spoke of the strike and what he had done in
all parts of the country to bring it to a victorious end.
Then he complimented the people of Cwmardy on their
patience, and deplored the action of the Communists, that
had brought Cwmardy into disrepute and had landed one
of their number in jail.

Mary's blood coursed through her like hot lead, and she
sprang to her feet, waving her arms wildly, while she
shouted : " Withdraw that. You are talking about my
husband."

The speaker smiled tolerantly and tried to continue
as though he had not heard the interruption, but from
various parts of the hall other cries arose and drowned
his voice.

" Withdraw that statement ! Give the girl a chance ! "

This support gave Mary strength and made her more
determined. She rushed from the gallery, down the stairs,
and entered the floor of the hall, by which time Ezra was
on his feet trying to get order. After a while the noise
subsided and the speaker began again, only to be checked
by Mary's voice.

" Withdraw that statement. Let me come on the platform ! "

The Party members edged towards her and uproar broke

out once more. Mary kept on shouting, hardly knowing
what she said in her excitement. She saw those on the
stage hold a hurried consultation with her father, and forced
herself forward towards them ; Ron and Harry, although
she was not aware of it, were at her side. She reached the
front of the stage, all the people now on their feet and
shouting, and with the help of Harry and Ron scrambled
up. As she did so, the others on the platform, in-
cluding Ezra, left it, so that when she looked around
it was empty.

She gazed dumbly at the huge blur of faces that confronted her, and her courage oozed away as she realised
that, having captured the platform, the people now
expected her to say something. She opened her mouth
and heard a pitiful little squeal which made her close it
again sharply.

Harry, who had scrambled on the platform behind her,
growled : " Go on, mun. For God's sake say something,
or let me do it for you."

The remark made Mary brace herself, and she stepped
forward to the edge of the stage, where, for the first time
in her life, she made a speech.

Her concluding words were accompanied by a burst of
applause, after which Harry took control of the meeting,
making it one of protest against the imprisonment of Len.
Mary remembered very little of what happened after this,
but before she reached home, she had joined the Party.

About two months after the meeting and Mary's entry
into the Party, she went with Big Jim and Shân on a visit
to Len. Shân spent the whole morning making little
round cakes on the bakestone, and insisted on packing these
up despite all advices that Len would not be permitted to
have them.

The massive, stony aloofness of the prison awed the two
women, but Jim strutted up to the huge iron gate as though
it belonged to him. The bell he rung announced their
presence with a sonorous austerity that chilled Shân's
blood. While they waited for the gate to open, Mary
read aloud the big printed notice informing visitors of all
the things they could not do if they wanted to come back
out. Shân listened attentively, and when Mary had

finished handed the parcel of cakes to the first child that came along.

They entered the little cubby, where Len was waiting for them. His face was sallow and thinner, but his eyes were clear and his whole body seemed to beam a welcome when they entered. Shân tried to touch his feet with hers beneath the table that parted them, but it was too wide and she had to give up the attempt, at the same time squinting from the corner of her eyes at the warder who stood rigidly at the end.

Len explained : " We are meeting in by here as a special favour from the governor. I asked him not to let you come to the usual place because I knew it would upset you to see me behind glass and bars, like they have in the other place for visitors."

His words were hurried and excited, as though he had to say something quickly to maintain a grip upon himself, but after the first spasm of emotion generated by the sight of them, he held himself in check.

Mary told him all the news and he supplemented her information with questions which he shot at her like machine-gun bullets. While this was taking place, Jim, trying to whisper quietly, but every word audible to the others, was telling the officer of the time when he was himself a warder in the military prison at Gibraltar.

"Aye," he said reminiscently, with a far-away look. " I have spent most of my time in gaol, between one thing and another. But, mind you, butty, I am not sorry for it. No, indeed ! Not by a long shot. There's many a poor old dab in the cemetery who 'ood be glad of the chance to be in gaol now."

But Len did not hear this. His whole attention had been diverted by Mary's news that the strike was on the point of collapse, and he felt heavy as lead when she told him that one of the coalfields had broken away from the strike and made a separate agreement. There was an awkward pause after this.

No one knew what to say until Mary tried to relieve the tension by saying : " Oh Len, I've joined the Party," and plunging into an account of the eventful meeting.

This lightened Len's despondency, and the little gathering

became more cheerful. Not a word was spoken of Ezra, although Len was bursting to know what he was doing.

All this time Shân had been eyeing his clothes, and on several occasions had opened her mouth to say something, but thought better of it. Now, however, she could contain herself no longer. " What is them old sacks they have put on you, Len bach ? " she queried.

Len gave a hasty and somewhat guilty glance at his suit before replying : " Oh, this is the clothes they give to all prisoners, mam."

Jim was about to add something, but Shân silenced him with a look. " Well, I am going to see the manager of this place about it. I have never reared a child of mine to put on clothes from other people's backs, and I am too old to let anybody start doing that to my own flesh and blood now."

Len hastened to placate her, but only finally succeeded after he had told a few lies about the good treatment he was having.

" It is like being home," he asserted with a twist of his lips that he thought was a smile. " All I do miss, mam, is the sight of you and dad and Mary. And what do you think ? The first day I came here they put a lovely Bible on my table, and I've got it ever since."

This finally dissipated any doubts she had. The warder now announced that their time was nearly up, and this news damped their spirits like a wet blanket. Mary sensed the loneliness induced in Len by the information, and choked back her own tears in an effort to cheer him up.

" It won't be long now," she consoled, " before you'll be with us again and back in the fight. All the people are waiting to welcome you, and Cwmardy will be like a flag-day when you come out."

Len saw through the attempt to cheer him, but it warmed his heart. " Don't worry about me, comrade," he said. " Look after mam and dad. I'm sure of food and shelter here, but our people outside are sure of nothing."

They caressed each other with their eyes before they parted, and Len was led away.

One day shortly after the visit to Len, and twelve months after the beginning of the strike, news reached the valley that the national leaders had called the strike off, and were advising the men to make the best terms possible in their own areas so that they could restart work immediately. Ezra and the committee called a general meeting where the position was explained to the people, whose haggard faces were bitter. There was no singing or cheering as Ezra pronounced their defeat, and when the meeting ended the people walked home with the same slow, measured steps they took at a funeral.

CHAPTER XIV

Breaking Point

WHEN Len was released from prison he found Cwmardy like a cemetery, although he received a joyful welcome at a meeting organised by the Party for this purpose. He had only been out a few days before he felt a weight press on him as the deadly blackness of the valley caught hold of him, and made the "chug-chug" of the pit engine sound like a wail. Mary was also affected by his depression, especially the night she told him all that had happened since his imprisonment.

"The company is only taking its favourites back," she reported. "And they are bringing in scores of men from over the mountain to work the pit. Our own men have left the Federation and the company is forcing them into its own non-political union. Everything is topsy-turvy, with everyone fighting for himself. They tell me," she continued, when he made no remark, "that things are worse than they have ever been and everybody is afraid to open their mouths for fear they'll be sent up the pit."

She made no mention of her father, and although he noticed the omission he did not comment on it. When she had finished, he remained silent for a long while, then caught her in his arms and buried his face on her shoulder. She knew the mood, but left him alone with his thoughts, while she stroked his hair. He trembled at the touch and raised his head to look at her. The shadows he saw on her face darkened his own, and he murmured huskily:

"Mary, my comrade, what's going to happen to our people ? To think, after all the battles they have fought and the things they have suffered, that they are now beat and broken up makes me sad." He turned away as though this helped him to think better, then burst out : "But it's not them who are to be blamed ; it's those who let them down and betrayed them." He lost his temper

and began to shout angrily : " This is what comes from
lack of faith. Aye, by gum, this is what compromising
with the company means—no organisation, no confidence,
every man for himself and to hell with everybody else.
No wonder the company is doing what it likes with
us."

She eventually calmed him with the reminder that
moaning would help no one. Her coolness strengthened
him, and they talked of other things till it was time to go
to bed.

They had hardly finished their breakfast next morning,
when Harry, Ron, and Will Evans walked in after a preliminary brief rap on the door. Len was glad of their
company, although he hardly knew how to talk to Ron in
case he said something that would revive the terrible
tragedy. But after the first awkward preliminaries Will,
as usual, gave the conversation a light turn.

" By gum, Len," he said, looking him up and down with
his head screwed on one side to get a more comprehensive
view, " prison have done you good, mun. You look more
like a man now than I have ever seen you."

Len laughed and turned to Harry, who was placidly
poking the fire, while Mary cleared the breakfast dishes.

" How is the Party going, since I've been away, Harry ? "

" Very good," was the reply. " Mary is a trump and is
fast getting one of our best speakers."

Len blushed and went warm all over. He hoped Harry
would keep on talking about her, but the latter changed
the subject.

" There's not much chance of the company taking you
back to the pit, now they've got an opportunity to keep
you out," he said.

Len started forward in his chair, but the other gave him
no time to say anything.

" That means you'll have to sign on the dole, like the
others who're not likely to start back again. We've been
talking about it, haven't we, boys ? " Turning to the
others, who nodded acquiescence, although they didn't
know what he had in mind. " And we think your Party
job is to get the unemployed organised on the exchange."

" But what about the Federation," asked Len in a
puzzled voice.

" Oh that's finished as far as the unemployed are concerned."

Len still looked dubious, but made no further comment other than to ask, " What do you expect me to do ? "

Ron helped him. " Since you've been inside," he explained, " we have been holding meetings outside the exchange each signing day. Most of the speaking has been done by myself and Mary, because Harry is away in other parts of the country very often now. We've had some of the unemployed to join up, but we must get them all. The Party thinks you can do this better than any of us."

Len sensed the implied compliment but for some reason did not feel flattered.

Shortly after this they left, Ron remaining behind for a moment to say he intended leaving the valley at the end of the week, as some friends were hopeful of getting a position for him elsewhere. The news saddened Len, but he made no effort to dissuade his friend.

Late the same afternoon, Len strolled down to see his father, who had just bathed and was beginning to enjoy a smoke when he entered.

Shân bustled to get her son a chair, and after he had settled himself, Len asked : " How's things going in the pit, dad ? "

Jim drew the black clay-pipe from his mouth, looked at it a few moments, then spat in the fire before saying.

" Hellish, Len bach. Hellish ! The company is making it a proper bloody muck-hole. Aye," he went on prophetically, " one day, there'll be another blow up ; then everybody will be saying ' Pity the poor miner.' Pity to hell ! " he shouted in sudden temper, while Shân glowered at him reprovingly. " There is no need for it, if the company 'ood only work the pit as she ought to be worked. Huh ! I hope you will never come back to it, Len bach. It's not fit for a dog, let alone decent men."

He paused, then added confidentially : " Do you know, Len bach, they have got spies in the pit now, and if us won't join the new union, they give us the sack. What think you to that, my boy ? "

" Ho ! So that's it, is it, dad ? Well, I'll be up with you in the morning to get my old place back."

Jim stared at his son in amazement, then burst out

laughing. "Your place back? Ha-ha! There is no bloody place there for you now, mun. We work here to-day, there to-morrow, and God knows where the day after. Not only this, mind you. If you do say anything about it, the officials get shirty straight away and are not behind in telling you that if you are not willing to do it, there is plenty on top of the pit who 'ood be only too glad of the chance. No, Len. There is not much hopes of you getting back, and if you did, you wouldn't be there a day, muniferni."

Jim painfully eased his body from the chair, tapped the bowl of his pipe on the hob, and made his way to the stairs, where he remarked: "I'm going to bed. Bring my supper up, Shân."

Len said nothing as he watched the bent bulk of his father go up the stairs, but Shân sighed.

"Your dad is breaking fast, Len. Aye, indeed, fancy going to bed this time of day! Well, well! He have had his best days and will never again be the man that he was. The work is killing him now. Well, well! And to think I do 'member the time when he could eat it."

Len rose with the first hooter at five o'clock next morning. Mary was already down, warming his working clothes and making breakfast. She looked more frail than usual, and her actions as she moved about were eloquent of weariness. "All this is waste," she grumbled. "Why can't you listen to sense, Len? We could be in bed now, instead of potching about down here for nothing."

He took no notice of her plaint and after he had finished his breakfast caught her to him and kissed her. "Go back to bed, my dear, you're tired," he said.

He found his father groaning and grunting as he struggled to pull a singlet over his head, unnecessarily shaking it and paying no heed to the cloud of dust which scattered all over the little kitchen. Jim looked for his pants among the remainder of the pit clothes drying on the rod before the fire, but failed to find them.

"Argllwydd mawr," he howled, "do you 'spect me to go to work naked, that you haven't put out my pants to air?" Shân glared at him, but made no reply as he flung the clothes from the rod to the floor, increasing the dust that was already heavy on the furniture.

Len helped him. " You are sitting on them, dad."

Jim rose from his chair as though it contained a pin, looked down dazedly for a moment, then said half apologetically : " Well, well. Whoever 'ood think of that, now. Fancy me sitting on my own pants and not knowing it. Ha-ha ! " The laugh sounded empty and Shân knew it to be an attempt to cover his discomfiture.

Before leaving for the pit, Jim warned his son : " You are only wasting your time, Len. There is no work there for you, and you will only have to bath all over agen for nothink."

" Perhaps you're right, dad, but there's no harm in trying."

They bade Shân good-morning, the latter responding with the remark. " I will wait down till you come back, Len."

The two men silently joined the long human line winding up the hill to the pit. Len noticed a large number of strangers, but said nothing until half-way to the pits, when a hooter suddenly blasted the morning. He looked at his father in surprise.

" What hooter is that, dad ? " he asked, unconsciously quickening his stride.

" Oh, that is a new stunt by the company. All the men have got to have their lamps out ten minutes before the last hooter do blow or they shan't go down."

Len would have asked more questions, but he had to save his breath to keep pace with Jim, whose gasps were mixed with curses as he practically ran to the pit, all the other men doing likewise.

They had passed the colliery officer and were about to go across the bridge when someone shouted harshly behind : " Ay, there. You by Big Jim. Where the bloody hell do you think you are going to ? "

Len stopped in surprise and looked back to see the colliery policeman hurrying towards him with waving arms. Big Jim stopped with Len, but the other men hurried on their way and took no notice.

The sergeant hustled importantly up to Len, and caught him roughly by the arm. " Come on, where are you going ? "

It was Jim who replied, " If he's coming the same place as me, butty, it's to the bloody workhouse."

" That's enough of it, Jim. Nobody's talking to you,"
said the sergeant before turning his attention to Len.
" Come on. Back past that bloody office you go, and quick
if you know what is good for you."

Len saw his father's face go white as snow, then red as
blood, and knew something was about to happen.

" Ha," said the old man. " At last. Just the chance I
have been waiting for, muniferni." He placed his box
and jack carefully on the ground and began pulling off his
coat, talking gloatingly all the while like a man about to
experience a long-desired pleasure. " You is a hell of a
big man and thirty years younger than me, but never mind
about that, because you is just about my dap. Aye, butty.
You have had your fling long enough. Now one of us have
got to pay the tune, and you can venture it 'on't be Big Jim
that is going to pay." His coat was off by now and he
pranced up to the sergeant with his fists outstretched, but
the latter, seeing the move, had drawn his baton in readiness. Len stepped between them.

" Don't be silly, dad. You'll only get the wrong end of
the stick in the long run. Put your coat back and hurry
or you'll lose the pit. He won't do anything to me."

Jim reluctantly obeyed. " Better not for him to, mun
jawly. Huh ! A big man like that pulling his truncheon
out like a babby. But there, I always did say they have
got no guts and that us can beat 'em every time, man to
man." He continued talking to himself as he made his
way over the bridge. When he neared its end he turned
and shouted : " If you do fancy your hand, butty, wait
for me on top of the pit finishing time and I will be with
you. Good morning, Len bach. If he do say anything
out of the way to you, us will settle it to-night." Len saw
him put his hand to his back and walk painfully out of
sight.

He paid no further heed to the sergeant and retraced his
steps down the hill. Shân was waiting for him, as she had
promised, but he told her nothing of the occurrence.

" Us did tell you that you was wasting your time," she
scolded.

" I know, mam. But it was better for me to see for
myself, wasn't it ? "

When he got home and had bathed, Mary tried to coax

him to go to bed for a while, but his brain was too restless
to permit him to lie down. All day he was tormented
by the transformation that had taken place in Cwmardy.
He likened the pit to a fortress which had to be besieged
before entry could be gained, and even then it could only
be done if he allowed himself to be chained and guarded.
The thought galled him, because all his life had been spent
in and around the pit and its every throb palpitated through
him like blood. He remembered the books he had read
and the speeches he had heard since he was in the Party,
and subconsciously he began to tell himself that the
pits really belonged to the people and not to the
company. This reminded him of some of the arguments
he had had with Mary before she joined the Party, and
again he thought of the struggle for power.

" That's what it means," he mused to himself. " And
the Party is right. Power to take over the pits for the
people who work and die in them." He paused a moment,
then told himself : " That means revolution, because Lord
Cwmardy and his tribe will never give them up." The
conviction soothed him, somehow, and he felt happier
because of it.

For many months after this he devoted himself to propaganda on the labour exchange, trying to get his old
workmates organised as unemployed. Every signing day
Mary and other members of the Party stood on the little
wall that separated the exchange from the row of ram-
shackle houses facing it. From this vantage point they
addressed the queues of unemployed, until Len eventually
became known as the mouthpiece and leader of the
local Communists. The people found his direct statements and eloquence very attractive, and always listened
attentively to all he had to say. The long unemployment
was painting a premature oldness on him, but these
activities prevented his becoming demoralised. Every
Tuesday evening he and the other Communists met in a
room lent them by old John Library, who had always
prided himself on his advanced views and was affectionately
regarded by the people as the philosopher of the oppressed.
At these meetings, the Communists discussed for hours the
problems confronting the workers and themselves. Each
year these became more complex and confusing, until the

Party was forced to intensify the political training of its members. Len was given the rôle of trainer in Cwmardy—a rôle that was the logical outcome of his tremendous influence with the people and prestige in the Party.

Always during the summer months, Len, whenever he had an hour to spare from his activities, tried to coax Mary to the mountains. Sometimes she refused for some reason, and on these occasions he went up alone and wandered aimlessly about, always eventually finding himself on a spot overlooking the Big House and the pits. One day, when the whole world was centred on Leipzig, Len, his thoughts fixed on Dimitrov, reached this point. He sat down in deep meditation for a while, before he saw what he thought was a familiar figure slowly make its way up the drive to the Big House. The more he watched, the more convinced he became it was Ezra, and began to wonder what reason prompted the visit of the miners' leader to the den of his enemy. He failed to find a motive, and was at last urged by the encroaching darkness back into the valley, where he met Mary, who said she had been looking all over the place for him. He noticed her wildness and broken breath, but asked no questions until they found a secluded spot where they could talk without being overheard. Something in her attitude bred a faint uneasiness in him, and he felt half afraid of the news she had, before she told it. He tried to soothe her, but she brushed the effort away impatiently, at the same time saying : " Don't, Len. I've got something awful to tell you, and we can't run away from it."

The words killed the impulse beginning to work within him, and he waited quietly for her to explain. The humid air, heavy with dampness, hung over the valley like a weight, emphasising the turmoil of the life it contained. The people who occasionally passed were silent, like bent shadows emerging from the darkness only to be buried in it again moment later.

Mary sighed and her hand searched for Len's, the thin fingers pressing his convulsively. At last she spoke again. " I can't tell you up the house, Len. I've got to be outside, the house seems to be a part of what I want to say. Oh, Len, dad has been up to Lord Cwmardy, who's given him a job in the office if he'll finish with the Federation."

The last words left her mouth in one burst, after which there was silence, while the young couple watched the burning glow from the pit furnaces. It seemed to crush the darkness with a grip that made the Big House look like a castle cut out of the hard bosom of the mountain.

When Len spoke the tones were low and emphatic. "It can't be true. I don't believe it." He suddenly caught her to him and felt the broken breathing that shook her body. The tremor made him weak, and he tried to avoid the fact contained in her words. "No, I'll never believe it. Ezra would never take a favour from his greatest enemy and sell his own fellow workmen to get it."

Mary shook herself free from the hard clutch of his hands and said resignedly. "Come. Let's go up the house to see him. Perhaps it's not too late even now," she added hopefully.

On the way up he kept muttering: "Good God! To think what our comrades in Germany are suffering, while we have to fight such things as this. Good God!"

They found Ezra pacing the kitchen in a manner that reminded Len of himself in the prison cell. He saw the struggle that had taken place pressed into the lines and furrows of the old leader's face and in the once vitalising eyes whose flame was now quenched.

The tragedy of the transformation gave Len the burning sensation of a bile and made him regret his mutterings. He walked towards the chair into which Ezra had sunk on their entry, and without any preamble pleaded: "Ezra, don't leave us. Don't let all that you've done for our people be buried in a colliery office. Remember you still belong to them and they'll come back to you again if you have patience and faith."

Ezra rose to his feet and began pacing the room again as Len went on: "Hell, man, don't sell out to the company after all these years of fighting. Think of Dimitrov facing the might and horror of German Fascism on his own."

Ezra stopped with a quiver at these last words, then turned sharply round to face his son-in-law. "Who are you to talk of my actions and my future?" he demanded harshly. "You and the gang you follow! Haven't you publicly branded me as a renegade and a rat before the people you profess to love? In't you responsible for

making them desert me and "—he hesitated a second and
fixed his gaze on Mary, then concluded—" yes, turned my
own daughter against me. Would Dimitrov have done
that ? "

Mary started to say something, but her father paid no
attention as he continued in tones of implacable conviction.
" I have been deserted because of the dirty lies bred in the
mouths of your Party members, and I'm now, after forty
years' service, alone, friendless, and penniless. This is
the reward for my devotion."

Len stepped nearer him with an eager interruption.
" But if you hang on a bit longer, Ezra, I'm sure the men
will come back to the Federation. They're bound to.
It's in their bones and their hearts."

Ezra looked him deep in the eyes before replying.
" Must I live till then on air ? Or do you want me to use
my influence to get a job that belongs to other people ?
No," he answered himself with a shout, and the next words
came with increasing momentum, " I'd sooner go to the
enemy and say, ' I'm defeated, Cwmardy, and helpless.
My fight is over and I ask you to let me do something for
the short time that is left to me.' " He paused to gather
strength, then said : " This need never have been if you
and Harry Morgan hadn't brought your foreign theories
into our valley."

Mary raised her gaze from the fire to say sadly : " That's
not fair, dad. If Len is a foreigner, then I am one, because
the both of us and yourself have been reared with the valley.
All we have been through, all we know and do comes to us
from the valley and the people. If the Party thinks
different from you, dad, it's not because we are against
you, but because we believe you are wrong. There's
nothing foreign in learning to do the right things for the
struggle of our people, is there ? Oh, dad," she moaned,
rising to her feet and catching his arm affectionately,
" there's no need for you to take this job that Lord Cwmardy
throws to you like we throw a crumb to a dog. You know
we can live happy together by here for the rest of our lives."
Her voice broke and she began to sob softly.

Ezra's head bent lower with each sentence. The silence
that followed made the crackling flames roar like thunder.
At last he shook himself and looked up to say : " It's no

good, Mary. I don't want anyone to keep me. I can
keep myself in the future as I've had to do in the past, ever
since that day I took your mother to her grave and came
back with you in my arms to an empty world. Yes, just
like that, Mary. To a world whose very fullness made it
empty of happiness and peace. That's what I want, what
I've been hungering after for years . . . peace. All my
life has been a fight, and the little that is now left me I
want for myself."

Some of his old strength found expression in the adamant
finality of these last words, and the others, realising this,
said no more. Shortly after, Len and Mary left the kitchen
like people leaving a tomb.

When the men left the pit next day and filed in a long,
ever-lengthening string across the bridge, they looked in
amazement through the office windows at the bowed
shoulders and grey hair of Ezra, with a pen in his hand and
a huge ledger before him. He did not raise his eyes from
the book and he was deaf to the remarks that spanged
against the window panes. On the way to their homes
the men could talk of nothing else. Will Smallbeer was the
most vociferous.

"Leaders, muniferni," he growled to those with him.
"What did I tell you years ago? Didn't I say put a
beggar on a horse and he'll gallop to hell? By Hell!
You can all see now that old Smallbeer was right, mun
jawly. They're all the same, give 'em half a chance and
they'll sell you."

Big Jim thought of Len, and grunted: "Huh! Us
can't blame a man for that, mun. It is human nature.
A man have got to live whatever he is, and you can't throw
blame on Ezra when rotters like you do leave the Federashon
and let him starve in the gutter. No, muniferni. I tell
you boys straight, I 'ood do the same my bloody self if
you played that trick on me."

Most of the older men felt Jim's sentiments were correct,
but the younger ones were equally vehement in their
condemnation of Ezra's action.

CHAPTER XV

Ezra's Death

For many months Len could not bring himself to concentrate on the significance of the change in Ezra's outlook and action. He subconsciously felt the tremendous personal tragedy embodied in the event, but hesitated to put into words the forces and ideas that had shattered so strong a man as Ezra. Len was pulled two ways, by his affection for his old leader and by the logic of the struggle against Fascism and war developing throughout the world. His own experience in the Party showed him the one way out, but the fact that he was still living in the same house as Ezra tended to make him subjective. At the same time he was worried about his own position. It hurt him to know that his father came home from the pit each day more bent and painful, while he himself remained to all intents and purposes idle around the streets and in meetings.

The horrible sense of dependence and inaction made him morbid. His body had been moulded in the pit and he felt it calling him like the pangs of hunger, a feeling he tried to escape by throwing himself even more vigorously into the work of the Party. The clear division of the people into employed and unemployed and the chaotic state of disorganisation among both sections appalled him. These things and the collapse of the official labour movement in many parts of the world became the basis for most of the discussions in the library. It became increasingly evident there was not unanimity in the ranks of the Party. One or two, led by Fred Lewis, concentrated on local affairs and were of the opinion that the only way to save the Federation and unite the employed and unemployed was by fighting for the appointment of a full-time agent in place of Ezra. The others, led by Len and Mary, thought the first thing to be done was to explain the dangers of Fascism to the people of Cwmardy, to get them back into the Federation as a basis for other things. The controversy lasted for weeks and became very bitter. At one meeting Fred Lewis accused Len and Mary of being influenced by the fact that they were related to Ezra and were jealous of anyone else taking his place.

Mary got up immediately the accusation was made and asked : " All right. Assuming your line is right, Fred, who do you think we should fight for to be the miners' agent ? "

Without hesitation, just as though he had already decided and the answer was involuntary, Fred replied : " Myself, of course. Who else is there in the Party who could do it ? "

This brought matters to a head, and Harry Morgan, who now worked for the Party nationally, was sent for to help. A special meeting was held to thrash the business out finally. Will Evans was elected the chairman, and opened the meeting with the statement : " This is going to be a most important meeting, comrades, because what we decide here to-night will be the policy of our Party that all of us will have to fight for in Cwmardy. I call on comrade Mary Roberts to give a report of what have happened up to date. After she have finished, we will have a statement by Harry. Then there will be open discussion, and we hope none of you will keep anything back. If you have got anything to say, let's have it straight out on the table, so that all of us will know where we are."

Mary spent very little time tracing the changes that had taken place in Cwmardy and the consequent differences in the Party. Harry Morgan followed with a survey of the political situation in general and its bearing upon the position in Cwmardy and the line of the Party ; but he did not commit himself on the issue before the meeting.

Len was the first to take part in the discussion. There was a tense feeling of alertness among all present when he asked for the floor. Mary inwardly prayed that he would keep calm and remember he was not in a propaganda meeting.

" Our Party," he began, " is based on loyalty to majority decisions, even if we in the minority are against that decision. This in my opinion is the only way we can work as a Party that has got to organise a revolution. But this revolution is not a thing of a moment ; it doesn't float

down to us from the air or bubble up from the earth. No.
It is made in the struggles and tribulations of our people,
it is born in the conditions that are imposed upon our
people by the capitalists, conditions that can only be altered
by taking power out of the hands of the ruling class. But
the problem for us is, how? Yes, that's the problem,
because what we do in small things will determine the form
of the big ones, and what we do in Cwmardy on this issue
must be done in such a way that it helps all the people
forward into organisation and unity, not only against the
company but against the Government." He stopped a
moment to clear his throat, then without taking his solemn
eyes from the chairman he continued : " I say, before we
can begin talking of new officials, we have got to build
organisation to such a pitch that full-time officials will be
necessary. We are not there yet because our people have
lost faith in the leaders who have let them down so often.
And we can't blame them. Let's build the Fed., smash
the non-pols., and get the people to elect a committee to
lead them. After we do this, then perhaps we will be able
to think of another miners' agent instead of Ezra."

He sat down, to be followed immediately by Fred Lewis,
who wasted no time with preamble. " If we follow Len's
line, we'll neither have a Federation or a Party," he
declared. " How can you expect organisation unless you
have leaders to build it ? "

A voice asked : " Isn't our Party the leader ? "

Fred retorted promptly : " Yes it is, but our Party is
made up of individuals, of men and women, not rag dolls,
and that's why I say we must put one of our members
forward for this position."

The discussion went on for hours before Harry summed
up all that had been said. " I think Len's line is the right
one. Build the organisation first, then the people can elect
their leaders after."

Everyone had been careful to omit mention of Lewis's
individualist stubbornness on other occasions, but when
the motion was put to the vote Fred's hand was the only
one that supported his present contention. When he saw
this he jumped up, put his cap on and made for the door,
shouting over his shoulder, " I'm not leaving the matter
here. I'm going to take it further."

Several members urged him to come back but he paid no heed and slammed the door behind him. Those left looked at each other blankly, before the chairman announced :

" Well, that's that. We know where we are now, and all I hope is he'll do what he said. The meeting is now closed."

But it was some time later before the Party members left the library and made their way home.

Memories of this discussion and Fred's attitude lingered with Mary for a long time. Her health was becoming worse each day, and on occasions she had the greatest difficulty in breathing. As a result, she could not devote so much time as she desired to the Party, particularly as she was further handicapped by the fact that her father was getting more morose and intolerant, while his whole body seemed to be fading away before her eyes. Len was hardly any consolation to her during this period, most of his time being spent with the other Party members, holding meetings, distributing leaflets, and campaigning to get the people back into the Federation. Mary, knowing this, never complained, and kept from him as much as possible her fears regarding Ezra.

But one night she was awakened by a loud knocking on the wall that separated their bedroom from her father's. She hurriedly shook Len, who sprang to his haunches in drowsy alarm. Before he could ask any questions, he heard the knocking that had alarmed her, and without even waiting to put on his trousers, ran into Ezra's room.

In a matter of seconds, Mary heard him call out : " Come quick, Mary, something's wrong with your father."

Pale with dread, she hastened after him, and saw Ezra struggling painfully to gulp air into his open mouth. Len held the old man's head in one arm while he used a newspaper as a fan.

" Dress quick, Mary," he urged his frightened wife. " Run down the house and tell mam and dad to come up at once."

Without hesitation she left the room, and the next thing he heard was the slamming of the front door.

Shân woke when the first pebble rattled on the window-pane. Pressing her nose against the glass she recognised

the dim shape of Mary, and hastily began pulling her skirt
on, at the same time waking Jim.

" Quick, James bach. Somethink have happened to our
Mary."

Jim needed no second bidding before he was out of bed
and half-way to the kitchen, stubbing his toes against the
stone stairs on the way down. He strangled the curses
that rose to his throat and opened the door to admit the
dripping Mary, who, instead of dressing as Len had advised,
had merely flung an old coat over her nightdress. Shân,
stumbling into the kitchen, saw this with her first glance,
and drawing it off replaced it with her great woollen shawl.

" There now, gel fach. Sit yourself down and take your
time," she tried to console. But Mary was too agitated to
dally.

" No, no. There is no time to sit down. You must
come up the house with me at once. Oh dear, dear," she
burst into sudden tears and moaned. " Something terrible
is happening to dad. He is groaning and fighting for air
while his eyes are fixed on Len in an awful stare."

She brushed her hand across her forehead and hurried to
the door, the old people close at her heels and Shân
muttering : " I knowed there was somethink wrong. This
is my dream working out. There, there, Mary fach, don't
take it to your heart so much. The Good Lord do always do
what is best, and everythink will come all right in the end."

Outside the howling wind clutched savagely at the rain,
throwing it against the houses, where it smashed into
running streams. The tears on Mary's cheeks were washed
away as the three people stumbled through the storm
towards Ezra's house, where a solitary light blinked in the
sweeping rain and beckoned them to hurry. They found
the miners' leader sitting up in bed with Len at his side.
His eyes were fixed on the window with an intensity that
was frightful in its obvious blindness, and his moustache
was thick with the saliva that dribbled to his chin as he
muttered incoherences to himself. His face shone with the
perspiration that oiled it. Mary sprang forward and put
her wet arms around him.

" Here I am, dad," she whispered chokingly. " You'll
be all right now. Big Jim and Shân are here to help you.
Cwtch up now and go to sleep."

She tried to press the bony body back into the bed, but he struggled against her efforts, gasping feebly : " Don't tie me down ; let me be free to fight."

His glaring eyes roamed the room when she released him, and Jim stepped up to take her place.

" Come comrade bach," he crooned, gently as a mourning mother. " Big Jim is with you now, and there is no need for you to fight while us is here."

Ezra looked at him and his stare softened a little as it focused on the bent form of his old workmate. His words came from deep in his belly when he said : " Ah, Big Jim. He'll not desert me like his son did. No. Old Jim will fight with me to the last."

He paused a moment, then began waving his hands weakly above his head, at the same time crying helplessly : " Let me get to my feet. Don't let it ever be said that I lay down when there was a fight to be won ! "

Jim forcibly held him in bed while Len rushed for the doctor and Shân went down to the kitchen to light the fire. Ezra's eyes became glazed and he breathed in choking gasps that stuck in Mary's heart like daggers as she sensed the outcome of the struggle taking place. All the passionate love she bore him now surged through her with a force that dried the juices in her body as he fought to get out of bed.

It required the joint strength of Jim and Len to hold Ezra down while the doctor examined him. At the end of the examination the doctor took Mary on one side. " There is nothing I can do for him," he said with professional hardness. " You must prepare yourself for the worst. I'll give him something to keep him quiet for a few hours, and I'll call again in the morning."

The storm outside the room shook the house with frenzied blasts that mellowed the moans of the man on the bed. He began calling for Mary and paid no heed to her mournful protestations that she was with him.

Shân's red-rimmed eyes were wet when she said. " Get into bed with him, Mary fach. Perhaps his body can tell him what his brain cannot."

Mary obeyed, and the moans ceased for a while as some subconscious faculty told him his daughter was near. His face lost some of its putty pallor and the pain-filled lines smoothed out, giving it again some semblance of its old

strength. Len looked on and felt a new confidence creep
over him at the sight. Shân busied herself making a cup
of tea and Big Jim stood near the bed, watching every
restless motion of the form beneath the clothes.

The night slowly dragged out its storm-wrenched hours,
and when the pit-hooters called the men to work in the
early morning, their blare startled the people in the silent
house. But the noise seemed to connect Ezra with the life
in the valley, and he stirred impatiently before eventually
opening his eyes to look about the room. He appeared
more normal, although his skin had a peculiar yellowish
tinge. He felt Mary at his side and turned to her, smiling
wanly when she pressed her hot lips on his forehead. A
knock sounded on the front door and Jim went down to
answer it. When he returned he replied to the query in
Ezra's glance.

" It was Sam Dangler's missus wanting to know if Sam
could do something to help before he went to work."

Ezra's face brightened, and Jim helped him rise to his
haunches as Mary left the bed.

" My people still think of me," he whispered.

" Of courst, they do, mun. They don't never forget those
who have been good to them," Jim answered confidently.

A sudden spasm of coughing seized Ezra, and it seemed
about to choke him until Jim cleared the mucus away with
a huge forefinger. For some time after this the room was
silent except for Ezra's terrifying gasps.

At last the dying man beckoned his daughter to him and
whispered weakly. " Open the window, my dear. I want
to hear the men going to work."

" But you will catch your death of cold," she protested.

His features hardened as of old when anyone tried to
thwart him. " I said open the window," he insisted.
" Chills or anything else can't affect me now."

Mary obeyed, and as she returned to the bedside the loud
tramp of hobnailed boots followed her.

They all fell in with Ezra's mood, and for an hour listened
silently until the hooters again blasted the dawn with their
announcement that the last man was down the pit. Ezra
sighed and whispered feebly, each word like a burden he was
unwilling to relinquish.

" There goes life, creation. They will give their bodies to

the pit all day, and their strength will be turned into coal.
Yes. Black lumps of coal which will be turned into gold
at the docks." He became reminiscent as he sank back
on the bed. " It is the flesh and brains of our people that
gives life to the world. Without them the world is dead.
Dead as I'll be in a very short time."

Mary sprang forward with a cry. " Oh, don't say that,
dad. You're looking better already."

Ezra gazed at her and gulped hard as she buried her head
in the clothes that covered his breast. " Don't grieve for
the dead," he admonished, while his fingers with slow
tenderness wound through the strands of her hair and
wandered to the lobes of her ears. The familiar caress
filled her with longing, and he went on more softly and
weak. " No, my daughter. And don't grieve for the living.
Fight for them. Yes, that's the thing." He borrowed
sudden strength from somewhere and jerked himself erect,
while Mary passionately clasped his hand to her bosom as
he shouted: " That's right. Fight, fight, and keep on
fighting until . . ." A dry rattle followed the last word,
and his body relaxed limply in Mary's arms.

Shân quietly led the sobbing woman from the bedroom
and left it to the two men and their dead leader. Len
looked down silently on the white face that had suddenly
become placid, and it danced in the tears he tried to blink
away. Big Jim blew his nose loudly before gently
straightening the cooling limbs and drawing the sheet
completely over the still form. This done, the old man
turned to the window through which the daylight was
struggling to enter and muttered brokenly.

" Poor old Ezra is gone for good. The company have
broked his heart so sure as they have broked the Federashon
and the spirit of our men."

Len looked at him, drawing the back of his hand across
his brow. " Yes, he's gone, dad. He's gone."

Shân took control of the household during the following
week, sleeping there at night so that Mary should never
be alone. Jim made all the arrangements for the funeral,
and Len received the visitors who came from everywhere
with condolences. It had been Ezra's wish that his body
be cremated, and the knowledge that Mary intended being
true to this desire excited the people of Cwmardy, because

it would be the first cremation that had ever taken place there. A further cause for speculation and gossip was provided by the Party announcement, on behalf of Mary, that there were to be no prayers and it was to be a red funeral with the Party in charge. Lord Cwmardy sent a letter which Mary read, then put in the fire. Len never asked what it contained, being too much concerned with her health to be interested in anything else. Her restraint and inner strength amazed him and made his love for her even more all-embracing than hitherto.

The miners kept out of the pit on the day of the funeral and from early morning began gathering about the street where Ezra had lived. Harry Morgan came down from London to speak on behalf of the Party. He brought with him a huge red banner with a gold hammer and sickle emblazoned in its centre. All the Party members in Cwmardy and many from outside turned up with red rosettes pinned on their breasts. Towards the afternoon large numbers of rich-looking cars rolled into the village, each containing top-hatted occupants.

The first intimation that something was happening in the house came when Harry Morgan beckoned six of the Party members inside. The huge crowd swayed forward as the coffin, covered with a red flag, came into sight through the window and was placed on trestles in the middle of the street. The mourners gathered around, Mary standing on the doorstep, with Shân at her side, and her eyes large and black in the dead-white flame of her face. Harry Morgan spoke a few words, which were followed by the rising cadences of the " Red Flag." Six Party members lined up on one side of the shrouded coffin and six old members of the Federation committee on the other. When the signal was given, they bent down simultaneously, and when they rose again Ezra's body rested on their twelve shoulders. The mass of people lined off in front and the mourners followed behind the coffin for the march to the crematorium, eight miles away. Lord Cwmardy walked with Big Jim at the head of the procession.

Len had a hazy memory of what transpired during the slow walk down the valley. He remembered seeing the lined streets and covered windows, but it all seemed like a passing panorama that floated by on a stream of hushed voices.

His faculties returned inside the crematorium chapel as he stood beside Big Jim and saw the coffin placed on the conveyor that led to a hole in the wall.

Harry Morgan went to the pulpit and his usually sharp voice was quiet as he began the people's farewell to Ezra. He pictured Ezra's life as steps in the struggles of Cwmardy, each incident and action irrevocably leading to a certain outcome.

" He weakened at the end," he declared, " but which of us dare say we would not do the same in similar circumstances ? He failed to see the struggle as a river flowing on against ever stronger dams placed there to stem its progress and divert its path. He took our people through many of these dams, but reached one that could only be broken through by a collective leadership, by a revolutionary Party that, knowing the strength of the obstacles, could mobilise the people into a unity powerful enough to overcome all barriers. Our Party did not regard Ezra as an enemy. We loved him for what he had been and what he had done. We grieve for him to-day, but we also glory in the knowledge that the foundations that he laid are safe in the keeping of the Party and the people."

His voice broke and Big Jim suddenly bent to Len, white and staring as he whispered : " Look, Len, look, the coffin is moving."

Len looked and saw the words were true. Every eye in the chapel watched the slowly moving encased body of the miners' leader advance towards the hole in the wall. The movement was eerie and awe-inspiring, and there was deathly silence until, at a signal from Harry, the Party members began singing the Internationale. The red-draped coffin went out of sight as the words :

> " Then away with all your superstitions !
> Servile masses, arise ! Arise ! "

filled the building, and two little doors closed on the hole that took Ezra from the world.

When Len got outside he saw every one gazing up, and, following suit, watched the heavy, ugly-looking black smoke that came through the crematorium chimney and mixed with the air of the valley. He went home alone and found Mary and Shân sitting quietly near the fire. He said nothing to disturb them, and was soon in a reverie himself.

CHAPTER XVI

Local Politics

THE old woman remained that night and the following week in the house.

" Not for the poor gel fach to think she is all alone with only Len, now that her father have gone, God bless him," as she remarked to Jim one night when they were disposing of Mary's domestic future. They tried to get the couple to give up the house and come and live with them, but Mary was adamant against this.

" It isn't because of the sticks and stones here," she said sadly, when they approached her on the matter. " They don't make a home. But the memories bound up in them do. That's why Len and me must stop here, where my father lived and reared me."

The old people grudgingly gave way to her, but Big Jim kept worrying about it.

One Saturday night he returned home from the Boar's Head leading a savage-looking bull terrier. Shân jumped from her stool and looked at the animal with startled eyes.

"Whatever have you got by there, James," she demanded, as Jim took the stool she had vacated and betrayed by his attitude that he was affronted by the welcome accorded his dog.

Len and Mary were sitting on the sofa, but he paid no attention to them when he replied : " What think you it is —a broody hen—that you do ask me so silly a question ? But there," he added resignedly, " whatever I do is always wrong in this house. I am fed up with trying to please everybody. After I give the last four pints I have on me, this is the thanks I get."

Shân softened at once. " Don't take it like that, James. I didn't mean to simple you, and you do know that, but the last time you brought a dog home it did nearly eat us out of house and home, and times is not so good now as they was then by a long way."

" Ho ! Don't worry, my gel, this is a different breed altogether. This 'un," bending to pat its head, " is a house-dog. You know, one of those that will let a packman or policeman, or somethink like that, come in the house, but won't never let them out, not while there is blood in their bodies."

Shân listened interestedly to this explanation, then asked : " But what is the good of stopping a man to go out, James ? I 'ood think what you want is to stop 'em coming in."

Jim turned to Len and Mary, who had not said a word, and the disgust in his look made them smile. " Now what do you think to that ? In't it like a woman all over ? "

" But what do you want a house-dog for, dad," asked Len innocently.

Jim lost his temper and shouted : " It's not for me, mun ; I can look after myself. I buyed this for you and that little gel who have got no father in this world."

The implication hurt Len, and he felt impelled to challenge it. " Don't you think I can take care of Mary, then ? "

Jim snorted, then laughed.. " Ho-ho ! You, indeed. Huh ! I 'ood like to see you in front of half a dozen burglars. Why, a puff of wind 'ood blow you from here to Africa, mun, in less than a minute. No, I can't be with you all the time, but Bonzo by here can—can't you, butty ? " He took the willing dog on his lap.

When Mary and Len left the house for their own that night, the dog accompanied them.

It was months before Mary got over the shock of her father's death, and even afterwards she occasionally ached for his presence. Everything about her conspired to bring back memories of him, and she detested being alone in the house. She accompanied Len as often as possible on his Party activities, and when for some reason she was unable to do this, she found a strange solace in the savage demeanour of Bonzo, who came to understand her every mood.

Shân spent much time with her, although, as she complained one day : " This old hill is getting too much for my poor old legs these days, Mary fach, and I do dread the thought that perhaps I 'on't be able to come here so often before long."

She came up specially on one occasion, bursting with news, and happened to catch Len in the house.

" What do you think ? " she asked, after she had squatted down and recovered her breath. " Your father, Len, have joined a club. You know, those drinking dens where, not satisfied with having beer in the weekdays, when they can get it, they do have it on the Lord's days, which was never made for such a thing."

Len understood his mother's agitation and tried to placate her. " Don't worry, mam. Since the old man must have a pint now and then, he might as well have it in a club as in the Boar's Head."

" Yes, yes," she interrupted impatiently. " He have told me all about that already. But what is worrying my heart out is that he will want to go there on Sundays, and you know the deacons is all eyes, Len."

Mary took up the cudgels on Jim's behalf. " Don't worry too much about them, mother," she exhorted. " Your Jim is as good as all of them, even if he will drink a pint or two on Sundays while they are in chapel."

" I don't agree with you, my gel. James might be so good as them, but he could never be better than old Thomas Jones. There's a Christian man if ever there was one," she piously exclaimed.

Len agreed with her. " That's right, mam. He's a real man that do practise what he do preach. It's men like him I would like to see in our Party."

The conversation was hushed as a rattle sounded at the door and Big Jim entered. Len got up to make way for him near the fire.

" Don't bother, my boy," Jim thanked him, at the same time taking the chair. " I will manage all right."

He stretched his legs towards the grate and pulled out his pipe, puffing at this until it glowed, then said casually : " The old 'ooman have been telling you 'bout the club, I s'pose."

Mary nodded acquiescence and Len added : " Aye, dad. Mam is afraid you will use it to go boozing on Sundays."

Jim drew himself erect in the chair to say with impressive dignity : " If I can't carry beer respectfully on a Sunday like any other day, then it's time for me to peg out. Yes. And let me tell you in front of your mother's face, Len," turning his own to the fire, " that if she do think them bloody deacons—— "

Mary hastily changed the subject. " How are things in the pit, these days, father," she asked.

Jim took the cue immediately and began a recital of woes regarding the pit. " It's more like a muck-hole than any-think else," he declared categorically. " I have worked underground for more than fifty years now—that's right, in't it, Shân fach ? " looking at his spouse, who nodded agreement. " And I have never seened such a shape on it all my born days.

" Colliers, muniferni ! " he paused to spit disgustedly into the fire. " Huh ! Give 'em a shovel and plenty of loose coal and they're all right, but ask them to dress the face and they don't know what you are talking about."

He bent down to relight his pipe, then spoke directly to Len. " It's a shame to see all your old butties who have been reared in the pit now on the streets, while strangers is working their places. Do you know," he added, " that nearly everybody except some of the old-stagers have all signed to be in the industrial union, instead of in the Federashon. There is going to be a hell of a stink about it one of these days, 'specially if they try to make me join it."

Len cocked up his ears at this, but said nothing, as his father rumbled on from subject to subject. After supper he and Mary accompanied the old couple down the hill, Shân declaiming against the bad times all the way ; but Len heard very little of it, his mind being absorbed in the information his father had given.

At the next Party meeting only two matters were dis-cussed : the election of a councillor and the development of the company union. Fred Lewis attended the meeting and took part in the discussion, although it was his first appearance since his last disagreement with the Party.

Len, in the chair, explained the issues involved. The

people in the crowded room listened intently to every word, and it was obvious they regarded the matters as very serious. The Party was a very strong influence in Cwmardy, and any decisions it took had far-reaching consequences both inside and outside the pits, a fact which made the discussion even more important than it would have been otherwise. A new member of the Party was the first to take part in the discussion. He was a small-framed, excitable, and quickly moving man who had originated in Berkshire. When he talked, his words came so quickly that they tumbled over each other, and occasionally he had to pause to re-adjust his false teeth which persisted in dropping.

"What we want," he declared, "is more news in the *Daily Worker* about Cwmardy. We can expose to everybody what is happening in the pit and nobody will know who's responsible. On the top of that, if we had such news, we could duplicate little leaflets to put in every one of them, asking the men in the pit to join our Party." He stopped a moment, then seemed to remember something else he had planned to say, and went on : " I for one would be willing to go to the pit-head to sell the *Daily Worker* if we could get this news in. You used to go there with the old pit paper, didn't you ? " he demanded. " And if you could do it then, I say we can do it now."

Fred Lewis followed, his sallow features and long body commanding attention.

"It's no good talking like Frank Forrest at this stage. Let's get down to fundamentals first. We can never tackle the non-pols. until we build the Federation, and we can't do that until we have a miners' agent. You all know what I think about this, but let's leave it at that for a moment and turn our attention to the election of a councillor. This is the second vacancy since Ezra died, and I think the time is ripe for us to fight the seat again."

This focused the discussion, and after he had finished others took the cue and it was eventually agreed that the Party should contest. Then came the question of candidate. The qualifications and eligibility of each member present was measured, and it was at last moved that Mary be the candidate.

Lewis went white as a sheet and, jumping to his feet,

exclaimed excitedly. " I'm opposed to Mary. We are only making our Party into a laughing-stock by giving our enemies the chance of saying that we are putting Mary forward because she is Ezra's daughter and should be supported because of this. I ask you," he pleaded, at the same time looking round the room, " is the council to be a family affair, such as the Labour councillors have tried to make it, or is it an institution we can use on behalf of the people ? If it's this, then we want a mass leader and a responsible comrade there, not a woman, good as Mary might be in other directions."

When he sat down Len checked the following clamour. " Let's be clear before we go on," he began. " None of us in this room is concerned about Mary as Mary. What we are discussing is our Party and what best we can do in the interest of our people. If this is so, then we must ask ourselves is it good that our people should have a Party woman in the council ? That's the first thing we have got to answer. If we say yes, then we must ask ourselves, does comrade Mary Roberts understand the line of the Party and does she fight for it ? As far as mass-following goes, she has as much influence as any of us."

Will Evans got up next and asked : " If Fred thinks Mary shouldn't be our candidate, who else have he got in mind ? "

The man to whom the question was addressed answered without hesitation : " Although I've got enough to do as it is and I don't want the position, I don't think anybody else can win the seat for the Party."

The colour had come back to his face and his whole attitude was now aggressive. After further discussion, Len put the two names to the meeting and for the second time on an important issue Fred was alone in support of himself. Without waiting for further discussion, he rose and left the room, deaf to Len's entreaties that he stop for the other matters. The meeting went flat after this, and the only other decision taken was in line with Frank Forrest's suggestion regarding leaflets in the *Daily Worker* and the selling of them on the pit-head the following Friday. Will Evans and Forrest were instructed to help Len and Mary get the leaflets out.

Neither of them had done this work before, but Frank

assured them that he'd soon get into the knack. The
Party typewriter and flat duplicator were taken up to
Len's house the next day, and for the remainder of the week
the latter was transformed into an editorial board-room
and a printing shop as they plodded through the initial
drafts of the leaflet. Will's pencil was more often in his
mouth than in his hand, but between them they had the
leaflet ready eventually.

"By the shades of Moses," Will stated with a sigh, "I'm
glad that's over! I 'ood sooner handle a mandril and
shovel than a pen, muniferni."

The task of cutting the stencil fell on Len, who gazed
dubiously at the old rebuilt typewriter, that looked more
like a mortar-mill than anything else. He scratched his
head and sat uncomfortably facing the machine for a while
before getting to work. He used one finger like a hammer,
which fell on the keys at long intervals as he looked for the
letter he had to hit. Mary, in spite of her protests, was
sent to bed long before the stencil was finished.

Dawn was breaking its way into the kitchen by the time,
coatless and hot, they began the last stage of production.
Will Evans separated the sheets of red paper and handed
them to Frank, who put one inside the duplicating frame,
jammed down the cover, which Len rubbed vigorously
with a roller, then shouted: "That'll do. Let's have a
look at it now!"

The three men crowded round the little frame as Frank
carefully raised the lid and pulled out the paper. They all
held their breath while this operation was taking place,
until Will, thinking his mate was too rash, hissed: "Careful there, butty. Steady or you'll be so sure as hell to tear
it."

No one took any notice, and at last the paper was through.
Frank turned it over carefully and for some moments they
stared at the blank sheet as though it were a skeleton.

Will was the first to break the silence: "Holy hell!"
he blurted out. "Us have been printing leaflets for blind
men."

Poor Frank still held the paper in his hand, staring like a
paralysed man at its blank surface.

Len sighed. "Perhaps we had better sit down for a
minute," he suggested.

His advice was taken, Will's glance alternating between the sheet and the duplicator. Suddenly he jumped and picked up the press to rub his finger over its skin.

" Got it ! " he declared dramatically. " Got it ! Frank put the ink on the wrong side. No wonder nothing come through. It's like cutting coal arse backwards."

Len became puzzled. Frank's eyes glinted viciously.

" It can't be that," he said pitifully, " because the comrade who had it showed me how to do it hisself."

" Huh ! " Will grunted. " Perhaps you had your eyes shut when he was showing you."

Frank started to his feet at the insinuation, but Len interrupted : " Come on, boys, or pay-day will be over before we start. Let's try it Will's way."

Will grabbed the roller with the command : " Hand me that tube of ink," and with one squeeze of the tube followed by a flourish of the roller he placed the paper in position. Again the trio watched, anxiously impatient, while the paper was taken away.

Before it was half off, Will looked up to announce triumphantly : " There you are, boys. Plain enough for a bat to read."

He switched the paper away and held it before the others. Their dazed look surprised him, and he slowly turned the sheet around, stared hard at its black, inky wetness for a moment, then exploded in a tirade.

" Hell fire ! Who done that ? " he howled, looking at the other two, as though he had just caught them committing murder.

The incongruity of the situation appealed to Len, and he burst into laughter, the others eventually joining him. The noise woke Mary, and wrapping a cloak over her night-attire she hurried downstairs. She was unable for some time to make head or tail of what they were trying to tell her, but Len at last managed to blurt out the whole story coherently. They cleaned the machine carefully, and, after an examination of the screws and other paraphernalia, Frank discovered what was wrong and they began again.

Mary was preparing breakfast and their hands were all blistered by the time they had printed all the leaflets they had planned, but everyone was happy in the accomplishment. That afternoon, all the available members of the

Party gathered at the colliery offices with bundles of *Daily Workers* under their arms. It was pay-day, and for a time the home-going miners provided a brisk sale until Mr. Hicks stepped out of the office to show he was present. His appearance slackened the sales appreciably, but they went up again when he returned to the office. A few minutes later two policemen hurried up the hill towards the sellers.

" Here they come," Len announced casually to his mates.

" Let 'em come. To hell with 'em ! Because they wear brass buttons, they don't own the bloody world, do they ? " Will replied, raising his voice to shout more loudly : " *Daily Worker*, one penny. Read how the Government is helping the blackshirts."

The two policemen, who were now quite near, stopped to consult each other, all the time watching the sellers from the corners of their eyes. Len kept close to Mary, and whenever she moved, he followed. The police appeared to have made up their minds, and approached him.

" Do you know you are on private property ? " the senior officer asked. The question was entirely unexpected, and Len floundered for a suitable reply. Mary filled the breach with a counter.

" Since when has this public highway been private property ? " she asked.

" It has never been a public highway," came the retort. " From that mark there," pointing back towards Cwmardy and away from the pits, " belongs to the company."

Mary said no more, but beckoning the others, she led them the other side of the mark, where they continued their selling.

The new move had the police guessing, and the sergeant went into the office. When he came back out, he went straight to Mary. " You can't stop here. You're causing an obstruction," he stated abruptly.

Will's jaw dropped for a moment when he heard this ultimatum, then his temper got the better of him and he shouted in disgust : " Well, if this isn't the bloody limit ! Put me back in a muck-hole and bury me. Us can't go on the other road because it's s'posed to be private, and now we can't stop on a public road because we obstruct

it when there is nobody about but ourselves, the sky, and
the smoke. If that's justice, I give in, muniferni."

This annoyed the policeman, who ordered brusquely :
" Come on there, quick now, and none of your bloody cheek
either, Will Evans, or we'll put you inside."

Frank bridled up at this ultimatum to his mate. " Ho !
So that's the game, is it ? " he asked, prancing challengingly
before the two officers, and glaring defiance. Before he
could say any more, the others herded round and
shepherded him away.

The sergeant gave a final shot : " Don't forget we're
booking you all for this."

He was true to his word, and in the middle of the next
week each of them received a summons to attend the
police court, where they were fined £1 each and costs for
wilful obstruction.

Things developed quickly in Cwmardy after this, as the
time for the council election drew near and the Party sent
a number of letters and deputations to Fred Lewis, asking
him to attend the meeting to define his position. He did
not acknowledge any of the letters and was never at home
when the deputations called. Hours were spent discussing
what was to be done about the matter, and just prior to
nomination day it was decided to make a final effort to
get his viewpoint. Len and Mary were deputed to watch
for him and invite him to a meeting of the Party which
would be organised to suit his time and convenience.
They failed to find him for some time, and it was Len who
eventually saw him in Ben the Barber's where he was
waiting for a haircut. Len broached the subject that was
uppermost in his mind, and when Fred met him with a
curt refusal began to coax.

" Good God, mun, you've been in the Party ten years or
more. Don't let all the good work you have done in the
past be wasted just because of this."

The other man scowled. " Don't lecture me. I was
working for the Party when you was toadying around
Ezra."

Len kept his temper. He was older than Fred and cer-
tainly more experienced, but he tried another tack.

" Perhaps that's true, but it's all the more reason why
you shouldn't jib now, just because you don't agree with

our line. More customers entered the shop at this moment, and the discussion was held over until both of them got outside, where, after a long argument, Len finally persuaded him to come to the meeting that night.

The Party meeting began promptly at six, and to avoid any semblance of partiality Len was removed from the chair and John Library took his place. The first thing he did was to ask for the minutes of the meeting where it was agreed that Mary should be the candidate. This was duly read out, after which Fred Lewis spoke.

" I think that decision is wrong and against the interests of the Party. In a personal sense I don't want to be a councillor, but I feel there is no one in the Party better fitted for it than myself. I want to say here, now, that if you insist on that resolution, I shall leave the Party, because I don't believe it is any longer fit to be called a Communist Party."

This statement created a temporary uproar, which the chairman soon quelled before asking a series of questions which he put directly to Fred.

" Why did you join the Party ? "

" Because I believed it was the only Party with the correct policy for the people."

" You know that the policies of the Party are worked out on the basis of a majority vote after exhaustive discussion ? "

" Yes."

" You know majority decisions are binding upon the minority, although the latter have the right of trying to convince the others where they are wrong ? "

" Of course I know that. I've been in the Party ten years."

" Do you think that has been the right method of deciding policy in the past ? "

Fred sensed the trend of the questions and began to hedge. " Yes, but what was good in the past isn't always good for the present."

John was very patient, and his clean-shaven face with its snowy thatch of hair almost beamed as he went on. " Tell us, Fred, where it is wrong to-day and give us a better method of doing our work."

Fred stammered, then coughed and lost his temper.

" Don't cross-examine me. I'm not a kid. I know you
are wrong, although you've all made your minds up
against me. But that doesn't worry me. I'm still a
Communist, which none of you have ever been, and I'll
go to the people and tell them so. And as far as the
election goes, I'm standing as a workers' candidate on real
Communist principles. Good-night." With these words
he straightened himself and walked with as much dignity
as he could muster towards the door. Len caught his hand
as he passed.

" Don't do this, Fred. You know what it means," he
beseeched.

Fred roughly brushed his hand away. " You can take
my resignation from the Party here and now," he declared
as he closed the door with a bang.

The silence that followed made the room seem dead.
Those present looking at each other dumbly, until Mary,
rising to her feet, broke the tension with the determined
declaration : " There can be no resignations from our
Party, and if he does what he threatened, there's nothing
else for us to do but expel him and make it an issue for
the election." This statement led to a further long discussion, which John Library skilfully directed until the
meeting became a committee of ways and means to win
the election.

Over supper that night Mary betrayed the anxiety she
had tried to hide. Len had drawn his chair away from the
table and was bending to light a cigarette when she said
slowly, as though not sure of her words.

" I wonder what makes Fred so bitter about me,
Len ? "

Len looked up sharply. " Huh ! He's only using you
because you happen to be the candidate. He'd do the
same if it was anybody else, and don't make any mistake
about that."

She stopped wiping the plate and asked : " But he put
it in such a way, Len, that he made me think he had a
personal grievance against me." Len smiled. " Aye.
He's got a grievance against the whole Party, because he
can't use it as he wants." He suddenly lost his temper.
" He's a rat and, you watch my words, he'll end up by
being our bitterest enemy." He paused a moment and

again bent down to light the cigarette. When he raised his head he had regained control of himself. " Come, Mary fach. Let's forget him and go to bed. We've got a hectic fortnight before us if we are to win this fight."

Mary hurried her washing up, but they did not go to bed for a long time after this, being too concerned with talking about the campaign, until the dead ashes in the grate reminded them of the late hour.

CHAPTER XVII

A Seat on the Council

For the next fortnight Len and Mary, together with the other members of the Party, devoted all their time to public meetings, leaflets, and the other work connected with an election. This culminated in a mass rally on the eve of the poll. Will Evans and his mates had specially decorated the hall for the occasion, draping the front of the stage with a huge red streamer on which was inscribed :

" Vote for Mary Roberts, Peace and Prosperity."

Long before the time for officially opening, the hall was full of people, who whiled away the time singing songs and hymns until they became impatient and began stamping on the floor and clapping their hands to the refrain : " We want Mary ! We want Mary ! "

The clamour made Mary self-conscious, and when she accompanied Len, Harry Morgan, and John Library on to the platform, she was as white as the silk scarf around her throat. The entry of the quartette was marked by a further burst of singing which drifted from tune to tune until it ended with the " Red Flag."

By the time John Library had risen and opened the meeting, Mary had recovered her composure a little, but still failed to distinguish individuals in the yellow mass that stared at her through the blue haze that filled the air. She was glad of this, because it gave her strength to concentrate. John's voice came to her from miles away, and its music slowly stirred her imagination, making her fuse all the faces into one, that of Ezra, her father. She saw again the dark eyes and strong mouth, and fancied she heard the echo of his voice in John's. By the time she was introduced, the strange thought seized her to speak as though she were arguing with him. She did so, and when she had finished her address the people were on their feet cheering wildly.

Next morning she and Len were up very early, Bonzo gazing curiously at them as though he wondered what they were up to so early in the day. Breakfast was a hurried affair, and it was not long before both of them, trying vainly to look unconcerned, were ready to go down to the school to examine the ballot boxes, prior to the voting taking place. Bonzo eluded Mary's attempt to keep him in, and she looked piteously at Len while the dog sat down contentedly some yards away and waited for them to move. Len looked at him helplessly for some moments, then shrugged his shoulders and turned to Mary with the remark :

" There, you've done it now ! He'll keep us busy all day watching that he don't fight."

" But it wasn't my fault, Len. I thought he was safe on the mat and never expected him to dodge us like that. Try to coax him to you," she added as a bright afterthought. Len bent down and snapped his finger and thumb.

" Come here, boy. Bonzo, good old Bonzo ! " he coaxed, at the same time sidling nearer the dog, who casually kept moving backwards as though he enjoyed the sport. Mary became impatient at last.

" Oh, leave him there. We'll have to put up with whatever happens now, I suppose. Come on or the boxes will be sealed before we get there."

Len disgustedly gave up his efforts to wheedle Bonzo and followed her, at the same time trying to keep an eye on the dog, who now bounded and pranced before them. When they got to the school where the balloting was to take place, they found Will Evans and other Party members already there, the former answering, in reply to their surprised query :

" We wasn't taking any chances and wanted to be here early to make sure there'd be no funny tricks at the start."

" But you've lost a turn to be here, Will," Mary expostulated.

" Turn—bah ! What's a turn in a man's life ? And, anyhow, what's a turn if we win to-day ? Do you know,

Mary, I had a couple of pints last night and when I went to bed I had a funny dream, mun."

Len shuffled uneasily. He had heard some of Will's dreams before, and was now nervous as a consequence. This one, however, proved to be quite innocuous and amounted to the fact that it had given Will an unflinching conviction that they had won the election already. The returning officer, who stood near, smiled grimly at the recital, but said nothing as the little group, satisfied the ballot boxes were empty when sealed, went outside, where they met the first voter coming in. She was an old woman over eighty years of age and had never voted in her life before, but had made her mind up to do so this time— " Because it is the only chance I have ever had in my life to vote for a woman, my gel," as she had told Mary when the latter was canvassing. She waved her hand as she entered the booth and turned her head to shout in her cracked voice : " Don't you worry, Mary fach. You do know where my vote is going, sure enough."

Things were very quiet throughout the morning, but towards the afternoon groups of children came to the parlour which was rented for the day as a committee-room and begged for red tissue paper and copies of Mary's election address with her photo on it. These were readily given, and for the remainder of the day the children paraded the streets singing :

> " Vote, vote, vote for Mary Roberts,
> Drive Fred Lewis out of town."

Fred, on his way to his own committee-rooms, a huge red and yellow rosette adorning his coat, passed them. He went white, although he gave a sickly smile as the children booed him lustily, until another procession of children, coming from the opposite direction, wearing red-and-yellow tissue-paper hats, swooped upon the first lot with wild shouts and a free fight ensued. After this he continued his walk in a better mood.

In the meantime Len was busy before a huge chart he had stuck on the wall of the committee-room. It contained the polling number of every voter in Cwmardy, and opposite every number was either a red, black, or blank square to denote the probable result of the canvassing and whom the number was likely to vote for. A Party member kept running between the polling booth and the committee-room with a paper containing the number of each vote recorded. Len hurriedly checked these on the chart. He found it very difficult work, because large numbers of people hung about the room all the time, anxious to do something to help. On one occasion he got exasperated and shouted to some Party members :

" For heaven's sake get out on the streets, not hang about by here. Can't you see our people are not turning up yet and the time is getting on ? "

Thus stimulated, the people filed from the room and gathered round the polling booth, their bright rosettes giving a splash of colour to the scene. Mary kept walking from house to house, accompanied by Will Evans, and urging the people to vote as soon as they could.

During the late afternoon, after the workmen had left the pits, a steady stream of voters entered the school. After voting the people gathered in groups and discussed the chances of the respective candidates. Jim and Shân came down arm in arm to record their votes, the former urging his wife even when they were at the door of the booth.

" Now 'member, Shân fach, don't make no mistakes. The last, do you hear ? The last name on the ballot paper." This done, the pair strutted out into the street as though they had just been crowned and all the people were there to cheer them.

Jim heard someone remark : " I don't think Mary have got much of a chance. She's a 'ooman, you see, and Fred Lewis is too well known."

The old man turned his head sharply to say : " What you said ? Our Mary have got no chance ? Huh ! She is in already, mun, and everythink is over bar the shouting."

" Don't talk so daft, mun," was the reply he received. " She haven't got a bloody earthly." Jim strode back at once, his hand digging into his pocket.

" Come on then, butty. If you be so sure as that, stand up to your beliefs like a man. I'll bet you five good pounds that our Mary have won by a thousand majority easy, muniferni."

" Right," came the quick retort. " Put your money down."

Jim opened his mouth in a pitiful gape and looked long-ingly at Shân who was again at his side. The people around became silent as they wondered what the old man would do in face of the challenge. Jim sensed the feeling and it helped him to grip himself. Drawing his body arrogantly erect and twisting one side of his moustache, he announced to all and sundry: "Huh! It 'ood be a pity to take the man's money so cheap, and I was never one to take advantage of anybody. No, butty. Keep your money. I don't want to take it from you—not that I couldn't put my hand on five hundred pound this minute if I wanted to, let alone five pounds." He said this with an air of superior contempt that left his challenger dumbfounded, then went on with magnanimous generosity: "But if you do want a little bet, just for the fun of the thing, I will bet you four pints. And if you win call in the Boar's Head or the club, and have 'em on my name."

The amazed man held out his hand helplessly to clinch the bet, and Big Jim, his head high in the air and humming a little tune, went proudly towards the committee-room, at the same time trying to make his rosette larger by spreading its folds. Once out of hearing of the people he bent to tell Shân: "Five pounds, indeed! Huh! He never seed more than five pence in all his life. Trying to take the rise out of Big Jim, see, Shân fach; but I was too old for him. Oh, aye, it will take more than a pup to frighten me with his bark."

He stopped to watch Mary's children supporters pass, cheering them loudly as they sang her praises. But before he reached the committee-room where Len was, Fred Lewis's supporters came along.

Jim scowled at them savagely. " Fitter if their mothers kept them in the house," he grunted to Shân, " instead of letting 'em strut about the place like hooligans. Huh! Come, let us go in from the noise. I don't know what Cwmardy is coming to, between one thing and another."

They entered the room and found Len in his shirt-sleeves swearing under his breath. The old man listened silently for a while, then asked sharply: " What is the language you are using before your father and mother, Len? Haven't you got no respects left, or have you forgot how I reared you? "

Len looked from the chart and a grin spread over his face for a moment, to be replaced by a worried frown. " I'm afraid we're down, dad," he muttered. " Our people are not turning up half so well as the others, and if they don't buck up we'll lose."

" Sit down, mam," he added, hurriedly reaching for a chair. Jim remained standing, a puzzled frown on his forehead.

" Losing ? Losing ? How comes that, my boy ? Good God, us have winned it already, mun ! What are you blabbing about ? "

The words sounded unconvincing and showed that Len's statement had shaken him. He drew his hand across his forehead and repeated : " Losing. Good God ! Four pints." Len began to grasp the significance of the disjointed statements, but said nothing until Mary came in looking worn out, although taut with excitement.

He immediately went into the kitchen and came back with a jug of tea and some sandwiches, which he shared out between her and Shân. While they were eating, he explained the position.

" Unless our boys keep on the doors, Mary, we're down the drain," he declared. A sudden thought struck him, and he turned to his father.

" Look here, dad, fetch all the boys except those in the booth here straight away. Tell them I want them very important." Without the slightest hesitation Jim obeyed.

While he was away, Len frantically jotted down names and addresses on to various strips of paper, and when the Party members came in he gave each of them a slip with the instructions : " These are our votes that haven't come in yet. Get after them and if necessary carry 'em to the booth." His excitement spread to the others, and Will asked.

" How are we standing, Len, by the chart."

Len hastily added up some figures and when he raised his head again there was a desperate look about him.

" Nine hundred and twenty of their votes have come and seven hundred and eighty of ours, and we've only got three hours to go," he declared, at the same time looking at the clock. The sight of it inspired him, and he turned again to the full room.

" Nothing for it but cars, boys. If we've got to carry every bloody vote we'll win this election."

Mary looked up in alarm. " No, no," she said determinedly. " We are not going to chance anything, Len. We've got to play for safety. We don't want the election declared void by the police."

Len glared at her as though he itched to strangle her where she sat. " Playing for safety to hell ! " he howled. " We're fighting to win. Fred Lewis has got cars flying around all day, and is sweeping 'em in from the cemeteries and wherever he can get 'em." He caught Mary's cool glance fixed on him, and calmed down immediately.

" All right, don't get your hair off," he pleaded, then turned again to the Party members. " On the streets, boys. Whip 'em in. We've got three hours and can do it yet if we get down to the job."

He put his own coat on and went out with them. Half an hour later three cars bearing glaring red streamers were racing to the booth, dumping voters there, then racing off for others before the first load had recorded their votes.

As eight o'clock drew near, the atmosphere became more tense and the main street crowded with people, many of whom paid frequent visits to the Boar's Head while they waited. Both Len and Mary had forgotten the chart, realising that everything now depended upon getting to the booth those supporters who had not yet voted.

Sweating freely and at the same time trying to smile at everyone, they scoured the streets of Cwmardy to make sure no possible vote was lost. When eight o'clock came they were both nearly exhausted, but Mary brightened to a startled thought.

" Where's Bonzo ? " she asked. " I haven't seen him since this morning."

Len grunted wearily. " Oh, he's been courting, I expect, or we would have heard him before now."

Mary frowned at him and led the way to the booth, where the people packed around the doorway. A police inspector politely made way for the couple to enter, closing the door tightly behind them. They found the four Party members selected to be present at the count awaiting them, each with a wide smile. Fred Lewis stood talking to the returning officer, his supporters grouped around them, but he came forward to shake hands with Mary.

" May the best man win, but I think I'm there," he stated with an uneasy smile.

Mary merely nodded her head and made no observation as she turned to her comrades, to whom Len was earnestly talking. Before the conversation was over, the returning officer and his clerk announced the procedure, and the supporters went to their places each side of a long table. They were placed alternately, a red rosette next a red and yellow, and so on round the table ; the returning officer and his clerk sat at the end.

The room became silent as the first box was turned upside down and a little avalanche of ballot papers spread over the table.

" Now count them into bundles of fifty," came the command, and immediately eight pairs of hands were buried in the papers and the counting began.

When this was over, there was another momentary silence, then : " Pass them down towards the right and check them as they come."

This was done, each supporter glueing his eyes on his neighbour's hands as the latter checked the number of papers in each bundle. The returning officer then checked the total with a number he had on a bit of paper and found both tallied. All the papers were again strewn over the table and he ordered the counters :

" Place all votes for Roberts in bundles of fifty on your left and votes for Lewis in the same numbers on your right. Pass spoiled votes down to me."

The atmosphere became tense, and Mary, standing on one side near Fred Lewis, felt her mouth go dry. Fred said something, but she failed to comprehend what it was and merely nodded, hoping this would serve instead of words. She saw the little bundles of paper mounting until she thought those on the right were like mountains. A grim little smile began to pucker the corners of her mouth, and, shrugging her shoulders, she began quietly walking about the room while the counting proceeded.

Len's whole being was concentrated on the papers that covered the table. He not only watched those of himself and his immediate neighbour, but let his attention wander all round, never for a moment losing sight of what was happening elsewhere. On one occasion he drew the attention of the returning officer to a bundle at the bottom of the table.

" I think there is a mistake there," he stated. " There's a Lewis on top of that bundle, but all the others are for Mary." He blushed and apologised, " Excuse me, I mean Roberts."

The bundle was investigated and the mistake rectified. The little error made everyone suspicious and more alert.

When the first box had been counted, the officer in charge ordered that the various bundles of fifty for each candidate be sent down to him. This was done and another box emptied, when the whole process was gone through again.

The piles mounted up slowly, but Mary kept her gaze away from them, although it required all her determination to do so. As the count neared the end she caught a glance from Len and hesitantly walked over to him. She saw a piece of paper with a mass of figures on his knee, and bent down to scrutinise them more closely. What she saw made her throat contract and she swallowed noisily, at the same time raising her eyes pitifully to Len and whispering :

" Oh, Len, it can't be true. Over five hundred majority for us ? No, I won't believe it. It can't be true."

Len caught her hand and pressed it silently to his side. " Pull yourself together, Mary, and get ready. He'll be announcing the official figures in a minute."

Even as he spoke a restless tremor ran through the people in the room. The man in charge coughed importantly and the others, with varying degrees of anxiety, watched his mouth. Fred Lewis's face was streaked like a ghost's, and Will Evans, thinking he felt sick, solicitously offered him a peppermint, with the remark : " Buck up, Fred, my lad. Better luck next time. Here, take this. It will help the bile from your belly."

Fred did not even turn his eyes from the returning officer as the latter announced. " I declare Mary Roberts elected as the councillor."

Mary felt the room twist about her, but Len's arm about her waist steadied her.

" What will I tell the people, Len ? " she muttered half
incoherently.

" Thank them for their faith in the Party and tell them
you don't represent any section or group now that you are
a councillor, but that you are at the service of all the people
in Cwmardy," he answered. The others grouped around
her with congratulations, and Will Evans gave her a kiss
that resounded through the room.

Mary felt the room swirl round and her knees melted,
but the arms of her comrades kept her erect as they slowly
escorted her, together with the official, out of the door and
towards the little iron railing that separated the school from
the road.

The clamouring people became suddenly silent as the
returning officer climbed on a pillar and, with a sheet of
paper held imposingly before him, read out the result.
His final words were lost in the roar of cheering that could
no longer be restrained. Big Jim burst through the crowd
and lifted Mary bodily on to the pillar, so that all the
people could see her, while Shân, alternately laughing and
crying, waved her arms about like a marionette.

After a while Mary checked the quiver running through
her body, and, holding up her hand, called for silence.
Then she began speaking, quietly and hesitantly at first,
then more strongly as the situation gripped her. Standing
above the people, her little form with its thatch of gleaming
hair looked twice its usual size as she exhorted them to
use her victory as a weapon to fight against the enemies of
the people and as a warning to traitors.

When she had finished, another prolonged shout shook
the air, and she was swept off the pillar on to the shoulders
waiting to carry her triumphantly up the street to her
home. Hours later the singing and shouting still lingered
over Cwmardy, and it was early morning when the last
echoes buried themselves somewhere in the mountain.

CHAPTER XVIII

The Unemployed

THE election victory and the return of Mary to the council changed completely the domestic conditions in Len's household. He had now to help with the housework so that Mary could attend the various committees and meetings which her new rôle entailed. But he was not sorry for this, because the demands on her time forced her to concentrate on other things than her health, with the result that the latter improved each month that passed. Nevertheless the changed routine in his life occasionally made Len irritable and fretful. He felt Mary's intense preoccupation in council work robbed him of her emotional company to a large extent. On the other hand, he felt she was over-stressing the importance of council work when she insisted on raising the matter in every meeting of the Party. But it was Will Evans who brought this latter matter to a head one night about two years after the seat had been won by the Party.

Mary was demanding a special public meeting at which she could report something that had happened at the previous council meeting, when Will jumped restlessly to his feet and asked :

" Is this a political party or a council clique, or what ? It's just about time we found out exactly what we are. All we hear in every meeting is council this, and council that, and there's no time for discussions on anything else."

Mary had remained on her feet during this outburst, but she saw the little smile that Len gave when he heard this echo of his own thoughts. The sight stiffened her against the challenge.

" I'm glad Will has had the courage to say what's on his mind," she began, " because it's obvious that more than him are thinking the same thing. I agree we mustn't concentrate the Party on one phase of the struggle, but neither must we neglect any phase. And all I've been trying to do is to get you comrades to see the importance of council issues to the people. It's these little things, such as parish, housing, child welfare, and so on, that affect the lives of our people in the quickest and most living way, and it's because of this the council can be made a mobiliser for bigger things and actions." She warmed to her subject as she saw the intentness with which the others followed her words.

"Take the question of unity between ourselves and labour. Where are the leaders of the Labour Party?" she asked; then answered: "In the Federation and the councils, isn't it? They are united with us in the Fed. against the non-pols. and the company, but they are miles away from us in the council. And that's just our problem. We've got to break down their opposition to us politically in one way or another, and I think the council is one way of doing it. If we can get Labour and Communist councillors marching together, on behalf of the unemployed for instance, I'm sure the mass of people would follow."

She kept on for some time and when she finished, three or four jumped to their feet together, each anxious to be first in the discussion that followed. Before the meeting finished, a better understanding prevailed and a clear plan of action was worked out.

During the afternoon of the next signing day at the exchange Len walked into the back kitchen with a weary droop to his shoulders. He pulled off his coat and placed it behind the chair before sitting down. There was a hopelessness in his actions that saddened Mary. She knew how keenly he felt the fact that since their marriage he had been unemployed most of the time and life had been a continual battle to maintain existence on insufficient means. She went to him and her hand dropped on his shoulder.

He buried his face in his hands and moaned: "Don't, Mary dear. You make things harder with your patience and courage, when your whole body yearns for things to prevent it wasting as it is."

She did not answer, but ran her fingers through his hair as he fixed his gloomy eyes on the fire. They remained in this posture for many minutes, until presently he took his unemployment pay from his pocket and handed it to her, with a gesture that seemed to ask for forgiveness and brought a sob to her throat.

" Oh, Len," she pleaded, " why do you worry so much about me ? Don't you realise if things were different, if we were not so poor as the rest of our people, we would not be together."

He started at her words, then answered slowly : " But Mary comrade, why need our people suffer this poverty when there is so much being destroyed and wasted in the world ? "

" Len, Len," she reproved him, " you are a Communist and should know all about the struggle and what it means." She sighed, then continued : " Dad always said you were more emotional than intellectual, more moody than rational."

This stung him to retort : " That may be, but it is only because I am made of flesh and blood, not stone."

She wormed her way to his lap and sat down, drawing his head to her bosom and soothing him with endearments. " There, comrade, have your bang out. You'll be better after."

She nursed him like a baby for a while before saying : " Think of the thousands in Cwmardy who are worse off than us. Then think of what they must do to save themselves from the ruin other people are making."

Her tones became softer as she let her mind roam through the realms of her political convictions. " Yes, as dad used to say, we must see things as they are in order to make them what we want them to be. Our poverty and misery is the expression of our class condition, but it is also the foundation of the unity that will sooner or later destroy both."

The confidence in her statements shook him, and placing his arms about her frail body, he pressed it to his and kissed her, before rising from the chair, still holding her in his arms. " You are right, Mary. We must not grieve over our condition, but fight against it. That is the way and that is what the Party is for. Forgive me, comrade, for being so childish. I couldn't help it for a moment when I came in and saw the suffering in your face, but you have given me sense again and I can see more clearly now."

He brushed a sleeve across his mouth and told her of the cuts in benefit that had been made in the unemployment exchange that day. "The people are in a ferment," he declared, " but no one seems to know what to do. It's all come so sudden that even the Party is not prepared."

Mary released herself from his arms and began to pace the kitchen, muttering to herself : " But some one *must* know what to do, our Party must *find* a way for the people." She stopped her pacing and faced him. " Len, we must call a Party meeting at once. You go round the comrades, now, while I make dinner ; then we can discuss the whole business."

The room in the library where the Party held its meetings was packed to suffocation, even people who did not belong to the Party thronging the corridors to hear what was going on and to take part in the discussion. Len, as chairman, opened the meeting with a brief explanation of what was happening on the exchange.

" Our people don't know where to turn to make ends meet, with the sudden and vicious cuts that have been made in their benefit," he declared ; " and as a Communist Party we have the duty of organising and leading them against it."

A shrill shout from the corridor floated into the room : " That's right. Tell us what to do and how to do it, and all of us will be behind you."

The people applauded this statement, which was followed by another from a middle-aged man. " That's right, fellow workers. I haven't been home with my dole yet. I have been cut ten shillings and am ashamed to take it to the old 'ooman. What can I tell her," he wailed, " when she'll ask me what's to be done ? "

This focused the problem for the people present and a loud hubbub of excited argument developed and held up the proceedings for some time before Len could obtain order and throw the meeting open for discussion.

Mary was the first on her feet asking for the floor. She wanted to direct the ideas and opinions of those present in a concrete way, so that the discussion could be positive from the beginning. Her quiet voice failed to carry beyond those in the immediate vicinity for some time, but as it rose higher and stronger it spread its resonance over the room and brought silence that enabled everyone to hear when she said :

" The problem is, what is to be done ? Our Party has the task to-day of solving this, and the first need is unity . . . whatever we do must be done together. We have called some of our leaders many things in the past and they are now full of bitterness, but this must be buried in face of this new attack so that we can go forward with them against those responsible for these cuts. I believe we can get the Labour councillors to come with us in this."

The applause prevented her continuing for some time, the women present clapping vigorously and stamping their feet on the wooden floor until the air in the room rumbled like thunder. Mary waited until the noise died down, then went on somewhat nervously. " But the first thing is to get all our unemployed together, so that we can find out how many have been cut and by how much. We must then take this to the combine committee so that we can bring the men in work on our side, then we should leave ourselves under the leadership of the combine and ask them to call all the people, with their M.Ps. and councillors, together next Sunday when we can decide what to do next."

Mary sat down and her beating heart made her deaf to the tumult that followed her words. Men and women clamoured to be allowed to speak in support, but Len wisely asked only those to speak who had different points of view. There were none, so he called for order to put the proposition to the vote and it was carried by a show of waving hands. Someone struck up the " Internationale," and the meeting closed with the last of its stirring words.

The road outside the library was alive with excited people, waiting for someone who would give a practical lead. Len got on the balcony, Will Evans and Frank Forrest either side of him, and shouted at the top of his voice.

" There will be a mass meeting of all unemployed men and women on the tip to-night." The announcement spread in wider circles till all were aware of it.

Without invitation and as a matter of ordinary practice the Party members accompanied Len to his home, where Mary immediately busied herself making tea for them all, putting hot water on the already used leaves in the teapot and pouring out the anæmic fluid without apology. Will Evans paused in his sipping to remark : " I think we ought to have a leaflet out straightaway ; this will force the combine to move."

Frank Forrest put his cup on the table, pressed his thumb against his loose artificial teeth to keep them fixed, and replied : " That's not the way to work. If there is to be a leaflet, the combine itself should have one out officially. We have comrades on the committee and it's their job to see to this."

" Aye," retorted another, " if we start monkeying about now, we'll drive the Labour people further away from us instead of bringing them nearer, as we must do if this fight is to go on."

Mary, sitting on the stool near Len, asked : " What about our meeting to-night. I believe there'll be thousands there, and it's from there the drive will have to be made. The best way of building unity is not by being content to talk about it and condemning those who don't come our way, but by getting the masses into motion. This will force the others to follow, or force them right out of the movement."

A wisp of smoke curled out from the chimney and, catching her throat, caused her to cough. The others remained respectfully silent till the spasm passed, Len patting her back the while. Then Will stated :

" I think Mary is right, but who's going to speak in the meeting and put our line forward ? "

" Why not yourself ? " came the immediate response from many quarters.

Will stared at each of them in turn before saying pitifully :

" Me ? Good God ! No, I can't speak, mun, and those who said I should, are talking all balls." He blushed suddenly and turning to Mary in the silence that followed his last words said hesitantly : " 'Scuse me, Mary, I forgot about you."

Len laughed and this eased the momentary tension. After this little interlude the discussion became heated until it was finally agreed that Will should take the chair and Len do the speaking, with Mary in reserve.

Will Evans remained after the others had left, to get a few tips on what to say. He appeared excessively nervous, and this was all the more noticeable because it was in such contrast to his usual devil-may-care demeanour.

Mary chided him. " What's the matter, Will ? You've chaired concerts in the Boar's Head—in fact, all your butties say you are a star turn—and here you are like a little baby with the belly-ache, because you have to chair a meeting."

" Aye, it's all right for you and the others to talk, Mary, because you haven't got to bloody do it, see. It's one thing talking to your own butties in a pub, but it's another talking to hundreds you don't know."

Len began saying something, but before the first word left his mouth Will turned on him. " Don't you say anything, Len. I remember the time when you was like a bloody kid because you had to speak."

" Oh, well," Len replied to the challenge, " it's no good arguing now ; the Party has decided, and that's an end to it."

Will glared at him as though he wanted to strangle him, but he said no more, and shortly after the three went to the meeting-place, calling in at the Boar's Head on the way to borrow a box for use as a platform.

The rubbish dump was already dense with people when the trio arrived, and there was a loud hum of excited conversation in the air. Will took the box directly to the centre of the throng, then waited hesitantly.

All the time the Party members were urging him to open the meeting, he was swallowing awkwardly, until the impatience of the crowd, acting as a stimulant, drove him in desperation on to the box, where he stood for some moments looking wildly about him before saying : " You all know what the meeting is about and I now call on comrade Len Roberts to address you."

He abruptly stepped off the box, his face steaming with perspiration, to make room for Len, who got into the heart of the subject without any preamble. The added height of the impromptu platform enabled him to see many of the councillors and members of the combine committee who were present, a fact which encouraged him to say : " There is only one body that can lead this fight successfully, and that is the combine. We must follow it loyally when it gives us its lead." He then continued with a recital of the things the combine should do immediately, chief among them being the calling of an official meeting of all men and women the following Sunday. The people present, when asked if they agreed with this, made no mistake about their consent.

That night Harry Morgan called a Party meeting, where the whole plan was discussed and decided down to the smallest detail, with the result that in the Sunday meeting called by the combine everything went smoothly, in spite of the fact that Fred Lewis refused to attend on the plea that the whole project was a Bolshevik manœuvre.

During the remainder of the week Mary and Len spent most of their time outdoors advertising with chalk, poster, and bell the mass demonstration that had been decided upon. Party members and committee men from the combine joined forces with Labour councillors to distribute leaflets round all the houses. Long before the time for the demonstration arrived everyone in the valley knew about it.

After supper the night before the protest march, Mary lay back in her chair and closed her eyes. Len saw the twitching of her cheeks, which he thought had become even thinner since the beginning of the week.

" What is the matter, my dear ? " he asked somewhat sadly.

She looked up and smiled at him, but the drooping lips still kept her teeth hidden, and he knew the effort was forced even as she said : " Nothing, Len, nothing. I am just a little tired."

He refused to be hoodwinked in this manner and rising from his chair went to her, taking her slim hand into both his own and bending down to bury his mouth in her hair. " Why try to hide things like this, Mary, when you know that your every mood affects me like an electric current ? " The mumbled words came clear to her through the strands of hair that tried to strangle them, and she shook her head slowly as though afraid to reply.

Len waited a while, then finding she made no further attempt to reply, he continued : " I know how hard you have worked this week for the demonstration and how

your chest is troubling you because of this, so why do you
keep so aloof when I ask you something ? You seem
sometimes to be miles away from me, and it is always when
I want to be closest to you, Mary. You are a comrade
and my wife, and there must be something very deep
between you and me, so deep that you are afraid to cross
it."

She caught his head and drew it level with her eyes, which,
dilated, stared into his with an intensity that robbed them
of vision. The hand on her breast involuntarily withdrew
itself when she said in a deep whisper : " Len, there is so
much for you to do in the movement and I am afraid."

He jerked his head away from the grip of her eyes.
" Afraid ? " he queried, as though not sure the word had
been used. " Afraid of what ? "

Before answering, she rose from her chair and went to
the settee, drawing him with her, and the two, half-sitting,
half-lying, faced each other.

" You love me, Len." The words were at once a statement of fact and a query, to which he nodded a humble
acquiescence like a boy caught pilfering. " Yes," she went
on, " and that is the danger."

Again something in her words and tone alarmed him,
and he stiffened his limbs although making no reply.

" You see," she went on, " if I let you see the world and
the struggle as something centred in myself, what will
happen to you if you were to lose me ? "

He jumped to his feet like a startled hare, and the whiteness of his face emphasised the blue veins in his forehead
and the pouches under his eyes.

" Lose you ? " he gasped incredulously. " Lose you ?
What on earth do you mean ? " An idea gripped him
even as he asked the question and he hurried on without a
pause. " You are in love with someone else." He flung
himself back on the settee heedless of where he fell, and
catching her roughly by the shoulders let his eyes bore
deeply into hers. What he saw there made him blink and
when he spoke again his voice, though quiet, was infinitely
sadder.

" Don't be afraid to tell me, comrade. I know I am
not the only man in the world, and that most men can give
you much better than I ever can." A lump rose to his

throat at the thought, but he forced himself to say what his whole being was fighting against. "Yes, my dear. Men and comrades who can give you all the things you have been used to with your father, and the comforts which your poor little body calls for." His head drooped and he felt a tear trickle down his cheek as he said : "Forgive me, Mary my dear. It is all my fault. I have been selfish and unkind. I have exploited your patience and your energy. It is only right that I should pay the price before it is too late."

He rose and stumbled to the fireplace, leaning against the mantelshelf and looking into the fire with eyes that were now dry as the cinders in the grate. Mary did not move after his outburst, but she watched his every motion while the tip of her tongue played about her lips, wetting them for the words bubbling there.

"So that's the sort of man you are ! So those are the ideas you've been nursing in your heart ! " She shot the statements at him with the momentum of bullets that twisted him half round to face the full blast of what was to follow. "You coward ! To believe such things for one moment and keep them to yourself, while all the time you were talking to me of love, pretending to be so kind and open when the other comrades were here and in the Party meetings."

The blood rushed to his head in waves, changing the white of his face to a flushing red. He made a mute appeal for silence, but she paid no heed to it and went on with increasing vehemence.

"You call yourself a comrade . . . and I believed you ! " Something clutched her throat like a talon, changing her words into hacking coughs.

Len sprang to her side and began rubbing her chest with his hand until she had recovered. Then he stood aside again and bent his head to wait for her further attack.

His action and his posture after the seizure melted the ice in her heart, and a tiny smile crinkled the corner of her lips when she realised how deeply she was misinterpreting his motives. "Let's forget what both of us have said," she pleaded softly, "and get back to what began it all." He nodded gladly and she continued. "What I was trying to say was that if we love each other to the exclusion of everything else, even while we are working for the Party, then something would be bound to suffer if one of us lost the other."

He followed the soft reasoning for some moments without appearing to understand its meaning, then it burst upon him like a flash what she was driving at. " You have been to a doctor ? " he demanded. " Come on. Tell me what he said."

She curbed his impetuosity with a glance. " Yes. I have seen Dr. Barnard, the specialist, and he says if I won't go to a sanatorium very shortly, I'll be in the cemetery inside two years." She tried to make the statement casual, but failed hopelessly, and the last words were moist with sobs, which acted on Len like petrol on a flame.

" Don't believe him," he shouted defensively. " Doctors pretend they know things when actually they don't understand more than you or me what is wrong."

" Hush, Len. You know better than that, and it is no good trying to run away from facts. For years both of us have been trying to hide what I showed you years ago in Blackpool."

Len bent his head and remained silent for a long while. At last he looked up and spoke to her in the deep musical tones that always came to him in a particular mood.

" My love, what can we do ? If you were penned up in a home, away from the workers, out of the struggle, you would die as quickly and surely as though you were poisoned. Your life does not exist only in your body, but in what your body and brains do for the struggle in which your father reared you." He broke down for some minutes and buried his wet face on her shoulder, eventually raising it to continue, without looking at her. " If I thought there was the least hope you would be cured or even get a little better by going to the sanatorium, I would gladly tell you to go. You believe that, don't you, comrade ? " he asked pleadingly.

She answered with a nod, knowing he was putting her own ideas into words without being aware of it himself.

The confirmation excited him and he spoke more hurriedly. " Yes, yes. What we must do is to plan your work in a better way. So much rest, a little activity, only the most important council committees, choose your food, then watch your weight. Aye, that's the thing. Weight is now life to you. We musn't let you lose an ounce one day without making it up the next." He laughed to hide his desperation, and she smiled in company. " If we maintain your weight we can't go wrong. And to do that I will pour my strength, this exuberant energy of mine, into you."

It was her turn to laugh now, as she ran her hand over his frame, but the spirit behind his remarks heartened her, even though she knew it would be eventually a losing fight.

" Come," she said, " let's leave the matter there and clean the supper things." They both rose, and he wiped the dishes as she washed, both working with happy smiles.

Later that night before she dropped to sleep he took her in his arms and, working her mouth open with his lips, he kissed her with an intake of breath that emptied her lungs and left her gasping, while he fought savagely to take the disease from her body into his own. The vigour of his continued caresses warned her of his intention, and she violently turned from his lips. He had extinguished the candle and failed to see the happy glow on her face as she bade him good-night.

Early next morning both woke like a pair of children and he passed joking comments as he watched her dressing. " We'll soon have to buy a corset for you," he twitted when he saw her small body exposed by the intimacy of her underclothes.

" What on earth for ? " she asked in feigned surprise, drawing another garment over her head.

" Oh, to stop your belly bulging out," he answered, at the same time breaking into a chuckling laugh, which she joined happily.

But he immediately became serious when she began pulling strong elastic garters over her stockings. " Huh ! Those have got to come off," he declared categorically.

" What have got to come off ? " she asked innocently. " My stockings ? "

He glared a moment, letting his naked legs dangle over the side of the bed before saying, in a dignified manner that reminded her of Big Jim : " Of course not. Do you want to catch your death of cold ? I mean those garters."

Mary was in a happily wicked mood. " If I do that my

stockings will come down, and I may as well go without any as let that happen, Len."

He swallowed noisily and came off the bed towards her, at the same time asking in what he intended to be a superior manner, although he would have died rather than go into a draper's shop : " Have you never heard of suspenders ? " Then he entered into an exposition of the harmful effects of garters, that act as ligatures and prevent the blood flowing freely. Mary laughed inwardly at him, but every simple word stamped into her the impress of the love behind it. When he had finished, she flung him a caress with her eyes and later in the day made herself a pair of suspenders.

CHAPTER XIX

Cwmardy Marches

DURING the week Mary had been busy among the women in the street, all of whom had pledged themselves to come to the demonstration. She had been particularly anxious about this, as she believed that each street should come into a demonstration as a contingent with its own banner, and not in the usual straggling individual manner. So, immediately after dinner, when Len had gone down to fetch his father and mother, who were to start from the same street as themselves, she went from house to house getting the women ready. In every home she was welcomed either with a smile or a joking remark, the little children, many of them with bare backsides, running to the door to greet her.

Half an hour before the demonstration was timed to start the women and children and the unemployed men in the street were lined up with a red banner at their head with :

" Sunny Bank Women want Bread not Batons "
sewn in white tape. Mary forgot her chest and the conversation with Len on the previous night as she looked behind her at the ranks of men and women who were ready to march. Each pair of eyes gleamed as brightly as her own and every mouth wore a smile, even the little babies', clutched tightly to their mothers' bodies in heavy woollen shawls. One of the Party members from the next street came up with a clarionette and two kettle-drums. The ex-servicemen present soon selected two drummers, and in a very short time the air was ringing with the strains of popular songs. The sharp notes of the clarionette kept everyone in tune and the tremor of the drums made feet itch to get into stride. Occasionally the clarionette gave a shrill scream as though its innards were twisted, but no one took any notice of this and kept on singing with unflinching gusto.

At last the music was interrupted by a cheer as Len and his parents came round the corner of the street. Big Jim, failing to walk erect, pretended he was doing so by stretching his head unnaturally far back and twirling his moustache arrogantly. But, not noticing where he was going, he stumbled against a stone in the roadway and would have fallen had not Shân gripped him tightly.

" Holy hell ! " he growled under his breath, while at the same time trying to regain his dignified posture. " These bloody roads are not fit for a dog to walk on, muniferni. It is time that the council do something about it."

No one heard his words in the excited clamour as the people prepared for the march off. Jim and Shân were given the place of honour in the front rank because they were amongst the oldest inhabitants of Cwmardy. Len and Mary stood either side of the procession to marshal it. The men with the clarionette and drums waited for the signal, every one held their breath for a moment, then three rolls on the drums, the clarionette blared into action, and the people began their march to the main demonstration. At each street-corner numbers of people saw friends already in the ranks and tried to break in to join them, only to be firmly told that they must go behind as the ranks were not to be broken. Whenever anyone was persistent, the women became vociferous and let the delinquent know, if he was not prepared to go to the rear of his own volition, he would be placed there. Shân and Big Jim, right at the head of the demonstration, with the blood-red banner streaming directly behind them, walked silent and erect, like soldiers, Jim jealously watching every stride she made to make sure she was in step. She stumbled once and, not knowing how, was unable to change her step to answer the music before Jim saw her.

" Change," he hissed, without turning his head. " Change, venw, for God's sake. You are a disgrace to the regiment, mun."

Shân felt deeply the indignity of her position. " I can't, James bach, I don't know how," she moaned quietly so that no one but he could hear.

" Iff arn daen, do scotch with both feet at once," he instructed. She misunderstood him and gave a little hop which only took her slightly in front without bringing her into step. Jim's eyes went blood-shot as he glared at her.

" Fall out," he ordered. " Fall out quick to the rear before anybody know you are with me."

Shân squared her drooping shoulders and planted her feet more firmly into the earth with each stride.

" Never," she declared emphatically, not caring now who heard her. " No, not for all the sodgers or sailors in the King's or anybody else's army will Shân fall out. Huh ! "

Len happened to come to the front of the procession at this moment and one glance at his parents told him what was brewing. He blew a whistle sharply, the impromptu band stopped playing and the people came to a halt.

" Just a whiff for the stragglers to draw up, so that we can march into the square in order," Len shouted, at the same time trying to convey with a glance a message to Mary on the other side. She unostentatiously made her way to him and he whispered in her ear. When the signal was given for the restart, Mary was marching between the old couple.

Sunny Bank contingent was the first at the starting point on the square on top of the hill near the pits, but in a very short time hundreds more had gathered and before the pit-hooter blaringly announced that the men were about to come up, the square was packed with men and women. Red banners and streamers speckled the air as the mournful strains of the drum and fife band floated up the hill. Miners in their working clothes and with coal-soiled faces joined the unemployed people, for the march round the valley.

The air was blasted by a roar like thunder when the gallant little group of bandsmen, puffing and blowing, staggered over the crest of the hill and came into sight. Their thirst was quickly quenched by the women, who ran into nearby houses and fetched out jugs of tea, water, and small beer, or whatever other liquid they could get. The lodge officials, some in working kit, now formed up in front with Len and Mary. Jim and Shân fell in the rank immediately behind, their temporary difference forgotten. The people of Sunny Bank made sure their banner was next to the one

belonging to the combine committee, this being the only
one to which they would grant precedence.

The signal was now given to the band leader, the drums
rolled, the fifes began to wail, and the long demonstration
against the cuts inflicted on the unemployed began its
march around the valley.

At the bottom of the hill, before turning into the
square which led to the rubbish dump where the other pit
contingents of the combine were waiting, Len looked back.
His eyes glowed with what he saw. The street behind him
looked like a flowing river of human beings, on which
floated innumerable scarlet banners and flags. He looked
far into the ascending distance, but failed to see any end.
His eyes began to water with the strain and he allowed his
ears to continue where the former failed. Although directly
in front of the band, he heard running beneath its thrumming
wails the deep monotone of countless boots tramping
rhythmically on the hard road. The potential power in the
sound tickled his throat, sending saliva into his mouth. He
had to gulp before he could say in an excited whisper to
Mary :

" It's the greatest thing that's ever been. Everybody
is on the march. Everybody." His emotion became too
deep to allow for more.

Mary, pride in her every gesture, murmured : " This is
the cure, Len, for me and the people. Unity. Unity in
action." Her voice rose into a shout on this last phrase,
and in a moment it was taken up by some young people
until it spread all through the ranks like thunder.

" Unity. Unity in action." The sound of the marching
feet was drowned in its tremor.

Mary turned to look at Shân and Jim. The old couple
were tight-lipped and silent, but they beamed with
happiness, although in Jim's eyes there was also a look of
dignity and discomfiture, as though his pride was beating
back something he badly wanted to do.

Mary sensed the situation and whispered to Len, who
immediately stepped back to his father's side and said :
" There's a urinal lower down, dad. You had better drop
out by there and join us on the field."

Jim kept his eyes fixed on the man in front of him and
screwed his mouth up to say : " What in hell think you I

am, Len ?   Do you think I can't carry three pints without
falling out ?   Huh !   I have drunked twenty-three before
now and marched eighteen miles afterwards without ever
thinking of losing a drop, muniferni."

Len felt abashed at this retort, particularly when he
glimpsed the proud smile on his mother's grim face, and he
hastily stepped forward to his own place, where Mary
glanced at him inquiringly.   He shook his head as an
answer to her unspoken query.

By this time the head of the demonstration had reached
the square, which was dense with people cordoned off to
make way for the demonstration to pass through to the
assembling field.   Uniformed ambulance men, lining each
side of the street, took their places alongside the marching
men and women, and in this manner for over half an hour
the people of Cwmardy poured through the square which was
their ancient battle-ground, into the field where most of
their vital decisions had been taken.

A short rest was taken there, while the various bands
competed for the loudest playing.   The valiant little fife
band was lost in the din of different marches blared with
brassy resonance into the air, which shook in the martial
strains.   The various committees now took charge of their
own contingents and began marshalling them up, after
Mary had had a conversation with the leaders, who agreed
that the women should head the march from the field.
There was some initial confusion while the people were
being sorted out, some women preferring to march with their
menfolk, but eventually everything, as far as possible,
was in order and ready for the next stage.   The bands,
each with its own vivid and distinctive uniform, were
scattered at regular intervals through the length of the
demonstration, adding to its vivacity and colour.   A bugle
sounded, drums rolled once more, the bands took up the refrain, and the procession began to unwind itself from the field.

The leaders of the combine committee marched in front
of the leading band, which was followed by the women,
but Shân and Big Jim still remained in the second rank,
having with adamant curtness refused to be parted or
shifted.   The procession marched twelve abreast through
the main street, most of whose shop windows still wore
shutters as mementos of past battles.

When the front of the demonstration was two miles
advanced, and on the summit of the hill to the east of
Cwmardy, people were still pouring from the assembling
field. Len lifted his head sharply into the air when he
fancied he heard the distant strains of music in the direction
left of the demonstration. He turned to Mary and the
workman next her.

" Can you hear anything ? " he asked.

They both looked simultaneously past Len, and he,
seeing their amazement, turned his head to look in the same
direction. He drew his breath sharply and his perspiring
face went a shade whiter. The mountain which separated
Cwmardy from the other valleys looked like a gigantic ant-
hill, covered with a mass of black, waving bodies.

" Good God," the man next to Mary whispered " the
whole world is on the move."

Mary did not reply for some time, unable to take her
eyes from the scene, although her feet kept automatically
moving her forward in time with the band. Then she
murmured, " No, not yet. But the people are beginning
to move it now." She said no more, and even the bands
were quiet. The people seemed overwhelmed with the
mighty demonstration of their own power, which they
could now see so clearly. Their voices suddenly became
puny, and articulation was left to their feet, which rattled
and sang on the roadways with music more devastating in
its strength than all the bands in the world.

Len momentarily felt himself like a weak straw drifting
in and out with the surge of bodies. Then something
powerful swept through his being as the mass soaked its
strength into him, and he realised that the strength of
them all was the measure of his own, that his existence and
power as an individual was buried in that of the mass now
pregnant with motion behind him. The momentous
thought made him inhale deeply and his chest expanded,
throwing his head erect and his shoulders square to the
breeze that blew the banners into red rippling slogans of
defiance and action. Time and distance were obliterated
by the cavalcade of people, whose feet made the roads
invisible.

The head of the demonstration now began to descend
the other side of the hill which led to the road leading back

to Cwmardy. As it passed Fred Lewis's villa, he ran out, hastily pulling his coat on as he ran.

" Hallo," he greeted them, waving his arm the while in a gesture of welcome, although his shaven face looked even sallower than usual under its dark skin. " All the people in the two valleys seem to have turned out to-day."

No one answered him and the band struck up another vigorous march. He tried to sidle his way into the front ranks, but was silently elbowed from one to the other until he found himself helpless on the side, dumb and open-mouthed in face of the flood that swept past him. At last someone took pity and allowed him to join in the ranks, where he was immediately lost to sight like something ephemeral that had come and vanished instantly.

Len's heart was now pounding madly as the significance of the incident gripped his imagination, and he turned again to Mary, who sensed his mood immediately.

" Like a moth around our bedroom candle," he told her softly, clasping her hand in his. " It comes and fusses about the flame, concentrating attention upon itself while it is buzzing around, then a little puff and it's gone again. Devoured by the very thing that drew it and gave it momentary prominence."

" Yes, Len. The people are like that flame. They give life, security, fame, and power to some. But they always give it on loan. And always, sooner or later, they collect the debt ; and the day they do that is the day that welshers disappear. Like a star falling in the sky, it comes out of nothing and for an instant the whole world that can see looks up to its radiance, and watches it fade and die, to be swallowed by the very void by which it came."

They both became silent again, while the men either side looked at them queerly, probably wondering if the demonstration had suddenly affected their minds.

" That is how the Party came," she mused to herself, although Len, hyper-sensitive where she was concerned, heard her muttered thoughts. " But the Party can never melt," she continued, unconscious of Len's interested attention. " It is moulded in and welded with the body itself, so that only the weakest and rottenest parts of it can ever drop off and be discarded."

She was suddenly attracted by a big building some

hundreds of yards in front, and she more or less subconsciously recognised the old mansion that housed the officers and staff of the new unemployment board operating the cuts. Little figures on the veranda scuttled out of sight as the procession came into view. The action gave her an idea and turning sharply she tried to spring past Len without disturbing the marching step of the demonstration. He heard a sound like something tearing beneath her skirt and his eyes opened wide with a quick-born suspicion of what had happened, but before he had time to question, she was past him and hastily whispering something to the foremost ranks of women, all of whom, he noticed, nodded their heads in agreement. When she returned to her place by his side, he was so curious that the incident of Fred Lewis completely slipped his mind. He noticed the determined twist that had come on her mouth and was too impatient to wait.

" What's in the wind, now ? " he asked.

She looked at him and the other men slyly, then replied loud enough for them all to hear : " The women are going in to see the chief unemployment officer."

The men stood stock-still for a moment, amazed at the casualness of the statement and the implications involved in it. But they were soon forced forward and had to argue their opposition to the project while they were marching.

" You can't do that," said one. " The committee never decided it."

" No," said the other. " This is a demonstration against the Government and I'm not one who is prepared for any hanky-panky bloody tricks. Everything has gone all right up to now, and we don't want you women kicking up a shindy for nothing."

Mary changed colour and Len started to defend her when she said determinedly : " I agree with you. But the Government isn't only a number of people in London. Government is of no use and can't act unless it has agents and officers and staff in every village of the country."

" That's it," Len implemented, unable to restrain himself any longer. " Isn't Parker, the new unemployment bloke, an agent of the Government carrying out Government orders ? Of course he is," he answered himself. " An Act of Parliament on a bit of paper with a king's seal stuck on it in London is of no more value than the paper itself and a spot of red wax. It is only when what it says is acted upon in Cwmardy and all the other places in the country, by people who are paid to operate it, it is only then that an Act of Parliament is of use to the Government. I think Mary is right," he concluded. "The Government in London don't make us suffer in London. No. It's here they make us suffer, and it's here we've got to fight them and the suffering they inflict on our people."

Before the other men had time to reply to this argument they were outside the offices. Mary and Len silently stepped on one side and let the band proceed, unaware of what was being discussed. The other men in front went with them, but the leading rank of women had stopped, their action followed in turn by every rank that closed up. The motion worked quietly back through the demonstration like a slow ripple receding to the rim of a pond. Police, white-faced and trembling, seemed to spring from nowhere, and their chief came hurrying towards Len and the others in the front.

"You can't stop here, Len," he declared. "Permission was only given for the march and the meetings in the field."

The air immediately became filled with excited clamour which drew the police together into a more solid phalanx between the demonstration and the building. Big Jim worked his way to Mary's side, followed closely by Shân, who kept her eyes on Len.

"We don't intend harming anyone," the latter told the inspector. "All we want is to send a deputation in to see Mr. Parker about these cuts."

The inspector hesitated, but only for a moment as the pressure behind began to force the front in. "Wait a moment," he asked nervously. "I'll inquire if a deputation will be received." He returned in a matter of seconds. "I'm very sorry, but Mr. Parker can only see deputations by appointment."

"That's not for him to decide," said Mary.

She looked behind her and sighed before turning again to the inspector.

"There are women in this demonstration who have carried babies more than ten miles already," she said. "And I don't believe they are willing to do that for nothing.

If you don't believe me, ask them," she invited, secure in her faith that the women would stand and that the men would stand with them.

The inspector looked at the mass of people, who stretched beyond reach of sight, and very wisely did not accept the invitation. Instead he shook his head resignedly, then warned her : " You will be held responsible for all that happens here to-day."

Big Jim, standing near, pushed himself between them. " Oh no, not quite so quick, boy bach. If anybody is to be blamed for what haven't happened, it's me, and don't you forget. Huh ! Fancy a bloody lump like you trying to put the blame for nothing on a little gel like that."

Mary caught his arm before he could say more.

" Don't worry," she told the inspector. " We shan't hurt anyone if your men keep their hands still."

The long pause while the conversation was going on made the people impatient and restless, particularly those too far off to see what was happening. They began to press forward and the weight increased as a shout rose :

" Don't let anybody stop us. Right on now and no turning back."

The noise stimulated them, and they surged forward with such vigour that the front ranks were through the police cordon before anyone knew what had occurred. The inspector made a grab for Mary as she was swept past him, but the pressure tore her from his grasp. In a matter of seconds the mass of women had surrounded the officers, and, helped by the men nearest them, were lustily shouting for the unemployment officer to come to the window and speak to them. But no reply came from the house, so the women rushed into the silent building, only to find all the doors barred against them.

A shrill voice, rising clear above the din, shouted : " Round the back."

In an instant the women poured out of the building and streamed with the remainder of their mates to the rear, where Mary, helped by numerous hands was already being lifted to the window. She had gripped the sill and was scratching wildly with her shoes on the wall to get a foot-hold, when Len saw her stocking slowly drop down over her leg, leaving its whiteness bare to the eyes that watched.

He was about to shout a warning when other women rushed forward ; at the same time a crash was followed by the tinkle of falling glass. No one ever knew who was first through the window and in the office, but the next thing the crowd outside saw was a dozen women waving and cheering from the room above.

The demonstrators responded and the cheering swept through the ranks until it resounded all round Cwmardy as the mile upon mile of street-packed people took up the shouts, although only a small proportion of them could possibly know what had happened in front. Mary, one stocking sagged over her shoe, looked at the women about her, and pride made her forget for some moments what they had come for, until a loud noise at the door the other side of the room drew her attention. The women all turned in that direction, and for the first time saw a slight, pale man, with a small moustache hardly the width of his nostrils, standing fearfully with his back to the wall furthest from the window. Some of the women began to laugh at the sight, but the noise at the door became more loud and imperative. " Open this door," a muffled voice was shouting. " What for do you keep me out here in the cold when you are all in there ? "

Mary recognised Shân's voice, and in a very short time with the help of other women she drew the bolts, undid the chain, and opened the door to admit as many of the people crammed in the passage as could enter the room.

Shân, quivering with temper, demanded to know who had dared to lock her out. Mary, putting her arms round the old lady's shoulder, soon succeeded in placating her, before turning to the man with the moustache, who was begging the woman nearest him :

" Don't touch me. I have got my duty to do even if I dislike it."

He shook pitifully as he made his plea. Mary stepped forward and the people noticed a sneer on her lips when she replied : " Duty ? That's what the policeman says when he kicks a woman he's batoned to the floor. And that's the excuse you make when you rob her of bread."

She paused to regain her breath after the exertion of climbing into the room and the passion that was now beginning to overcome her. Another woman, her eyes as heavy with fatigue as her stomach was from bearing too many children, filled the breach.

" We haven't come here to touch you," she declared, her voice still carrying traces of the music that once used to stir concert audiences. " But neither do we want you to hurt us, whether you call it duty or not."

" But what can I do, what can I do ? " he wailed, rubbing his hands helplessly through his hair.

" Don't operate any more cuts and send a wire to the Government telling them of our demands," shouted Mary.

This excited the other people in the room, and they all began shouting together. The people outside thought something was happening to them and the shout spread in wider circles until the unemployment officer thought the world was being deluged. A look of absolute fear came into his eyes and when he saw a group of men wildly clambering about the window to get inside, his heart gave way and he dropped to his knees moaning like a child being cruelly beaten. Mary glanced at the crouching form and a spasm of pity ran through her for a moment, till she saw Len and Will Evans with other men, sitting astride the shattered window-sill, from which point of vantage they could see all that was happening both in the room and among the mass of people outside, who now began to sing again.

She bent down, and putting her hand under the official's arm helped him to his feet, where he stood, swallowing hard, as Mary asked him in quieter tones :

" Well, what is your answer ? We don't want to be here all day." She glanced round the room. " Some of these women still have over ten miles to march before they get home."

The man looked helplessly at her, then managed to whisper. " What if I refuse ? "

The answer came from all the women simultaneously : " You'll stop in this room till you change your mind."

Mary began making her way to the window. He sensed her intention and stopped her with a cry that seemed to stick in his throat. " All right. I'll do as you say."

The women could hardly believe their ears for a moment, and looked into each other's faces as though seeking answer there, until Mary rushed to the window and, with a flurry of skirts, was lifted bodily by Len and Will on to the sill, where they held her safely while she told the people outside what had transpired.

Like an electric current the news flashed from mouth to mouth so quickly that it seemed all the people in Cwmardy knew of it in an instant.

The air crackled in the shouts and cheers, while Mary and the other women left the building and took their places back in the ranks. The band had now returned, and striking up a Welsh battle march the demonstration started on its final trek to the field where the meetings were to be held.

For hours the people remained on the rubbish dump, listening to speeches, singing, and cheering themselves hoarse, before black shadows creeping slowly over the mountains warned them it was time to begin the tramp home.

Len and Mary went home with his parents. They found the fire burned out and the coal nothing but a white ash. Jim started to swear miserably.

"A man can't leave his own house for two minutes, muniferni, without the bloody fire do try to spite him out." He was tired and sore and wanted to vent his spleen on something. He chose the fire knowing it couldn't answer back, but Shân was also tired.

"For shame, James bach," she scolded. "If you haven't got no 'spects for me, you did ought to have it for these children by here, who can hear every dirty word that do leave your mouth."

Jim grunted and lowered his huge body very slowly and carefully into the armchair while Len with some paper and sticks drew the fire into a new blaze on which Mary soon boiled the kettle and made tea.

The supper revived their spirits and their eyes flashed again as they recited the various happenings of the day and competed with each other which was the most stirring thing that had occurred. Big Jim thought it was the march of the Sunny Bank contingent up to the meeting-place.

"Only one thing did spoil it," he commented. "If it wasn't for your mother by there, with her bad legs and what not—I told her 'nough not to come out—it 'ood have been a better march than any guardsman could make."

Shân half rose from her chair, but Len forestalled the threatening storm.

"I don't know, mum and dad," he said, "but the best thing of it all to my mind was when our Mary climbed up that window with her stocking hanging down over her shoe. Ha-ha!" He laughed boisterously at the memory, while the others looked down in surprise at Mary's bare leg, which in her astonishment she lifted without thinking what she was doing.

Big Jim chuckled wickedly at the sight. "Well, well," he remarked like a professor stating an unchallenging thesis, "that's a lovely little leg for you, Shân fach."

But Shân did not hear this remark. "There," she declared. "Now I know why you do cough so much. How do you 'spect your chest to be helfy when you do leave your legs naked like that?"

Mary blushed, but had no time to make any reply before Shân continued. "How come it you is like that, my gel? Tut-tut! No wonder half those men was mad."

"Oh, mother," Mary eventually managed to blurt out, her face red as the fire, "I didn't know it was down." She turned to Len and began to upbraid him. "Why didn't you tell me?" she demanded.

He burst into another laugh. "I knew, but I forgot all about it in the excitement," he answered.

Big Jim broke in. "I am not the only man who do forget things then! Ha-ha! That's one for me, Shân."

He suddenly stopped laughing and doubling up in his chair began to groan. "Oh, hell! This bloody back and the rheumatics will be the death of me. Help me, Shân," he growled out, "not stand staring by there at a man dying, mun."

Shân sprang to the cupboard, bringing back with her a bottle of something which she shook vigorously.

"Pull his shirt off, Mary fach," she commanded.

Mary went to the old man, who continued to grunt as they helped him remove the shirt and exposed the huge hairy chest beneath.

"I have told you before, Shân," he grunted, "that that stuff is like dog's piss for all the use it be."

Shân took no heed of his grunts and began rubbing the evil-smelling stuff into his chest, after which she turned him round and did the same to his back. He twitched his shoulders once when she happened to be a bit rough.

" Holy hell ! Trying to kill me on the sly, are you ? Don't forget I have got witnesses here if you start any of your bloody nonsense."

" Hush, James bach," she retorted placidly, " don't draw sin on your head without need. You have got enough there as it is."

Before the treatment was finished, the sound of singing came from the mountain that separated Cwmardy from the other valley. It was so sweetened by the distance that they looked at each other.

" It's the people going home from the demonstration," Len said.

Without another word they all went to the door and looked at the black sides from which crept the music of the men and women still making their way homewards. Other people in the street heard it and were drawn out of their houses to the doorstep, where they silently listened to the slowly receding harmony, that brought odd little twitches to their throats. Suddenly, Big Jim, still without his shirt, strode into the middle of the road and waving his arm in the air, let his voice boom out : " Three cheers for unity—Hip-hip ! "

The " Hurrah " that followed spread over the valley like a blanket, and was repeated till the sounds of singing were lost in the distance.

CHAPTER XX

Stay-in Strike

THE action taken in Cwmardy against the Government's attempt to lower the standards of the unemployed spread through the country like a flame. The Government grew alarmed at the growing heat and strength of the protest and issued a " Standstill Order " that restored the cuts already made.

This victory acted like a tonic upon the people, particularly those in the pits. The prestige of the Party increased tremendously as a result of the struggle, and many of its members were made officials of the Federation, Harry Morgan becoming chairman of the combine and Will Evans chairman of the lodge.

Strengthened in this way and now having to act as administrators as well as agitators and propagandists, the Party members held many discussions on how best to get rid of the company non-political union.

One Friday, the men themselves brought things to a head. A hurried 'phone message sent Harry and Len scurrying to the pit-head, where they found the men who had just come up holding a meeting. Although Will Evans was busily addressing them, the men were broken up into little groups each discussing something that appeared to upset them considerably. Big Jim was the most vociferous, and the only one whose words were decipherable above the din.

" Do they think I am a dog," he bawled, " that they give me boy's pay after a week's work ? Muniferni, if Hicks do think he can do that to me, he is climbing the wrong pole, and he can put his shirt on that. Good God, if I tooked this pay home to Shân, she would chuck it and me out through the bloody window ! "

Will Evans tried to get order. " Come, boys," he pleaded, " let us have some sense about it. Let's know first of all how many of you are under your money."

Into the air went a number of hands each holding a pay sheet.

"Hold 'em up, boys, while I count 'em."

This done, he asked for the amounts the individuals were short of, and immediately the din rose again.

"Ten bob. Twelve and six. Fifteen bob." The shouts came from all parts of the crowd.

Harry and Len had worked their way to the improvised platform by this time and the former got up alongside Will. His uplifted hand, commanding silence, for some reason reminded Len of Ezra and took his mind back over twenty years when the fight for the minimum wage began. But he had no time for meditation before Harry's piercing tones broke into his thoughts.

"The first thing to do, comrades, is to appoint a deputation to see Hicks straight away."

This was speedily done, Harry, Will, Big Jim, and Len being appointed for the interview.

Mr. Hicks hastily dodged back from the window through which he had been watching the scene, and when they entered the office they found him surrounded by his officials. He did not invite them to confront him, but addressed them over the heads of his subordinates.

"Well, what do you want now? And why in hell is it those men have not gone home? If they were doing justice to their work they'd have gone long ago."

Harry started to speak, but Big Jim got in before him.

"Pull your feet off that table, mun, when you are talking to better men than yourself, and meet us face to face, not with this pack of bloodhounds between us."

"Let me alone, Len," he continued when the latter tugged his sleeve to calm him. "Do you think I have put my body into this pit all my life to have a pay like this after a full week's work." He dragged his hand from his pocket and exposed a ten-shilling note and some silver, flourishing it around his head so that all could see. He grunted disgustedly. "Huh! I have pissed more than this against the back wall of the Boar's Head on a Saturday night before now."

Mr. Hicks rose from his chair and the officials opened out to admit the deputation to his sight. The heavy pouches under his eyes quivered with temper when he spoke, and he clutched his stick so tightly that his knuckles were as white as his face.

" So that's what all the fuss is about, is it ? You expect me to pay men for loafing about all day, do you ? Well, let me tell you all now, that those days are over for good."

Harry interrupted him. " Don't forget, Mr. Hicks, there is a minimum wage Act, that some of our men died for, still in existence, and you can depend on it you'll pay that whatever goes."

Hicks turned on him in a fury. " What ? Are you threatening me ? Get out." He turned sharply to the official nearest him, and snarled : " Here, 'phone up the police. Tell them I'm being intimidated."

Jim's bent shoulders straightened so erectly that his body seemed to fill the room. " Police, police," he stuttered. " Ah ! They 'on't be much bloody good to you. You had to send for sodgers when us fought for the minimum wage in the first place, and you'll want 'em now before you make us work for nothing."

It was obvious by now to all present that Mr. Hicks was not in a condition to negotiate anything with the deputation, and Len nodded to his friends a hint to leave. As they were going out Mr. Hicks raged like a lion losing a prey it thought secure.

" All right," he roared, waving his stick like a baton. " If you won't listen to sense, Jim Roberts, call in the office for your cards. There are plenty of better men than you waiting and willing to do your work, and that goes for the others as well."

Jim, who was on his way to the door, turned at this to snarl : " Aye, I know. The Federashon have been a bone in your guts for a long time now. That's why you have brought these non-political foreigners in to take our places, and you do think now you will sweep all the old hands out and fill the pit with non-pols. Bah ! " Spitting his disgust. " I have seened better things than you in a dog's bile. Ach ! But don't you think you have winned. No, us have still got a couple of cards up our sleeve."

With this the deputation went out to the men who were impatiently waiting.

Later that evening a meeting was held in Len's house. Party members looked their perturbation. They knew Mr. Hicks had precipitated the inevitable, but were not sure how best to counter his move. They discussed the position for hours, Len remaining silent for a long while until an idea breeding in his mind reached maturity. When he spoke it was in a whisper, as though he were afraid of what he was saying.

" Comrades, we've been bullied and battered for staying up the pit. What about staying down for a change ? "

The brief sentence was followed by a momentary pause, then a gasp of surprise as the audacity of the idea made itself felt. When the Party meeting broke up, the decision was made and worked out the same night in a secret emergency committee of the Federation.

During the small hours of the morning the throb of the pit engines seemed more subdued and hesitant, and the black air quivered as though with the suppressed excitement. Shadows slipped silently from house to house leaving a message in each, but no word leaked out from the quickly closed doors. Police officers, smelling trouble as a fox smells fowl, snooped around the street-corners and back lanes vainly trying to pick up information.

Mr. Hicks, rather more subdued, had called all his leading officials together in the consulting-room on the pit-head. The general manager's face shone white in the sooty atmosphere of the overheated office as he addressed his subordinates, most of whom were in their pit-clothes.

" It's strange," he muttered disconsolately, " that none of you know what the men are up to. Usually when they are going to strike we know all about it, but this time everything seems so still and ordinary, yet we know there is something in the wind." He rose from his chair and restlessly scratched his head as though the contact of his finger-nails with his scalp would give him inspiration. The faces of his listeners emphasised his own bewilderment when he asked : " Did none of you hear the men say something in the pit to-day, just one little hint ? "

Williams, the under-manager, his black moustache drooping over his mouth, shook his head slowly. " Yes. It was shameful to hear what some of them were saying. A stranger would have thought they were pounds under their money instead of a few paltry shillings."

Evan the overman interrupted. " But a funny thing, they seemed friendly with the company union members. I can't understand it at all." He pulled a brass box from his waistcoat pocket and put a huge wad of tobacco in his mouth.

Mr. Hicks watched him, with an absent look, and when the pouch was replaced, the action seemed to fix something in his mind.

" All right," he declared, " we will know soon enough. All of you be up half an hour earlier than usual in the morning. I have told the police to stop those reds distributing any leaflets on the pit-head, and all you want to do if the men try to hold a sudden meeting is to urge them down as quickly as possible. That's it," he declared, his eyes beginning to gleam with enthusiasm, " get them down." The officials left the office with this exhortation echoing in their ears.

Next morning, as the men queued up to await their turn for going down the shaft, a whisper ran through their ranks. It was as delicate as the swaying of a rose in a breeze and was inaudible above the rhythmic intonation of the machinery to all but those interested. " Be careful with your grub and water to-day, boys," it ran sibilantly from mouth to mouth, never becoming louder as it slipped through the ranks, but manifesting its existence by a restless tremor. The men seemed unusually anxious to get down out of the daylight, which as a rule they were loath to leave for the blackness of the pit.

Officials scattered here and there about the surface were amazed at the eagerness with which the men filled each cage and sank out of sight. When the wooden droppers had banged loudly after the last human load, Mr. Hicks came out of the consulting-room. A broad smile split his face as he approached Williams, the under-manager.

" Well, it seems our suspicions were unfounded, Mr. Williams. Very good. Very good indeed."

He twirled his walking-stick happily as the under-manager replied : " Yes, Mr. Hicks, they went down, thank goodness, and we are right for to-day again."

The colliery sergeant butted in. "Not even Roberts and his bolshies troubled us, sir. We were expecting some nonsense from them." Mr. Hicks nodded, but made no reply as he turned and made his way back into the office accompanied by his under-manager.

Meanwhile the men in the last cage lingered a little on the pit-bottom, but not long enough to cause suspicion. They fancied the trudge to their working places, past huge roof-holes and overhanging rocks, had become much shorter, and many of them sang quietly as they walked with bent heads and bowed shoulders. The hymns they sang were old and mournful, but the voices, though deep, were happy. The younger men were especially exuberant, galloping noisily down the steep inclines, making the men in front scamper hurriedly to the rubbish-plastered sides in the belief that the horses were stampeding. Will Evans, however, seemed to have lost his playfulness, and he walked quietly behind Dai Cannon and Big Jim, hardly listening to the remarks flying around him.

"I don't like this new stunt we are planning," Dai told Jim, a blob of sweat dangling precariously from the end of his nose. "I always like to see a straight fight, and not these foreign affairs that sound all right but don't lead nowhere."

"I don't know, mun Dai," Jim grunted, his huge body bent nearly in two under the low roof. "Us have always got to find new ways of fighting if us do want to win. And, any fight is better than the pay I had yesterday. You ought to have heard Shân when I gived it to her!"

"Huh! New ways, muniferni. The old ones was good enough for my father and his father before him, and they are good enough for me too."

Jim unconsciously lifted his head to reply, hitting it sharply against an overhanging piece of rock. "Hell fire!" he roared, forgetting all about his answer as he rubbed the injured spot vigorously. "This bloody pit is getting more like a muck-hole every day. They will want dogs to pull the coal out before long if they don't do some ripping to this blasted top."

Will Evans noisily shifted a lump of tobacco into his cheek. "Aye, you are right, butty. The company have forgot all about repairs. So long as we give them all the

coal they want, never mind a hell how we get it. This old
pit will soon only be good for swopping for a broody hen.
They tell me," he added confidentially, " that they are
going to get rid of all the horses and are going to buy mice
to pull the trams out because the roof is so low."

" Mice," growled Jim. " Huh ! No decent mouse
would work in the bloody hole. It's only daft beggars,
like us, will do that, and fight each other for the chance.
No wonder the bosses are laughing, muniferni." He kept
on grunting and swearing for the remainder of the distance
into the face.

Once there, the men were not long stripping to the waist,
and in a very short time the signal passed down the face :
" Let her have it." After a few preliminary coughing
" phot-phots " the conveyor began its voice-shattering
jerks that always kept it empty. The air became heavy
with coal-dust that added to the heat and made it more
intolerable. The diffusing light from the lamps was
blanketed by the dust, which left nothing but green pin-
pricks to stab the darkness. Bodies, gleaming with sweat,
lost tangibility and became emphasising shadows in the
blackness. Big Jim lay flat on his side, slicing through the
coal with deep, reiterating blows from his needle-pointed
pick, while Will Evans, on his knees and bent in two,
shovelled the product on the troughs, which he fancied
were always shouting : " Fill me up quick . . . Fill me
up quick."

Suddenly the terrific clattering of the conveyor ceased,
leaving the men dangling helplessly in an aural void until
a heavy voice boomed up the face.

" Who the bloody hell put this muck on the troughs ?
Do you think I am a cockle girl, or what, spending all my
time picking stones off the conveyor ? Play the bloody
game, you up there."

An authoritative voice sounded from the roadway.
" What's the matter, boys bach. Why the hell is the conveyor on stop ? Do you know you are losing coal every
minute and the journey is waiting for you ? "

Big Jim could not stand this ; flinging down his mandril,
he lifted himself on his knees until his naked back touched
the roof. " Coal ! Coal ! That's all I can see and hear,"
he shouted. " That's all my bloody life is. Never mind

about money. Never mind about food. Give the company coal and the world can go to hell." He exhausted himself, picked up the mandril and started hacking the coal as a vent for his temper. The conveyor began again as suddenly as it had stopped, and for the remainder of the day it dominated the bodies of the workmen.

At the end of the shift the men lay back on the roadway for some time, stretching their limbs to cure them of the cramp induced by their work, but Will Evans seemed to have gathered a sudden excess of energy and ran from place to place like a rabbit, saying a few words to the men in turn. When he returned to his own road the workmen there were already dressed and waiting for him, Big Jim whiling away the time with yarns about Africa and Gibraltar.

" I 'member once in Gib," he said, while Will put his clothes on, " an old Dutchman who owned all the oyster beds, mun jawly. One day he comed to our commandant with tears in his eyes as big as dog's balls. I was batman to the commandant at the time and knowed all that passed. ' Somebody is pinching my oysters,' he did say, ' and I do want you to put a stop to it.' He said a lot more than this, waving his hands about all the time like if he wanted to chuck 'em in the air and bring the fief to him there and then. Our C.O. didn't say a word till he had finished, then he said, short like, ' All right, butty. I will put a guard on the beds.' But next day the Dutchy comes up agen with the same tale, only worse. The chief did scratch his head funny-like and grunt to hisself : ' Hmm. Peculiar. I will put another sentry on.' And he did too, muniferni, but on the third day the Dutchman comed up agen with the same yarn and crying real this time like a man whose dog has been poisoned. After he finished—and it was a hell of a long time before he did, mind you—the C.O. said stern-like : ' All right. There is nothing for it but to double the guard.' The Dutchman gived him one look for a minute then let out a yell that nearly broked the windows, and beginned to dance about like one of those dolls us used to see in the circus, shouting all the time at the top of his voice : ' Double the guard ! No, by damn, take the bloody lot off before they eat the beds and all ! ' " All the workmen joined in the laugh that followed.

On the way out Dai Cannon asked " Was that true, Jim,
or one of your usual ? "

Jim stopped in his stride and turned round, at the same
time lifting his lamp to have a better look at his mate.
" Have you ever knowed me to say a lie, Dai bach ? No,
never in your life. That yarn is so true as I am standing
by here this minute, God strike me dead."

Dai said no more as they continued their way with the
other men towards the pit bottom. At every road junction
and parting others joined the progressively lengthening
line until the pit seemed full of veins pulsating with men.
Each step forward intensified the quiet excitement that
had developed in the ranks. Tired feet became lighter
and gave a jogging motion to the swinging lamps that made
the long stretch of light look like an undulating streamer of
ribbon. The scampering hoofs of the horses in front sent
dust whirling in the air ; but no one noticed this or seemed
to be inconvenienced by it, as the men turned off the main
roadway and silently followed the horses into the stable,
letting the compressed air close the door behind them with
a bang.

Mr. Williams, the under-manager, and Evan, the overman,
stood waiting on the pit bottom. The last tram of coal for
that shift had whirled up the shaft five minutes ago, and
the two officials were now uneasily waiting for the men.
Ordinarily the latter were ready to go up before the last
trams had left the pit-bottom. Williams looked at his
watch, then turned the whites of his surprised eyes to his
subordinate.

" Good God ! It's gone three o'clock ! " he declared,
like a man who sees an unexpected and unpleasant vision.
" What on earth can have happened ? " he asked helplessly.

" I can't make it out," answered the equally puzzled
overman. " If there had been an accident, we would
have heard of it long before now. Let's ask the
hitcher."

The two men strode over to the workman responsible
for loading and unloading the cage and handling the lever
controlling the knocker on the surface.

" Funny the men haven't come out yet, Tom."

" Aye, mun. But perhaps they are having a whiff somewhere."

The under-manager lost his temper. " Whiff to hell ! " he blurted out. " This is a pit, not a bloody hospital."

" Aye, I do know that, but funny things do happen in a pit sometimes."

The manner of the reply convinced Williams the man knew something. " Come on," he ordered brusquely. " Out with it. Where are the damned fools ? "

Tom carefully wiped his face in his cap before replying. " Well, if you look in the stables perhaps you will find something there."

The two men looked at the hitcher for some moments as though they thought he had suddenly gone mad, then a slow suspicion began to form in the under-manager's mind. His face went pale beneath its coal-crusted blackness.

" Come," he ordered. " There's something fishy about this business and I believe I know what it is."

The two officials stumbled hurriedly towards the stable, leaving Tom unconcernedly squatting at the pit bottom. Before they reached the stable door, they heard voices above the clamour of the wind squeaking and howling through its cracks. Without a word they put their shoulders to the planks and burst the door open.

The whitewashed stable, with its row of stalls in which the horses were placidly munching, looked like a huge circus in the lights of the lamps hung about its timbers. The men were gathered together in a compact mass listening to one of their number who was mounted on a tram of manure. They all turned their heads when the door opened and the two officials entered. After a brief hesitation Williams and his mate walked towards the figure in the tram, the men quietly making way for them to pass, then equally quietly closing in behind them.

Williams confronted the man who towered above him on the foundation of horse-dung, and from force of habit raised his lamp to have a better view, although its light was indistinguishable in the scores of others.

" Well, what is this damn' nonsense ? " he demanded. " Do you know it's long past the time you should have been up the pit ? "

Someone began laughing, and in a matter of seconds it was taken up by all the workmen and the stable quivered with hilarity.

" Ho-ho," Big Jim exclaimed, the echoes of his voice booming in the enclosed space like pebbles in a drum, " Fancy Williams worrying 'bout us being down after time. Ho-ho ! Life is worth living, muniferni, if it was only to hear that ! "

Williams sensed the determination and all that it implied in the laughter, and began to cajole immediately he could make himself heard.

" Come, boys. Don't be silly now. You will only make things worse for yourselves if you have any grievance."

There was no reply, and the stable became like a vault in the stillness. Williams swallowed hard, then tried again. " Be reasonable, boys. If you have any grievance, elect a deputation to discuss the matter with Mr. Hicks in a proper way."

Someone in the crowd shouted out : " Be reasonable be damned ! Haven't we been reasonable and patient for months, trying to get the management to pay us our proper wages and withdraw the blacklegging non-pols. or make them join the Federation ? "

" Aye," broke in another. " And what have been our thanks ? Scores of us getting the sack, forced to join the scab union, spied on and summoned by the police, and no pay after doing our work ! "

A deep murmur began to drone round the stables. Its intonation turned Williams' face even whiter beneath its coat of black, and he started to stammer. " B-b-b-b-but w-w-what good can you do by stopping d-d-d-down here ? "

Will Evans, on the tram, answered him. " That is our business. Yours is to get out and tell Hicks we are stopping here until he cleans our pit of scabs."

Evan the overman, who had been silent all the while, felt it was now time for him to intervene. " But you can't do that, mun. You'll starve to death and your lamps will all be in the dark before much longer."

Big Jim inflated his magnificent chest. " Huh ! Funny to hear you worrying 'bout us, Evan. Don't bother your head, mun. Us can look after ourselves and the pit without your help, take that from me."

Will Evans began laughing. " Ho-ho ! Boys, this is good. When we don't come to the pit they send their bobbies running like blue hell to drive us down and their magistrates make us pay for stopping on top. Now they are falling over each other to get us up. Ha-ha ! "

Again a wave of laughter flooded the stable and the two officials retreated through the door and back to the shaft bottom.

While this scene was taking place underground, Mr. Hicks looked through his office window on the surface. The noisy clang of passing trams had long since ceased, its place being taken by a strange silence. Mr. Hicks' uneasy eyes saw large numbers of pale-faced men in pit-clothes scattered about the colliery yard, but what surprised him most was the large proportion of other men who walked about excitedly. His grey moustache looked limp when he turned to the chief clerk at his side.

" Quite a lot of men looking for work to-day," he commented dubiously. The other man did not reply for some moments, then : " I don't understand it," he said. " They can't be looking for work, and even if they were, what are all those women doing here ? "

The general manager looked again, screwing his eyes up to have a more accurate view. He stared hard for some moments, picked his stick up from the corner where it rested, hastily ordered his clerk to get in 'phone communication with the pit bottom, and strode out into the crowd.

He spied Len, with Mary and Shân at his side, in the middle of the throng, and made his way directly to them. " What are you doing here ? " he demanded. " You know you have no right on these premises."

" Huh ! Who are you then ? Lord Muck ? " asked Shân indignantly. " Anybody 'ood think to hear you, mun, that you do own the place."

The people gathered around the little group, the women immediately siding with Shân. " That's right. Let him have it," exclaimed one. " It's through him and his sort that our valley have been ruined and our men are now down the pit till God knows when."

This stung Mr. Hicks into a frenzy. " What ? " he howled. " Aren't the men coming up to-day ? "

His only reply was a joint yell from hundreds of throats. " No. And they won't come up until you get rid of the scabs and pay them their wages."

The noise of the challenge struck the air like the detonation of artillery and swept down the valley, bringing men and women to their doors and into the streets, which they hurriedly left as they made towards the pit. In a short time Cwmardy had emptied all its occupants, except the invalids, on to the pit-head. Even dogs, barking joyfully into the vibrating air, scampered between the tramping feet of their owners and added to the noisy multitude that now filled the colliery yard.

The frantic general manager, accompanied by other officials and hardly conscious of what he was doing or saying, strode among the men in working clothes.

" Get down at once," he ordered, " or go back home for good."

" Go down your bloody self and stop there ! " was the only reply he received.

He turned to his officials. " Don't stand there like damn' clowns," he shouted, while his eyes glared. " Get those idiots up at once." He would have continued his raving had not the clerk come from the consulting-room with a message that he was wanted on the 'phone at once by Williams the under-manager.

He had some difficulty in forcing his way through the crowd, but sweating and swearing he eventually accomplished the task and grabbed the 'phone.

" Hallo. Hallo there," he growled impatiently into the mouthpiece. " Yes—yes. It's me. What the hell is wrong down there ? "

A long pause during which he turned from white to purple then back to white again, as the under-manager explained the position. Before Williams had finished his report, Hicks' body was rigid. He turned to the officials who had followed him into the office, staring as though he could not see them, the receiver still dangling from his hand. At last he pulled himself together and swallowed hard, before saying to no one in particular :

" That's finished it. They're going to stay down . . . stay down." He lingered over the last two words as though they stuck to his tongue and their taste was bitter. He walked slowly to the window, his head bent and his hands behind his back, looked at the mass of people surging outside, then seemed to gather new rage.

" 'Phone the police. Clear the yard. 'Phone Lord Cwmardy," he yelled in one burst of words, at the same time flinging his stick into the corner and himself into a chair. Outside the people were shouting : " Where's Fred Lewis, our executive member ? "

Down in the stable the men were holding a meeting with Will as their chairman. They were all both confident and jubilant with the exception of Dai Cannon, who now demanded the platform of dung, which was immediately vacated for him by the chairman. Willing hands helped the old man mount the tram, where the lights turned his greying hair to silver, as his deep voice rolled round the stable.

" Boys," he began, Big Jim looking up at him with open mouth, " you all know me, and know when there is a fight on I am in it with all my heart."

" Aye, aye, Dai bach," someone shouted, " especially if there is a pint behind it."

The quip put Dai on his dignity immediately. He pulled his overhanging belly back under its leather belt. " This is not the time for tomfoolery," he declared with great and emphatic solemnity. " At this hour of destiny, only fools and donkeys dare to guffaw. All of you think the company will give way in a very short time. I want to warn you—and me and Big Jim know this company better than any man alive now that Ezra has gone." Jim nodded his head in proud confirmation as his mate continued. " I want to warn you that this company will be prepared to starve us to death rather than give way on this vital principle, but I believe they will give us the back money without fighting at all."

A loud shout greeted this remark, " Tell us what to do, mun, not gabble by there like a bloody goose."

Dai lost his temper. " Don't you shout at me," he yelled, lifting his foot and stepping forward over the edge of the tram. Before he could say any more his arms rose in the air for a moment then followed his head as he plunged off the tram into the waiting clutches of Big Jim. He tried to get back again, but impatient shouts of " Put it to the vote," prevented him.

Will Evans got on the platform. " All right," he

declared. " If you are all ready we will vote. Every man take his lamp in his hand and we will decide by a show of lamps. I believe that will be better down here." The light in the stable seemed to bubble frothily as the lamps were hastily taken from the various resting-places.

" All in favour of going up the pit and appointing another deputation to see Hicks, please show."

A moment's pause, then a solitary light lifted itself above the others as Dai declared his conviction against them all, in a silence as deadly as that of a cemetery.

" All in favour of fighting it out down here, please show."

Immediately the lamps went up, burying the ground in darkness but turning the roof into a light-drenched sky.

A loud cheer followed the vote. " Good old Cwmardy." It broke in shattering echoes on the timbered walls and dug itself deeply into the hearts of the men. The last notes were slowly dying in the shuddering atmosphere when someone took them up and moulded them into song which sprang simultaneously from throat to throat, pouring into the stable a flood of melody that emptied the enclosed space of everything else :

> " The land of my fathers,
> The land of the free.
> The home of the harp,
> So dear to me."

The sweet tenors seemed to draw the baritones with them like magnets, lifting them up, then drawing them down, as they ran longingly over the notes of the anthem.

At last it was finished, and Will from his point of vantage carried on with the meeting.

" I have been told to say on behalf of the Party to which I belong and on behalf of the combine committee," he declared, " that we believe that all boys under eighteen, men over sixty except Big Jim, and those whose health is not so good ought to be sent up the pit."

The men became divided instantly, those affected by the suggestions being opposed to them, while the others agreed.

The chairman was about to put the matter to the vote when a fracas in the middle of the crowd sent ripples of excitement through it.

"Half a minute, Mr. Chairman," someone shouted. "There is a fight by here and we want to see there will be fair play all round."

Will forgot the dignity of his position and immediately jumped off the tram to be nearer the combatants, pushing his way forward until he was close to them. Big Jim, however, was before him and was already holding Dai Cannon's coat, as the latter, his fists extended, pranced about like a young cockerel in front of Will Smallbeer, who was hurriedly pulling his shirt over his head.

"What is the matter?" Will asked in bewilderment. Dai did not stop posturing as he answered.

"Nothing much, boy bach. Nothing much. You leave this to us. No man can insult me. No, not if he is so big as two houses."

"But what is it all about that two butties have got to fight to settle it?"

Dai stopped a moment to spit disgustedly. "Don't call that man my butty," he pleaded dramatically.

Will looked helplessly at Jim, who was complacently chewing a lump of tobacco.

"What is it, James?" he asked.

"Oh, Will said Dai was years older than him and would never see sixty agen if he lived to a hundred. Dai called him a bloody liar and Will offered to fight him for it, the loser to give in that he is more than sixty and the winner to stay down with the boys."

Smallbeer had by this time relieved himself of the shirt and stood with his head bent nearly to his knees and practically hidden by his whirling arms. Occasionally the bald pate shone through temporary gaps in the defences.

"Come on," he challenged. "You are very good with your tongue, let's see if you be half so good with your fists. And after I finish with you," he added, "I will fight any two who do say I am more than forty-five at the most, barring Big Jim, who have got more sense in his little finger than all of you put together have got in your bloody heads."

Before he could continue, Dai let go his fist and a howl at the same time, as the former landed smack on the bony head. He danced about more vigorously than ever, rubbing his injured knuckle the while.

" Stand up and fight like a man, not twt down by there like a monkey," he beseeched. His adversary only laughed at the taunt.

" Ha-ha ! Bit off more than your mouth can hold, eh ? " he gloated, at the same time advancing cautiously towards Dai, while the human ring drew in more closely about the combatants.

Fred Forrest pulled Will's sleeve as the latter, interestedly and oblivious of anything else, waited for developments. He turned at the tug and bent his ear to the whispering of his Party comrade. " You've got to stop this."

" Stop it ? What in hell for ? Let the old men enjoy themselves, mun."

" We can't have the men fighting each other, Bill. We want to keep all our fighting for the boss."

Will seemed on the point of refusing to interfere, hesitated a moment, then a second thought determined him.

" All right," he declared, " leave it to me."

He pushed his way back to the tram and began shouting at the top of his voice : " No more fighting among our-selves, boys. Let's carry on with the meeting. Make those two put their clothes back on. Give a hand, Big Jim." His sharp command pierced the air like a stiletto, and the words brought the men back to the fact there was important work still to be done. The two loudly protesting battlers were unceremoniously bundled back into their clothes, after which the meeting went on.

The youngsters and old men were rounded up and dug from the hiding-places into which many had retreated during the excitement. They were marshalled in front of all the others, the huge door was opened and the procession wound out of the stable towards the pit, its progress marked by the dust that floated around it.

Half-way out Will Smallbeer suddenly burst into tears. " It's not fair," he sobbed, " to send a man out like this. I can work and fight and drink as good as any man half so old as me, and here you send me up the pit like a baby to be a laughing-stock for everybody. But I 'on't go," he howled, flinging himself headlong on the side, where he crouched up like a ball.

Big Jim looked at the prostrate form sympathetically for some minutes before saying : " Pity, mun. Pity. Don't

he look 'xactly like a hedgehog by there when a dog is
nosing it." No one laughed.

Far away came the sound of a cage in motion, followed
a very short time later by two lights that floated towards
the waiting procession of men.

" Who the hell is this ? " Will asked of no one in particular.

" Must be old Hicks coming to see us," someone else
remarked.

" Whoever it is, no giving way now without a signed
agreement," came from a score of whispering voices, as the
lights stopped at the head of the long line. Will Evans,
accompanied by Big Jim and a few others, made his way
to the front, where he was surprised to see Fred Lewis
and a stranger squatting down comfortably on the side.

" Hallo, boys," the former greeted them affably. " Made
your minds up sudden, haven't you. I have been away,
as you know, and only heard this morning at the executive.
This is Jack Hopkins, our area member," he added. " They
have sent him up with me to help in this affair."

" Oh aye. That's good," said Will. " But what sort
of help are you going to give us ? "

The stranger replied : " Well. We first of all want all
of you to know how much we admire what you are doing.
But now you have made a demonstration and shown your
spirit, we think you should come up the pit and let us tackle
the business constitutionally."

The message slipped from mouth to mouth till all the
waiting men were soon aware of it, a fact that found
expression in a groan that grew louder.

" Constitution to hell ! Now we're down we're sticking
down till Hicks gives in."

Will turned again to the leaders. " That's how it is," he
declared.

" But listen to reason, mun," Fred pleaded. " You
can't keep down any length of time without serious harm
to some of you, and when you are finally forced to the surface you'll be worse off than you are now, and we'll be
further away than ever from smashing the company
union."

The listening men began shouting again their disapproval,
and Will, encouraged by this, declared : " If the executive

is not prepared to help us in a better way than that, ask them to keep their hands off and leave the fight to us."

The stranger became desperate, his squat, burly figure shaking with the feeling that gripped him. " If you come out," he promised, " I guarantee we will get your money to-morrow and clear the pit of scabs within a month."

" Who told you that ? " asked Big Jim. " Cwmardy or Mr. Hicks ? "

" No. Not yet ; but they will be bound to when you have the whole weight of the executive behind you."

" You tell that to the marines, butty. I knowed old Cwmardy before you was pupped and he's not so bloody simple as you think."

" No," commented Will to loud cheers from the men who were impatiently waiting for a definite statement. " We'll come up when you have it signed in black and white that our money is there and that the company union have finished forever in this pit. And mind you," he went on, " we 'on't take it from no one except Len Roberts."

A burst of applause made further conversation impossible, and the men lifted Will Smallbeer from the side and carried him bodily to the pit bottom.

The two miners' leaders went up with the first batch of old men to convey the news to the waiting people. Fred Lewis jumped on a coal tram and held his hand up for order, which he soon got. All eyes present were fixed upon him with concentrated attention, and Mr. Hicks, watching from the office window, felt his heart gladden when he saw the black-grimed men who had ascended with the leaders.

" He's persuaded them to come up," he whispered to his subordinates, as Fred Lewis's voice crept through the closed door.

" Fellow workers," it rang in the air which was already beginning to carry the germs of dusk, " they have decided, despite the advice of the executive, to stay down until the scabs are cleared out. They are now sending all those too young, too old, or too weak up the pit."

There was a moment's breathless silence, during which no one seemed to breathe, then a roar swept the valley : " Hurrah ! Hurrah ! The fight is on. Down with the company union." Fred looked mutely at Jack Hopkins, and the eyes of each showed the other that further argument was useless. The former jumped off the tram and the two were soon lost among the people.

Mary's eyes shone happily as she clasped Shân's arm and looked at Len, who stood erect as a dart nearby. The pride and happiness in the demeanour of all the people stirred her heart.

" Isn't it wonderful, mother, the way our men fight ? " she asked.

Shân nodded her head nonchalantly, although her posture betrayed how deeply she was gripped.

" Aye. They have been reared to it, you see, Mary fach."

The dense crowd of men and women began to sway spasmodically, and suddenly, without a word or warning sign, Len felt himself lifted in the air and carried to the tram, where he was gently placed down feet first.

" Speech. Speech," came the insistent demand. Although taken by surprise, Len remembered the discussion in the Party the previous night and knew exactly what to do.

" We must all go home now," he declared, " and prepare for the morning, when we must all be ready to be on the pit first thing with hot tea and food for our boys down below. There is no need for anyone to worry," he exhorted, " if we stand fast we can depend on it our boys in the pit will stick." Loud cheers interrupted him for some minutes, then he went on. " Perhaps it would be well if we picked a deputation to go down and see exactly how the boys are fixed." This was agreed to, and Len, with half a dozen others, was selected for the job.

Mary squeezed his hand as he made his way to the cage, and Shân instructed him to tell Jim : " Mind to keep his flannel shirt on. I will send him a blanket and some 'bacco to-morrow morning."

The cage with its little party of emissaries dropped out of sight as quickly as a falling bomb, and Len once more tasted the pit in his mouth. The hitcher was waiting for them on the bottom with a greeting.

" Hallo, boys, come to pay us a visit in our new home, eh ? You'll find all the family quite well, thank you."

Len smiled and asked : " Where are all the boys ? "

" Oh, you'll find them in the bedroom."

" Bedroom ? What do you mean ? " lifting his lamp to have a better look at the man.

" Aye, aye, mun. They have turned the stables into a bedroom."

Without another word, Len and his mates made their way towards the door behind which they now knew the men were settling down. The whistling air tried to prevent them jerking the door open, but with a concerted tug the men broke its grip and stood for some seconds looking in amazement at the scene before them. All the available brattice cloth had been hastily gathered, shared out, and was now being used as blankets. With a sheet of this under them three men were squeezed closely together on the manure tram, sleeping as peacefully as babies. Many of the younger men had taken possession of the mangers in the stables and were nestled down to rest while the horses' lips moved wetly about their bodies, hunting the stray fodder scattered about. The remainder of the men had made their beds on the floor of the stables, using fodder sacks, old timber, and whatever they could find as pillows.

Many, unable to sleep in the strange surroundings, were quietly whispering yarns or chatting, when Len and his party opened the door. Immediately the stables became silent of everything but the whistling air and the occasional clang of a chain as a horse restlessly shook his head. The scene struck Len with majestic force. The silence turned the stables into a cathedral where anything but whispers and bared heads would be sacrilege. He had known the pit and the men in all their moods, but never had he imagined the former as at once a battle-ground and a home for the latter.

He blinked away the moisture in his eyes and called out : " How be, boys. It's only me and a deputation."

Big Jim sprang to his feet like a catapulted ball. " Hurrah," he howled. " It's our Len and his butties. Up to it, boys."

Instantly all the reclining men were on their feet and gathered about the little group of pale-faced emissaries.

One, still rather suspicious, asked : " Come down to try and get us up, have you ? "

The deputation felt the resentment and determination

in the words and hastened to explain. "No, no, boys. We have been sent down by the men and women on top to help you carry on the fight."

A roar of cheering drowned the remainder.

Then another asked : "What are the women doing up there ? "

"Oh, they turned out to make sure that everything is all right with you."

Another burst of cheers followed this remark, and Big Jim's voice rose above it : "By damn, those gels is good boys, muniferni."

Will Evans, who was one of the three ensconced on the dung, now came forward.

"Hallo, Len. Glad to see you, butty."

Len's looked his mate up and down. "Good old Will. What do you intend to do now ? "

Will scratched his head for some moments and was then about to speak when another of the men forestalled him. "We are going to make this stable our headquarters. Then to-morrow we'll divide up into squads, to keep the place clean, fetch the water, and what not. We have already decided to have an Eisteddfod to-morrow, and Big Jim is going to be the adjudicator. There will be four choirs and variety turns as well."

The determined sangfroid of the man amazed Len and it was some moments before he could ask another question. At last he managed to inquire : "But won't your lamps all be in the dark by then ? "

"Ay. We 'spect so," Will replied offhandedly ; "but that 'on't make any difference to us. If horses can manage in the dark, I'm bloody sure we can."

Even now many of the lamps were beginning to lose their power and the light in the stable was like the smoky dusk of the surface. Len bent his head and could find nothing more to say other than : "Stick to it, boys, and don't worry about the people up above. They'll play their part."

Another member of the deputation continued : "Aye, you can bet on that. We'll have food and hot tea down to you in the morning."

Someone shouted : "Don't forget some 'bacco, butty, and the Racing Special."

The remark gave Len a new idea. " Boys," he shouted out, " I'm going to stop down with you."

For a moment there was complete silence, then Will replied : " No bloody fear, you don't. Your place is on top, seeing to things there."

" Who'll stop me staying down ? " demanded the crest-fallen Len.

" You'll see now," was the quick retort, as Will jumped back on the tram, from which position all the men saw his dim form.

" Where is Len's place, boys ? Up or down ? " he asked them.

" Up," came the unhesitating response, like a roar of thunder over the mountain.

Len sensed the men were right and made no further effort to persuade them otherwise. After some more discussion, the deputation, escorted by all the men, left for the pit bottom. When they ascended the shaft, they heard singing fade slowly as they left it in the earth, but immediately the cage burst the wooden droppers from the pit-head it seemed the same singing was born again as those on the surface welcomed them. The deputation reported the position, and the people, their minds contented, slowly made their way over the bridge and down the hill to their homes.

CHAPTER XXI

A Victory for the Workers

THAT night Mr. Higgins and Lord Cwmardy, hurriedly called from London, held a conference in the Big House with their chief officials. There was a bright gleam in Cwmardy's eyes as Mr. Hicks excitedly reported the events of the day. When he had finished Mr. Higgins stopped his restless pacing to remark :

" Scandalous ! The men must be evicted from the pit at once, by whatever means are necessary to accomplish this."

Cwmardy, his pipe clenched tightly in his teeth, nodded his head slowly. " Yes, that's so. But what men, what men ! " He became reminiscent as he went on. " It's their courage and audacity that makes them such splendid workmen." He gave a short sigh, then entered into the discussion that followed. The conference did not break up until the red streaks of a new day began shooting over the mountain.

Throughout the night Mary and Shân, with the other women, remained up cutting bread and butter, making sandwiches and tea. Shân was as excited as a young girl about to be married. She supervised the proceedings from her seat in the corner of the canteen, got up by the Co-operative, occasionally rising to do again something not done to her satisfaction.

" Pity they did send old Smallbeer and Dai Cannon up," she remarked. " I am sure the both of them do feel it awful."

The women ceased working for a moment, while one of them remarked : " The men did quite right. Us can't risk any chances now, and God knows what 'ood happen to old men like that if they was kept down for long."

" Aye," said another sympathetically, " They could have fits easy."

This started a buzz of conversation in which Mary joined. After a while the conversation took a serious turn as the women let their thoughts drift to the menfolk underground. One middle-aged woman sighed deeply and looked on the verge of tears. Mary noticed her and queried.

" What's the matter, Mrs. Davies ? "

The woman gave a little sob, lifted her apron, and replied : " Only yesterday afternoon my little Ianto, God bless him, asked me for a shilling to put on a horse, and I wouldn't give it to him. And now he's down in the pit and perhaps I'll never see him again. Oh dear, dear." She broke down completely and it was some time before she controlled herself sufficiently to add : " But he shan't suffer. Oh no. He shall have the racing paper down every day like the clock, and I will never refuse him a brass farthing again as long as I live." This pledge consoled her, and they all continued with their work.

Early next morning the people of Cwmardy, led by the band and a lorry full of food, made their way to the pit-head, which they found surrounded by police and officials. Len tried to pass the cordon, but was grasped roughly by the shoulder and pushed back. " No one is going near that pit to-day," remarked the police inspector. The people looked at each other in amazement for some moments, until Mary, with Shân clinging tightly to her heels, brushed past Len and the inspector and, without looking back, shouted over her shoulder : " Come on. Our men need food." Her action electrified the people, and in a second the crowd plunged forward with a roar and burst through the uniformed barrier that vainly tried to hold them back. Shân, her fists flailing wildly in all directions, fought like a tigress.

" Want to starve my man, do they ? " she grunted to herself as she ploughed her way towards the pit.

One of the policeman lost his head and, drawing his baton, began lashing at the unprotected heads. For some moments he had it all his own way and a number of men and women lay around him stretched on the dusty earth. Then something caught him behind the ear and he collapsed like a deflated concertina to join in the squirms of his victims. Without leadership or organisation, but driven by a common urge, the people fought their way to the pit-head. Apart from the thudding of blows and an occasional groan, the battle was eerily silent. Food parcels, burst open and their contents exposed during the melée, were scattered all over the colliery yard and crushed by trampling feet into the mud.

Mary felt herself pushed and huddled till she became giddy in the moiling crush. Her eyes lost focus and turned sightlessly in her head, so that she failed to see the truncheon land on Shân's shoulder, but she heard the moan as the old woman sank slowly on her knees into the black mire. The world seemed to burst into a red blaze for a moment, then she flung herself around the old woman, screaming at the top of her voice.

" Oh, Len, Len, they've hit mother."

Shân, half-squatting, half-kneeling, opened her eyes and looked dully at her daughter-in-law for some moments before asking : " What is the matter, gel fach ? I am all right, mun. It'll take more than that to upset your old Shân." She closed her eyes again, her face the pasty whiteness of dough, as the pain from her damaged shoulder spread down to her fingers, stiffening them into rigidity. Mary cuddled her more closely as Len pushed his way through to the crouching couple.

Hatless, his face streaked with coaldust, his breath short and rapid, he eventually reached them and carefully placed his arms around his mother's shoulders, drawing her erect. Mary got the other side and between them they worked a passage through the fighting people to some timber nearby, where they sat down.

Shân was quickly recovering her usual composure, although a few tears trickled down her skinny cheeks as she thought of what Big Jim would have done had he seen her being struck. She shook these away with a sharp nod and catching Len's head declared: " Us will never get food down to our boys."

Len looked about him at the police and officials, who were once again between the people and the pit. The showers of stones and sticks which darkened the air seemed to melt about the attackers, giving them greater vigour to charge with lashing batons, forcing the people back upon each other until everything became confusion and pandemonium.

" Come," he gulped, " or we will be left by here at the mercy of the police."

They skirted their way around the timber and behind some waggons until they again found themselves mixed up in the mass of people.

In the pit the men were making preparations for the Eisteddfod and concert. All the lamps had exhausted their light and the company had cut off the electric current that normally lighted the pit-bottom, so that everything was done in a darkness more dense and heavy than black ink. It seemed to break into bubbles when the men spoke, and location became a matter of sound.

A voice, which could only belong to Big Jim, rose above the murmur of the others : " Are you ready, boys ? "

The question came from the roof, and betrayed the fact that Big Jim had mounted the tram of manure as a platform from which to conduct and lead the singing.

" Right, boys. Now 'member, no funny tricks and fair play all round, because this is more 'portant than any 'Steddfod in a Chapel. Us will go by numbers. Are you ready, number one ? "

" Aye," came a deep responsive chorus from one part of the stable.

" Right then. When I do count three, start off. Now ! One, two," a long pause then, " three."

Before the word had interred itself in the darkness it was caught in the wave of melody that came from choir number one. The men not participating listened attentively to the rippling air that broke harmoniously on their ears. The universe was drowned in pleasing sound and made them hold their breath lest they disturb it. No one spoke for a while after the conclusion of the song, then a clamour took its place as the men discussed the merits and otherwise of the choir. The occasional clanging of horse chains made it appear that even the horses wanted to join in.

Big Jim eventually took charge again. " Not so bad, boys bach, not so bad. Damn, they is worth a clap, mun."

The hint was taken and a loud clapping of hands followed in which the choristers were as vigorous as any.

" Now us will have number two."

A shuffling of feet resulted, then silence followed by :
" Same thing agen. One, two . . . three."

Half-way through the second piece a loud voice, peculiarly
like Will Evans', shouted disgustedly : " Those tenors are
all to hell, mun. Damn ! They are swamping the baritones."

No one took any notice except Big Jim, who hissed :
" S-s-sh ! Fair play all round, boys. If anybody think
they can 'judicate better than me, they can come up by
here, muniferni."

After the fourth choir had competed, the men remained
quietly awaiting the verdict of the invisible adjudicator.
Jim took rather a long time before starting, then began
" 'Scuse me, boys. I have been looking for some 'bacco,
but my pouch is empty. Anybody got a bit to spare ?
What about some of you boys I have been keeping in
'bacco for years ? " He sensed the hands stretched towards
him and cautiously felt them. His fingers closed on one
that appeared to have a bigger lump than the others.

" Thanks, butty. I will do the same for you some day,"
drawing himself erect again immediately to roar " Fire in
hell ! Who was it who gived me that lump of horse dung ? "

A rumble of laughter made his further words inaudible
until someone shouted : " Come on, let's have the bloody
'judication. We is all waiting."

The laughter died down and Big Jim, spluttering and
cursing, was again heard. " Some men are not fit to die,
muniferni."

" Come on, let's have the result."

" All right, all right, keep your bloody hairs on. There
is nobody here afraid of you, whoever you are."

A further short silence then, after spitting loudly, Jim
began the adjudication.

" Well, boys, us will start with number one. Very good
song and very good singing with this one, but they raced
the tram a bit too high, eh, boys ? All of us do know if
you build a tram too high to pass the low timbers, the whole
bloody thing is ruined. Now number two did not do that,
but what they did do was not to put enough coal in the
bed of the tram, so that all the time it was sounding like
loose T-head rails under a journey running on wild."

A loud surge of laughter prevented him going on for a

while. When it had died down into spasmodic gurgles from various parts of the stable, he went on.

" Choir number three was very good, too, on the whole, but sometimes I did fancy I was listening to somebody sawing a empty tram in half, mun jawly. I think, putting it all together, and fair to everybody like, that number four was about a pair of rails in front of the best. What say you, boys ? "

There was loud clapping and boos for a while. Then Will Evans took charge, blindly groping his way to the tram and stumbling over bodies to do so. " Now we will start the concert."

For hours the men took it in turn to sing and recite, even while there was growing a vague unuttered uneasiness in their minds. The promised food had not yet arrived, and the men sent back to the pit before the lights went out to await its coming had not yet returned. Mingling with the music was this wonder of what was wrong. Fred Forrest quietly opened the face of his watch and let his fingers follow the hands, trying thus to estimate the right time. He thought he had it and immediately his stomach became empty and began to rumble for food. The chairman found ever greater difficulty in getting volunteers, and at last gave it up when someone shouted : " Cut it out, it makes us more thirsty."

This focused the thoughts of all the men and hands groped towards water-bottles to discover that the contents had been finished long since in the belief that more was coming.

The stable became silent but for the restless stamping of horses' feet.

A voice shouted : " The poor things are hungry."

" Aye," broke in another, " who had the feed-sacks last night ? "

The men concerned immediately got up and drew the bags which had been their beds from stall to stall, filling the manger in each before leaving to the sound of teeth crunching oats.

A further long period of quietude followed, during which many of the men dozed off, their eyes tired of the darkness which made it impossible to know if their lids were open or closed.

Will Evans stumbled and crawled about until he found
Big Jim. "Something must have happened on top,
James, or Len and the boys would have grub down long
ago."

A loud grunt and a movement prefaced Jim's reply.
"I could fancy my back is broked, mun, but there,"
resignedly, " what do backs count if the heart is
good? " A pause followed while Will meditated on
this.

"You must be getting on a bit now, James."

"Aye, my boy. Gone sixty-five and over fifty years
underground, and not a bald hair on the whole of my
head. What think you to that? "

"I don't s'pose I will ever live to that age and still be
of any bloody use."

"Huh!" patronisingly. "Don't break your heart, boy
bach. You have got plenty of time to grow old yet, and
don't forget my father was so young as you once."

A loud shout interrupted the conversation. It ran
through the stable like a wail.

"Can't anybody stop this bloody snoring by here? "

A number called out : " Get to sleep and forget it."

"Sleep to hell. How can a man sleep when that bloke
makes me think the missus is in bed with me? "

More joined in. "Watch him, boys. If he's got strength
to think of his missus in bed, he must be picking grub
from somewhere."

"Order, boys. What time do it go dark? "

The question was answered by a chant : " It never goes
dark till your eyes are shut." Everyone joined in this,
after which there was quiet for another spell.

Jim took advantage of this to whisper : " I'll go back
to the pit bottom to see if there is any news. Tom, the
hitcher, is sure to know something."

"I'll come with you," Will replied.

"No, no! You stop by here to make sure that nothing
out of the way do happen. If anybody say they are thirsty
or hungry, tell them to chew timber."

Back came the retort : " If us chew much more timber,
muniferni, us will be shitting sprags."

This left Jim somewhat crestfallen, and without another
word he quietly made his way to the stable door. He was

on the point of tugging it open when a sudden panicky
scrambling and a muffled yell stopped him.

" Quick boys, quick ! " came the hysterical plea, as
someone stampeded violently at the bottom end of the
stable. " A mouse have got inside my shirt and I can't
get him out ! "

Laughter covered the open door and Jim's retreat
through it.

Slowly, hands outstretched each side of him, Jim went
towards the bottom of the shaft. He lifted his knees carefully with each stride before jerking his foot out so that
the toe of his boot should be the first to make contact
with any obstacle in front of him. Mice and cockroaches
scuttled wildly among the timbers at the noise of his
approach. Winged insects droned past him like
miniature aeroplanes. The darkness was impenetrable.
Unable to stand the strain any longer he began to
shout.

" Hallo-o-o-o ! Hallo there ! Is there anybody about ? "

The echoes battered their way about the timbers, until
another shout from far off chased them away. " Aye,
straight on."

Thus encouraged, Jim soon reached his objective.

" Well, what have happened ? " he asked the invisible
men.

" Nothing. We have been clanging blue hell on the
knocker, but not a bloody sound or a move have us had
in reply."

Jim pondered this for some time, then commented :
" Huh ! That's funny, because our Len said there would
be food and tea down in the morning, and here we are
with another night nearly gone already, if my guts know
anything about time."

He would have carried on, but the iron knocker above
his head suddenly brazened out the " clear-away " signal
which meant the cage on the surface was about to
descend.

" Ha-ha ! That is Len so sure as hell. He do know what
I say if I was a million miles away, muniferni."

No one answered him, and they all listened to the roar
of the air as the cages, rushing in opposite directions,
crushed it into wild squeals. They faintly heard the crash

when the ascending carriage struck the wooden droppers and lifted them from the shaft-top as the other cage came into sight on the bottom.

The men's eyes were instantaneously fixed on the two lamps it contained. Their light failed to illuminate, and the white beam only made the darkness more dead. A long pause while the men wiped the wet mist from their eyes, then Jim grunted impatiently :

" Come on, Len bach. Let's see what you have brought with you, mun. Don't stand by there like a lump of paralysed mutton."

" Len isn't here," came the reply. " It's Mr. Hicks and Fred Lewis."

" Oh," the monosyllable sounded like the moan of an expiring martyr.

The two men came out of the cage, their swinging lamps throwing more shadows than light round those waiting on the roadway.

" Ah," the comment came from Mr. Hicks as he squatted down near Tom, the hitcher, while Big Jim, still standing, towered above both. " Now we can talk sense."

Apparently without noticing the general manager, Jim asked Fred Lewis : " What have happened to the food that you was going to send down ? "

" Oh, there has been a bit of a squabble on top," the latter replied uncomfortably. " But we have not come down to discuss that," he added hastily.

" Huh ! " broke in one of the men who had been sent back to wait for the food. " What squabble do you mean ? "

Thus faced with a direct question, Fred hesitated a while, then blurted : " The police refuse to let our people send food down, and there's a riot up above."

This was followed by a gasp of amazement from the expectant men.

Big Jim was about to say something, when Will Evans' voice exhumed itself from the darkness behind. He had followed Jim in spite of the latter's injunction.

" The rotten bastards ! " A pause, before he continued in a sharper tone. " But it's not the police, it's Hicks and the company, who, not satisfied with half-starving us on top, are now trying to starve us down here."

" Listen, listen," pleaded Mr. Hicks. " I don't want to starve any of you. I want to live in harmony with you all."

" Ha-ha ! " the laugh broke in cackles. " Want to live in harmony. Ha-ha ! And want us to live in harmony with non-pols., who are cutting our throats and ruining our pit. That's what you want—harmony in everything that is best for you and the company."

Jim's bent shoulders painfully squared themselves erect. " That will do, butties bach," he declared. " If these men want to talk, let them come into the stable to do it, where all the boys can hear what they have got to say."

The men accepted the advice, and the little procession, one lamp in front and the other behind, made its way from the pit to the stable, obliterating its progress with the dust that followed.

The beams of light that stabbed the darkness through the open stable door brought all the men to their feet with a bound, but nothing was said as Mr. Hicks walked straight to the tram of manure, Fred Lewis close behind him. From all quarters black bodies merged into the lighter shadows cast by the lamps and eyes became blobs of liquid whiteness glaring at the two men.

The miners' leader spoke first, clearing his throat noisily before beginning. His lank form and dark features fitted into the general surroundings, making the latter appear to an onlooker like the picture of a meeting in hell.

" Well, boys, as you all know, I give way to no man for militancy and support for those I represent." He paused, as though expecting applause, but the deadly silence urged him to continue more quickly. " But there are times when leaders must do things which the men don't like at the moment, but which are best for them in the end."

This brought an uneasy shuffling of feet in the dusty manure of the stable floor, and a low growl from many of the listening men.

" We are in that position now," went on the speaker. " I speak with the full authority of the executive when I say we are united in asking you to come up the pit and trust us to settle the matter to your complete satisfaction." Again the silence egged him on, and he began to plead. " Think boys. Our people on top are being battered about and our women are grieving for you while you remain here. Damn it all, if we are to fight, let's all fight together."

A loud howl followed on the heels of this statement.

" We are fighting ! "

" The executive wants us to give in ! "

" Our leaders are ratting ! "

The slogans rang in the air, stirring it into a fermenting turmoil, that made nerves quiver with excitement. An old workman jumped on the tram alongside Fred Lewis, his black face glistening. " Fellow workmen," he bellowed hoarsely, "when we put a rank and file executive in the Federashon, we all thought that everything would be all right, but here we are now again faced with the same tricks and the same old lies. Bah! All of 'em are the bloody same. Put a beggar on a horse and he'll ride to hell."

Claps and shouts completed his statement. Mr. Hicks raised his hand and tried to get a hearing, but the shouts swelled into a roar through which came the reiterated demand :

" Pay us our wages and clear the pit of non-pols. and we'll come up."

Its repetitive insistence dominated everything else for a while. It crowded upon Mr. Hicks, bowing his shoulders and putting deep lines and dark shadows into his face. He turned to Fred and whispered something, but the latter shook his head as though he could not hear in the din. Both men, worlds apart but dominated by the same impulse, looked with mutual desire upon the scene beneath. Each movement gave birth to monstrous quivering shadows that chased each other all round the stables. Faces seemed to be detached from the bodies to which they belonged as they dangled from and merged in the moving shadows. Only eyes appeared fixed as they threw back the glare from the two solitary lamps. One of the men suddenly threw his arms above his head and sunk slowly to his knees, moaning as he subsided.

" O God ! Give us the light of day, which the company has taken away. Give us food, give us water. O Christ, give me my family."

The last words ended in a scream that silenced the other men as those nearest bent down to lift the sobbing man to his feet.

" There, there," they soothed him as though he were a baby. " Don't take it like that, mun. Perhaps you have got a touch of 'flu."

The last word spread till everyone knew it. It became an entity of its own, robbed of its context.

Again a slow, dim murmur rose steadily into a roar.

" Up the pit with him."

" Send him home, he's done his bit."

Fred tried to take advantage of the incident. " There you are, boys," he shouted. " That's what will happen to all of you in this damned hole. Let's go up together," he pleaded.

Will Evans flung himself into the ensuing silence. " Give us the agreement and we'll come."

This was immediately taken up. " The agreement. The agreement in black and white ! "

Will felt something gnaw inside him and turned away to be sick, but nothing except thick, sticky mucus rose to his mouth, burning his throat like acid as it came up. When he recovered, the men were already lining up, Mr. Hicks and Fred in front, followed by two men holding the man who had collapsed, then all the others in ranks of two. He fell in with them, vaguely wondering what they were about to do, while his feet rose and fell automatically. The roadway widened near the pit bottom and enabled him to get nearer the front just as the general manager, miners' leader, and disabled worker were stepping slowly into the cage. He felt the rush of air that followed the clang of the knocker and saw the two lights jump suddenly up the shaft and disappear like two bubbles on a pipe. The men around him were immediately transformed into intangibility that found expression in sound, which lifted in ascending tiers until it filled the black air with invigorating ripples :

> "Bread of Heaven,
> Bread of Heaven,
> Feed me now and evermore."

The plea became a defiant challenge as voices moulded into moods. The final stanzas were repeated twice before someone shouted : " Home, boys," and they all turned so that the rear became the front as they slowly stumbled back to the stables.

Very late that night two meetings were held in Cwmardy, one in the colliery offices, where Lord Cwmardy presided, and the other in the new workmen's institute, where Harry Morgan chaired. Harry's usually beaming face, with its high, glistening forehead, was now drawn and puckered as he faced the mass of men and women whose features betrayed the agony of the past hours. Shân, her shoulder still helpless and painful, sat with Len and Mary near the first row of seats. The latter's eyes looked twice their usual size in the unnatural pinkish glow on her face, the muscles of which twitched spasmodically whenever she moved her head. Len, nervous and irritable, sought her hand on the seat against his side and pressed the fingers between his, knowing the contact would help to settle his frenzy.

" I'm opposed to the line," he whispered. " The men are in the mood to fight and we have negotiated and played about long enough with the problem of the non-pols. Our Party dare not act as strike-breakers now the men have taken action."

" S-s-sh," she replied equally quietly, as Harry rose from his chair and Fred Lewis bent forward with his elbows on his knees. " Fellow working men and women," the chairman began. " We have reached a decisive moment in our history. Our men have given us the responsibility of leadership, but this does not mean they have no responsibilities themselves. If they trust us to lead, we must lead in everything that concerns the pit and the Federation."

Someone in the back of the hall shouted out, " Well, lead right then. When the men are fighting, don't try to lead them away from it."

Loud applause from all parts of the building greeted this, and Harry's eyes gleamed behind their spectacles as he felt the indomitable courage of the people. He held up his hand, but for some time could not get order. When he did he went on calmly, as though there had been no interruption : " That spirit, that courage which our people now display can be used in certain circumstances to defeat us. It is not sufficient to fight ; we must always know how to fight to win. Perhaps what seems defeat at the moment is necessary to take us to eventual victory. As it is now, we are not only fighting the company, we are fighting each other. It is anarchy," he shouted excitedly, as the din provoked by his words grew more emphatic and vociferous.

" Let the executive lead, not rat," the people shouted. " You are as bad as the old bunch once you get in power —you forget all you used to stand for and preach."

This stung Harry and he went white, but he waited until there was silence before replying. " You have made me chairman of the combine and because of that I have to see all the people and not only those in one pit. Believe me, boys," he cried dramatically, " the executive will never betray its trust, come what will. We are pledged to sweep the non-pols. from the coalfield and we intend to do it. But we cannot do it in the way the men are acting now."

Another loud howl of dissent swept the hall, during which Harry, waving his hand despondently, retired to the chair and began a conversation with Fred and the others on the platform.

Len watched them dully. He knew from the Party meeting earlier that evening what Harry was saying, and his heart burned within him. He turned again to Mary.

" Oh, my dear, our line is wrong," he moaned.

" Never mind," she consoled. " Right or wrong, it is the line and we have to be true to it."

" But it means we have to become strike-breakers."

She swallowed at the implication, but straightening up, said : " If that is necessary for final victory, then it must be done. Don't forget, Len, we must sometimes swim against the stream, although that is much harder than going with it."

He gulped and turned his attention to the meeting which was now out of control, the people on the platform appearing to be lost in the wilderness of noise that surrounded them. Len looked at his immediate neighbours and met wild staring appeals that he say something for the men below.

His own eyes grew momentarily misty and blind, then something swept through him like fire and he sprang to his feet with a jerk, still clasping Mary's hand and half-dragging her with him. Mary understood his mood and, sitting down again, let him feel her body near his, knowing her close presence would check any tendency to irrelevant wildness on his part.

His sudden action had run through the crowd like a current and commanded attention. Harry saw this and immediately took advantage of it, recognising his Party comrade even through the smoky fog that hung over the hall.

" Order," he shouted with upraised hand. " One of your fellow workmen wants to speak."

Others took up the cry. " Order, order," until the appeal became more noisy than the previous uproar, but it died slowly until at last silence took its place and Len began to speak.

" Comrades," his voice low and tremulous, " we are called upon to-night to make one of the most serious decisions of our lives. Our executive and our chairman, Harry Morgan, have told us what they think. Our men down in the pit since yesterday morning without light or food are also showing us something, and I want to say now that, right or wrong, I am proud of them." His voice rose into a crescendo of passion with this last phrase, lifting with it a tumult of cheers that lasted many minutes. Mary, sensing what was happening, let her hand creep upwards till it felt his and he clasped it tenderly in his firm fingers.

Someone in the middle of the hall began weeping loudly, causing a little stir in the immediate vicinity until someone shouted : " It's all right, Len, carry on."

Len did not heed the exhortation, but it heartened him for what had to come. " Yes. Proud of them, as we all are. And what are they doing, comrades ? " He paused, then answered himself. " They are fighting to keep a principle which they and their fathers won through suffering many years ago. They are there in the blackness of the pit so that we above it can keep our freedom and the right to join what union we desire without asking the company."

The whole gathering was now tensely silent and alert to every word as it came from his quivering lips.

" Our pits were swept clean of blacklegs in the big strike, but since then the company has been clever and used the poverty of our own people to turn some of them into scabs. They have forced us out of our own Federation into their union if we wanted work and wages, bread and home. They have kept our men down the pit through fear of starvation on top, unless we accepted all the conditions the company imposed on us through its union. Yes," he went on bitterly, as his memory traversed the past in quick panoramic flashes, " they made us sell our freedom for a job."

The people on the platform, led by the chairman, clapped their hands vigorously, but Mary began to get nervous as she saw the trend of Len's remarks. Her adamant loyalty to all Party decisions made her on occasions fear her husband's vehemence when he felt a thing deeply. She tightened her grip on his hand and tugged it softly, sending a message through it to his brain in the hope that the latter would calm the tumult she knew was boiling in him. It appeared the effort was successful, because when he continued, it was much more quietly.

" For months and years our executive has been negotiating and pleading with the company to let us choose our union without fear of victimisation or reprisals, but each time they have been scorned and called dictators ; and now our men have lost patience and taken things into their own hands. Think of it," he beseeched, " during the strike, some of us wondered why the police should be sent in against us. But since then, we have learned the Government doesn't keep them just for chasing criminals. No. They keep them to maintain law and order and everything that we do that is in our own interest and against that of the company is illegal and disorderly. They use the police to smash us with their batons ; then summons us for a riot which they themselves have made. And after this, before we know where we are, they use magistrates and judges to twist the law and turn us into criminals, then send us to jail. Isn't that true ? " he shouted, his face red with the pressure of words, while Harry Morgan began to fidget uneasily, even though he felt his flesh tingle with the stark truth of the assertion. "Yes," the speaker went on. " We have nothing to expect from the company, from the authorities, from anyone. No, nothing can serve us but our own strength,

determination, and unity." The last word seemed to
awaken a new line of thought in his mind. "That's it—
unity. Whatever happens, we must be united. Never
mind how we differ in other things, we must be united
against the things we suffer in common at the hands of the
boss and his government." His voice broke a little and
became sad as he continued : "That is why I believe the
executive is right and we ought to ask our men to come up
the pit. Look," he swept his arm dramatically through
the air before him, "everywhere our men are split. Some
are fighting underground like ours, others are on the surface
and working. That's what Harry means by anarchy.
That's what he means when he says we must on this issue
fight together or lose the fight."

He sat down abruptly and unexpectedly, leaving the
people in a welter of surprise and conflicting emotions.
Most of them had expected anything but this from him,
and his actual pronouncement left them clammy with
disappointed expectancy. The meeting continued in an
atmosphere of dull apathy for some time, but it ended in
an uproar of dissent and indecision.

As the people left their meeting and poured into the
lamp-lit darkness of the main street, they spontaneously
hushed their voices when a line of buses filled with blue-
uniformed and bright-buttoned men passed by on its way
to the pit-head, where the meeting in the colliery office was
still proceeding. Lord Cwmardy's white hair made his
face look softer as he said.

"Mr. Higgins is quite right. We can't let the men con-
fiscate the pit in this manner." He bent his head as though
he were meditating over some deep thought. "No, the
day shift of loyal men must proceed to work as usual in
the morning, and the rebellious elements must be removed."
He drew his hand across his brow and sat down tiredly,
leaving his underlings to work out the details.

Big Jim carefully moved his recumbent, pain-filled body
to a more comfortable position, whispering curses beneath
his moustache as he did so. Will Evans, whose squirming
entrails refused to let him sleep, felt the slight movement
and closed nearer to the old workman.

"What time is it, Jim ? " he asked in what he tried to

make jocular tones, but his weariness made the effort a hopeless failure.

" Oh, it's not dark yet and the barmaid in the Boar's Head haven't shouted ' Stop tap ! ' " was the nonchalant retort.

" Hell, Jim ! Don't talk of the Boar's Head. I could drink a pint as big as a barrel now."

Jim's tongue unconsciously ran over the dry rim of his long drooping moustache, leaving it moist enough for his lips to smack with longing as he said.

" Ah ! A barrel full as big as a pond, muniferni."

Both men let their minds wander for some time until a new thought struck Will.

" I wonder what won the three o'clock that day we came down," he asked wistfully.

" Hmm. What race did you say, my boy ? You see, my remembery is not so good as it did used to be, these days."

" The three o'clock."

" Oh, aye. I heard you first time, mun, but I did want to make quite sure, you see, because Shân have turned that set of ours into a proper Chapel goer, muniferni. That's all you can hear on it—sermons and hymns. Only a deaf man can understand anything else it do say, mun jawly."

Will became invigorated with the indomitable courage and optimism of the old man. He laughed loudly and woke other restless sleepers, although he was not aware of it till some of them shouted : " What the hell is the matter ? Have the bloody circus started or what ? Have a bit of respects for other people, mun, whoever you are. You're not in a workhouse or a gaol now."

Will laughed more loudly than ever at this, and others joined. in, waking everybody up and filling the stable with confused sound that made the horses neigh restlessly.

Someone rose to his feet and the tremor in his voice exposed the weakness in his limbs when he shouted hoarsely : " Come on, boys. Time to feed the horses."

When this was done the men crawled more closely to each other, each finding his way to his own group of mates by the directing voices that led him over reclining and squatting bodies. After this everything became quiet for a while and a vague common desire filled all their minds.

Everyone kept it to himself even as the longing urged him to open his mouth and speak. At last the desire broke its bonds in an initial sibilant whisper that slowly seeped its way through the ranks and fixed everyone's thoughts.

" Water, water. Where can we get it ? "

The intensity of the need that gripped the men killed its vocal expression for some time after this first outburst, when an idea shaped in their minds and again the thought was given life.

" There's water in the pipes between the stop tap and the boshes." The elementary simplicity of the fact that only now had dawned on them stupefied everyone until Big Jim began to laugh clamantly.

" Ha-ha ! That's good ! The next thing us will forget is that there is always coal in a coalpit."

This broke the tension, and arrangements were made for tapping the pipes and filling the empty water-bottles.

Bottles were being passed from groping hand to groping hand, jokes and laughter accompanying the operation, when the stable door suddenly banged open and disclosed a large number of lights. Men stood still with outstretched hands, in stupefied amazement at the unexpected sight. Pit-blinded eyes became blinder still as the lights from the lamps struck them with pain-inducing beams.

A voice, emerging sharply from the ring of light, ordered : " Get ready, there. All of you have to go up the pit, and the quieter you go the better for yourselves. This pit is going to work to-day, and we've got men ready to work it."

The lights began to move forward in a solid block that was harder than the blackness which tried to crush it. The strikers involuntarily began to retreat before the menacing advance, until someone shouted from the rear :

" We can't go back any further, we're up against the end."

But still the lights advanced with nothing but their motion to mark their coming. Will Evans felt his hair bristle uncomfortably as his quick temper began to rush the blood to his head. He had understood the new move even as he heard the order, and the despairing call from behind now snapped something in his head.

" Pick up something for a weapon, boys," he howled,

" and let us fight for the door. The officials and non-pols. are trying to beat us out of the pit."

The cry was followed by a flurried shuffling as the men stooped to pick up from the floor pieces of wood, iron, and whatever else they could get hold of. Then the strikers stood, wordless and immobile, waiting for the outcome of the new development. The lights they had prayed for now became their greatest enemy, making everything invisible to their eyes, filling them with tears and making their heads throb. But the menacing halo did not stop its advance until it came and broke on the first wave of strikers, who lashed out in all directions without knowing what or who they were hitting. The action ran through the stable with electrifying speed and effect.

The attackers had never expected such a determined resistance, and their first ranks, which of necessity had to take the brunt of the onslaught in the confined space, pressed back upon those behind them, throwing the latter into increasing confusion as the strikers bore on. Groans and grunts mingled with thuds and curses. Lamps were whirled wildly in the air and used as weapons which fell like shooting stars upon the soft flesh in the way of their descent.

Suddenly a whistle shuddered through the stable with a shrill squeal, followed by a warning :

" Look out there ! " as a long nozzle peeping through the ranks of the attackers burst into a roaring crackle. The compressed air thus released, drove itself like a solid wall against the men before it, sending some squirming to the ground and the remainder into a panicky retreat to the sides or anywhere they could escape its annihilating fury. Screams found company with appeals as the blast did its work.

" Fair play, boys, fair play. For God's sake give us a chance ! "

The answer seemed to come from the very nozzle of the pipe : " You've had it, you bastards, and wouldn't take it, now take this," and the terrifying tumult rose higher still as the tap was opened fully.

The strikers felt that everything was lost and were on the point of declaring their readiness to go up the pit when a loud clang of rolling iron challenged the blast for noisy supremacy. The dung-filled tram, released from its wooden anchors and driven into greater momentum by the strong hands of Big Jim and the energetic ones of Will Evans, plunged wildly into the swaying mass of men behind the blast pipe. The latter gave way immediately and ran headlong for their lives towards the pit, the tram hurtling after them like a tornado in which was merged the cackling laugh of Will Evans as he picked up the blast nozzle and switched off the air.

Lamps scattered about the floor of the stable acted as footlights for the grotesque scene. The noise of the battle had stampeded the horses, who were now kicking wildly in all directions, driving the men into bundles on the sides until some sprang on the wooden fences that separated the stalls. Unloosening the chains which held the horses' heads, the men turned the steeds round so that their hind-quarters pressed against the mangers and the walls.

Then the survey of casualties began. Wounds were bound with shirt or singlet strips and no distinction was made between friend or foe. When the ambulance men reached Big Jim they found him squatted on the floor clutching a man to his body as though he were nursing a child.

"Good God! Is he badly hurt, Jim?" one of them asked.

"No. Not much yet. But he will be unless he use his head from now on. He tried to run away with the others when the tram went on wild, but I had him, muniferni, before he could get far."

"Who is it?"

Jim's mysterious demeanour filled the others with a curiosity that made the query more than an ordinary question.

"Oh, you will find that out soon enough. I bet you 'on't guess, none of you, in six times."

The men grew impatient and bending down, took the man from Jim's grasp, raising him erect so that they could all see him. A gasp of astonishment echoed round the stable as the white features of Mr. Hicks reflected the light from the confiscated lamps.

"Holy Hell! Big Jim's collared the big boss!"

The men held an immediate meeting to discuss the new

developments, after which all the non-pols., officials, and
badly hurt miners were sent to the surface with a message
to the authorities that Mr. Hicks would remain down with
the strikers until a satisfactory settlement was made by
the company and that no harm would come to him if food
was sent down immediately. This done, the men began to
discuss the next moves. Big Jim never moved from Hicks'
side, and it was Will Evans who declared :

" That have settled it, boys. No more bloody stables
for us. It is nothing but a death-trap. The only thing
now is to get inside to the double parting and make that
our home. Put out all the lamps except one. We don't
want to be in the dark agen if we can save light."

The men agreed and all available sacks, brattice cloth,
and other soft material was taken along as they made their
way to their new earth-embowelled home.

The solitary lamp turned the line of men into dim
shadows that quivered and danced on the timbered roadway. The eeriness of the tramp stole into Hicks' heart,
and he whispered to Jim in a trembling voice.

" What are they going to do to me, Jim ? "

" Nothing, boy bach, nothing, if you will keep your
head and do what you are told."

" But why do you keep me down ? "

The manner in which the query was made implied a deep
fear that tickled Jim, whose reply became a gloat : " Ah !
That's the puzzle, see. Ha-ha ! Before now you was the
big boss, shouting and ordering and sacking. But the
boot have shifted to the other foot. Yes, catching you
have made us the bosses, and for once in our lives we will
do the ordering and you will do the listening."

Something in the statement and the silence that followed
it turned the manager's blood to water. He began to plead,
raising his voice so that the other men could hear : " Let
me go, boys, and I'll see you get fair play."

There was no reply other than the stumbling, muffled
tramp of feet and the quickened tremor on the shadowed
walls.

Hundreds of police surrounded the pit-head when the
injured came up, but the ranks of people who pressed upon
their outermost ranks saw that a battle had taken place
underground. They burst into wild cheers when they saw

that most of the injured belonged to the non-pols. and officials, and the police made a baton charge to clear them from the yard. This action was followed by a shower of stones and coal lumps that precipitated another fight which lasted for hours before the people were finally driven down the hill into the streets of Cwmardy, which became tremulant with exultant shouts : " Our boys have captured Hicks. Now it won't last long ! "

Shân's eyes shone brightly at the glowing embers in the fire grate of her little kitchen.

" Dear, dear," she mused proudly, " our James is the oldest man down, yes, the very oldest, and I am so sure as this hand is fast to me," holding it out for Len and Mary to see, " that he will be the very last to come up."

Neither of them answered her, so she turned again to the fire.

" Him and me have been together a long time now. Yes, forty years or more, and it is 'bout time he left the pit for younger men. He have done his share and did ought to have rest and comfort in his old days."

Mary stirred on the chair and placed her hand on the old woman's shoulder with a gesture that was itself a caress.

" Never mind, mother. One day we will put this old world of ours right and use the good and beautiful things it has for all the people and not for the few who now take it all."

She changed the subject abruptly and turned to Len. " What is the next move ? " she asked sharply. He shook his head despondently.

" It is out of our hands," he replied. " Everything now depends on the boys down below and what the company will do about Hicks. One thing we can depend on, and that is there'll be no more fighting down below, and they'll let food go down now if only for Hicks' sake."

Each morning during the five days that followed the people of Cwmardy plodded up the hill to the pit, with food and material for the strikers. They remained until nightfall, only leaving when they knew there were sufficient pickets to ensure all necessary information reaching them in the shortest possible time.

A mass meeting was held on the eve of the morning

which marked the tenth day of the strike. A report was here given to the people of the latest negotiations between the executive and the company, after which Len was appointed to go down with Harry Morgan and Fred Lewis to interview the strikers. On its way to the pit, the deputation was inundated with flasks of hot tea and packets of food. Shân handed them a tin of tobacco with the solemn injunction :

" Now, 'member, you must put it into his own hands and nobody else's, because I do know it is the only thing he is worrying about . . . and me, of course," she added as an afterthought.

The tramping feet reminded Len of the Big Strike and Ezra. He wondered what the once dour body now looked like in its earthy blanket. The thought made him shiver, and he automatically looked for Mary in the following throng. He saw her with his mother, the latter limping doggedly to keep pace with her people. His body again warmed at the sight of his two loved ones trudging together in the lines of their fellow workers. He smiled grimly as he noticed Ezra's heritage of determination stamped indelibly into Mary's features, and his heart beat more quickly in its significance.

The setting sun sent blood-hued rays to linger over the valley as the members of the deputation stepped into the cage, where they dangled on the thread that was to drop them to their mates. A loud heartening shout followed them into the pit and the rush of the carriage was accompanied by a rush of the people, which broke through the police cordon and gave them possession of the pit-head, where they waited patiently for news from below.

Meanwhile Harry and his colleagues had passed the now empty· stable and were dragging their feet through the dust to the double parting where Tom, the hitcher, had told them the men had established themselves. Their lights were seen a long time before they reached their destination. A husky voice halted them.

" Stop there and don't move another step till we know who you are."

The trio immediately obeyed, holding their lamps still so that the others could see they had stopped walking. Some minutes passed before two shadows broke through the darkness into the lamplight, both walking slowly and hesitantly, like babies just learning painfully to stand erect for the first time. Len looked, and recognising his father and Will, his eyes became dim. But neither of the two saw anything, for their eyes were closed tightly, the compressed lids drawing wrinkles all over their faces. The couple walked on until Big Jim bumped into his son, when he stopped abruptly and threw out his arm to grasp Will and prevent his going into danger.

" Well ? " he asked in a voice that he strained up from his belly. " Who is there and what do you want ? "

The very weakness of his tones implied a challenge which the deputation sensed immediately.

" Dad, dad," Len cried, " it's me and Harry and Fred."

Will felt his body melt away from his head, leaving the latter whirling around even as he maintained his senses and wondered what was wrong. He gave a little moan.

" Oh, God ! What is the matter with me ? " and began to slither weakly to the floor, but before he reached it three pairs of arms were round him, holding his body and bending his head towards his knees. Big Jim rested his shoulders against the sides and dumbly waited while the others attended to Will.

Harry forced a hot sip of tea between Will's clenched teeth. This revived him, and he shamefacedly urged them to let him go.

" I'm all right now," he declared. " Keep that tea for the others, who deserve it more than me."

Harry and Fred, however, insisted upon helping him back to the men, but Jim refused assistance, pretending the heavy hand which clasped Len's shoulder was there to steady the latter, because " he wasn't used to the pit for a long time."

In this manner they reached the double parting, where the remaining men, some lying and some sitting, were awaiting them. The lamps were fastened on the high cross timbers to keep the glare from the men's eyes. Big Jim introduced the deputation and a weak cheer welcomed them, but this evaporated into dry coughs that spread like fog among the strikers, whose thin bodies and slack skin began to shape in the light from the lamps.

Harry noticed the pitiful dignity with which the strikers

tried to impress the deputation, and swallowed the lump in his throat to say : " Well, boys, you have done your duty, and the fight is over. Our people are waiting for you with open arms and happy hearts on top. You did the trick when you kept Hicks down."

He expected, as did his mates, a cheer to follow these words, but none came, and he was astounded to hear after a brief silence the quickly uttered command :

" Let Len show us the agreement. That's what we said on the first day and that is what we say to-day."

There could be no mistaking the determined self-abnegation behind the whispered words, and Len wasted no time in arguing.

" Let's be quite straight from the start, boys," he began. " We haven't got an agreement for the simple reason that the company thinks it is saving its face if it can get you up first and then let you have the agreement in the office. They want to make sure that Hicks is safe and sound."

A murmur of disbelief came from the men, and Len hastened to add : " But there can be no mistake about it. The company is prepared to take a free ballot and let every man join what union he wants to."

This time a small cheer managed to trickle into the air, and Big Jim quickly stepped into the breach thus offered. " Us can take his word, boys, because he do know if he said a lie to do us down, I 'ood cut his head off 'xactly like if he wasn't my own flesh and blood, muniferni." He took his hand off Len's shoulder to give greater vehemence to his words, but the action only made him sway drunkenly. His statement nevertheless decided the men, and a quick vote was taken to clinch the issue.

Then began the faltering walk to the pit. Each of the men refused aid from the members of the deputation and the provisions they had brought with them.

" There is not enough for all of us," said one as he rejected the offer. " And we might as well stick it till we can all get some."

" Aye," said another, " and we have had to depend on ourselves all this time, so we might as well depend on each other now at the finish."

And in this manner, the weaker leaning on the stronger and all leaning on each other, they made their way behind the deputation to the bottom of the shaft, where some officials were waiting for them. This started another upset, the men refusing to ascend till the officials had left.

" Hell fire ! " Will tried to shout and in so doing turned his voice to a croak. " We came down without 'em, and by damn we'll go up without 'em." Hicks shivered weakly and instructed his subordinates to get up out of the way.

The ultimatum and instructions produced surrender, and the officials stepped into the waiting cage and were whisked away, Fred Lewis going with them to acquaint the people that the others were coming. When the first carriage full of strikers banged its chains against the droppers, the rush of released air was smothered in the terrific cheer that rolled and crashed over the valley. Police and officials were scattered about like coaldust when they tried to keep the people away from the pit-head. The strikers were tenderly lifted out of the cages and tended by loving hands while they waited for the remainder to come up. Kisses mixed with happy tears and both were lost in the singing and cheers as the cage slowly emptied its final load. The last man to step out was Big Jim, whose trembling hand arrogantly twirled his long moustache. Shân rushed towards him.

" James, oh James bach," she sobbed, as she flung both arms around him and pressed her face to his black one when he bent down to kiss her. " I knowed everythink 'ood come all right."

He raised his head and seeing Mary nearby, stretched out his hand affectionately to stroke her brown hair glistening in the electric lights.

No one ever remembered exactly what followed, everything was excitement and tumult. But the blare of a brass band took command of the situation, and, in step with its lively march rhythm, the people took their victorious strikers down the hill to Cwmardy, where banners and streamers waved a breezy welcome home.

CHAPTER XXII

A Party Decision

A FEW months after the excitement of the stay-in strike news began to appear in the press about an armed insurrection against the government of Spain. The people of Cwmardy wondered what it was all about until the truth slowly leaked through, and then they began to learn that the insurrection was developing into an invasion. This fact caused furious discussion, and Spain became the main topic of conversation wherever two or more met.

One evening in Mary's house she paused in the act of powdering her nose and looked at the clock ; then, with a hasty : " S-s-sh ! It's time for the news " to Len, who was noisily washing his face, she switched the wireless on. The piercing oscillations that accompanied her efforts to find the station startled the dozing Bonzo, who sprang to his feet with a growl and looked disgustedly for some moments at Mary fingering the set, before subsiding back upon his mat in the corner with the stately motion of a dowager at her bankruptcy examination. The dog waited until the voice came over the ether with its deeply intoned announcement : " This is the first general news bulletin," then slowly dozed off again with one eye half open.

Len came near the fire-place and continued wiping his face, although he now did so more slowly like one who wanted to deaden any foreign sound. Mary leaned over the table and fixed her eyes on the instrument as though this would enable her to see the words. Both of them unconsciously tensed their bodies when the word " Spain " came across, and they were afraid even to breathe properly in case they lost one item of the following statements. When it was finished they looked at each other silently for some moments before Len asked in what he thought was a casual manner : " Do you want to hear about the price of gold ? " She shook her head somewhat sharply and he hastened to switch off, leaving the kitchen in a quietude so deep by contrast that Bonzo again cocked his two eyes open to see what was wrong.

Mary bent to pat his head, at the same time remarking : " It's looking pretty black in Spain, Len, if we can depend on the news."

Len flung some small coal on the fire. " Yes, Mary, very black ; and we'll have to do something about it soon."

Both seemed fearful of saying too much in case their emotions overcame them. Mary took a final look round the kitchen, made Bonzo more comfortable on his mat, then said : " Let's go, Len, or we'll be late and you know how sarcastic Harry is when there's important matters to discuss."

They locked the door behind them and hurried to the meeting place, returning an occasional salutation on their way down but not stopping to chat with any of the acquaintances they met. When they arrived at their destination they found all the Party committee already present, with the exception of Will Evans, who was working afternoons.

" Hello. Slept late ? " Harry asked as the couple took chairs next each other.

" No, we waited a couple of minutes to hear the news," replied Mary.

" Oh, aye. Well, we'll get more than the wireless gave before we finish to-night."

He turned to the others. " Can we have a chairman, please ? "

Len was nominated and carried, and without wasting time he left his seat and went the other side of the table alongside Harry, who whispered something to him for some moments. Len nodded his head in approval, then began the business of the meeting.

" Harry has got a report to give us to-night about the situation in Spain," he announced. " It appears there have been some very big developments and we have now got to take some definite and practical steps in the matter."

The room seemed to go suddenly cold although the air outside was humid and close. Mary felt a queer trickling through her spine, and drew her coat more closely, at the same time bending her head to the table so that only the top of her brown hair was visible to the others.

Harry did not rise from the chair when he addressed them with slow deliberation. " Comrades, the civil war in Spain has reached a new stage. It has now become an armed invasion by foreign countries—open intervention by Germany and Italy, the countries of Fascism. Yes, the fight in Spain is no longer one in defence of Spanish democracy ; it has become a war for the defence of world democracy and it can only end when we make Spain the graveyard of international Fascism and all that it means."

He continued for more than an hour giving his report, his voice often shivering with emotion, but Mary never raised her head during the passionate discourse.

An idea germinated by the wireless news was taking more definite shape in her mind with each word Harry uttered. It thrilled even as it drained the blood from her thin cheeks. She knew already that it was what she wanted, even while she tried to drive the thought away.

Suddenly some words of Harry's drew her taut and for the first time she looked up, to see Len's eyes fixed on her with an intensity that drew the blood back to her face in pink flushes that burned her ears as Harry's pronouncements buried themselves there.

" That's the position," he declared. " We must continue with protests, we must help financially and with foodstuffs, but more important still, we must help with men. Yes, comrades. We must fill the gaps that the Fascists make. For every democrat they destroy we must find two more to take his place. Our workers have fought in the wars of imperialism. The time has come when they must now fight in defence of democracy and all the ideals that they cherish."

For a long time after these closing words there was a silence which made the room as callous as a tomb. Harry's report had brought the war from the realms of theory and news and had made it a living, individual fact that burst like a bomb in the consciousness of everyone present. Len found his mind fixed on one sentence in the speech. It thrust all other thoughts aside and flayed him like the burn of swishing nettles :

" The national leaders of labour are dragging the honour of British people in the mud, and it is only the Party and the working class can redeem it in the eyes of the world."

He couldn't tear himself away from this and the implications it involved. His brain automatically separated the problem into its parts and focused upon the one that posed the question of individual responsibility and obligation. Without thinking of doing so, he let his gaze wander to Mary, who returned his look with eyes that didn't appear to see him.

At last the tension was broken by a voice which asked : "How can you expect us to recruit workers for Spain if we don't go ourselves ? I could never, for one, bring myself to ask another to do what I couldn't."

Harry appeared to be prepared for this question, and answered without hesitation : "That's not the point. We shall send our best and most trusted comrades out, you can depend on that. But the main thing is to get workers, particularly those with war experience, to go."

Mary followed immediately with another question. "Does that mean that only men who were in the last war can go ? "

"No. Party comrades who have no military training but who have a wide political experience are going to volunteer."

"Ah." The sound escaped Mary's lips like the sigh of a mother who suddenly feels again the long dissolved grief of the parting from her child.

Then, for no apparent reason, the room became full of excited voices. From all quarters came the assertion : "If that's the case, then I'm the man to go."

Harry raised his hand and for the first time got on his feet. "Comrades, let's be clear. The matter is entirely in your hands, but I have a suggestion to make which I hope you will seriously consider before coming to any final decision."

Len had not said a word throughout, but he knew what was to follow as surely as though the words had already been spoken. All his life he had been temperamentally opposed to physical violence, and even now, despite all his experiences of brutal actions against his people, he felt an inward shrinking when it forced itself upon him. It was in this that he differed most fundamentally from his father. Big Jim was urged to violence by the sheer exuberance of his physique, while Len was impelled to it by intellectual realization of its necessity. Because of this Len went into every action with a calculating, cold hardness that was foreign to his normal self, whereas Jim swept into action with joyous whoops that betrayed his pleasure in battle.

Len's thoughts were canalised by Mary's quiet question : " What is your suggestion, Harry ? Who is the comrade you want to recommend ? "

The brief hesitation that followed was sufficient answer, but Harry rather nervously replied : " Len Roberts—he's the comrade I've got in mind, and I think he's the best for many reasons."

Mary's hand jerked to her breast, which she squeezed convulsively, but she soon calmed herself in the discussion that followed the statement.

" But he can't go, he's wanted here," said one voice.

" The front-line trenches of democracy are now in Spain, not Cwmardy," came the retort.

" Let's send a single man. What about myself ? " asked another.

" We want the best, the most able," was the instant reply.

" What about Will Evans—he's just the man ? "

" Will's working and we can't draw him from the pit for the time being."

" But what about Mary ? She can't live on air."

Mary sprang to her feet at this. She felt the question an insult to her whole life and, quite irrationally, resented it. " I'm not here to bargain about him," she announced heatedly. " If he is necessary to the fight I give him freely, whatever the result might be. But don't bargain over him. Don't ask me to sell him."

The vehemence of the utterance subdued her, and then she realised how unfair she was. No one answered her insinuation, but it put an end to the questions, although Harry tried to put everyone at ease when he asserted : " Mary'll get what she's having now to live on. The supporters of democracy will see to that."

Shortly after this the meeting broke up into chatting groups, Harry taking Len and Mary on one side to tell them : " You'll have to go in three days, Len, so you'd better come down to-morrow to see about your passport

and the other things that are necessary. There'll be about
twenty others going with you."

Len's face was hard as stone when he replied : " That's
all right. It'll give me nice time to square things here.
What do you say, Mary ? " turning to his wife.

She squeezed his hand proudly in hers and looked at
Harry. " Whenever the Party says, we'll be ready."

" Good. What about having a little private celebration
somewhere before you leave ? " Mary half started, but
Len made the objection first.

" No, Harry. It's not a time for celebrations, and I'd
sooner go the same as the other boys. There can't be any
fuss made over their going because of the authorities, so
I'd sooner if we didn't."

" Good lad, Len. I'm off now. See you in the morning."

" So long, Harry."

The couple waited until he had left the room, then joined
the others. They chatted for some time until Len, noticing
Mary's impatience, made an excuse and got away.

" Are you worrying, Mary ? " he asked as they walked
homewards.

" Oh, Len, I don't know what's the matter with me.
I've got a funny kind of pain in my belly and yet I feel
so proud somehow."

A wanton thought flashed through his mind for a moment
and he expressed it in a whisper. " Do you think you have
gone ? " Then he laughed before she could answer.
" Ha-ha ! Of course not, worse luck. But, duw, Mary,
wouldn't it be nice if you had a baby coming while I'm
out there ? "

He allowed the pleasure of the thought to control him
for some moments, and Mary did not interrupt him. At
last he said, as though talking to himself. " Why not ?
I know of women who have had babies after twenty
years."

Mary looked at him wistfully, one small hand clenched
so tightly by her side that the knuckles stood out white.
" Don't Len. You know it's impossible and you only
hurt the two of us by wishing for such a thing." She could
not refrain from adding : " But it would be wonderful
to have a baby waiting for you when you come back. He'd
have hair like mine and eyes the same colour as yours,

and . . ." she stopped and a pitiful little smile hung on the corner of her lips.

Len caught her arm and pressed it to his body. " Never mind, comrade," he consoled, both himself and her. " If we can't create anything with our bodies, we can with our minds and the work we do for the Party. That's something to go on with, isn't it ? "

They laughed together, then Mary suddenly had another thought. She stopped and stated abruptly : " Len, you must see your father and mother to-night."

He coloured a little before excusing himself. " Oh, we can do that some other time. There's plenty of time before I go away."

" Oh, Len. How can you say that. To-morrow you'll be off meeting Harry and making final arrangements. Then the next day you'll be going."

The reproach in her voice hurt him more than the truth of her statement. He had a horror of fuss and dreaded the scene with his mother, which he knew was bound to occur when she was told what he intended doing. Already he felt his tongue going dry as he vainly tried to find excuses he could validly call reasons. He wished now he could slide away with no one but Mary to know he was going, thinking this would cause his mother less pain. Then hard upon this thought came the knowledge that it was born of selfishness, that it came out of the fact he was himself afraid to face the pain of parting from his parents.

Mary sensed the battle taking place within him, and tried to help. " Let's go in now, on our way home," she suggested, and Len somewhat shamefacedly agreed without further comment.

Shân was busily wiping the brass candlesticks when the couple entered, but she immediately replaced the one she had in her grasp and queried with feigned surprise : " Well, well, fancy seeing you. I thought you had forgot you ever had an old mam, Len, seeing how long you have been coming to see me."

" I've been pretty busy, mam, between one thing and another," Len replied as he took a chair and sat down. " Where's dad ? "

" Oh, he's out the back. I don't know how long he's going to be, but he have been there about a hour already."

She bent to whisper : " Your father is not half the man he did used to be, Len. No, indeed. He is getting more childish every day." She sighed, then abruptly ordered : " Here, Mary fach. Sit on this stool. It is better than that old chair."

Mary did as she was bade and had hardly made herself comfortable when Big Jim came in.

His body was bent slightly forward from the hips and his hand was pressed tightly to his thigh, but the white moustache still had the arrogant stiffness of the days when it was black. He greeted them with a glad : " Hallo. Where have you two felled from so sudden ? Ah, come to see the old man agen before he peg out, I 'spect."

He grunted his way to a chair, while Shân looked at Mary with eyes that seemed to assert : " There, what did I tell you ? "

Len, knowing he had neglected his parents in recent weeks, felt a little awkward. He wondered how to frame a feasible explanation, but before he could succeed Jim asked sharply : " Have you put me in the 'surance, yet, Len ? "

It was Mary who answered : " No, father. And we don't intend to either. You have got years before you, mun, and it would be a waste of money that we can't afford to lose from our dole."

She tried to laugh the idea away, but Shân pursued it. " You did ought to, Mary," she scolded. " 'Surance is always handy when something do happen. And, mind you, it can happen to anybody. Yes, indeed. It is back to the earth us have all got to go. Huh ! You must put the two of us in before it will be too late. Duw ! Think, gel fach—there will be mourning to buy, without counting anything else that you have got to get for funerals if you want to be 'spectable."

Jim interrupted her with a remark to Len, at the same time puffing heavily at his newly filled pipe between the words. " Her words is right, Len. But 'member this, the old 'ooman do want a oak coffin ; a orange box will do for me. And she do want us to be buried in the same grave, but, muniferni, she will have to alter a lot before ever I will agree to chance my arm to have her nagging me after I am dead."

Mary laughed loudly, and this prevented Shân making the retort that trembled on her lips.

" Let me help you to make a cup of tea, mam," the younger woman offered, at the same time rising from the chair and taking the tea-pot from the hob.

The hot beverage had a soothing effect upon the old people, although Jim tried to depreciate its qualities with a solemn declaration : " Tea is all right in its place, and that is in a 'ooman's belly. But for a man, ah, it is beer that he should have. Duw, I 'member the time, years ago now, when us could have a pint for tuppence. Beer, mind you, not the muck us have got to pay sixpence for to-day."

Shân shrugged her shoulders impatiently and advised : " Oh, left the old beer there for to-night, James bach," then immediately remarked : " Don't you fancy our Len is looking not half well, somehow ? "

This query turned the conversation, and for some time they became reminiscent about their offspring.

" Do you 'member the first day he did start school, and us put that lovely new velvet suit on him, James ? "

" Aye, my gel. He did look well that day. Just like his old man."

He addressed himself to Mary, half turning in his chair to do so : " You are too young to 'member that, Mary fach, much too young. Your little arse was no bigger than a shirt-button in those days. But if your father was alive he could tell you that I was a good-looking chap then. Aye, by damn. Straight as a line, wasn't I, Shân ? " He twisted his moustache proudly as the old woman nodded assent.

Len and Mary let their elders wander through the past in this manner, wondering the while how best to break the news that was burning within them. At last Jim made an opportunity when he said appraisingly, looking Len up and down much as a farmer scrutinises a cow : " Our Len is a pretty smart chap too, come to think of it. Not so big as his old man, mind. No, not by a long chalk. But that is Shân's fault. Still, I can 'member the time when a man like him could make a mark in the army."

Len and Mary glanced simultaneously at each other and opened their mouths together, but it was her voice that was first heard, as she blurted out : " That's just what our Len is going to be—a soldier."

The crash of a saucer as it fell on the floor passed unheeded. Shân sat erect in the chair, her fingers bent as though the saucer were still in their grasp. Her bottom jaw had sagged loosely and her eyes had the same look as a playful dog's that had been unexpectedly kicked.

Jim leaned forward, his shoulders becoming more hunched, and hastily thrust a paper spill into the fire to light his already glowing pipe. But Len saw neither as he kept his gaze on the dancing flames and let his imagination frame pictures in them. The tin clock on the mantelshelf broke into the silence with a hollow " tick-tock . . . tick-tock " that beat on the brains of the people in the kitchen.

Suddenly Shân sprang from the chair, her body rattling the table as she rose. " What did you say, Mary ? Our Len going to be a sodger ? " Something gurgled in her throat for a moment before she made a pretence of laughing. " Ha-ha ! Come, don't tease your mam in her old age."

No one answered and no one looked at her. She glanced at them in turn, her eyes dilated and her face grey, as she waited for the reply. Then she spoke to Jim, her words dropping with increasing impetus from her lips. " There you are, satisfied now, are you, that your nonsense talk have brought us to this ? It is you that have put all these things into his head."

The continuing silence drove her frantic for a while, but she began to weep in sheer impotence as the reality of the assertion made by Mary forced itself into her unwilling mind.

Mary went to the old woman and quietly led her back to a chair, where Shân could lay her head upon the table. The convulsive sobs that sounded like wet sighs infected the others. Tears began to trickle from Mary's eyes, came more quickly each moment, although she tried to check them, then she broke down completely and, burying her face in Shân's hair, moaned : " Oh, mam, mam," at the same time squeezing the elder woman to her own body.

Len gulped and blew his nose to provide an excuse for wiping his eyes, while Jim poked the fire savagely as if seeking revenge for something it had done to him.

For a long time the monotonous song of the clock was

merged in the women's sobs. Then Shân raised her head, turning it so that her lips pressed on the wet cheeks of her daughter-in-law.

"There, there, Mary fach, forgive me. It is my fault that your heart have come so heavy," she soothed while her own face burned redly from rubbing with the tear-sodden canvas apron.

"That's right," Jim supplemented hopefully. "Come, my gel. Wipe your eyes and tell us what have happened."

This reversal of rôles made Mary feel ashamed, and she kept her head down while she battled against her emotions, leaving the explanation to Len, who made it with hesitant and unconvincing sentences.

Big Jim and his wife remained motionless during the recital, but when it was finished Shân was on her feet again, a defiant blaze in her eyes. "What? Do you mean to tell me that you are going to fight and die for foreigners millions of miles away from Cwmardy? No, never! If you have got to fight it will be here by your mother's side, where I can look after you. Huh! Spaniards indeed! I have never seened one of them and don't owe them a single penny. No, Len. You stop home by here with your mam and dad in their old age. They 'on't last long now."

The air pressed heavy as lead and the crunching of Shân's boots on the sanded floor sounded like the crackling of a forest fire as she paced the narrow length of the kitchen. Jim felt impelled to help her, although in his heart he was proud of Len's action and claimed it entirely as a product of himself.

"Good old Len," he muttered. "You are 'xactly like I used to be when I was your age. Aye, indeed. But you must listen to your mam now. She do know best. Many a time have I learned that in the old days when I used to be a little bit wild. If it wasn't for her then, God knows where I 'ood have been to-day. Yes, you listen to your old 'ooman, Len."

Seeing that Len made no response to this plea, Jim tried another track. "You can take it from me, butty, those Spaniards are no bloody use. Duw. When I was in Gib, mun, I comed to know them inside out, and I have never yet in all my born days seened one with any guts. No, muniferni."

The innocently conceived insult ran through Mary like a burn, and, hastily patting the moisture on her cheeks, she defended the Spanish people. The argument went on for hours, Jim eventually siding with Mary, but Shân remained unconvinced, although she finally accepted the position with the best grace she could.

" Righteousness must prevail one day, I suppose," she muttered in Welsh, before warning them fatalistically : " You will find that my words will come true and then you will all be sorry for what you are doing against me now."

A short time later Len and Mary sadly left the house and went to their own home.

Not a member of the family slept that night. Shân wept while Jim smoked and cursed, between vain pleas that she keep quiet so that he could have the sleep that was nowhere near him. The younger people had also been deeply affected by the events of the evening and especially by Shân's fight to keep her son at home. But they said very little to each other as they prepared for bed. Bonzo seemed to sense something untoward had occurred and kept on petting Len, muzzling his nose affectionately into the latter's hand and springing up to him.

Mary was the first to undress and get into bed, Len sitting on its edge for a time, playing with her hair while he tried to give expression to the emotions bubbling within him. But for some reason he failed, and at last got into bed by her side. Her cool flesh against his hot limbs steadied him, and he began aimlessly fondling her breasts.

" Put the light out, Len."

He obeyed, and the little room was buried in a blackness which gave both of them courage.

" Do you still think the same about me going, Mary ? " he queried. He felt the nod of her head on the pillow, which was her only reply. Somehow he felt disappointed, for although he detested fuss from other people, he found an emotional satisfaction in being fussed over by his wife. He felt her hand creep in tickling motions over his body, and turned on his side to squeeze her more closely to him.

" Len," she whispered, " Harry's arguments to-night were right. You are the best man to go."

" Yes, I know," he answered, and there wasn't a tinge. of egotism in the bare statement.

He let his mind roam among the incidents he had heard regarding the war in Spain and began planning what he would do, although he had not the slightest idea what would be expected of him once he got there. But he knew by the versatility of his own experiences that whatever it was he could fit in. The thought gave him a warm glow of pride, and his fingers, without conscious volition, wandered over her legs. When they reached her buttocks he became sad again, and all his mind centred on her physical condition.

"You are going thinner, you are losing weight," he complained. "Oh, Mary. You'll take care of yourself when I'm away, won't you ? " he begged.

She did not answer, and a recurring thought made him nervous of the darkness, so he lit the candle again. The little flame rose and fell in grotesque shadows on the walls. He watched them for a while and was likening the monstrous shapes to Fascists when Mary gave a horrified little scream and, springing to her haunches, caught him round the neck.

"What is it, Len ? " she gasped, her perspiring hands upon his flesh. Len looked dazedly around, then saw a big moth weaving in and out among the shadows. His quickened pulse gave away the falseness of his laugh when he twitted her. "Ha-ha ! There's an old baby for you."

But Mary, whose face was still squeezed tightly to his chest, muttered in muffled tones that echoed her dread : "It came from the window. It was big and black."

Len reassured her and gently raised her face from its hiding-place. "It's only the shadow of a moth, Mary. What's the matter with you to-night ? " The tremor that shook her was sufficient reply, and his body responded to it in a surge of physical desire. Both of them quivered for some moments while he mumbled incoherently in her ears. At last he made himself articulate, although the words sounded far away, as though he were talking to something in his past.

"Oh, Mary, it is not good that a man should love as much as I do, should give himself so completely to another. Everything that was me I have given to you, until now I have nothing left of all that I was. No, not even dignity, or I wouldn't be talking to you as I am." He sighed as the measure of his emotional capitulation took hold of him, then continued : " But I am not sorry, Mary. Everything that I have been you have become. All that I once was you now are. So that our long life together has been creative after all, hasn't it ? "

The question was a plea. Mary moved restlessly by his side, but said nothing. She knew all his moods and was aware he was now unburdening the feelings he had been nursing secretly for years. He had turned on his back and, with his hands behind his head, went on musing.

" Yes. By God, I have loved so much that it hurt me more than pain. I have followed your every thought, echoed your moods, and wept in your sufferings. You have become part of me so that I float loosely like a lost balloon when you are not near. Oh, Mary, my dear, I have no life apart from you. My mind always wanders to where you are, and I wonder what you are doing, to whom you are talking. Thoughts creep into my mind and I try to crush them. But they keep on coming until they are too strong for me and I become their prisoner. Yes . . . their prisoner."

The last word was said like the " amen " that follows a prayer.

Mary softly placed her hand upon his head and let her fingers play with the strands of his hair. The touch seemed to give his thoughts a new channel.

" But you have given also, my dear. You have given me your body, have let me have your mind. Yes, your strength has made me stronger, made me more determined, so that both of us have benefited by our life together. Ha ! Do you remember, Mary, how I used to tell you that you must have initiative, audacity, and temper as well as political understanding to become a leader ? "

Again he felt her affirmative nod.

" Well, it's still true, and you have them all. You are now a leader of our Party, whatever might happen to me. Because of this I shall be happy in my heart whatever I may feel in my mind or my body. What more can a comrade want than to know that the future is safe in the hands of those who follow him, especially when they are the ones he has lived with and loved ? "

Something triumphant and stimulating swept over him

and he turned abruptly on his side. Clasping her body to his he laughed happily before pressing on her lips the burning moisture of his own. He felt the pulsing of her heart, but did not see the tears in her eyes.

Some time later Mary turned back upon her side and asked : " Len, are you afraid to go ? " The query was put as gently as the echo of a child's song far up in the mountain, but it stung him like the fangs of a snake.

" Afraid ? Afraid of what ? " he demanded harshly.

" Oh, ever so many things."

" Such as ? "

" Well, perhaps you are afraid to leave me."

The words were like a blow, stunning him for a few seconds before he could gather his thoughts again. He felt the reproach of the statement and became apologetic, although at the same time he tried to avoid the implied query.

" Oh, Mary, why do you say that ? You know I have been to gaol. You know I have been beaten up on demonstrations. You know all that I have done in the struggle, and now you say that I am yellow." He waited expectantly, but her silence eventually impelled him to continue :

" Yes, I am afraid to leave you," he challenged. " I'm afraid something will happen to you while I'm away."

Mary rose to her haunches. " I thought so, Len. Yes, I thought so." There was a happy tremor in her voice, but she pulled herself together before betraying it too deeply. " Don't worry about me, my comrade. I shall be all right with your father and mother, and don't forget we have the Party. I know it's going to be hard, Len, not only for you but for all of us, but look how happy we'll be when it's over and you're back in the ranks again."

She caught his hand and rested it against her breast, swaying her body like a mother with a baby. Len let the soothing motion capture him and filled his nostrils with the scent of her flesh as he murmured : " Yes, Mary comrade. There is no question of fear. It's just another job that has got to be done in order that we can carry the struggle of our people forward."

There followed a long pause after this till she asked curiously : " What are you thinking of now, Len ? "

Very slowly, as though he were manufacturing the words

in his mind before giving them expression, he answered :
" I was thinking of all the little kiddies who think so
much of us. Of how they rush to us when they come from
school and shout ' Hallo, Len. How be, comrade ' before
asking for fag photos. They are so true. They follow
us into our meetings and on our demonstrations ; and yet,
when we go, what will they have to remember us by ?
Nothing, Mary. Nothing, except the fact that they once
knew a man who had always been unemployed—a man
who wandered from meeting to meeting and street to street
always looking for something he never seemed to find.
Ah, but now ? When they look back upon their youth
they'll be able to say : ' We knew Len. He fought for us
in Spain, and Mary helped him.' Yes, my love. How much
better a memory is that than the deadness of the other.
It will help them when they are men and women to be
active in the fight. That's what we want, activity that
leads to action, not the inertia of pessimism and despair.
And what our children see us doing, they do later for themselves. Remember the funeral of the little dog and the
passionate loyalty of those kiddies to a playmate that had
become a carcass ? That's the love and the loyalty we
must cherish."

His words had become slower as though he was loath to
lose them, or let them lead him immutably to the next
idea. " Who knows ? Perhaps, when they look back on
the past, they'll be able to brag to each other : ' Our Len
died in Spain.' "

Mary jerked her body taut and stopped him. Her
breath came in quick gasps as she implored and challenged
in a single statement : " Don't ever say that to me again,
Len. You are going to Spain to fight, not to die."

It now became his turn to soothe and placate. His
caresses and endearments helped him, and they were both
asleep, clasped in a mutual embrace, when the window
blinds leaked the crimson glow of dawn into the bedroom.

Next day, while Len was away making arrangements
for his departure, Mary spent all the time with Shân, both
of them pretending nothing unusual was about to happen.
Shân busied herself making round cakes on the slab of
iron kept for the purpose. Len was very fond of these,

and the old woman intended them to supplement the food he ate whilst travelling.

Mary scrubbed and cleaned the kitchen. When she reached the fire-place with her bucket, Jim obligingly lifted his huge feet on the hob out of her way.

"Damn! You are a pretty little workman, mun," he commented appraisingly as she rinsed the moisture off the flags and treated them with blue stone to leave them white.

"It is a pleasure to watch you working, muniferni," he continued as he put his feet back on the fender, but before he could fix himself comfortably they were all startled by a loud "plop" that came from the tiny room beneath the stairs.

"Hell fire! Somebody is trying to shoot us," Jim roared, at the same time looking wildly at Shân, whose eyes were full of apprehension.

Mary had a suspicion, after the first shock, of what had happened, and, with a hurried glance at the old woman, rose from her knees and opened the door leading to the dark, web-strewn cubicle. She hesitantly put her hand inside and withdrew a flagon bottle from whose neck some fluid was frothily gurgling.

Jim gave it one look, then sprang to the dresser for a cup, which he hastily put under the dripping fluid. While the cup was slowly filling he muttered disconsolately : "Well, well, Shân, I never thought that you could be so mean. Me dying of thirst by here all the week and all the time you have got home-made wine in by there! Huh! For shame on you! Don't never call yourself a butty agen."

Shân drew herself erect and her face shone with dignity when she replied to the accusation : "I had thought to keep that for our Len's birthday, and had to hide it away from you or you 'ood have gutsed it long before now, more's the shame on you than me. But since he is going away, us will have it to-night instead."

A tear dangled insecurely on her eyelid, but she proudly shook it off without raising her hand.

When Len returned late that night he found his people all sitting around the fire in his own house. This surprised him, because he knew Mary had been down to his mother's during the day and that the old couple liked having her there. But he understood the reason for the gathering immediately he saw the bottles on the table and the pile of corned beef sandwiches arranged in neat little tiers in the middle. A lump rose to his throat, but his eyes gleamed happily as the significance of the scene came to him. He fancied Mary looked sweeter than usual, in the dress she only wore on special occasions, and his wandering eyes noticed that his parents also wore what they called the best clothes.

The wooden dresser had been removed and its place was taken by the piano which had been one of Ezra's presents to Mary in the days of his prosperity.

Jim sat in Ezra's chair, a glass of wine in his hand. He held this up to the light appreciatively while he murmured : " Very good. Very good indeed. But not half so good as a honest pint of beer," before swallowing the wine in one gulp.

Len pulled his coat off, hung it on the hook behind the door, and turned to find Shân waiting for him. She held a half-pint glass full of wine in one hand and the flagon from which she had emptied it in the other, completely ignoring the empty glass in Jim's outstretched hand as she ordered : " Here, Len bach. Drink this down. It'll do you the world of good. Better than all your old beers, whatever your father do say."

Len took the glass and put it to his lips, while Jim pleaded : " I wasn't meaning *your* wine, mun, Shân fach. Ha-ha ! Good God, no. I was talking about that muck Dai Cannon do make. Ach, it is not fit for pigs to drink. Huh ! But your wine, my gel, ah, I 'ood sooner have a flagon full of that than a pint of beer any day."

The sentiments bribed Shân and she refilled his tumbler.

They sat in a ring around the fire, placing the big plate of sandwiches on the stool between them. Then they began talking of old times, carefully refraining, however, from referring to any of the sad occurrences of the past. Mary, whose eyes were beginning to shine wickedly (Len always said they were full of dancing imps when she was in this mood), related the story of the times he had followed the marchers to a certain town, in spite of orders she was not to do so. " Our Len was like a wet rag by the end of

the day," she asserted, "and was just crying like a big
baby when he brought me to the station to send me back
home."

Len, who was also starting to look a little flushed, took
umbrage at this smudge upon his manhood. "Oh, fair
play, Mary. I wasn't worse than any of the others, was
I? And in any case, even if I was, it was because I had
to lug you most of the way because the back of your shoe
had rubbed half your heel off. Fair play now. If we're
going to have it, let's have the truth."

They laughed at his vehemence and Jim bawled out:
"Ho-ho, Mary fach could march your legs off, mun.
Haven't I seened her do it many times on the demon-
strations?"

Len thought this an unscrupulous reference to the time
he had dropped out of a demonstration because of an attack
of giddiness, but he said nothing further about it as he
saw his mother beginning to nod drowsily.

"Come on. Let's have a sing-song," he announced.

Shân immediately opened her eyes and Mary drew her
chair to the piano. "What shall we have, Len?" she
asked.

"Let's have something bright and happy that we all
know."

Mary, her thin shoulders swaying to the rhythm, immediately began playing a jazz tune. When she had finished
it she asked: "Did you know that one, mam?"

"Yes, my gel. Of course I did. It was *Bwthyn bach* with
some fancy tra-la's, wasn't it?"

"Duw, duw, no. That was 'The Blues,' mam."

"Huh. Never mind, Mary fach. Don't worry. I
haven't got my specs on and it is quite easy to make a
mistake with my eyes so old as they are."

Len laughed loudly, but after some more tunes the
music got into him and mixed with the wine. He rose
from the chair and stood by Mary, lifting his voice to the
refrains she played. They went through song after song,
and, as they exhausted their repertoire of modern music
and the wine took more effect, they unconsciously drifted
to the old hymns of the people.

Shân became wide awake when the sad tones moaned
through the kitchen. She clothed them in their Welsh

words, her low contralto throbbing an accompaniment to the voices of Len and Mary, who eventually stopped singing and left the field clear for the old lady.

Jim took the pipe from his mouth and used it as a baton to keep time, smiling happily as Shân crooned her way back into the past where they both immersed themselves to the temporary exclusion of the present.

Whenever Mary was in doubt about the hymn they were singing, she simply paused a second, then let her fingers trickle over the keys and follow the tune as Shân sang it. Len sat down near his father and felt a deep sadness begin to weigh on him. Tears came to his eyes as each song brought back flashes of his youth. Then he became ashamed of his sentiment, and hoping that no one had seen the tears, put his hand out and lifted a glass from the table. It was nearly full, but before he had time to put it to his mouth Jim had taken it from him and, still conducting with his pipe, nodded to the other half-empty glass nearby.

Len took this without a word, looking his thanks at his father over the rim.

The more Len drank the more he worried about its effects on Mary, knowing that wine sometimes made her irritable and excitable. But he need not have bothered his head, because Mary was holding her emotions rigidly in check. Then a wave of new sentiment engulfed him as Shân sang a pathetic ballad. He rose unsteadily to his feet and began by kissing Big Jim, who looked at him stupidly. After this he insisted on stopping the song to kiss Shân and Mary, the tears streaming from his eyes as he did so.

He felt a little more satisfied after this and again let his voice join the others, but when Shân floated into the plaintive melody of *Dafydd y Gareg Wen*, everyone but herself became silent.

The old woman was weeping openly before she had completed the ballad. The last time it had been sung in the family was just prior to the death of Len's sister, and now, although neither of them gave words to the thought, it developed a significance that overwhelmed them.

Shân and Jim did not return home that night. The former slept with Mary and the latter with Len in the bed that used to be occupied by Ezra. They had hardly closed their eyes before it was time to get up. Len immediately

went out the back and let cold water from the tap run on
his head and bare shoulders. He wanted to be in his
highest spirits this morning and was taking no chances.
Although all of them pretended there was no need to be
excited, they only succeeded in adding to the tenseness
of the atmosphere. Shân followed Mary wherever the
latter went, fearing, for her own sake, to lose sight of her
for a moment. Big Jim strutted around like an unconcerned stag, filling the room with his bulk.

It had been agreed that only Mary was to accompany
Len to the station. When this was first mooted Jim had
protested, but gave way when Len said it would be necessary for him to look after Shân.

The time slipped by as if it were anxious to steal them
from each other, and when everything was ready Mary
went out first, unwilling to be a witness of the parting
between Len and his parents. Shân caught her son to her
with a gentle grasp that slowly developed into an all-
embracing passionate clutch that left him breathless. But
her eyes were brightly dry when she released him and said :
" Take care of yourself, my boy. 'Member us will be
waiting for you. Yes, waiting and watching, and your
mam, for one, will be praying for you every night."

She turned her head away and stooped to lift the hem
of her apron to her eyes, but suddenly remembered herself
and left it untouched as she stood erect. Len looked at
his father, whose hand was already outstretched, and felt
his own lost in the grip that bade him a silent good-luck.

Without another word and fearing to look again at either,
Len followed Mary down the hill to the railway station.
At every step Len felt himself pulled from behind, but
steeled himself not to look back at the old people, whom
he knew were standing on the doorstep watching him recede
from their sight. His gaze wandered to the pits instead,
and the floating smoke from the stack made him think of
the changes that had taken place in his life since the days
when he first saw it and heard the palpitating throbs of
the pit engines.

He remembered Cwmardy when it was a tiny village
made up of smoke-grimed cottages and the pit. Pride
swelled him as he now looked at its hundreds of streets and
big buildings with bright windows. The Big House looked

lonely on its crest, and, instead of dominating Cwmardy, was now dominated by it. He felt run through him the tremor of the life that Cwmardy held, and, catching Mary's arm, he whispered proudly: " Cwmardy and our people are worth going to Spain for, Mary." There was no answer, but when they turned the corner that hid them from Sunny Bank they heard a mournful howl from Bonzo as they went out of sight.

The couple had barely reached the station before the train steamed in with screaks and blasts that unnerved Mary. Len found an empty carriage and, leaning through the window, put his arm round Mary's neck, giving her a long-drawn kiss that was simultaneously a sigh. The wheels were beginning to turn when he released her lips. She bent her head and dimly saw the wheels take him away. Suddenly she jerked up and looked ahead to see him hanging through the window waving his hand in affectionate farewell. Her feet lifted involuntarily and she started to run towards him, her arms outstretched as though she wanted to pull him back. The speed of her feet increased in pace with the quickening revolutions of the wheels and she was deaf when he shouted above the noise of the train. " Stop, for God's sake, stop."

She kept on running. The porter who caught her round the waist heard the pitiful murmur that died on her lips as he pulled her back. " Oh, Len. Oh Len, my comrade."

For the remainder of the day she hardly knew what she was doing, but her spirits revived in the Party meeting that was held that night. She was made organiser of the branch in Len's place, Harry being unable to undertake the responsibility because of his work as chairman of the combine. This new rôle gave her the feeling she had a two-fold obligation to fulfil, and when she went home she was both happy and weary.

Shân, who had insisted on sleeping with her till Len returned, had supper waiting. Although she had no appetite for food, Mary ate some to please the old lady, who broke down before the meal was over. This helped Mary overcome her own emotions, and she tried to console the other, whose sobs kept time with Bonzo's padding feet as he searched round the kitchen for Len, smelling everything that belonged to him.

CHAPTER XXIII

A Letter from Spain

LEN had been away eight months, during which time Mary had thrown herself completely into the work of the Party, happy in the fact she heard from him more or less regularly. Her health had improved to such an extent that she spoke at more public meetings than she had ever done hitherto, and found no harmful effects. Her infectious enthusiasm impregnated the people and they all came to regard her as their own, belonging to them as surely and solidly as the Square where they had fought so many battles.

They dropped the prefix " missus " and she became plain Mary to everyone. Even the enemies of the Party had to respect her for her indomitable courage and the *élan* with which she entered every campaign.

Shân tried to restrain her and one day took her to task. " You are doing too much, Mary fach. What with the council, meetings, committees, marches, *Daily Workers* and what not, your little body will be so sure to break as my name is Shân."

" Don't worry, mam. What we are doing is nothing to what our Len is going through."

" Ah well. You will listen one day, when it is too late," said the old lady before she fatalistically gave way and relapsed into silence.

Mary never put the wireless news on when her parents-in-law were about, but each night before they went to bed she read out the news from Spain, which she had carefully edited beforehand. Quite unconsciously she gave them the impression that Len was responsible for all the Government victories and the Fascist defeats. Big Jim carefully hoarded all she said and every Saturday night retailed the news again over a pint or so in the Boar's Head. On one such occasion, when he had taken more beer than usual, he bragged to his cronies.

" I knewed it years ago. I always did say that boy would
be a general one day. Of course. What else could you
'spect from such a father as me ? Aye. And I pity those
poor dabs of Spaniards if he wasn't out there helping them
now against all those Shermans and Bracchis." No one
ever laughed at these statements.

The longer Len remained away the more thrilling a
legend his name became to the people of Cwmardy. He
came to be regarded as a sort of chivalrous crusader linked
up inevitably with the Party and Spain. As a result of
this, her own personality, and the work she was doing,
Mary had an open entry to most of the houses, being treated
as a member of the family. Her smiling presence gave a
welcome brightness to some of the drab homes whenever
she called at them. She knew the exact circumstances of
most families and was aware of the best time of the day to
drop in to collect the weekly payment for the *Daily Worker*.
Bonzo always managed to catch her up each time she went
out, although she took every measure to ensure he was left
behind. She was fearful of the many fights he engaged in
and also shy because in practically every street were dogs
hardly distinguishable from him.

She had been longer than usual without a message from
Len, but thought little of it until the weeks became a
month, then six weeks, then ten. The long silence began
to worry her, and she pestered Harry Morgan each time
she met him between his visits to London. But all he
could tell her was that the last time they had heard Len
was well and doing good work. This news heartened her
the first time she heard it, but constant repetition made
her introspective and she started searching in her own mind
for the real reasons. At night in bed her imagination
scoured every conceivable possibility, so that she woke
each morning more depressed and listless than she was the
morning before. She felt herself losing weight and the
cough returned.

Shân noticed the symptoms and watched her like a cat,
although Mary had kept her fears from them and always
managed to fabricate a story when they inquired about
Len.

The Party members saw the change taking place in her
and often commented about it, but it was left to Harry to

approach her on the matter. He pleaded with her to take a holiday and even offered to arrange everything for this. But she was adamant.

Then, quite unexpectedly, news came through the usual channels that some of the men who had gone out the same time as Len were returning home. The information made Mary's heart skip some beats, then spring with greater vigour into action.

She told Shân and Jim about it the same night and ended with the remark : " Now we'll know something definite about our Len."

Immediately the statement left her mouth she realised she had made a mistake, but Shân, rigid in the chair, spoke before she could cover the error.

" Know something about our Len ? Whatever do you mean, Mary ? Us thought you knowed all about him without this."

Mary swallowed before answering dubiously : " Of course we do, mam. What I meant was perhaps Len, who is very important out in Spain, will have to stop there for a bit yet."

" But you did not put it in that way," Shân insisted, still not satisfied. Mary felt herself in a trap and tried desperately to wriggle out of it without saying a direct lie.

" But, mam, I was only thinking that if Len is not coming back with the boys, perhaps he's sent a special message with them to us."

Jim took up the cue and entered the discussion. " That's it, mun. Like I always used to do, Shân, in the war, when the boys was coming home on leave. Don't you 'member, gel ? "

This settled Shân's doubts.

Mary called the Party committee together the following night to make arrangements for the welcome home. There was a full attendance at the meeting, every member alert with subdued excitement. It was decided to organise a demonstration and a mass welcome meeting in the new workmen's hall. Mary agreed to ask the women of the Co-operative and other Guilds to make banners for street decorations. Another Party member, who was also in the town band, stated he knew the latter would turn out in full strength. Harry Morgan, as chairman of the combine, raised the matter in that body, and it agreed to approach all the other organisations in Cwmardy to take part in the welcome home. As a result of all these efforts, a joint committee was formed to take charge of the complete organisation for the day.

Posters were exhibited in the shop windows, leaflets distributed to the houses, and preliminary meetings held in every street. The hall was decorated with red streamers, banners, special Spain prints, and *Daily Worker* posters. The lights were covered with delicate silk so that when they were switched on the whole hall glowed a deep crimson.

Artists belonging to the Party were commissioned to make large canvas paintings of the men who had left Cwmardy for Spain. When these were completed they were fixed on the red plush curtain that backed the stage. Len's wavy hair and big eyes occupied the centre. His picture was painted from a photograph he had taken on one of the marches, and his face looked longer than it actually was in real life.

The intervening days passed like dreams to the members of the Party and the organising committee, but at last the day arrived. The town band was ready to play the battle-hymns of the people. Women had hung banners of every description from their windows and spread long streamers of bunting across the streets, until Cwmardy looked like a lake of waving fire.

The schools were empty of children, all of whom anxiously awaited the street teas that had been organised for them by levies on the wages of the workmen and donations from the Co-operative Society and other organisations.

The men in the pits had already agreed to remain home for the event as a reply to a letter sent to Mary by the chief of police banning any demonstration through the main street.

The people in each street followed the example of Sunny Bank during the unemployed demonstrations, and marched as street contingents, converging on a common point for the mass demonstration through Cwmardy. The police realised it would be impossible to execute their threat and made no attempt to provoke the people.

Long before the train was due the approaches to the

railway station were crammed with demonstrators. Most of them heard the train steam in, but very few saw what happened after, until an insistent blare from a motor car urged them to open the ranks for the procession of three cars. The first contained the returned soldiers, with Mary among them. Officials of the committee occupied the other two. The ranks reformed immediately the cars had passed and by the time the latter had reached the Square, they were at the head of a densely packed mile-long stream of people.

The occupants of the cars got out on the Square, the waiting bandsmen formed up before them, the returned soldiers were lifted on unknown shoulders, and, to the deep throb of drums, the march up the hill started.

Mary never knew how the old couple got there, but when her blazing eyes looked round they saw Jim and Shân right behind, the latter waving her arms and shouting at the top of her voice though no one could possibly hear what she said in the deafening tumult that was part of the demonstration.

Mary's heart twitched at the sight and it gave her greater strength to go on, her feet hardly touching the earth till they reached the hall. She managed to get inside, Jim and Shân still following. Those who could not enter were catered for by loud-speakers, which relayed to them every word said in the hall.

Harry Morgan, Mary, Len's parents, and officials of the organising committee surrounded the soldiers on the stage. Harry, who had been elected in charge, beckoned the brigaders to the front, where they stood for many shy minutes listening to the roars of welcome that greeted them back to Cwmardy.

When some measure of order had been restored, Harry called upon them all to sing the Red Flag. The request was heard by the band outside, who immediately struck up the initial chords, which were followed by the massed voices of the people.

When the mighty intonations died down Harry began his speech of welcome. Mary leaned forward, elbow on knee and chin in her hand, the better to follow the proceedings. The faces before her were melted into a huge grey blob framed by the red of the decorations. She heard

Harry's piercing voice cut the air with "Comrades and Friends," then felt a nudge. She looked around and saw one of the soldiers beckoning her with his finger. Bending back to hear what he wanted, she noticed subconsciously that he carefully avoided her eyes as he handed her a packet.

"This is from Len, Mary, and there's one from me as well. I thought I might just as well bring it with me, since I wrote it."

The conversation was carried on in a whisper and as soon as he had finished the messenger sat back and fixed his attention on the meeting.

Mary didn't know what to do for some minutes. Her heart was beating into her ribs with an intensity that added to the glow on her cheeks. She felt it would be a sort of sacrilege to read the letters while the speakers were on their feet and before all the eyes in the hall.

Yet all the time she hesitated her whole being demanded that she read them quickly. Her body began to tremble with excitement and, unable to contain herself any longer, she rose quietly and tip-toed off the stage into one of the ante-rooms behind.

This was in darkness, but the many Party meetings held there had taught her where to find the switch. After a little groping she pressed it, and in a moment the room was filled with a glaring light that hurt her eyes after the subdued crimson of the big hall. She paused to ease the quiver of her flesh, all the time looking with intense concentration at the packet in her hand. She was burning to open it, but reluctant to start doing so. At last she pulled herself together and with a haste that made her fingers clumsy tore open the covering and found two mud-stained letters inside.

She recognised Len's writing at a glance and a pathetic half-smile flickered on her face as she remembered the occasions she had twitted him about his terrible scrawl. She pulled the letter from its envelope and began reading to herself. But in a short time her lips began to move, and she read on half aloud.

DEAR MARY AND ALL AT HOME,

      I don't know when you had my last letter because postal arrangements are rather wonky, so I'm giving this to one of the boys to make sure that you'll get it, as it looks like he'll be coming home shortly. Well, Mary, I hope everyone at home is O.K. and that the Party comrades are putting their backs into the campaign to help Spain and save democracy.

Obviously I can't tell you much of what is taking place here, but I have been in this hospital for the last few weeks (just a little scratch) and am going back into the line to-morrow. You will be happy to know Ron is here with me. He was one of the first to come out and has made a name for himself as a fighter and a leader. You can just imagine that the two of us stick together as much as possible. He hasn't changed much since the old days, except that he is perhaps a bit thinner. We are gaining the upper hand now and are beginning a new offensive, of which I am glad.

It's marvellous to see how our boys go into action. You know them all and will remember how they were on the demonstrations and marches, but that is nothing to the way they act out here. It makes me proud of our people and of myself for belonging to them.

But it's strange, Mary (or is it ?), that while there are certain differences I could swear sometimes I was still in Cwmardy and that the Fascists are not far away in a strange land, but are actually destroying our birth-place and all it means to us. The men who are dying don't seem to be strangers, but our comrades as we know them at home. The same old hills are somewhere around here, and I know the same old smoke-stack and pit is not far away. The faces I see about me are the same faces as those in Cwmardy. It is only when they speak that I notice any difference.

Yes, my comrade, this is not a foreign land on which we are fighting. It is home. Those are not strangers who are dying. They are our butties. It is not a war only of nation against nation, but of progress against reaction, and I glory in the fact that Cwmardy has its sons upon the battle-field, fighting here as they used to fight on the Square, the only difference being that we now have guns instead of sticks.

Yes, Mary my love. And to-morrow I am happy to go back to them. All our lives we have been together. In our homes, the pit, the streets, the Federation, and the Party. The strikes and demonstrations and marches have led us unerringly to this, the battle-field of democracy.

It is in the nature of things that we can't all come back to Cwmardy, that some of us will be left here with, perhaps, a cross to mark the fact we were once living, but were robbed of life by Fascism.

Yes, that is inevitable, as it is at home that after every

action in defence of our rights they stick some of us to rot in prison.

Some of the boys we knew have already gone, but not in vain. They have helped to stamp into the earth an invisible barrier of bodies from which breathes a new spirit of hope and love and invincible courage. Fascism may kill us, Mary, but it can never kill what we die for. No, never! Our very death is creation, our destruction new life and energy and action.

I know, my love, that you appreciate all the possibilities and that whatever happens to me you will carry on building the Party, drawing our masses into a unity that will save Cwmardy for the people. Even as I write I know that you are near and I can almost feel your breath upon my neck as you bend over to read this. I know every throb of that wonderful heart that is too big for your little body.

It seems so long since I touched you with my hands, but I see you in every battle; you are at my side in every action. Remember the day we marched together in the big demonstration, Mary? Well, like that. You are with me wherever I go, whatever I do. And never forget, whatever happens, we were brought together because we belong to the people and it is only the cause of our people can ever part us.

If that should happen, if it becomes necessary, then don't grieve too much, because belonging to the people, you will always find me in the people. Give my love to all the comrades at home. Throw your whole weight into the Party. Tell mam and dad not to worry about me. Sleep happy in the knowledge that our lives have been class lives, and our love something buried so deep in the Party that it can never die.

So-long, Mary, my comrade and love,
LEN.

A roar of cheering swept from the hall into the little room and Mary raised her head to see what was the matter, but the lights glistening on the tears that filled her eyes blinded her to everything. She felt there was something within her that wanted to escape. It seemed to clog her body and make it hard to breathe. She lifted her hand slowly to the pocket on the left breast of her coat and drew out the red silk handkerchief with its emblazoned hammer and sickle which had been Len's gift to her from Spain. She looked at it dazedly and saw it dancing in her tears.

Equally slowly and methodically she raised it to her

eyes and wiped them, then getting a sudden grip on herself she read the letter again before picking up the other.

It felt heavy as lead in her hand as she opened it. Her eyes fixed instantly on one sentence that stood out before her like a neon sign.

> We found him lying among a group of Fascists and brought him away from them to bury him with his own people. He had been with them all his life and we left him with them in death.

Mary read this over and over. She could not tear her gaze away from it until something gripped her by the throat and she could not breathe. She sprang to her feet and the grip was released. When she ran headlong from the room she left a moan behind : " Oh, Len. You are gone for ever."

She was on the stage before she knew it and the immediate deep silence that followed her entry brought her to a dead stop. Looking around like a woman in a trance, she saw the blur of faces before her, then the weeping form of Shân with Jim pathetically stroking her hair, nearby.

In a flash she knew that the people had been told that Len was dead and she turned her head to see his portrait stand out among the others with its draping of black cloth. Someone caught her arm and led her to a chair near the table, on which she bent her head. When she raised it again the hall was nearly empty and Shân, red-eyed and heaving, was standing near her, with Jim, who kept swallowing hard all the time.

" Come, Mary fach. Our Len have left us for ever, and this is no place for us. Let us go home."

Mary looked again at the painting and fancied she saw the lips form into a smile and the sad eyes soften with encouragement.

She stared at it for some moments and the feeling grew on her that Len was saying : " Go, Mary. Follow the people, they are your hope and strength."

Jumping up, she caught Shân about the shoulders. " You go home, mam. I can't come yet ; the people's day isn't over and I must be with them till the last, as our Len was."

Shân straightened her body. " Us will go, Mary, when you come and not before."

They followed the last figures through the hall doors and found the demonstration getting further away every minute, the smoke from the pit curling round it before dissolving into the air and leaving the scarlet banner dominating the scene. They heard the barely audible strains of the band, and the people singing :

> " Then away with all your superstitions,
> Servile masses, arise ! Arise ! "

Mary started to run. " I must go before they get too far," she muttered.

Jim and Shân slowly followed, the former shouting, " Go on, Mary fach. Me and Shân is not quite so quick, but us will be with you at the end."

Mary stumbled, but kept on her feet. She began mumbling to herself : " I must catch them up. I must catch them up." When she reached the tail of the demonstration she thought the beats of her heart were centred in her throat and stumbled again. This time she would have fallen, but eager hands caught her and a cry ran through the ranks towards the front : " Send the car back. Send a car back." When it came they placed Mary gently inside and sent it back again to the head of the march.

Jim and Shân limped far behind. He put his arm about her waist. " Us can never keep step with 'em, Shân fach. Us have got too old. Yes, too old. But never mind, my gel ; they have got to come back sooner or later before they can get home, then us can join 'em again."

Shân halted to get breath. Floating towards them came the voices of the people muted in a common unity :

> " Though cowards flinch and traitors sneer,
> We'll keep the red flag flying here."

THE END